With best regards
to Doris.

Oliver Akamnonu
Aug. 14, 2012.

KONGANOGA

Mauling the Polity

Dr Oliver Akamnonu and
Professor Ndu Eke

AuthorHouse™
1663 Liberty Drive
Bloomington, IN 47403
www.authorhouse.com
Phone: 1-800-839-8640

© 2011 Dr Oliver Akamnonu and Professor Ndu Eke. All rights reserved.

No part of this book may be reproduced, stored in a retrieval system, or transmitted by any means without the written permission of the author.

First published by AuthorHouse 3/15/2011

ISBN: 978-1-4567-4542-4 (e)
ISBN: 978-1-4567-4543-1 (dj)
ISBN: 978-1-4567-4544-8 (sc)

Library of Congress Control Number: 2011902837

Printed in the United States of America

Any people depicted in stock imagery provided by Thinkstock are models, and such images are being used for illustrative purposes only. Certain stock imagery © Thinkstock.

This book is printed on acid-free paper.

Because of the dynamic nature of the Internet, any web addresses or links contained in this book may have changed since publication and may no longer be valid. The views expressed in this work are solely those of the author and do not necessarily reflect the views of the publisher, and the publisher hereby disclaims any responsibility for them.

This book is dedicated to our wives Chika and Felicia and to our children: Olisa, Chibu, Ure, Kechy, Somto, Ikedi and Chuka

Contents

Chapter 1.   Pen Pals Meet 1
Chapter 2.   Jekyll on the Mound 7
Chapter 3.   Locum Tenens 13
Chapter 4.   As Amiable as They Come 18
Chapter 5.   A Companion for a Career 23
Chapter 6.   On the Homeward Job Trail 30
Chapter 7.   The Federal University of Science and Technology, Kiba 40
Chapter 8.   Erudite International Scholar 46
Chapter 9.   All Change, Heading Home 54
Chapter 10.   Starting from the Head 62
Chapter 11.   Senior Academic 70
Chapter 12.   The Family Relocates to Konganoga ... 77
Chapter 13.   Never a Dull Moment 85
Chapter 14.   Cashing the Gift 92
Chapter 15.   On Your Marks, Get Set 99
Chapter 16.   Meeting the Challenge Head On ... 106
Chapter 17.   At the Pinnacle 112
Chapter 18.   Aretha Is Not Tarzan for the Jungle ... 120

Chapter 19.	One Incubator and the Bubble in Activity	128
Chapter 20.	Board Room Games	134
Chapter 21.	Points of Order	141
Chapter 22.	Becoming a "Learned Gentleman Lady"	148
Chapter 23.	The Burdens of Office	155
Chapter 24.	The Battles Within	160
Chapter 25.	Mr Vice Chancellor the League Member	169
Chapter 26.	The Realities Unfold	179
Chapter 27.	Fulfilling the League Member's Promise	194
Chapter 28.	The Downward Drift	205
Chapter 29.	An Eye on the Promise; a Family in Ruins	214
Chapter 30.	Dash for Reparations; Dinner with the Devil	222
Chapter 31.	Making the Best of a Bad Situation	233
Chapter 32.	The Limits of Diplomacy	246
Chapter 33.	The Last Straw	260
Chapter 34.	The Bigger Flight	273
Chapter 35.	The Startling Revelation	280
Chapter 36.	Back to Base to Maul the Polity	298
Chapter 37.	Coalition of Polity's Wreckers	309
Bibliography of names		325

Also by the same authors

- Suppers of Many Dishes part I (By Dr Oliver Akamnonu)
- Suppers of Many Dishes part II (Odyssey to the West and beyond) (By Dr Oliver Akamnonu)
- The Gods Have Not Yet Spoken (By Dr Oliver Akamnonu)
- Taste of the West (By Dr Oliver Akamnonu)
- Nation of Dead Patriots (By Dr Oliver Akamnonu)
- Coming Late to America (By Dr Oliver Akamnonu)
- Bature (The Forbidden letter "B") (By Dr Oliver Akamnonu)
- The Honorable (By Dr Oliver Akamnonu)
- The Trial of Monogamy (Phased polygamy in God's own country) (By Dr Oliver Akamnonu)
- Earth's Man of Color, Genes, Agenda or Genes (By Dr Oliver Akamnonu and Professor Ndu Eke)
- Soldier Ants of War, 40 years after (By Dr Oliver Akamnonu and Professor Ndu Eke)
- Arranged Marriage and the Vanishing Roots (By Dr Oliver Akamnonu)
- Heroines and Chameleons (By Professor Ndu Eke)
- Comedy of Naked Vampires (By Dr Oliver Akamnonu)

Prologue 1

Even when the forces of evil, avarice and greed appear to triumph and overwhelm the forces of good, humility and progress, for any people or nation, these events must always be seen as only temporary.

Humanity must never despair or succumb to intimidation from these forces of darkness which nonetheless must be given no hiding place.

The joy in witnessing the ultimate triumph of good over evil even in spite of the inherent pains at sanitizing the polity will always be worth any consequent suffering in the end.

Oliver Akamnonu

Prologue 2

Evil is evil, no matter by whatever name it is called.

There can be no attenuation of evil by dilution with terminologies employed, or by attempts at classifying evil as a culture of any people.

Nations whose leadership decide to wear evil as a badge of honor can never hope to attain enduring peace or progress.

Try what they may; amass for themselves as much of their people's resources as they wish; garb themselves in as much colorful regalia of gold as they please; they labor in vain. They can never earn the genuine respect or admiration of other nations or well-meaning people.

Oliver Akamnonu

Prologue 3

Thieving has mushroomed to a most thriving industry
As the world has become a global village
One's destiny lies not with tribe or country
It lies with humanity.

Ndu Eke

Prologue 4

At the end of the day what counts the most is what good we have left for society, not how much silver and gold we have accumulated.

What counts the most is how many faces we have put a smile on, how many souls we have lifted out of physical and spiritual poverty; not how many mansions and islands we have to our names.

Certainly what counts the most is whether on our tombstones it is written:
"Here lies the man who acquired the most gold;"
or whether it is written:
"Here lies the man who did the most good."

Oliver Akamnonu

Prologue 5

Those who were imposed on us as leaders were traitors who successively beget others like themselves. Our ... leaders are mostly characterized by unbridled selfishness, blind egocentricity, voracious appetite for ill-gotten wealth, Machiavellian orientation, boundless corruption and shameless opulence. We ... have a political class that is largely ideologically bereft, morally bankrupt, socially irresponsible, politically barbaric, intellectually fraudulent, and spiritually anemic.

Chinedu Nebo

Chapter 1

PEN PALS MEET

In the beginning, the Commonwealth was accessible to the common man. Thus, when Dr Okon Johnson graduated from Premier University, Oluba as the first medical doctor in his province in Konganoga, he set his sights far away. Zeland was the country to which his native country Konganoga had been partitioned during the scramble for Africa. Zeland thus colonized Konganoga and somehow included all her colonies into a politico-socio-economic group called the Commonwealth of Nations. There was freedom of movement from one place to another within the Commonwealth. While the euphoria of overtaking her neighbors persisted in Ebume clan, Dr Johnson bought himself a flight ticket. Without preambles or ceremonies, he landed in the capital of Zeland. As a student in Premier University, he had become acquainted with Clough McAndrew who was also studying Medicine in his native Zeland but was in his final years. Drs Johnson and McAndrew were pen pals. Although Dr Johnson was excited about his new overseas friend, he had not planned to travel out to a foreign country. He nevertheless was not lacking in inquisitiveness and adventurism. The idea to travel came on gradually, goaded by the contents of his exchanges with Clough McAndrew. Once he took the decision, he did not waver. He saved money for a one-way flight ticket. Next, he began to save for feeding. Dr McAndrew had offered to help him with accommodation for up to three months, by which time he would have fixed himself at a hospital, as a 'locum tenens', for starters.

Dr Johnson had been given the direction to the hospital where Dr McAndrew worked. On arrival at the Edward International Airport, he was to take a bus to the Princess Victoria Central Bus Station. From there, he was to take the night bus heading north to Calcouth. It was a 12- hour journey. The service was labeled express. Both the driver and his guard sat in the front. This surprised Dr Johnson. In Konganoga, the mates of drivers usually sat at the back, to keep an eye on the back as it were. When the bus pulled up at a service station, Dr Johnson thought it was only to refuel. He was surprised when the driver announced that passengers who wanted coffee could alight for it and that the bus would resume movement in precisely 45 minutes. He followed the others although he did not take coffee at night. The last time he did that was during the preparations for the final examinations. He needed it to keep awake. He knew it was a counterproductive effort. Coffee could keep a student awake but it was at a cost. It was one thing to be awake. It was a very different thing to assimilate what one read. However, students needed to be seen to have burnt the midnight oil. It was a consolation in the undesired event of a failure. Where the bus stopped was not just a fuel station. It was a shopping centre with restaurants, gymnasium and game stations. There was a casino for gambling. Dr Okon Johnson considered it a sin to gamble. His pastor said so. He had thought that the food was part of the bus fare. He was observant of others. He saw them pay for what they took. By the time it got to his turn to pay, he had put back what he had taken from the rack. The server noted that his tray was empty and ignored him to attend to 'Next, please'.

Another surprise for Dr Okon Johnson occurred when they set out to continue the journey. The driver's mate had become the driver. In Konganoga, whatever the distance of a journey, regardless of the roughness of the road, however 'manageable' the passenger lorry was, one driver started a journey and ended it at the destination except for refills or the call of nature on the driver, his mate or some vocal passengers. When the lorry broke down everyone waited, sometimes for days until it was repaired. In such circumstances the place where the lorry broke down became an instant camping ground for the passengers and their belongings which often included fowls, dogs and goats. One passenger lorry was captioned, 'Will is way'. For coffee, the driver chewed the kola nut without ceasing. He always had a mate who sat at the rear of the lorry. Up a hill, the mate was expected to trot after the lorry with a heavy wedge in hand. This would be handy to wedge one rear tire if the first gear failed. The mate was not expected to know how to drive, lest he displaced the driver from his job. If he was discovered to have learnt to drive on the job, he was relieved of the mate's duties.

On arrival at the Calcouth bus station, Dr Johnson took a cab to the District General Hospital where Dr McAndrew worked. The later had left a message with the security men at the gate about an African gentleman who he was expecting. Thus, when Dr Johnson was asked who he wanted to see and he mentioned Dr McAndrew, the security man did not say anything further. All that Dr Johnson noticed in five minutes was the arrival of Dr Clough McAndrew. The two had not met before. They had not exchanged photographs. However, it did not require rocket science for both to spontaneously know they had found themselves.

'Dr McAndrew', said Dr Johnson.

'Dr Johnson', said Dr McAndrew.

They embraced each other. Dr Johnson paid his fare and was shown into Dr McAndrew's two-door Mini. His one piece luggage was taken from him by Dr McAndrew who pulled forward his seat to put the luggage in the back seat. He opened the passenger door for Johnson. He entered and drove the car to a block of buildings. When he stopped and brought out the luggage, the two doctors went into one of the buildings. It was like a dormitory. The usher took both men to a room. This was self-contained. The usher checked that the water, hot as well as cold, was running from the taps. There was a clean towel with a soap tablet in the toilet/bath room. When the usher left, both men sat down.

'This is the nurses' hostel. This wing is for men. However, anyone can visit anyone but visitors are not allowed to stay the night. There is a cafeteria. The food is actually nice and it is cheaper than you can get outside. I thought you should be here to have your freedom within the rules as I have stated. I have reserved here for you for three months. When you get a place, you are free to leave. I will not be debited unspent time. After work this evening, I will take you to show you my place and we can go and have a bite somewhere nice. I know there is a lot to catch up with. Let me leave you to take a bath. The reception will show you the cafeteria where you can have some breakfast. After that you can take a nap. Lunch is served at the same place. I take it that you have some money with you. The banks are in the town centre in case you need to cash some checks. You can call me Clough, I take it your first name is 'Okn', am I right? Now, mate, I will see you sooner than later'. Dr Clough McAndrew excused himself and left.

It was like a speech from the throne. The accent was familiar from Premier University where most of the lecturers were from Zeland. Okon Johnson's eyes were opening rather too fast. All the time he was corresponding with Dr McAndrew, he was not sure how to pronounce Clough. Was 'ugh' silent or was it pronounced as if it was 'f'? He had heard it from the horse's mouth: 'Clof'. He wondered whether he should have corrected Clough about his own name. The 'o' after 'k' was not silent. He should have got him to pronounce every letter. In less than 15 minutes, he had been told all he needed to know to take him through the first three months in Zeland. It was said with little to spare. It contrasted with events in his home place in Konganoga. Dr McAndrew would have started by asking about Dr Johnson's father, mother, brothers, sisters, cousins and others. Then he would be asked about his goats, his yams and his other crops. He would, after the inquisition, take his turn to put Dr McAndrew on the spot as if in retaliation.

Okon did as Clough had suggested and in the order that he was advised. He had a shower and found his way to the cafeteria. He pointed at items as he went along the line with others. Okon was a careful person and he lived within his means. He took a glass of orange juice, omelets, smoked bacon and potato chips. Each item was put in his plate by the chef. At the end, the cashier pressed his machine and announced the total. Okon gave him a pound note. The cashier pressed something else and the till opened. She took the 'change' from there, dropped Okon's money and pressed another button. The till sprang back. Okon noted the details in amazement. Everything seemed to have been worked out in advance. He kept repeating to himself '*oyibo, na waa* for you' (*white man, you are something else*). After the breakfast, Okon went to his room. He opened the luggage and brought out his wrapper, a six feet by four feet piece of cloth. He removed his clothes, except his singlet. He wrapped himself up in the cloth and lay down. He was to catch up with the jet lag and the 'express' bus journey. The catching up was interrupted by a tap at his door. He got up and opened it. Dr Clough McAndrew was there with Ingrid. It was 5 p.m.

'Well, never mind. Ingrid, this is my pal Okn. Okn, this is Ingrid. You'll get to know more about her'.

'You are both welcome. I am sorry, I must have overslept'.

'Oh no, you are entitled to all you get, mate. The night is yet to come. So get yourself dressed. I don't know about you, but we are hungry. We just go and get a bite, or take a bite. Which one, Ingrid?'

'I think Okn will decide. He is new here, I believe'.

Ok, Okn. We give you five minutes to change although I do not think Ingrid is shy'. Without waiting for anyone's response, Dr McAndrew pulled Ingrid along and they left the room. Dr Johnson changed into his clothes quicker than the five minutes prescribed by Dr McAndrew. He opened the door and found the couple holding on to each other on the corridor even as people men, women, boys and girls were walking to and fro. They saw Dr Johnson too and moved quickly towards him. They entered his room only to come out again. They went to Dr McAndrew's Mini car. Dr Johnson had to enter and go into the back seat. Ingrid gave the direction as Clough drove. Soon they reached their destination, the *Jekyll on the Mound*.

Chapter 2

JEKYLL ON THE MOUND

Through their correspondence, Clough had guided Okon about when to get to Zeland. He had used the word summer but Okon did not know which months were summer months until Clough told him. Thus, when Okon arrived, it was quite warm in Edward International Airport. However, the temperature was noticeably lower in Calcouth just 12 hours away by bus. It was warm inside the *Jekyll on the Mound*. There was a crowd of young people, men and women mainly in groups, chattering away and smiling. The cigarette smoke from a few was perceptible to Okon. Although he objected to it, he did not complain. Soon the three of them found a space. Clough asked Okon what he would like to drink. He was taken aback on two counts. First, he expected that Clough would have asked Ingrid first. It was later, when he thought about it, that he realized why. He knew what Ingrid drank. The second count was that he did not know what drinks were on offer.

Out of modesty, Okon requested a glass of wine. It was now Clough's turn to be surprised. Okon did not know that wine in a pub, by the glass or by the bottle, was more expensive than most patrons would budget for. 'Red or white?' Okon said 'red'. Clough did not want to ask any more questions, such as rare or medium, to avoid more problems. He went to the bar and soon reappeared with a small glass of wine, a pint of 'bitter' and a shot of gin and tonic. Ingrid was the first to take hers, the gin and tonic.

'Here is yours my friend from Konganoga', and Clough handed the glass of wine to Okon. Okon thanked his friend. All three clanged their glasses in a ceremonial welcome gesture to Dr Okon Johnson. Ingrid, after a few sips of her gin and tonic, asked the gentlemen what they would like to eat. In the meantime since they entered the pub, Dr Okon Johnson observed that there was no one being served rice, beans, yam, garri or plantains in any form. He recognized fish and chips. One of the Zeland lecturers in Premier University had invited Okon Johnson's tutorial group to his house for a light supper. He and his visiting fiancée had prepared fish and chips for the group. For the group, that was equivalent to a banquet on their staple food. It was discussed for a month afterwards.

Clough, in response to Ingrid, asked for fish and chips. When his eyes caught up with those of Ingrid, all that Okon could say was a single word: 'same!' Not only had he said the safe thing, he also showed that he was not that native in any case. Ingrid brought the three meals and each took one portion, found a space on the bar table and began to eat. As a person next to one of the three left the pub, one of the other two moved to take up the vacated space. Soon, all three were seated together. That was when Clough and Ingrid had the opportunity to ask Okon questions about his travel. These included the airports of departure and arrival, the airline, smoothness of the flight, etc. He was asked if there were any differences between Konganoga and Zeland in terms of infrastructure. Once he realized that he had not gathered enough evidence, Okon was brief in his response to the last question. He had learnt about evidence-based medicine. It was not only in medicine that people operated on the available evidence. It was Okon's turn to buy the next round of drinks by Clough and Ingrid's expectations and according to their culture. Okon was unaware of the reasons why there were no drinks for the food. His hosts were not aware that he did not know. They merely thought that he was a scrooge. It was months later that it occurred to Okon that he had strayed from etiquette. In Zeland, when a group of friends went out for some entertainment, everyone was expected to pay for what he or she ate or drank. If one of the group started buying, each person in the group was expected to do the same or each would contribute his or her share of the item consumed. In Konganoga, people were used to receiving and were happy to show gratitude. In Konganoga, unlike in Zeland, begging was not regarded as an antisocial behavior. Receiving gifts without reciprocating immediately was not regarded as antisocial either. It was expected that whoever had the most money or whoever was hosting the party would shoulder all the expenses alone.

After the supper of fish and chips, Clough drove back to his flat. There, he offered drinks to Okon and Ingrid. Okon observed that Ingrid did not really live with Clough, in spite of their intimate posture on the corridor when they got to his room to take him out. To round up the evening's entertainment, Ingrid wanted to know if anyone wanted a cup of tea or coffee. While Okon declined either, the other two helped themselves. Clough took tea, while Ingrid had her usual black coffee without sugar or milk. When they were through, Clough sought Ingrid's permission to take Okon back to his room, offering to take Ingrid back after that. Okon thus confirmed that she did not live with him.

'Okn, I am on call tomorrow. However, I will see you about 6 p.m. the next day. In the meantime, if you need to get me urgently, use the phone in the Nurses' Home and page me'.

'What page is that? Okon asked. He was not familiar with 'paging'. In answer to Okon's question, Clough explained that there was a telephone linked to a hospital switchboard. If one needed a person carrying a hospital phone linked to the switchboard, all that the person needed to do was call the hospital operator who would then connect the caller to the person who was being called. One could not directly reach others except they go through the switchboard operator. The switchboard operator often listened in to a conversation between those using the hospital pager.

Since Clough was going to be busy the next day, Okon figured that he should take it as a free day for himself. He asked about how to get to the shopping places. He was told it depended on what he wanted. He had no particular items in mind. He just wanted to do some window shopping. He was told the buses he could take to the Town Centre. After a late breakfast, he got into Bus 23 and sat down. Soon the bus conductor went round collecting fares depending on where one wanted to alight. He told the conductor he wanted to stop at the Town Centre.

'First or second stop?'

Okon just looked at the man. One elderly lady in front of him noticed that Okon was probably a visitor and volunteered to mediate between him and the bus conductor. She asked Okon whether he was going shopping. When he answered in the affirmative, she told him to stop at the first stop. He paid and was given his change. The same lady told him when they had reached the first bus stop. When he came down, he saw several shops in a large expanse of land. There were no residential houses within walking distance, as far as he could see. Several people were milling around, pushing what appeared to Dr Johnson to be prams. Those were shopping trolleys and the area was a shopping centre. He followed people into a large store. It seemed to contain several other stores. The prices of the goods were pasted on the times, each with its own price tag. He went to the clothing section. There were shirts, trousers, suits and underwear. Each item had its price tag. Dr Johnson liked to wear white underwear. He saw them in pieces and in bundles. Just at that point one of the staff in her uniform was passing. Dr Johnson called for her assistance.

'Please what is the last price on this?'

'It is written there, sir', and she made to leave.

'Yes, I can see it. I am asking for the last price'.

The shopping assistant could not work out what the problem was. Besides, she was actually busy and had been attending to someone else when Dr Johnson called for her attention. 'Excuse me, sir; I was actually attending to someone else. Perhaps you could get the assistant covering this section to sort it out, all right? She smiled and hurried on.

Dr Johnson left the store to enter a different one. He did not really have any particular item in mind. He went into several stores. At the end of all that, he was able to buy two Mars bars with chocolate written on the wrap.

Back in his room, Dr Okon Johnson began to ruminate over recent events in Konganoga. The country had become partitioned into more entities. The partitioning came about as the only way to resolve the conflicting interests of the tribes that had emerged from a bloody internecine war. He fell asleep. The next day in the canteen, he met one of his countrymen doing a doctorate degree program in political science. Sule Ojo was the son of a member of the ruling house in Jalango Province of Konganoga. He was a free thinker. He told Okon about life for settlers in Zeland. There was a Zelandic Council where he should go and register. The Council coordinated human development activities in the Commonwealth. Occasionally, grants, conferences and social activities were advertised there. Other information available there included naturalization, ownership of property and access to legal advice.

There was also Konganoga Students Union which Sule recommended, although he did not really have much need for that kind of group. They were mainly poor students or students who he felt were misinformed. This later group thought the country belonged to everybody. They did not know that there were the real owners to whom the erstwhile colonial masters had bequeathed power. Sule belonged to the group of inheritors. Furthermore, he was not minded to abdicate what had become a birthright. Although Okon and Sule had never met before, they instantly became polarized. Each had a different experience of Konganogan citizenship. They were rivals rather than patriots of a common cause. Their names informed so.

Chapter 3

LOCUM TENENS

A few weeks after he arrived in Zeland, Dr Okon got a locum tenens job at Kirkurd District General Hospital. He was to hold brief for a doctor in the Casualty department. Apart from the unfamiliar accents of a few patients, he fitted in with confidence. He was given accommodation for the one month he was to serve. He soon got details about how to obtain specialist training in Zeland.

Dr Johnson was on duty on a quiet Saturday evening. There was a local derby in the national soccer league. Dr Johnson retired into the call room to revise his Anatomy for the primary examinations in surgery.

'Doctor Johnson, Doctor Johnson, please come', the student Nurse Fiona, was shouting.

Dr Johnson listened again. Rather than wane, the noise waxed. He put on his white coat and rushed out of the room. As he got closer, he heard some of the vilest profanities he ever heard. He followed Fiona who had been sent to call him. As they reached the bleeding patient, Mr. Murphy, seeing a black man in a white coat and suspecting he was a doctor, screamed.

'Keep your bleeding distance, mate! We are not here for a sick joke'.

Dr Johnson took the notes from Fiona. He read the name, noted his age and his occupation. 'Murphy Kinnock, age 42 years, unemployed'.

'Mr. Kinnock, I am Dr Johnson. What happened?'

'They brought me here to see a doctor. You bring a janitor who calls himself a doctor Johnson. What health service has this turned to? Let me go instead of being messed up with by your doctor Johnson'.

In an attempt to get the remaining important information, Dr Johnson asked: 'Where do you want to go to, sir?'

'Janitor Johnson or what, I am sure they did not bring me here to see a witch doctor. Do I look like your tribesman? If there is no proper doctor, then let me go and die in my house'.

Meanwhile, Fiona had set up the dressings and sutures by the side of Mr. Kinnock, waiting for Dr Johnson to stop the bleeding. As soon as Dr Johnson removed his white coat, put on the apron and began to scrub, Mr. Kinnock demanded to see the Consultant. He gave his reason as not wanting to be touched by a colored janitor. This message was relayed to the Consultant who was also colored. He told the Matron to get the client to sign that he did not want to be touched by a colored person.

Mr. Kinnock was not the first white Zeland person to make the demand he had made. A necessary document had been designed for that. The paper was given to him to sign. He signed and left the hospital still swearing. It was winter. He had, in his drunkenness, been waiting at the bus stop, not knowing that there were no night buses at that stop. The police who normally drove around did not pass through that street the rest of that night. In the morning, his body was brought to the Casualty. Dr Johnson saw him and certified him dead, from hemorrhage and exposure to cold.

Fiona followed him to the call room to collect the death certificate. Dr Johnson was sad. It would have been a few sutures and Mr. Kinnock would have lived. Perhaps.

'Doctor, it was not your fault. That is how some of these people behave. This time, he has caused his own death. There is no one else to blame.' She sat down as the doctor filled the certificate.

'Fiona, I thank you for your sympathy. Can we go out for a drink next time you are off duty? She smiled, collected the completed certificate and left. The date was neither accepted nor rejected. Both noted. Fiona was the first to act on the date. She looked at the doctors' duty roster and found a date both Dr Johnson and she would be off duty. Soon they were on duty together again. A chance to chat came up.

'Dr Johnson, was that your offer to go for a drink a threat or a promise?'

'What is the difference? I am ready when you are'. He did not drink much. Besides, each person, according to Zeland culture, paid for himself, for platonic encounters. Dr Johnson thought it was for all encounters.

The evening selected by Fiona arrived. She came to Dr Johnson's room in the doctors' quarters at the scheduled time. They walked to the *Pond*. The *Pond* was a quiet pub near the hospital. Most of the patrons worked in the hospital. They met there for occasional functions. It was a tryst on many occasions. Fiona and Okon sat at a far corner. That would reduce the number of those who would see them. Fiona did not mind. Dr Okon Johnson was a shy man, not by nature, but by upbringing. His father was a catechist in the Church of Zeland. He lived as prescribed by the scriptures. That was until he came to Zeland.

Okon asked Fiona what she would like to drink. She replied that she did not drink into an empty stomach. That sounded like the girls in Dr Johnson's Premier University. He had always avoided the occasions that led to that response. Things were changing fast for Okon. He merely raised his eyebrows, as both went to get some 'bite'. There was lamb stew and potato chips. Fiona asked for both. Okon did likewise. When they got to the cashier, Fiona paid for herself. Okon noted the difference from Premier University girls. He paid for his. As they got to their table, Fiona went and brought two bottles of cold water. They talked as they ate. Fiona was asking the questions. Okon responded with answers.

'Can I call you by your first name?'

Sure, but please pronounce it correctly'. He remembered the difficulty Dr McAndrew had with his name. He told Fiona that the 'o's in Okon were not silent.

'What is your surname?'

'Fergus'.

'How do you pronounce it?'

'Fegos'. How long have you been in Zeland? Did you come straight here? How did you know about here? Will you be going back?'

Dr Johnson kept answering until the last question. He was aware that some of his countrymen who came to Zeland to study graduated and stayed back to work. Some of them even married 'foreigners', having foreclosed the notion to return to the native country. The trend seemed to be increasing. There seemed to be a good life in Zeland compared to Konganoga. He was yet to experience it. He was just starting. He gave a straight answer to the last question.

'I have just come. My main aim is to get the Fellowship and take it from there'. Do you want me to go back already?'

'No, I was just asking'.

They finished eating.

Dr Johnson asked Fiona what she would like to drink. 'A glass of cider, please. I have a light brain. Besides, I am on duty in the morning'. Okon went to the bar and brought a glass of red wine and a glass of cider. He did not see a bottle of *small stout* on the rack. He sat down and they continued to chat.

'How long is your nursing training? How far have you gone with it? Are you enjoying it?' It was Fiona's turn to get under fire. She answered, not in syllables but, with elaboration. They were both more interested in the conversation than in the drinks. Dr Johnson thought that they could have stayed in his room and ordered the food from the hospital canteen. A bottle of red wine in the shop was cheaper than a glass of wine in the pub. However, there was no need to cry over spilt milk.

'You can visit me any time you like. I can cook you some Konganoga food'.

The name of the country was quite funny. Fiona hoped that the dish would be fun to eat. 'I will think about it. Thanks anyway for the offer. I think we should be going now. I am on early'.

They got up and Fiona put on her coat. Dr Johnson had not removed his overall, all that while. Although the pub was warm, it was cold to him. They got to the bus stop that served Fiona's destination. They continued to chat until the bus came. She entered and said to Dr Johnson 'Cheerio, see you later'.

'Take good care, see you.' Dr Johnson replied.

Chapter 4

AS AMIABLE AS THEY COME

Dr Johnson was taken aback on the first and last time he went to the Church nearest to where he lived. There were only a few worshippers. Apart from the members of the choir, the average age of the worshippers was about 65 years of age. He was familiar with some of the songs. He remembered *'Abide with me...'* He remembered *'When I survey the wondrous cross...'* At the end of the service, the congregation split into smaller groups on the grounds of the church, exchanging pleasantries while heading to the cars. Dr Okon suddenly realized that he stood alone. People just looked at him, grinned and sped off. A few waved a few fingers and walked on.

An elderly woman came to him.

'Nice to see you', she said

'Thanks. How are you?' Dr Johnson responded.

'I am all right, thank you. Where do you come from?'

'Konganoga.'

'Where is that?'

'Africa.'

'Which part of America is that?' She had expected Okon to say Mexico and was disappointed to expose her ignorance to the stranger.

'No, ma. Africa is south of the Mediterranean Sea.'

'Oh yes, my husband fought in the desert during the 2nd World War. Benson was a lovely man. We had a daughter following his last visit to Zeland. I know he is resting in peace. He did not come back at the end of the war.' Some tears followed the last sentence. 'I am sorry to embarrass you. Did you get converted here in Zeland?'

Dr Okon Johnson was on night duty later that evening. The conversation did not seem to have an urgent benefit to him.

'My father was a catechist'. She did not wait for a response. She excused herself and left. 'If they do not think I am a faithful, let them please themselves,' Dr Okon mused. He did not go to that Church or any other one after that conversation.

Dr Johnson was described by one of the Consultants, Mr. Owen to be of amiable disposition. He had learnt, through training at home and in the school, to be obedient. He believed that empty drums made the loudest noise and lived this aphorism. He also had very firm beliefs. It took him time to observe a circumstance, digest it and form an opinion. He was tenacious once he formed that opinion. What the Consultant noticed was the observation stage of Dr Okon Johnson's appraisal of the situation in which his ambition to be a specialist placed him. When the doctor he held locum for returned, Dr Johnson was asked if he would kindly cover another doctor whose leave was due. The same scenario recurred a few times. A substantive position soon arose. Dr Johnson was asked by his consultant to apply. He was a bit surprised. He felt he should have just walked into the job. The system was too orderly. The administrators knew their job. If a Consultant or other person had an interest in the filling of a vacancy, they would have to show it at an interview. Mr. Owen was a popular surgeon in the hospital. He was abrasive, but anyone in the hospital who needed an operation preferred him to do it. He often took delight to ridicule the hospital administration whenever they fumbled. This was often. He was in the interview for the position which Dr Johnson applied. It was his turn to field questions for the candidate.

'Dr Johnson, how long have you worked in this hospital and in what position?'

Dr Johnson narrated how he started off as a locum tenens. By the time the first job ended another doctor went on leave and he was asked to continue. Soon the doctors made a duty roster for their leave and put his name to cover them.

'How many complaints have been filed against you since you became a career locum tenens doctor?'

At this, others in the panel, including the administrators, laughed. It was rare for Mr. Owen to induce laughter in business. Rather, he was known to cause tears.

'I have not been queried, Sir'.

'You have not crossed the path of any nurse?' Matron Ogilvie was on the panel. She did not know where Mr. Owen was heading to. She certainly did not want the interview to be used to cast aspersions on her 'children' as she fondly called them. She has been in the business of nursing and running battles with doctors.

'Objection, Chairman. Dr Johnson was not in the nursing department. If he has any problems, it would be with the medical committee.'

The Chairman, who had become interested in the interview with regards to the candidate, responded.

'Objection sustained.' There was another round of laughter. This was to the relief of Dr Okon Johnson. When the question about crossing path came up, his mind went to Fiona. 'Did Mr. Owen know something? He had come to regard the white man with awe. In his private moments, he would recall the saying '*bekee wu agbara*' (the white man is a spirit). Matron Ogilvie saved him from that question.

Mr. Owen used that remark on crossing the path to divert the attention of the panel. There were two more candidates to interview. It was obvious that Mr. Owen wanted Dr Johnson. He asked the other candidates intimidating questions until each showed his soft underbelly. At the conclusion of the interview, Mr. Owen summarized his own assessment. He preferred Dr Johnson over and above any other candidate. He then excused himself 'to go and rescue my registrar who was stuck in a patient's abdomen'. He left the panel to continue. One of the administrators on the panel was the first to speak. They knew the amount of trouble Mr. Owen would throw up, especially after he made it clear who he wanted. They suggested to the Chairman to let Mr. Owen have his say and his way. The Chairman, a retiring Manager, had been envisioning Mr. Owen rushing into the theatre, perhaps with a sharp knife, going to rescue his registrar. How could the poor chap have got into the patient's abdomen? Was he swallowed? He was ruminating when the plea was made by one of his staff.

'Any objection, ladies and gentleman?'

A pin could have dropped. No one said anything. No one wanted any scene from Mr. Owen. He had his say and would have his way.

Four days later, Dr Okon Johnson landed his first substantive post in the Zeland Health Service as a Senior House Officer (SHO). He phoned Dr McAndrew. He wrote letters to friends in Konganoga. Success has a way of begetting success. However, the same applies to failure. The result of the Primary examination taken two weeks earlier was released. Dr Johnson got his success letter by post. He showed it to Mr. Owen. The latter was very happy, not just for Dr Johnson, but also for himself. His support at the interview had been justified.

Dr Johnson spent four years working in Kirkurd General Hospital with Mr. Owen as his mentor. After two years as SHO, a Registrar job came up. The interview went very much like the SHO interview in which Mr. Owen virtually intimidated the panel into voting for Dr Johnson. This time, a few people had met Dr Johnson in his professional capacity. He was popularly known to be a caring surgeon, not abrasive like his master but equally effective. On completing the fourth year, he sat the final examination in surgery and passed. He thus became a Fellow of the College of Surgeons. With that, he shed his title of 'Dr' and replaced it with a reversion back to 'Mr.' He became Mr. Okon Johnson. He decided to specialize further, this time in Ophthalmology. Mr. Owen helped him to get a training position in that specialty. In a further period of two years, Okon obtained the Diploma in Ophthalmology. He began to look for a permanent hospital appointment. That was when he began to see the proverbial glass ceiling. He could see where he wanted to be, but he could not get there.

Chapter 5

A COMPANION FOR A CAREER

While Dr Johnson was preparing for his examination in surgery, Fiona was preparing the grounds to cement their relationship. After the first date in which they ate lamb stew and drank cider and red wine, they were to meet several more times. They were getting familiar. Fiona would sometimes bring him food she prepared in her flat. They became regular companions at hospital social events, to the notice of their contemporaries. She got to know everyone in Dr Okon Johnson's album of photographs. He had come from Konganoga with his album of photographs. They had visited her parents twice. It was at the second visit that Mr. and Mrs. Fergus raised the eyebrow to each other, as Fiona and Okon left to return to Kirkurd. After he passed the final examination in surgery, they decided to get married. They had weighed in the reaction of several parties in that marriage. Whatever, Mr. and Mrs. Fergus had not been looking forward to having in-laws in 'darkest

Africa'. It just did not fit with their environment. However, they knew that that their opinion would count only up to a certain point. Beyond that point, they would have to rue and grin, if the push came to a shove. The next they knew was the engagement of the couple, surgeon and nurse. Mrs. Fergus was the first to congratulate her daughter, and by implication, Dr Johnson. In order to keep the ceremony to a low key and acting to the dictates of the economic reality, the couple arranged to limit the celebration to a registry marriage. Dr Johnson invited Dr McAndrew and his wife, Ingrid. They attended. Mr. Owen and Audrey could not attend but they sent a warm greeting card. A few common friends from Kirkurd District General Hospital were there, all by invitation. The couple did not bother with a honeymoon. Dr Okon Johnson's convincing argument when he discussed the matter with Fiona was 'what is new?'

Dr Johnson applied for accommodation for a married couple and got one, a two-bedroom flat. It was a nice comfortable pad. Heating cost was moderate because the windows were double-glazed.

In four years, Dr Okon Johnson successfully completed the specialist training he had sponsored himself by working and studying in Zeland. His specialty was in Ophthalmology. He was quite pleased with himself. In the Zeland system, a surgical specialist was addressed with the title 'Mr.' instead of 'Dr'. Okon Johnson took offence at any of his acquaintances, including the staff of the hospital, who persisted in referring to him as Dr Johnson.

His employment in Hospital was coming to an end. In spite of several applications and a few interviews, he was finding it difficult to get attached to the healthcare system where he would deploy the skills he had spent close to a decade acquiring.

While he worked and studied Ophthalmology in

Zeland, Mr. Okon Johnson shared a leftist political philosophy with a few friends from different parts of the Commonwealth. He spent a lot of time participating and organizing rallies, protesting one thing or the other. What to protest about were rather too many. The Zeland society was fast developing into a capitalist economy driven by the few against the interests of the many. In one of the protests, immigrants, classified by the state of Zeland as illegal, organized to confront the government to declassify them and legitimize their stay in Zeland. To them, nature did not declare any person illegal. It was all contrived. It was therefore, the duty and moral obligation of those who contrived the classification to dismantle it. Appeals were made to the appropriate sections of the governing organs, while violent protests were being planned against the government. Mr. Johnson was vocal about the inequalities in society. He assigned himself at the vanguard in the crusade to equalize the society. He preferred peaceful protests. He however, began to notice that violent radicals were infiltrating the ranks of the protesters and were about to *hijack* the movement.

Fiona had delivered two young daughters in succession. She was also working in Kirkurd District General Hospital. She commuted to work. Frustrated by his inability to secure a substantive job, Mr. Johnson often took time off to search for work. At such times, he went on the dole to receive unemployment benefits. During such periods, he participated in a few demonstrations against the capitalist economy and the policies of the capitalist-oriented government.

The government proposed a clamp down on immigration. Some of the politicians on the far right advocated for the 'rehabilitation' of all foreigners in their home countries. No exception was made for the citizens of the Commonwealth. Rehabilitation was interpreted to mean expulsion. If he could not be given a job, the system had found him a cause.

Mr. Okon Johnson, the tenacious eye surgeon, now had a cause to engage his attention. He took it full-time. He was involved in the organization of rallies and marches. With the threat of expulsion, the group upped their plots by one more ratchet. They began to employ fire bombs and the demonstrations became more violent. The activities of these dissidents, as the press daubed them, were often in the news. The violence put off even the sympathizers. The government doubled efforts to confront them 'within the rule of law', while covert counter measures went on. It was not long before the 'dissidents' began to feel the heat from government's counter action

Mr. Johnson soon began to concentrate on his own plight of being unemployed in spite of being skilled and employable. Fiona had been sympathetic to and supportive of her husband initially. However, she was not going to let him destroy himself, thereby his family, by his radicalism. If only her husband would imbibe professionalism, they would be fine, she thought. She decided to go and seek advice from Mr. Owen. He had retired to York with Audrey, to enable them study the intricacies of the Yorkshire pudding. Audrey had been a caterer before she too retired. Fiona Johnson had phoned to set up an appointment. She arrived on schedule.

'You are very welcome. How is Okon and did he manage to get a permanent appointment?'

'No, Mr. Owen. That is why I have come to see you. I think you are the only one I know that Okon would listen to. He reveres you. When he could not get an appointment after several locum appointments, he drifted into full-time radicalism. I have encouraged him to return to Konganoga and offered to follow him with the children. The rallies are becoming violent. I just do not want to be a widow, with children without a father'. She began to sob. Audrey had come in as Fiona narrated her mission. She brought a box of tissue papers for Fiona to wipe off her tears.

Mr. Owen was sorry about the situation. He added that something had to be done. 'Certainly, tears are not it'. He would get in touch with a pal at the foreign office. 'Which country did you say?' he asked Fiona

'Konganoga'.

Mr. Owen picked up his gold fountain pen and scribbled what he thought he heard. 'Audrey, any tea? I am famished. I don't know about you two.'

'If you are hungry, you just have to say it. I'll fix something in a jiffy'. She went into her kitchen while Mr. Owen diverted attention by asking after Fiona's two daughters.

Audrey soon appeared with an apple pie big enough to serve three. She brought ice cream. Each person helped himself or herself with the pie, the ice cream and the tea. Fiona meanwhile kept watching the time. She knew what train she wanted. She thanked her hosts and craved their indulgence at her disturbance. She told Mr. Owen to please help her and Okon and the children. She did not know what exactly she wanted him to do. She merely cast her bread upon the waters. It was now up to the return of the waves. She went to the road to catch a bus. She arrived at the train station with a few minutes to spare before the train arrived and took off again.

Mr. Owen had a friend whose son worked in the foreign office. He had been Chairman at the wedding of Martin Spencer. He had established contact with Martin, in addition to his ties with the father. He rang Martin Spencer up.

'Hello Martin, its Mr. Owen here'.

'Hello, Mr. Owen, it is nice of you to call'.

'Yes. Tell me, do you know anything about Konganoga?'

'Well, yes. All I know about the place cannot fill my cupped hands. Yes a little bit'.

'I'll go straight to the point. There is this properly trained doctor from there who is finding it very difficult to land a job here. This is causing his young family enormous hardship and disharmony. I was just wondering if it will not be better for the chap to go back there, considering the manpower needs of Konganoga'.

'We don't really get to know about the internal events in these colonies, but I can make some enquiries.'

'Precisely! Do me that favor, will you?'

'I will get back to you as soon as I hit something'.

The timing could not have been more auspicious. There was a cocktail party at the Konganoga consulate scheduled for the following Saturday and Martin had been invited. He had forgotten what the party was for. Mr. Owen's call upgraded that invitation to a 'must do' status. He attended, and on time too. He met the secretary of the Consul, Mr. Wadinga who he had made an acquaintance with not long ago. They exchanged pleasantries. During this exchange, Martin found out what the party was about. A delegation from a new University in Konganoga was visiting for the purpose of interviewing academic staff for this University. The Consulate had received applications following a recent advertisement by the new University for academic staff. Martin had not asked Mr. Owen for details of his candidate. He did not foresee his stumbling on to something soon after the telephone request. He therefore, did not ask the secretary whether the candidate had been shortlisted for the interview. By virtue of his stint at the intelligence section of the foreign office, Martin was aware of the need to pursue a trail with speed and vigor, in order not to let pass a quarry. He stepped aside from the party and called Mr. Owen. He informed him that a team had come from Konganoga to recruit academic staff for a new University. He asked for details of the doctor. He got his name and his qualifications. The later would be quite applicable if the University had a school of medicine.

With the information he got, Martin sought out the secretary to the consulate and passed on the same information he had obtained from Mr. Owen. Mr. Martin Spencer relished being at his former role in the service. It was a rather familiar and intriguing turf. The files of the candidates to be interviewed were on the secretary's office. It was a simple matter for him to go and check. He did. The name Okon Johnson was not there. He reverted to Mr. Spencer and revealed his findings. He revealed more. The interview was for four days. The candidate could still apply and would be given a special privilege to do so as the closing date for receiving the application had lapsed for a week. Mr. Spencer then took a chance on Mr. Owen being asleep. The old fox was not only awake; he was going through the day's *Financial Times*. Mr. Spencer's call went through and he relayed the information from the secretary.

Chapter 6

ON THE HOMEWARD JOB TRAIL

Mr. Owen phoned Fiona Johnson and relayed the information about an academic position in a new University in Konganoga. Mr. Okon Johnson was away to take part in a protest rally. It was his instruction not to be disturbed at such occasions. Luckily, Fiona had access to his curriculum vitae including Mr. Johnson's previous application papers. She assembled them and wrote one for the present recruitment exercise. The application was sent to Mr. Owens. He forwarded the material to Martin Spencer. The later transmitted the application material to the secretary of the consulate. Mr. Wadinga read it, but was not personally interested. However, Mr. Okon Johnson's credentials were relevant for the purposes of the interview. The new University was cited in Wadinga's home area of Konganoga, Kiba. From his name, Okon Johnson was not from there. Based on the recommendation of Mr. Spencer, Mr. Okon Johnson's name was added to the list of the shortlisted candidates and was scheduled for the last day of the interview.

Fiona had initially concealed from her husband the contacts for a job which she had made on his behalf. She was not very sure that Okon would give 100% approval to the initiative. He had once in a while expressed a desire to go home but his involvement in the foreign national's movement had for some time taken center stage in all that he was doing. He had, despite his professional training begun to relish opposition and anti government agitations.

Fiona wanted to ensure that the contacts began to materialize before she would inform her husband about what she had been able to achieve towards the family's resettlement.

She was not sure what the future held for her and her family in a foreign country far away from home, an area which, right from her early years had often been associated with barbarism and all kinds of unpleasant stories. She and her friends prior to her meeting and falling in love with Dr Johnson had always associated people from areas such as Konganoga as colonies that Zeland was beginning to succeed in civilizing.

Indeed Fiona had experienced some difficulty initially with pronouncing the name Konganoga. For the first few months after her marriage to Dr Johnson she occasionally still pronounced Konganoga as *Konagoga*.

When, eventually, the invitation for interview arrived and Fiona made a clean breast of her contacts to her husband, the latter initially thought that his wife was playing some April Fool's Day fun on a July 1st day. It was only when the invitation papers were produced and Dr Johnson saw the official letter heading of his country that he began to feel convinced. He was exceedingly proud of his wife and after giving her several kisses for her excellent initiative he said:

"Fiona, I feel daily more convinced that you were really born a combination of two cultures Zeland and Konganoga. You daily surprise me with your intelligence, your enterprise and your doggedness on issues that you believe in. I am truly grateful. And whether this venture materializes or not, I will always be grateful to you."

There were five members of the interview panel. The panel had interviewed two candidates before Dr Johnson was called in. Although he felt unease at being addressed as Dr Johnson, he did not protest. It could be misinterpreted as arrogance if he started explaining to the interviewing team that he should professionally be addressed as Mr. Johnson. Besides, it did not matter in the circumstances. He was shown a seat in a chair opposite the interview panel. The Chairman introduced himself and the members of his panel. The interview had started. Without any further protocols, the Chairman switched his attention to Dr Johnson.

'Dr Johnson, briefly tell us about yourself.'
'I am Mr. Okon Johnson. I come from Konganoga'.
'Where in Konganoga?'
'Madibua,' Mr Johnson answered.

Mr. Park, who represented the Assistant Registrar, was excited to find such a high ranking officer from his tribe. He could not restrain himself, even though it was not his turn to field questions.

'Madibua!?' Mr. Park exclaimed.

Over the years with perceived feelings and accusations of tribal discrimination, of which the victims included the people from Madibua, many people had begun to disguise their names. One way to do so was to adopt foreign names as surnames and first names as well. In Konganoga, there were several tribes with distinct languages. In some languages, the dialects of the same language differed significantly enough for these dialects to be mistaken for different languages. Traditionally, people answered names that had meanings. Thus, one could answer a name or its translation and retain the same meaning. If a group in a tribe, for some material gains decided to be known as a new tribe or nationality, they could translate their original tribal names to a foreign translation of that name. Madibua was a new nationality from the Agbaland tribe. A person who was known as *Ngozi* when Madibua had not declared itself a separate nationality from Agbaland would change his or her name to 'Blessing' which represented the English translation of the name. This was to mask the earlier identity. Some people would see that as an example of a complex or *inferiority complex*. Those who changed names would see it as emancipation from tribal subjugation, a sort of declaration of self rule.

Mr. Johnson did not know the reason for Mr. Park's excitement. He answered the question. 'Yes, Madibua.'

Mr. Park had realized that he had intruded into the process inappropriately. He allowed the interview to proceed according to the laid down protocol. He was careful to avoid leading questions. This would have been construed to mean a declaration of interest. The interview eventually came to an end. Mr. Johnson was told that each candidate would be communicated with the result of the individual's interview by post. Okon returned to his family, unexcited. He told Fiona what transpired. She was not really versed in Konganoga ways. They would have to wait for the outcome of the interview. One thing was sure; Okon was minded to find employment even in Konganoga. Over the course of his residency years and, in consideration of his marriage to a Zeland citizen he had gradually grown to fall in love with Zeland culture and ways of life. He would have loved to stay back. His wife had a life in the system and his little daughters though still tender in age, were coming up in school. Apart from the raw facts that he was not absorbed by the system and but for the subtle acts of discrimination by a certain percentage of the population, he was enjoying himself and was happy with the system.

The interview results came out two weeks later. Mr. Johnson's letter was an apology that his specialty had not yet been established in the new University. The Registrar wished him better success with future applications.

The same reason given to reject his application could have been used to justify his employment. If the University had not established the specialty, Mr. Johnson was an opportunity to do so. He was a qualified academic. And a Department of Ophthalmology or at least an ophthalmology unit was a *sine qua non* for a comprehensive medical education system. The truth of the matter was that Mr. Jonson's first name Okon gave away his tribe. His tribe did not fit the job. Okon found out later that instead of himself, one Dr Kwame of Tangonga, who was not as qualified as Dr Johnson and who was not even from Konganoga, secured the employment. The system felt safer and more sympathetic to a foreigner than a national whose tribe did not *fit* or sound exactly right.

Mr. Johnson's attitude to the letter was defiant. He had continued with the protests against state capitalist policies. The protests were attracting the attention of the mobile police force. On one occasion, Mr. Johnson had been arrested and detained overnight at the police station. When the Divisional Police Officer (DPO) learnt about it in the morning, he was quick to have him released. The likes of Mr. Johnson attracted the human rights activists. Following several letters detailing infringements of fundamental human rights, the central police Chief embarked on a campaign to stop or reduce police infringements of citizens' human rights. The DPO was not keen for the attention of the central police chief or that of the Zeland's snoopy press.

Fiona had continued to complain to Okon to free himself from the protests and concentrate his energies on the welfare of his family. He now had three nagging issues. He needed a job. That would probably address the other issues that included his relationship with his peers at the protest group and his family. He decided to visit Konganoga to look for a job. Fiona paid for the travel.

He decided to go and find out why he was not successful at the interview conducted by the University in Zeland. He had talked to two other candidates at the interview. One of them had got a letter of appointment. He had been given six months to make up his mind. The offer included his expected salary as well as responsibility of the University with regards to shipping his belongings to Konganoga and flight tickets for him and his family. That was what Mr. Johnson would also have received if he had been successful. Further, his friends told him that the administrator at that interview was his tribesman. His name was Mr. Park.

The more Mr. Johnson considered his prevailing plight, the more determined he resolved to find out why he had not got the job earlier. At the University, Mr. Johnson found the office of Mr. Park. He had a secretary. That meant that he was fairly highly placed. When he called at the office, he was happy to find that Mr. Park was on seat.

'Good morning, Mr. Park. Do you remember me? I am Dr Johnson. I was among the candidates you and the recruitment team interviewed recently in Zeland. Unfortunately, I did not get the appointment.'

'Oh, yes. You are the doctor from Madibua. I remember you very well. I was even more disappointed that the offer was made to a foreigner in preference to you. I argued passionately on your behalf but some vested interests prevailed. Have you secured an appointment now? I drafted the letter to you and the others. This is civil service. You do as you are directed to do. You guys out there probably think that we are better off than you there are. We are not.'

'Well, home is best. However, there are not many people in my field. I therefore expected to be given an appointment following the interview.'

'That is the point.'

Mr. Johnson did not understand what Mr. Park just said and indicated so by his body language. Mr. Park did not want to bias the mind of Dr Johnson. He looked at Dr Johnson full in the face. He was immediately sympathetic. He also had a score to settle with the leader of the interview panel, Prof Ewere, the Deputy Vice-Chancellor. Dr Johnson's case was not the first time their paths had crossed and clashed. Mr. Park knew his job as an administrator and bided his time.

'I think you should write another application and take it to the Head of Department of Surgical Sciences. He was the one who requested somebody in your field. He has mildly protested to me that no one had been appointed from the interview. He will minute in your application. Ultimately, the Dean will do the same. There will be no reason to recommend negatively. I wish you all the best in your endeavors.'

Mr. Park had the knack to go straight to the point, often with anticipated effect. It would have been futile for Dr Okon Johnson to expect more at that point from Mr. Park. He left the Deputy Registrar's office and found his way to a business centre. His Curriculum Vitae was in a flash drive. He also had hard copies of his documents in his portfolio. He edited his application letter and printed out the most recent and appropriate copy. At the Department of Surgical Sciences office, the head of department was on seat.

'Good afternoon. I am Mr. Okon Johnson, visiting from Zeland.'

'Good afternoon to you, sir. My name is Dr Ziebu of Surgical Sciences. You are very welcome. It brightens our day to see you people who are out there. With you there, all our hope cannot be lost. However, we need you guys here in spite of the constraints.'

It was as if he read Okon Johnson's mind.

'Thanks for the kind sentiments. I actually came home to look at the prospects.'

'Prospects? There is a gaping need for manpower in virtually all areas. In this Department alone, we call it a Division to mask the serious manpower deficiency. There are several units that should be departments but the staff are not here. What is your specialty? Don't tell me surgery or O and G.'

'As a matter of fact, I applied for a position in Ophthalmology and I was interviewed in Zeland last month. However, I was not successful. I am told you prefer foreigners here.'

'Foreigners or citizens, we need all we can get. We got someone from that interview but there is no staff in Ophthalmology. I am covering some aspects and the man you referred to also does likewise. An Ophthalmologist comes here once in a month from another State, mainly to teach the medical students. Now that you are here, please bring me your application. This country is sick. By the way, I know that in Zeland, specialist surgeons are referred to as Mr. It is done the American way here. If people coming to see you realize that you are a Mr., they will refuse to see you insisting to see a Dr.'

'I carry the necessary documents as I visit places. My application into your department is here'. Mr. Johnson brought out the application letter as well copies of his certificates. Dr Ziebu took them and glanced through them. He usually kept a step ahead in his thinking. *Here I am sitting here and what I need presents on a platter of gold. This is what this University spent quite a bit by organizing an interview in Zeland and still did not get it. The gentleman is carrying relevant documents as he tours. The very next place he presents with these, we've lost him.*

'Do you have time? We should go to the Dean's office and see if he is in the office.'

Both men left Dr Ziebu's office for the Dean's. At the time they got to the office, the Dean was coming into his office.

'Our timing is nonpareil, sir. This is Dr Okon Johnson just visiting from Zeland. Dr Johnson, meet Prof Kemji, Dean of the Faculty of Clinical Sciences.'

'Let us get into the office, gentlemen. In my place, you don't receive important visitors on the corridor. You do not offer them kola nuts there either. I do not want to miss an august visitor.'

As soon as they entered the Dean's office, the Dean went straight to his chair, to secure it, as it were. He showed his visitors their own seats. He then switched on the air conditioner on the window. He also switched on the ceiling fan. Dr Ziebu excused himself momentarily but soon came back. He introduced his companion's mission.

'Has he applied?' Prof Kemji asked.

'Yes, Dean, the application has been sent to your secretary.'

The Dean pressed the bell and the secretary promptly appeared. 'Do we have any correspondence to deal with?'

'Yes, sir. One just arrived. I have documented it and will bring it.' There was a system for tracking documents. They were usually entered into an in-coming register.

Those being dispatched from an office were entered in a dispatch register. The sources and targets of each were also appropriately documented. This practice arose from experience. Some administrative staff sometimes engaged in sharp practices and sometimes were irresponsible, or both. Applicants were well advised to follow their submission from one office after another.

Prof Kemji glanced at the document brought by his secretary but chose to hear from the Head of Department. Dr Ziebu explained and reminded the Dean about shortage of staff in the Surgical Division. He further explained that a team had been to Zeland and back. The team reported that they did not see many applicants whose applications were listed. Dr Johnson was actually interviewed and was later told that his department was yet to be set up. Yet in the establishment of the Faculty, the department was listed but no staff had been recruited due to lack of applications.

Chapter 7

THE FEDERAL UNIVERSITY OF SCIENCE AND TECHNOLOGY, KIBA

Prof Kemji was aware of the dirty politics and inefficiencies in the University system in Konganoga generally. He had been fighting such dirty politics and inefficiencies in his previous University until he was frustrated out. Thanks to the new Federal University of Science and Technology (FUST), Kiba, where he was relieved to transfer his services. At the time of his appointment, there was a serious shortage of teaching staff. The founders of the University appointed anyone who had the requisite qualifications. Accreditation of the new University by the Council of Universities was *sine qua non*. Prof Kemji was a renowned Physiologist. He was described as an asset in the panel report following his interview. Over the years in 'Science and Tech', he began to notice the rot as it set in. Academic excellence was graded inferior or, at best, at par with primordial considerations (using his phrase). Federal University of Science and

Technology, Kiba was due another accreditation visit. The Vice-Chancellor had announced in the University Senate that if any program failed accreditation, heads would roll. Yet a panel travelled to Zeland, interviewed a candidate, found him worthy but rejected him because the department had not been set up. Prof Kemji wondered in his balding head about who was to set up the department other than qualified individuals. It just did not make sense. Not much made sense to Prof Kemji. He received the application and told Dr Johnson to see him in two to three days. He preferred the title Dr to Mr. which Okon Johnson was used to in Zeland.

The days to the accreditation visit were drawing near. The nearer the date, the faster it seemed to be approaching. Prof Kemji carried the file of Dr Okon Johnson to the Vice-Chancellor. He had written a covering memorandum in case he did not see the Chief Executive. Without first ascertaining whether Professor Ozanda was in or not, he gave the letter personally to the VC's correspondence secretary or clerk who duly entered the submission in the appropriate register. Professor Kemji appended his signature because he brought it. In the Memorandum, he had subtly mentioned that the essential documents were to be given to the VC's confidential secretary. Therefore, the clerk did not object to Prof Kemji taking Dr Johnson's file along with him.

The Vice Chancellor, Prof Ozanda, was in his office with the personal assistant to the V-C (PAVC). Prof Kemji tapped on the door, opened it and entered. He sat down in a sofa to give the PAVC time to conclude his brief and leave. The VC respected the Dean for his outspokenness. Reports reaching the Vice Chancellor from informants had clearly excluded Prof Kemji from the shenanigans rampant in FUST. He did not indulge in harassment of students or staff, whether sexually or financially. He also did not condone such misdemeanors from others. He was a stickler for laid down rules. In his Faculty, the pass mark in every subject was 50%. Anyone who scored 49.6% did not pass, 'according to the regulation', as he would remind those pleading otherwise. The Vice-Chancellor would rather attend to Prof Kemji. The PAVC knew when to leave and did so.

'Good afternoon, VC, sir'.

'Dean, you are welcome, please sit yourself down. I hope there is no problem, not that we expect problems from your students. You know your Faculty is the jewel on the crown of this University and I am not kidding you'.

'Thank you, sir. We appreciate. You know that accreditation visit is just two months away. Time has a way of pacing up nearer a set date. I have this application for Ophthalmology. There is no staff there at all. This applicant is visiting from Zeland. I noticed that he has sets of these applications in his bag. I suspect that each place he goes, he drops a set. I am not sure of the institution in which will receive this application and let it pass. The Head of Surgical Division saw him this morning and brought him right into my office as I was returning from my lecture. The papers are here. I have gone through them. I think we should not allow him to go.'

'Dean, what precisely are you recommending? Remember that there is an embargo on employment, although accreditation takes precedence over those paper embargoes. What is your prayer?'

'Thanks, VC. I have recommended that he be given temporary employment, pending a formal interview. That way, he enters our staff list for the Accreditation visit. If, at interview, he does not satisfy the panel, so be it'.

The Vice Chancellor remembered his injunction

regarding failing accreditation. He knew that Prof Kemji would have documented his prayer. He was that careful. He took the file from Prof Kemji. He looked at the application itself. The Head of department recommended interview. The Dean recommended exactly what he prayed the VC to do. It was a simple matter for the Vice Chancellor. He answered the Dean's prayer in writing, signed and dated it. Both Professors exchanged some banters, mainly on the impending accreditation visit. The Dean thanked the VC and left with the file in his hand. The document was entered as received and as dispatched. Each was countersigned by Prof Kemji

The Dean knew the next move. He was to take the file himself to the Registrar who would summon the Deputy Registrar, Establishment, to issue the letter for temporary employment pending an interview to regularize the appointment, so to say. At the Registrar's office, he had the letter of application endorsed by the Vice-Chancellor recorded in the register. He then took it to the Registrar. After reading it, the Registrar told Prof Kemji that he would process it.

'Reg, you know how fast and risky the movement of memos can be here. That is why I have come by myself. The VC is aware of the need to grab this doctor. So endorse it as you would. The lecturer is still in my office on his way to the University of Konganoga in Kumbrujaa. I want to stop that trip'.

The Registrar looked at the author of the application and assigned an ethnic group to the author. He did not have a personal grudge, nor did he have any enthusiasm for the applicant. He endorsed the application to the Deputy Registrar, Establishment to issue the letter. He called a messenger to take the letter. Prof Kemji thanked the Registrar and followed the messenger. There was no taking of chance on this application. As soon as the Dean and messenger walked into the office of the Deputy Registrar, Establishment, it was obvious that the matter was fairly serious. As the messenger handed over the application with its numerous endorsements, Prof Kemji added that he was together with the messenger. The Deputy Registrar requested the Dean to go and promised to do the letter and pass it on. Prof Kemji thanked him but informed him that he would take the letter himself. It was futile to argue, not with all the endorsements on that application. The appointment letter was written and signed. The dispatch register was signed by Prof Kemji as having collected it. Prof Kemji was done. He returned to his office and called the Head of Division of Surgical Sciences to see him. Before he arrived, Prof Kemji made a photocopy of the letter of temporary appointment. When the Head of Division of Surgical Sciences, Dr Ziebu came, he was pleasantly surprised at the letter of appointment, in spite of its being in the interim. He collected the letter.

Dr Johnson came to the Dean's office in two not three days after his last visit. The Dean welcomed him. He did not offer him a seat. He told him to see the Head of Surgical Division. As Dr Johnson got to the door, the Dean called him back.

'By the way, when can you start?'

Dr Okon Johnson was confused instantly. The way the Dean received him less than a minute previously appeared ominous. He recovered his calm and told the Dean that there was as at the time, nothing to start on.

'See me after you have seen Dr Ziebu. I am sure he will be in the office now.'

'Sure, I will do, sir.'

Dr Johnson soon returned to see Prof Kemji. This time he was grinning from ear to ear. 'I saw him, Prof Kemji. I am grateful for this. May be I can answer the question that

I did not understand earlier. I will go back to Zeland and prepare to return. I suppose I can do so in two months.'

'Actually, that will defeat the object of the whole exercise. An accreditation exercise has been scheduled to hold here in three weeks. The team must sight everyone on the staff list. If you are not here when they come, it really means that you were not on ground. Perhaps you should see what adjustments you can make in order to be physically present during the exercise'.

'I'll do so, sir. Again thanks for this opportunity'.

When Dr Johnson left, Prof Kemji sat down to go through the keynote address he was to deliver in New Jersey. He was requested to give a keynote address to a group of upward bound young men and women from Konganoga with a notice of one year. He took his time to prepare the lecture as well as search for the best fare deal he could get. He asked his secretary to pack 20 copies of each of the latest two books that he published. The meeting in New Jersey was to hold in one week. His flight ticket, hotel reservation and personal travel allowance had been secured. Time was racing. At the close of work, Prof Kemji put his lap top in the bag. He switched off the appliances in his office. Although the secretary would check these before going home for the day, Prof Kemji always wanted 'to make assurance double sure'.

Chapter 8

ERUDITE INTERNATIONAL SCHOLAR

Prof Kemji would appropriately be described as a versatile scholar. He carved out a niche for himself in the academic world nationally and internationally. His friends could not understand his apparent lack of ambition; especially political ambition. He would not hustle for any appointment. He was brought up to work hard. For him, there lay the key to success. He was also contented with himself. This satisfaction was borne out of personal experience and philosophy rather than orthodox religion. It was difficult to know which religion he professed, Islam or Christianity. He could actually fit into *Chrislam* if there was such a religion.

Prof Kemji had written a few books. He decided to use the opportunity of the visit to New Jersey to market his books in another country. He packed a total of 40 copies of his two recent books into two suit cases. Luggage to be checked in to aircraft in Konganoga was manually searched by a group of personnel at the international airport at Kumbruuja. In view of pervading lack of patriotism in Konganoga, workers contrived ways and means to enrich themselves by hook or by crook, preferably by crook. The customs officer asked Prof Kemji to open the first case. It was packed full with books. The eyes of the customs officer opened wide. Whether by joy or by ecstasy, Prof Kemji did not know. He also was not interested. The customs officials were interested.

'Sir, does the second box contain the same?'

'I am afraid so.' The understanding to the customs officer was that the Professor was afraid that he had been 'caught'. This emboldened him.

'Are these for sale?'

'Not really. I am going to present at a meeting of an academic club to which I belong.'

'Sir, are you exporting these books or are you importing them?'

'What is the difference? If I am not allowed to travel with the books by the law, let me keep them here. Someone will come to collect them at a convenient period before I return'. He soon recalled that Konganoga was a democracy that endorsed free speech; at least it did on paper. The professor was travelling out of Konganoga and yet a customs officer asked whether he was 'importing or exporting' 40 books in two titles written by him!

The motive for the question soon became clear. The officer requested to take a copy. The plan to intimidate Prof Kemji into negotiating with something had not cut ice with the professor.

'You can keep it,' Prof Kemji said and went on to the next stand, dragging along his two suitcases. He was eventually through with the officials. In a few hours, passengers were advised to board the aircraft. The pilot and head of the cabin crew each made their routine broadcasts. The pilot welcomed the passengers on board. He explained the flight route and expected arrival time. His broadcast was informative. The passengers were requested to enjoy the flight. The head of the cabin crew, a lady, an iron lady, was not going to be left out. Her announcement was packed with prohibitive directives. Bags and boxes were not to be left on seats or on the tables for food. In the event of an emergency, no one was to block the aisle, etc, etc. At this point, passengers usually went mute and blank. There was to be no smoking in the aircraft. Smoke detectors were installed in the toilets. Violators would be prosecuted on land. Mobile phones were to be switched off during the duration of the flight and lap tops could be used when the aircraft was cruising at its maximum altitude. Even Prof Kemji could not rationalize the new craze concerning the 'chit chat gadgets. The pilot ordered the cabin crew to do final checks. They dutifully complied.

'Cabin crew, please take your seats for takeoff.' The craft taxied out into the runway and waited. Soon, the engine roared into full blast and the huge bird was on its way. The pilot stepped on the throttle. The big bird responded by lifting her nose up. This dragged the rear tires in the upward bound direction. In seconds, the bird was up fully in the air. This was the risky part of the travel for two reasons. It was a point of no return. The process of getting airborne could not be aborted at that point. The aircraft was at it maximum vulnerable situation. After 9 hours of smooth flight, the jet liner landed safely and smoothly at the John F Kennedy Airport.

At the immigration, two areas were created and people filed in to each one that applied to each disembarked passenger. One area was for the citizens. The other area was designated 'Other Passports'. As the line moved forward, two police officers were walking about with dogs. Prof Kemji was not bothered about the police or the dogs.

According to him, they were sniffing for hard drugs. He was not in possession of any. Suddenly one little dog went to an Asian passenger and jumped on to her handbag. People became curious. She was a pretty woman in her forties. The police woman running the dog quickly seized the bag and asked the woman to open it. Inside was an apple. The police woman asked for the Indian woman's customs form. There was no entry there to indicate that there was a fruit. The passenger was made to sign that an apple was recovered from her. The police woman then congratulated the dog and gave her a piece of chocolate. She quickly ate it up. Prof Kemji thought in his mind 'what a bitch' and moved on.

When Prof Kemji got to the desk of the immigration officer, the officer smiled and greeted Prof Kemji. He returned the compliments, also with a smile. That was the end of civility for the Professor.

'Passport please'.

As soon as Prof Kemji brought out his Konganoga passport, the immigration officer's countenance dipped. He straightened up in his seat.

'Where have you come from?'
What is the purpose of this visit?
How long are you staying?
What address will you be staying at?
Have you been here before?
Who will be responsible for your stay?
What is the proof that they will?
What is the room number in the Hotel?
What is the telephone number of the hotel manager?
Where do you work?
What as?
How did you get promoted to the rank of Professor?
How many publications are required to make one a Professor in *Konga*? Is that how you call it?

Was your father a Professor?

Where is your wife?

The more answers Prof Kemji gave, the more questions reeled out.

Is she expecting you back?

'Officer, I am not in a position to know what my wife is thinking right now but, considering the inquisition that I now face, I just hope she will have me back'.

'Professor, you are to answer my questions.'

'I just did.'

'No, you didn't.'

At that point a supervisor, who from a distance noted that the visitor had spent too long with his officer, came to them. The immigration officer said the visitor was very rude when he fielded routine questions at him. The supervisor looked at the passport and invited Prof Kemji into his office. The Professor was sweating and looked angry.

'What are you here for, please?'

'I have come to deliver a lecture at the International Civil Rights Convention in New Jersey. The conference is scheduled for tomorrow and I needed to rest because of the jet lag.'

As he talked the supervisor was glancing through the passport pages. The Professor had travelled to Europe several times. He had spent some years in the United States.

'Where were you here?'

'I was at Berkeley as a student of Biochemistry and got my PhD before continuing to study Medicine at Hopkins.'

The supervisor could not help but apologize to Prof Kemji for all the trouble. He said if he had the chance, he would like to attend the lecture 'provided that there would be no fees for attending.' Prof Kemji thanked him and went to 'Baggage collection.'

KONGANOGA

Prof Kemji was late coming out of the immigration area. The chauffeur who was sent to pick him up went back to the organizers and reported that he was not on the flight. Meanwhile, after looking for a small placard bearing his name and not seeing any, he took an airport taxi to the venue of the occasion in Dukes Grand Hotel. He had explained to the taxi driver that his fare would be paid by the conference organizers. They arrived as one of the organizers was exchanging words with the driver. The organizer said the Professor had phoned while in the plane before it took off from Edward International Airport, Zeland. The chauffeur ought to have phoned before leaving the airport. From the conversation, Prof Kemji knew that he was the subject.

'I am Kemji, Professor Timothy Kemji from Konganoga. Are you one of the organizers of the conference?'

'Yes, Professor Kemji. My name is Karl, we were in correspondence by e-mail and we talked before your flight took off. I am really very sorry about what happened at the airport. This chauffeur was detailed to pick you up. He did not. Instead, he mocked it up. How was your trip, sir?'

'It was ok until the airport. Your immigration has changed from visitor-friendly. I had to know what was in my wife's mind and what she was doing, for crying out loud.'

'I am really sorry. Since the ugly event called 9/11, some people have taken certain unwarranted liberties. I think you need to relax and rest. I have a nice suite for you and the people here are far more decent than the immigration chaps,' Karl said.

The next day, Professor Kemji delivered his lecture. There was a rapturous ovation, an hour after he started and after Prof Kemji cleared his throat and declared: 'I thank you for being a listening audience.' His public lecture was as much an entertainment as it was an intellectual harvest for the audience. He took a few questions, as time would allow.

The convention included closing events which included a bus tour to the Waterfalls of Buffalo. Prof Kemji used the opportunity to visit two of his contemporaries in the College of Medicine, Buffalo. Two days later, he went back to the airport en route home via Zeland. He felt that this time, no one would maltreat him at the immigration. He raised his tolerance level for what he might consider to be an abuse. He checked in his luggage electronically and obtained a boarding pass. He was still to meet the ground staff of the airline for his luggage to be tagged.

'How long will you spend in Zeland?' the airline ground crew asked.

'Two days', answered Prof Kemji.

'Do you have a visa for Zeland?'

'Yes.'

The ticketing officer looked for the Visa in the current and immediate previous passports and could not find it. Meanwhile, Prof Kemji stood there unruffled and confident. There appeared to be an international conspiracy bothering on revulsion about the Konganoga passport. Konganoga had brought notoriety upon herself with her citizens indicted for such international transgressions as cyber crime, advanced fee fraud, money laundering and credit card scam. It was a convenient opportunity for certain officials to exploit to give vent to prejudices. Prof Kemji was aware. He was also not guilty as an individual and showed no remorse for the actions of his countrymen.

'Please show me,' the ticketing officer demanded.

Prof Kemji took his passports from her and showed the page in the previous passport where the Zeland visa for 10 years was stamped. The ticketing officer thanked Prof Kemji and wished him a safe flight. Soon, his flight to Edward International Airport in Zeland was called. He boarded with others. Ten hours later, the pilot announced that he was commencing descent. Some 20 minutes later, the cabin crew members were instructed to prepare for landing. Soon, the jumbo jet hit the ground running until it came to a complete halt for passengers and later, crew to disembark. Prof Kemji followed the direction for flight transfer. He waited for 14 hours for the overnight flight to Logos International Airport in Konganoga.

Chapter 9

ALL CHANGE, HEADING HOME

Dr Okon Johnson recalled his predicament in Zeland. Peaceful protests were degenerating. If care was not taken, there could be mortality. He had his own country but, he chose to be fighting another people in their own country. He hardly slept at night, especially with his wife stressed. He had not realized that he was her stressor in addition to he, Dr Johnson, being stressed also. He decided to stay for the accreditation. He could still change his mind if the need arose and if the circumstances in Zeland turned round in his favor. The new circumstance of employment in the Federal University of Science and Technology, Kiba presented an opportunity for a turn around. He would not miss it.

Professor Kemji had returned from a 10-day absence on the tour to deliver the keynote address in New Jersey. Dr Johnson signed the letter of appointment, signaling an acceptance of the offer. He made a photocopy of it before he returned it to the Registrar.

'Dean, welcome back. I hope your trip was successful,' Dr Johnson said.

'It went very well, thanks. Have you decided what to do with the offer of appointment?'

'Yes, I will stay until the accreditation. After that, I will get back to Zeland to pack up and call it quits over there.'

'In that case, we had better start looking for accommodation for you.'

'How do I get about that?'

'You apply to the Housing committee in writing. Indicate the size of your family and the ages of the children. It is 12 days to the accreditation.'

Something did not quite fit. That was the impression Dr Johnson had of Prof Kemji. He was in a pensive mood. He appeared abstract.

Back in the house, Prof Kemji needed to talk to his wife about their son in America. He did not know how to do it. He did not know whether he should say his mind to her. He knew that two good heads had always been considered better than one. There was also nothing to lose talking to Vylin. She usually would understand. For an American black sister to marry a brother from Africa and follow him home was a testimony of love.

'Honey, you know I took a flight to go and see Curt. I actually spent five days with him at the flat.'

'Now, was it not good of you? And how was my boy? Did he feel good?' Vylin excitedly said.

'Not good, at least not by my opinion. I wonder if he is not lonely. He certainly appeared to be a loner. He did not seem to have many friends. I am not sure he has a girl-friend,' Prof Kemji continued.

'There was no proper food in the kitchen. He seemed

to go from frozen to oven. He lives there alone. He has no kettle to boil water. He cooks it. He has no toaster. Therefore, he bakes his toast in the oven. He has no coffee. He drinks organic tea. The heater is on, even in this summer. He has two spoons, teaspoons. Thank God he didn't look malnourished, like me. I was worried over these things because you had been to see him a few times.'

Vylin's eyes were wet with tears. She was patient to allow her husband to finish.

'I have to go and see him,' was Vylin's response. She always liked to travel 'to see the children.'

'I do not know what you are going to do now. All the items listed have been addressed except girl friend. Are you going to take one to him?' Prof Kemji asked his wife sarcastically to make her put up her usual smile.

By the time Prof Kemji finished talking, Vylin was on him, her head on his laps. 'Is this supposed to be my supper?' the tired Professor asked.

Dr Johnson was present at the accreditation visit. He acted as the Head of the Department of Ophthalmology although he was the only qualified full time academic staff in the 'Department'. The leader of the accreditation panel was also an Ophthalmologist of the rank of Professor. Professor Vanchees was an Indian. He congratulated the Faculty for having an Ophthalmologist. There were only a handful of them in Konganoga. He advised that young doctors should be encouraged to enter the field. With that, he was optimistic that the department would be adequately staffed in about four years. The Professor asked Dr Johnson his rank. He said lecturer I. 'How many papers have you published?'

'Eight, Prof, two others are with editors.'

Prof Vanchees looked at the Dean and said 'that's

enough for a Senior Lecturer. People should be encouraged to do this job.'

After the accreditation visit, Dr Johnson returned to Zeland and related his experience to Fiona. So much had happened in such a short time. It appeared that there was never a dull moment in Konganoga. From the time she sought advice and help from Mr. Owen and got both, she set her mind to migrating to Konganoga with her husband and their two daughters. She was apprehensive about it all right. However, the happiness of her family was a priority. Many of her countrymen and women had worked in Konganoga as teachers, engineers, doctors or colonial office staff.

Konganoga was only underdeveloped. Which place was not underdeveloped at one point or the other? She mused.

'I think we should give it a try', Dr Johnson said. 'I will go first and sort out issues of accommodation and school for our daughters. I will also look at your own employment prospects. Even if I fail, we still have here to stay.'

'We will not fail', Fiona assured her husband.

He was touched. "You know, in my quest for relevance in this society, I have brought you moments of anguish. It was because you took up our responsibility for these children that I took it for granted. I am really sorry. I promise that with your continued support, we shall triumph.'

They both grasped each other the way they had not done in at least two years after the birth of the second daughter. Dr Johnson had expected a boy. In Konganoga, a boy child was it. Subconsciously, those protests and rallies were a vent to his frustration over futile searches for a job and also over his disappointment in not having a male child. This was an opportunity to return to basics. He was not going to miss it. They explored each other the way a blind man does a piece of fruit. They kissed with passion.

Fiona surrendered herself the way a lioness does to the head of her park. Okon the lion lived up to the beat. They woke up in the morning and gave each other a loving kiss. The two girls were already up and doing. Kem, the younger one was playing with her toys. Her sister Eno, was brushing her teeth.

Fiona was off duty the day after Okon returned. She fixed breakfast and took Eno to school while Kem and her dad played for the first time in a long while. Fiona returned and the plans for Okon to return to Konganoga began in earnest. As they agreed, Okon was to return alone and begin to sort out anticipated problems. He just needed his personal effects like clothing and books. He had promised Prof Kemji and Dr Ziebu, another Faculty member and Coordinator of surgical sciences who he had developed good rapport with, that he would return in a month. Prof Kemji understood. He too had returned from the same Zeland not too long before. Dr Ziebu would have wanted Okon back, suggesting that his wife could just pack up things and ship them. The University would be responsible for the costs of shipping and clearing at the Konganoga seaport. He also mentioned that as a nurse, there should be no problem about employing her in the Teaching Hospital. It was all to entice Dr Johnson. It worked. He noted it although he did not mention that to Fiona. She would probably have followed Okon immediately to 'try' Konganoga.

Okon and Fiona went to visit Mr. Owen and Audrey. They took a box of chocolates. The purpose was to thank Mr. Owen for his mentorship and other kind gestures. Okon handed the packet to Mrs. Owen and turning to Mr. Owen, he went down on his knees. Mr. Owen recognized that as a mark of respect in Konganogan culture, although he felt embarrassed by it.

'Mr. Owen and Audrey, Fiona and I are eternally grateful to you for the way you took me up and put me through the system. I have acquired enough skills to enable me contribute to society and take care of my family, immediate and remote. We have come to inform you that we are beginning the process of returning to my fatherland. I got a job the last time I visited in the same University that interviewed me here and said there was no vacancy. I have already started. They needed me for an accreditation visit and I obliged them. I will go like John the Baptist, to prepare a place for Fiona and our kids. We will forever keep in touch. Thanks.' He then stood up.

Mr. Owen was not really impressed by the John the Baptist analogy. He professed Christianity but was aware of the hypocrisy of many 'church goers' that he knew.

'Well, in the circumstances, I think what you have done and plan to do make a lot of sense. Life is full of phases. I think one should do the best he can at any particular instance. All those days I was huffing and puffing in the hospital, I did not reckon with retirement and the consequent total loss of power and influence. Of course you are welcome to this country and our home any time. Take good care. If there is anything we can do, please let us know. Audrey, this is a free country in case you have more to say.

'Fiona, you and the kids should come and spend a week end from time to time when we are home.' Audrey said.

With that, Okon and Fiona drove back to their flat. A week later, Dr Okon Johnson bided his family farewell as the cab drove him to the airport. He had purchased a return ticket valid for one year. He would determine to hold his job in Konganoga and keep out of politics. 'Once beaten, twice shy.' He mused.

He went through the Immigration and customs without event. Soon his flight was called. Seven hours later, Dr Johnson was back in Konganoga to resume work as an academic staff of the Federal University of Science and Technology, Kiba.

Dr Ziebu was pleasantly surprised to see Dr Johnson back sooner than he expected. He had even thought the latter would not return, considering the poor state of development or rather underdevelopment of the country. There was a general feeling of frustration and despondency in Konganoga. Not many people in the country would forego an opportunity to seek out greener pastures elsewhere.

'Good man, Dr Johnson. You are very welcome. I hope you came back with your family and belongings. As we say here, I hope you packed your bag and baggage.'

'Well, I have for now, come back alone. I think it will be easier to start the work, concentrate on it and make adequate arrangements for my family before they actually arrive. Right now, accommodation is critical.'

'By the way, I was discussing with the Dean the other day when we wondered if you would return. We said that if you did not, perhaps we could offer you a Senior Lecturer position. Your publications merit it. Left to me, that offer remains on the table.'

'That is very kind of you, sir. Let me go and see Prof Kemji and return.'

'Yes do that. Our little chat remains confidential. However, if the issue comes up, you know how you can treat it. I will wait for you because we have a lot of work to do.'

Dr Johnson did not see the Dean in the office. He

was on the campus but the secretary did not know where he had gone. Dr Johnson informed the secretary that he would be back later.

Chapter 10

STARTING FROM THE HEAD

The Coordinator of the Division of Surgical Sciences, Dr Ziebu was waiting for Dr Johnson to return from the Dean's office. He returned, but much earlier than he anticipated. Dr Johnson explained that the Dean was not on seat.

'I want you to study the lecture time tables. This is modeled after the Premier University, which we are lucky you attended. Roughly, we are 50% short of lecturers. That simply means we will double up the lectures for the lecturers. You will head the department of Ophthalmology. It is your assignment to attract Professors from outside or raise same from inside. Charity, they say, begins at home. Have they given you accommodation yet?'

Dr Okon had listened attentively He was impressed with the obvious sincerity of Dr Ziebu and his undisguised good wishes for the establishment. He then replied.

'Thanks. I will go through the timetable. Before I complete it, I will call a meeting of the department quickly so that everyone knows the other. As for accommodation, they said they did not know I would arrive yesterday. I have a room in the guest house. I am required to report at the Director's office tomorrow to sort it out finally'.

Dr Ziebu took Dr Johnson to his departmental office. The secretary, Naomi was at her desk. She stood up as the Coordinator and 'the other gentleman' walked in. Dr Ziebu introduced the two 'strangers' and left. Naomi fetched the key to the Head of Department's office and opened it. It was hot but neat. The cleaner took her job seriously and anonymously. She understood her job to mean cleaning the office of the Head of Department. They did not say 'when he is in'. Naomi switched on the air conditioner because electricity was on. That was the exception rather than the rule in the new Konganoga. She left immediately after. Dr Johnson looked at a few files on the table. The contents did not refer to recent events. He soon rang the bell and asked for the academic staff list. Five were on the list. He would be the sixth. The others were virtually all part-time lecturers referred to as adjunct lecturers. He had met them during the accreditation exercise. Virtually all the adjunct lecturers were "borrowed" for either the private sector or from other institutions that had no formal affiliation to the Federal University of Technology Kiba.

Back in the guest house, Dr Johnson made a few adjustments to the schedule but would confirm the adjustments with the lecturers concerned. This was one of the items listed on the agenda of his inaugural meeting as the head of the department. The final adjustments were ratified at the meeting. The secretary was instructed to type out the revised time table by the close of work that day. Whatever shortcomings Naomi might have, using the word processor was not one of them. Dr Johnson was pleasantly surprised when she promptly returned the new lecture schedule. He would also go straight to the coordinator of the program and impress him.

Dr Ziebu was in his office just ambling away a few minutes before he would go to pick up his son from school. He often did that when he wanted to be nice to his wife and save her the trouble.

'Hello, Dr Johnson, how are things?' Dr Ziebu asked.

'Not bad, thanks. We have just had our inaugural departmental meeting. We have ratified the lecture schedule. Here is your copy,' Dr Johnson said.

'Already? That's nice. We are not used to express services here. It is as if time is limitless. I am impressed. Lest I forget, have you seen the Dean about your ranking as was mentioned during the accreditation?'

'No I have not. I did not meet him the other day. I will try again tomorrow. Today is already gone. Please when you have had time to go through the schedule, kindly let me know so that I can officially post it on the notice board.'

'Since you have consulted your staff, what else am I supposed to do? Post it, man. Going back to your rank issue, try to see the Dean. They have called for appraisals. I am due for promotion to Reader. Strike while the iron is hot. I'm off to do a school run. See you.'

Dr Johnson wasted no more time in pursuing the rank issue. He had been advised to strike while the iron was hot. He was prepared to do just that. He was quite knowledgeable of the often repeated saying that "opportunity only knocks once". He remembered the singer Jimmy Cliff's admonition to "grab it or you lose your chance". Indeed as he hurried up to the Dean's office he hummed the song in his mind.

'Hey my good man, you are back? Good of you to keep to your word. I was quite pleased when the secretary told me you came to see me.'

'Thanks Dean. I have started work in earnest.'

'Good. Did you see the coordinator?' Professor Kemji asked.

'Yes, I am just coming from his office. He said I should see you to remind you about the accreditation chairman's remarks about my status.'

'Remind me again please.'

'During the accreditation visit, Professor Vanchees asked me how many papers I had. When I told him eight, he said that was enough for a Senior Lecturer.'

'That is quite right. The fact is that you have not yet been interviewed. Therefore that can still be sorted out in due course. If applied now, you would be required to spend three years before consideration. There is an ongoing appraisal. Since you are new, send me your CV and copies of the publications. I will have to call for a meeting of the Faculty Promotion committee soon.'

'Thanks, Dean.'

True to his word, Professor Kemji soon summoned a meeting of the Faculty Appraisals and Appointment Committee (FAAC). Dr Ziebu represented the Division of Surgical Sciences. His papers were among those to be appraised. When it got to his turn, he was told to leave the panel and told he would be called back. There was no objection when his data were read out. Each member had a copy. He was therefore recommended for promotion to Reader at the Faculty level. He was recalled into the room. After a few candidates, the Dean read out Dr Okon Johnson. He explained that he was new.

'Dr Johnson had come to visit Konganoga prior to the recent accreditation visit. He agreed to apply so that he would be employed for his department that had no full-time lecturer. He agreed. An interim appointment letter was given to him in a hurry. He also decided to stay permanently. He went back to Zeland ostensibly to bring his family. Ladies and gentlemen, we often hear that from some of our people domiciled in Zeland, America or Europe. Recall Dr Jumbo the minimal access surgeon. It is now four years and no word from him. Well, Dr Johnson is back here and has already started work. I looked at his CV and publications which are in your files. He should be considered for appointment as a Senior Lecturer.'

A pin could have dropped with a din. Initially no one said a word. Then Dr Ezemtubo, acting head of Pharmacology, raised his hand. The Dean saw him through a furtive glance but decided to see if other hands up would be up.

Dr Ezemtubo and the Dean were not the best of friends. His department was also not popular. The staff members there were too lazy to publish papers. They were usually not enthusiastic to give their lectures as scheduled. Dr Ezemtubo was coerced to publish papers in any medical journal to justify his promotion. There was need to elevate someone in the department which was said to be 'bottom heavy' with all the staff at Lecturer I or below. With his promotion, he was the only Senior Lecturer in a department of 10 academic staff. Many of them had been in the University for over five years. An academic staff member was expected to be promoted every three years until the rank of Professor. Those who had not been promoted from a rank for more than three years were said to have expired on the job. Dr Ezemtubo was unmindful of the adage that those who live in glass houses should not throw stones. He was under a self-imposed compulsion to find a fault with the Dean. He felt that there was something irregular with the Dean's presentation of Dr Johnson. The Dr had not even been interviewed, he thought.

Dr Ziebu also raised his hand, obviously to support

the Dean's recommendation. The newly employed Acting Head of Ear Nose and Throat, Dr Usene also raised his hand. Prof Kemji had facilitated his employment when some vested interests were opposed. Dr Usene also came from the same ethnic background as Dr Johnson. The Dean decided to let Dr Ezemtubo speak first. Dr Ziebu would counter it later, he hoped. Hopefully also, subsequent speakers would back Dr Ziebu.

'Yes, Dr Ezemtubo, you have the floor.'

Dr Ezemtubo stood up. The Dean told him he could sit as they could all hear him. Dr Ezemtubo, about 5'3" tall, joked that he already had a handicap with height and would likely be ignored if he sat down talking. He remained standing and began to talk.

'Mr. Chairman sir, Dean, this University has a clearly articulated policy on promotion of academic staff. You tell us that Dr Okon Johnson joined us at the last accreditation, just 10 weeks ago. According to you, he has not even been interviewed. Now you are asking us to promote him after those 10 weeks. Is there a special reason to fast track the man's promotion? If so, when is he penciled for promotion to Professor? I would not be here to take part in the gross disregard of the University regulations. It is an abuse of due process.'

Dr Ezemtubo was brief, succinct and obviously sarcastic in his contribution especially with the allusion to professorship. He took back his seat soon after his speech, removed his glasses and appeared to be waiting anxiously for who would dare to counter his statement.

'Dr Ezemtubo, I thought I made my presentation very clear. You should have told us what precisely you are here to do rather than what you are here not to do', Prof Kemji said. A few members chuckled. The Dean had thrown the ball back to Dr Ezemtubo's court. The Dean was also not going to allow him play the ball. He called on Dr Usene to speak.

'I think the Dean made it clear how Dr Johnson came here. I would think the man means well for this University. He could have stayed back in Zeland, considering how we have run down this country. We should be encouraging people to join us. This promotion exercise is also aimed at keeping our morale high. We should look at the publications if we do not trust the Dean. This Committee is also responsible for appointments. We can call him for an interview if again we do not trust the Dean and the Vice-Chancellor who have so far discharged their responsibilities in this material circumstance credibly. If the publications are scored and they meet the required total, he should be recommended for senior lecturer'.

Immediately Dr Usene ended his contribution, Dr Ziebu raised his hand again and the Dean, looking towards him, said 'yes, Dr Ziebu, you have the floor.'

'Thank you Chairman. Let us not forget how desperately this University requires qualified academic staff. Dr Johnson, strictly speaking, is not a confirmed staff of this University. Therefore the charge of accelerated promotion does not arise. Let us not waste our time here. As Dr Usene suggested, are the publications enough for a Senior Lecturer? The answer is an unequivocal yes. The Chairman of the accreditation panel Prof Vanchees, an expatriate, was the first to point this out. We checked the publications of Dr Johnson in the Surgical Division. He has enough scores and more to spare. But, anyone interested can rescore using the University guidelines.' Then the room went quiet.

'Shall I split the house? The Dean asked. Two people out of the five in the room said no, that it was not necessary. The Dean followed on. 'Approved?'

Despite the vote that weighed heavily against his opinion, Dr Ezemtubo was not a man that would give

KONGANOGA

up so easily. He immediately sprang up to his feet even without being invited to speak.

'What are we approving?' Dr Ezemtubo asked.

Dr Usene and Dr Ziebu in unison from different points in the room answered 'Appointment as senior lecturer.' The room was quiet again and the Dean repeated what he said before.

'Approved?'

'Approved' was heard. Dr Ezemtubo did not say more. The Dean went to the next candidates one after the other until all submissions were deliberated upon. At the end, the Dean read out the recommendations of the Faculty. It included Dr Ziebu for Reader and Dr Johnson for Senior Lecturer among others. The recommendations and necessary documents were sent to the University Registrar for the upcoming central appraisals and promotions exercise. When the time came, all the submissions from the Faculty of Health Sciences sailed through. Three weeks later, the Registrar wrote to all the candidates for promotions and appointments up to Senior Lecturer, informing and congratulating them accordingly. Dr Johnson got his own letter.

Chapter 11

SENIOR ACADEMIC

Dr Johnson, by virtue of being a senior lecturer and acting head of department, became eligible to many committees in the University. There were the Senate and several committees where the senate had representations. He was in the appraisal committees of his department, the Surgery Division as well as the Faculty. He got information about who said what at his recommendation for senior lecturer. However, only Dr Ezemtubo was antagonistic to some extent. He had to be careful of him. It was part of University politics. One avoided enemies and rallied round friends.

In the early days of his return to Konganoga, Dr Johnson found events and attitudes of people comical. As time went on, he began to assess the situation as tragic. He seemed to find faults with everything. He was right to observe that things were done more from a political perspective than from a logical viewpoint. While he whined at what he perceived, he believed that things would get better. He had complained so much, often interjecting 'in Zeland,...' as he tried to lay emphasis on his stint abroad. For some time, some of his colleagues joked that he had not yet landed on the ground, implying that he was still acting in a foreign land.

Dr Johnson's profile was rising in the Department. Once he got on top of the job as acting head of department, Dr Johnson turned his attention to getting things ready for his wife and two daughters to join him. He was a friendly person and people liked him for that. He soon got a three-bed room University accommodation. He got a housemaid from his village. Her name was Umanamaa. He bought a used but fairly new Japanese car popularly known as *Tokunbo*. There was the departmental driver, Jonas, who was very dutiful but felt a compulsion to divulge whatever information that was saved in his brain. The redeeming feature was that his memory was like a sieve. Whatever he did not divulge in 24 hours was deleted automatically. He was instinctively using others to store information. The problem was that he would not remember where to retrieve the divulged information. Jonas was a happy-go-lucky. Dr Johnson noted this handicap and factored it into his attitude in the presence of Jonas. This included telephone conversations. It was not only necessary to avoid unnecessary direct information to Jonas, it was also important to do the same with people that Jonas was wont to show his garrulous disposition to, including the departmental secretary, Naomi.

Dr Johnson took leave to travel to Zeland to bring his family to Konganoga. Before his arrival in Zeland, a shipping company had collected the household effects including a car, a petrol engine electrical generator, beds, a deep freezer and a refrigerator. These had been put in a container and shipped to the main port city of Konganoga in Apupa, before Dr Johnson arrived in Zeland. He helped Fiona with her bank records and tax returns. He decided they would not claim back their social security payments. Konganoga was obviously unstable and they could be forced by circumstances to return to Zeland.

Since Dr Johnson attended the wedding of Ingrid and Dr Clough McAndrew, they had not met physically. They kept in touch with occasional telephone calls and exchange of Christmas greeting cards. Clough had been the initial motive for Dr Johnson to get to Zeland and had cushioned his landing to make it a soft one. Dr Johnson decided to go and visit his pen pal friend to formally inform him that they were returning to Konganoga. To Clough, the Johnsons were relocating but, to Okon, they were returning home. As far as Clough was concerned, Okon Johnson was no less entitled to stay in Zeland than himself. Besides, Fiona and the two daughters were citizens of Zeland. With very strong subconscious ancestral stranglehold, Dr Okon Johnson and not a few of his countrymen in Zeland felt strange in their adopted country. It was 80 minutes drive between where Dr Johnson's family lived and Yolanda, where Clough and Ingrid McAndrew lived. Dr Johnson drove with his family in Fiona's Morris car. Dr Johnson had called to give an estimated time of arrival in Yolanda. They were to drive to the railway station where Clough would wait to pick them up. He was already there when the Morris car, driven by a man of color pulled up. As soon as Dr Johnson saw Dr McAndrew, he cleared the car and came out. The two men embraced themselves and went over to Fiona. She wanted to come out but Clough dissuaded her, as they would drive to his house at once.

'Ingrid is keen to see your lovely daughters. Don't tell me their names yet. I think Ingrid will understand the meaning. She graduated first class in Linguistics. Okn, drive behind me. It is just about 25 minutes to the house', Dr McAndrew told his visitors. It was as if Clough refused to pronounce Okon the way he should.

The two cars drove out of the railway station, with Dr Johnson following Dr McAndrew. The road was clear. In 25 minutes, Dr McAndrew drove into his street, followed by Dr Johnson and his family. Ingrid saw them through the window as they drove in. She opened the door and went straight to Dr Johnson's car. Ingrid greeted Dr Johnson perfunctorily and quickly diverted attention to Fiona and her two daughters. She continued this preferential attention as they all entered the sitting room. The two girls saw a few toys lying about and went for them. Ingrid brought them drinks and chocolate biscuits. When Ingrid was satisfied that they were occupied, she went over to Fiona and asked what she could offer them. Dr McAndrew decided for everyone to have sherry or red wine. They all ended up having a shot of each.

In spite of the many years of their friendship, Clough still could not pronounce Okon properly. He had learnt to avoid the name, if he could. Dr Johnson thanked Ingrid and Dr McAndrew and without much ado, said the reason for the visit. It was to inform them that they were relocating, rather returning home. Then Dr Johnson thanked Clough and Ingrid for all the help they received from them. They would of course keep in touch. The visitors left to get home to send the children to bed. They were to travel down to Campden the next day for the night flight to Logos International Airport.

Check in at Campden airport was smooth. In the waiting lounge, Eno and Kem continued to play while their parents tried to have them restrained. They had not the faintest idea about where they were travelling to or what to expect. Fiona had also not been to Konganoga prior to this relocation or return 'home'. Six hours after take off the jumbo jet aircraft landed smoothly at Logos International. There was a connecting flight to their destination in a few hours. The weather was hot and humid but the fans were working inside the VIP lounge. Dr Johnson had paid for the use of the VIP lounge. Eno said she was hungry and Kem admitted the same. They had merely picked on their food on the flight. Food was being served in the lounge. They all went to the counter to see what they could eat. The only items the girls were familiar with included cakes and rice. With the latter they had the option of fried rice or white rice. They all chose the latter. The food was heated up in the microwave oven before they ate it. As usual, the girls did not take much and asked for cake. Fiona found the pepper a bit hot. However, she had to eat it to encourage her daughters to do the same although they soon abandoned the food for the cake and soft drink.

The connecting flight was announced. It was strange to Fiona that they had to walk through the tarmac before climbing into the plane. It was free-sitting, implying that one sat in any vacant seat. This often meant that a few people with tickets could not find seats. In such circumstances, they had to find another flight. There were a few carriers but the tickets could not be endorsed to a different carrier. This often meant that for a flight, one sometimes had to purchase two or more tickets to increase the chance of flying. Dr Johnson knew about this problem and gave a generous tip to a staff in the VIP lounge to secure them seats on their flight. A member of the cabin crew got some of the tip to secure four seats for Dr Okon Johnson. As they climbed into the plane, he mentioned his name to the cabin crew welcoming passengers aboard the plane. One of them quickly took them inside and gave them four seats. It was an hour flight. The weather was bright and dry.

The pilot landed his plane safely. The departmental driver, Jonas, was waiting. A porter loaded the belongings of the Johnsons into a trolley and they moved out of the arrival lounge. Jonas was the first to spot Dr Johnson. He did not know that Fiona, his *oga*'s wife, was a white woman. At first he thought she was just another passenger on the same flight as Dr Johnson. It was when he saw the two girls following Dr Johnson and this woman that he 'added two and two together.'

'Welcome, sir. Is this madam?' As Jonas asked the question, he immediately turned his ear closer to Dr Johnson in the manner of one who would not want to miss any information that he would readily relay.

He also at the same time guided the trolley to where he parked the departmental car. The luggage was transferred into the car. Dr Johnson gave the porter money. The porter checked the amount quickly and thanked Dr Johnson. He was obviously satisfied with what he received. Otherwise, he would have politely or rudely complained to Dr Johnson. Jonas opened one door for Fiona and the daughters, while Dr Johnson entered through the other side. The drive to the house took some 45 minutes because of traffic congestion popularly referred to as 'go slow'. Jonas started to download to Dr Johnson some of the events that occurred in his absence. Whatever came into his mind was spoken, without regard to the level of importance.

'*Oga*, there is go slow on Akiri street. That is why I am taking this way although the road has a lot of pot holes. Madam welcome, you hear. I hope your people are fine at home?' Jonas did not wait for a response once he had something to say. Neither Okon nor Fiona engaged him in his one-way conversation. Eno and Kem were busy sizing up the places they were passing.

'Mummy, the grass here is too tall. Will you allow us to play in them?' Eno asked.

'No, my dear. There may be snakes or other dangerous creatures in there' Dr Johnson interjected.

'Oh, snakes? I want to see them. Some of the ones they show on television are really cute. Can I touch it when we see one?' she continued innocently.

'Oh, no, the snakes here are different from the ones on television. The television snakes are friendly. These ones here are deadly. They have poison in their teeth' Dr Johnson advised his daughter.

Jonas turned left off the major road into the University campus. He finally arrived at Dr Johnson's house and stopped the car. He again opened the door for Fiona and her children. Dr Johnson was surprised that Jonas opened the car doors for Fiona. He never did that for the female staff, lecturers and others who occasionally rode with Dr Johnson. He hoped that Jonas would not remember the names of the ladies who he sometimes drove, either with or without *oga*, in the car. His garrulous disposition was not going to be acceptable to Dr Johnson and he made it known to Jonas as soon as both were alone.

Chapter 12

THE FAMILY RELOCATES TO KONGANOGA

Umanamaa, the housemaid opened the door and rushed out to Dr Johnson excitedly.

'Welcome, sir.' Then she looked on to see Fiona and the two daughters. 'Welcome, ma. Baby', she now addressed Fiona and Eno. She tried to lift Kem. The little girl screamed as loud as her voice could go and ran to her mother, shouting 'no, no, no' as she did that. They all entered the three-bed room flat, with Umanama and Jonas carrying the luggage. Jonas dropped what he carried in the sitting room. Umanamaa subsequently sent all the pieces of luggage into the master bedroom. She now went to the kitchen. Fiona and Okon and the children sat down in the sitting room.

'Sweet hearts, you are all home. After we have cooled off, I will show you the house. Do not expect too much. However, it is functional. Let me show you the toilets, in case anyone needs to use them. He got up and Fiona followed him with her daughters. Kem was toilet trained and in Zeland used to make a fuss if there was anything in the toilet. They returned to the sitting room.

'Okon, dear, are there any drinks? I would like a cup of tea. Girls, tell your dad what you want.'

Okon called Umanamaa and told her to boil some water and bring some cold soft drinks. She acknowledged by half-stooping and left. She soon brought some orange drinks together with biscuits. Eno and Kem took what they liked from the tray. Soon the kettle began to whistle a signal that the water had boiled. On hearing the whistle, Okon went into the kitchen. He pulled out a tray and a flask. Umanamaa knew what he wanted to do and told him that she would complete what he wanted to do. She poured the boiled water into the flask. She then put two mugs in the tray and then cubes of sugar. A small carton of tea bags and a jar of instant coffee were put in the tray. She carried all into the sitting room, took a stoop and left. Okon made a cup of tea for Fiona and went to the kitchen to fetch a bottle of beer from the refrigerator. He remembered when he used to smoke and drink beer. Fiona helped him to kick the habit of 'dragging a fag'.

Fiona took her daughters to the bathroom and helped them to have a bath. She also had her own. After that, she went into the kitchen with Okon. Umanamaa showed her where the food items, condiments, cooking utensils and plates were kept. Fiona knew it was her house and she had to assert ownership without delay. It was an apparent instinct with many women. 'See kitchen, seize it,' seemed to be the motto. She decided to prepare egg omelet which everyone could relish. Soon the family had a proper breakfast.

'Fiona, you should take the girls to their room so that they can sleep. You can take a nap too, after all the travel. What items would you like me to go and buy? Later, I will take you to the market. I still have a full week of my holidays left.'

'I think we can have boiled rice for lunch. I saw fresh vegetables in the kitchen. We can have pounded yam or garri in the night. Can *Umamaa* prepare soup as we used to have in Zeland? I bet I can cook better than she can' Fiona bragged. She had practiced the pronunciation of Umanamaa several times and thought she had mastered it.

When they were courting, Okon had fascinated Fiona with his 'African dish'. He might have enticed her with it. It was fun for her to prepare the 'African recipe' as she called it. Soon, she began to go to the Indian shop where the special food items such as black eye beans, semolina, okra, spinach, stock fish and others were sold. She also developed a genuine appetite for 'African dish'.

They both smiled as they remembered.

'You are the boss in these culinary matters. Therefore, you have the last word. Umanamaa had prepared vegetable soup in anticipation of our arrival home yesterday. The soup should be fresh but, you are the boss' Okon said.

No decision was taken. They both retired into the master bedroom. It was not long when Kem, the younger daughter, pushed her way into the room and announced that there was no television in her room. She wanted to watch cartoons.

'Kem, darling, they show television only at night here,' Fiona said.

'But, where is the television set they will show it at night?'

Don't worry, your daddy will buy it.'

'Today?'

'Yes, or tomorrow'. Fiona had just parried the question. She knew Kem would come back on the issue. She had forgotten to tell her that it was in the shipment they sent from Zeland. It was not only in the children's room that there was no television. There was none in the whole house.

Taking the opportunity of his remaining leave days, Dr Johnson went to the hospital to talk to the Chief Matron, Mrs. Ama Green, about employing Fiona. He explained that his family had just come back to Konganoga to join him. The Chief Matron was popular in the hospital for her motherly and amiable disposition. She was hardly ruffled in the discharge of her duties. She had attended some management meetings with Dr Johnson and occasionally exchanged ideas on certain issues. Dr Johnson had, before the return of his family mentioned the need for Fiona to join the hospital service. Chief Matron told him to bring up the matter as soon as she joined him. Thus, Dr Johnson was reminding her of her earlier advice.

'That is nice. How are the children? I hope it is not too hot for them. Let me have her application as soon as you can. It will help if copies of her certificates are attached.'

'Thank you, madam. The application is ready. I will come back tomorrow,' Dr Johnson said and left.

Dr Johnson knew the hospital routine. People often reported late to work. However, certain heads of units were responsible enough to lead by precepts. In this, Mrs. Green was of the 'old school'. The official time to start work in the morning was 8.00 o'clock. She made it her habit to come in time to receive the report from the night shift and discharge the staff to attend to their home chores. Usually, by 10 a.m. the Chief Matron would be relaxed to attend to *paper work*. That was when Dr Johnson returned to her office with the wife's application. The Chief Matron asked him to sit down. She glanced through it and appeared pleased.

'She did all her studies overseas?'

'Yes, she did. As a matter of fact she is from Zeland.'

'That is really interesting. We need the injection of new blood in the nursing service here to infuse some desirable work attitude into the staff. There is also a shortage of capable hands. As far as I am concerned, there is no need to waste time. She can start work tomorrow, pending a formal interview.'

'I thank you so much, Chief Matron. It is already Wednesday. Can she start on Monday to enable us get the children into a routine?'

'Sure. I understand. Let her start as soon as possible. There will be an interview soon. She will have a head start when she attends the interview from inside, so to say.'

The routine about the children that Dr Johnson was referring to, involved school, nursery and feeding. Okon felt that with the few days remaining on his leave, he would be able to orient Umanamaa on some of the 'routines'. Another important 'routine' was to take the children and Fiona to his ancestral home, the 'real' home. The latter could however be done at his convenience. Fiona also had to sew the Nurses' uniform. The fastest that it could be done was one week. However, she reported for work the Monday after the husband submitted her application.

The Chief Matron was pleasantly surprised to see that Mrs. Fiona Johnson was a white woman. She saw the situation from a positive perspective. She would take pride that she had an international nursing department. Mrs. Ama Green invited the deputy Chief Matron, Mrs. Pretty Abat to her office for introductions. 'Pretty' as she preferred to be called, had returned from Zeland with her husband Professor Abat of Philosophy Department when their children came of school age. Professor Abat did not want his children 'de-culturised' in a foreign environment. He believed fervently in people clinging to their roots. He could be described as ancestral. Besides, his wife, while in

Zeland, no longer enjoyed the sort of social interaction that prevailed in Konganoga before she joined her husband. Her incessant nagging about 'white' nurses was the catalyst for Professor Abat's philosophy on roots and culture. Part of Mrs. Abat's problem was attributed to the appellation "Mrs. Abat". It was suggested that the professorial attachment to her husband's name had gone into her head.

Someone had once jokingly said that Mrs. Abat was so obsessed with her husband being a professor that she would have preferred to be addressed as Mrs. Professor Abat. Luckily Mrs. Abat never insisted on this appellation.

'Deputy Chief, meet Mrs. Fiona Johnson. She is the wife of Dr Johnson, Head of the Department of Ophthalmology. She is joining as a staff nurse midwife. You may have met yourselves in Zeland,' the Chief Matron said. 'We will sort out the postings to know an appropriate place to put her for maximum benefit to the hospital,' Mrs. Green concluded.

Both ladies acknowledged each other cautiously. Fiona did not want to take any false steps. Pretty noted that Fiona was her junior and did not want to transfer aggression to her. She asked which city Fiona lived in Zeland. She said Chisterton, where her parents lived. That was not where Pretty and Prof Abat lived. Therefore, they were unlikely to have met in Zeland.

Mrs. Green took Fiona to the administrative office for her to complete some forms. She was given papers to undergo medical examination for fitness to work as a nurse. When they came back to the Chief Matron's office, Fiona was given a design of the nurses' uniform. She had a choice to have it sewn by the hospital tailor or to use another tailor, provided there would be no fancy frills. 'The hospital tailor is good and the material is one approved for the supplier. Although, it could take a couple of days longer, the labor is

KONGANOGA

cheaper. Besides, with some interest from here, they could sew it in good time. I advise you to try the hospital tailor in this instance until you find your feet around. You can attend to your domestic matters, pending when the pair of uniforms is ready. I will give them to your husband. Just take your time. We are not terribly fast here. Therefore, you will not find it difficult to blend into the system.'

Fiona opted to have the uniform sewed by the hospital. The cost would be deducted from her first salary, if she did not mind. That was acceptable to her. She thanked the Chief Matron. 'I will report for duty as soon as Okon brings the uniform.' She left the office to return to her house, driven home by Jonas the Departmental chauffeur. Okon was at home with the girls when Fiona returned.

'How did it go?' Okon asked.

'Very well indeed. The Chief Matron was particularly nice. I was not quite sure about the deputy Chief Matron. Guess her name' Fiona told Okon.

'I do not need rocket science to tell you that one. It's pretty easy, is it not?' Okon answered. They both laughed at the pun. Most people knew Pretty. It was not the kind of name to hear and quickly forget. More significantly, she would not be described as stunningly beautiful. Yet, that was her name and she was called that.

Some of her subordinates in the office who Mrs. Pretty Abat occasionally bullied, and who consequently did not particularly like her, often joked that their boss's parents must have taken measures early in their daughter's life to give her a name that would counter her lack of natural endowments by giving her the name "Pretty".

'When do you start?' Okon asked.

'It's up to you. That is what the Chief Matron said. I mean it,' Fiona answered. Okon smiled, thinking that it was a joke. Fiona repeated what she said.

'Am I now the High Chief Matron?'

'I was just pulling your legs. The Chief Matron will give you my uniform. I will then wear it to work. That does not require rocket science either.'

'You may have figuratively pulled my legs. Pull it factually' Okon said and held her by her hand and took her to the bedroom.

Eno and Kem often found things to attract them outside, including various types of insects, butterflies, grasshoppers, crickets and chicken all of which appeared to be busy. However, they did not actually know what these living things were doing. The weather appeared to be summer for them. Fiona and Okon often took advantage of the distraction of their daughters to engage in other things.

Chapter 13

NEVER A DULL MOMENT

'When you said the Chief Matron said I would decide when you are to resume work, my mind went to whether she wanted us to make another baby.' At that point, Kem burst in as usual to report the sighting of a creature that looked like a 'small train'. She insisted that her mother must see it before it drove away. Kem was cutting the character of a 'she who must be obeyed'. Fiona followed her to the back of the house. She had herded the creature into a corner to prevent it from 'driving away'. 'That is a millipede,' Fiona said.

'What is a migipig?'

'It is actually called millipede and it is a creature with a thousand legs.' Fiona corrected.

'It must move very fast, mummy, if it has a thousand legs. I have only two and I can run fast. That is why I blocked it there.'

'No. Too many cooks spoil the broth and too many

legs slow the millipede down,' Fiona told her daughter. She returned to the bedroom, allowing Eno and Kem to enjoy their picnic. She too was enjoying her version of a picnic.

Fiona started work as a Staff nurse midwife at the University Teaching Hospital a week after her husband submitted her application. She was on temporary appointment pending a proper interview and a successful medical fitness examination. She was assigned to take charge of the children's special care unit (CSCU). There were only two babies on admission. They were premature deliveries and needed to be in the incubator. The consultant had prescribed it. He was unaware that the facility was unavailable. The one that was 'on display' in the unit stopped functioning two months earlier after a series of electrical power fluctuations. There were children who required the facility. They were referred unofficially to a private hospital in the city. Those who could afford it went there. Those who could not took their chance in the University Teaching Hospital. Most of these did not leave the hospital alive. The nursing staff had become inured to the handicaps in the hospital, including poor and erratic electricity supply and lack of potable water. Relations of patients brought water from their homes. The source ranged from bore holes to open streams. Fiona got to know all these on her first day at work.

Obele, a young and bright student nurse, was her informant. Initially, Fiona thought that Obele was joking. That was until she found out that the tap in the unit was dry. The basin attached to it was used to 'store' broken plates and other unserviceable gadgets. She noted all these in a jotter. She asked Obele whether the Chief Matron was aware of the situation. She said that Mrs. Green had quarreled openly with the maintenance engineer when the engineer could not repair or cause a replacement of the unserviceable equipments in the unit. 'The parents of these two babies have been told to take them to a private hospital. They say they are unable to fund it,' Obele concluded before she went to sign off duty.

Fiona handed over to the next shift and went home.

She got to the house quite exhausted mentally and physically. Mentally, she could not believe that people were allowed to stay in the hospital without treatment. That was certainly strange to her. Also, she could not assign the attitude of the workers to their responsibilities. She wanted to know about the professional nursing ethics in Konganoga. Physically, the heat and the consequent sweating to regulate her internal milieu made her feel drained. Dr Johnson was at home with the daughters. Eno and Kem were, as usual, outside, exploring the habitat. The return of their mother was not a priority. It was taken for granted.

Dr Johnson knew that Fiona was tired physically. He did not know about the frustration and mental fatigue. 'How was it on the first day?' Okon asked.

'It was fascinating. It was different from Zeland, anyway. Just tired,' Fiona responded.

'Now I know why siesta was invented. You need to rest your feet off the ground. Go and get a nap. We can stroll to the tennis court later.'

After supper, Fiona helped Eno with her home work and read some rhymes for Kem before getting them off to sleep. She spent about an hour narrating her experience in the children's special care unit. She did not think it should be regarded as part of the hospital. She felt that things could be better. It was not just a matter of economic poverty. There was also a bankrupt attitude. Fiona thought about all those wastages in her last hospital in Zeland. She had requested the Chief Matron to reserve some discarded materials for her. This was sequel to Dr Johnson's account of events in Konganoga. She had scissors, needle holders, bowls, kidney dishes etc in mind. She now mentally added incubator. She wrote a letter to the Chief Matron of her last hospital. She gave a graphic account of what was on ground in her University Teaching Hospital. She reminded her of the request she made before they returned 'home'. This time, she added operating table and accessories as well as an incubator. The letter was posted by air.

Mrs. Allis Barnton was the manager to who the letter of request was directed. Her son was doing a one year volunteer work as a doctor in Darfur in Southern Sudan. His graphic presentation of the state of the hospital there worried her for the sake of the people suffering 'somewhere in the forest of Africa.' There was nothing in particular she could do about it beyond worrying. She remembered the saying from one of her teachers. 'Things without remedy should be without regard.' It was line of least resistance and she took it. Then this letter from Konganoga came from a former nurse at her hospital. It was going to be 'yours for the moving'. There was an inventory of unserviceable hospital equipments. Many were in service but the manufacturing companies had new equipment to flood into the market. They pressured hospital managers until they took those new equipments off the manufacturer's warehouses into their hospital wards and theaters. Among these were two analog incubators recently decommissioned to create space for the digital versions that had zero tolerance for electrical power fluctuation. There were other materials ranging from hard ware such as two operating tables to clothing materials. Mrs. Barnton asked the service manager to check all the equipment and select those to send to charity. The store man (this was the old name for the 'Service Manager') was anxious to create some breathing space in the store.

He soon reported that he was ready to 'ship out.' He was to use this apt phrase to Mrs. Barnton several times in a few days.

In three weeks of her airmail letter, Fiona Johnson received a reply signed by Mrs. Allis Barnton. There was a long list of hospital equipment including two analog incubators, theatre wares, hard and soft, ready for shipment out, at the recipient's cost. Fiona took it to work and showed the Chief Matron, Mrs. Ama Green. She was very delighted. Mrs. Green always saw only the bright side of any encounter. She has taken a liking for Fiona even before they met face to face. That liking was now being vindicated. The Chief Matron took Fiona straight to the Chief of Administration (CA) of the Hospital, Alambo Mungo Park. Mungo Park rose from the ranks in hospital administration. He was well connected. Elevations were his for the asking. He did not need to ask. His interests were of interest to those who made things happen. He was once promoted twice in a year 'to fill an important vacancy' in the hospital administration. In spite of his good connection, Alambo Mungo Park was very corrupt. Money had a special attraction for him. He had a string of women to help themselves with his loot. If he expended some of his loot into culinary or sartorial exploits, the latter were not evident on him. Alambo was a title he appended to his name. It was not any body's business to verify that he had been so elevated in his community.

What did anyone have to lose by addressing *Mungo Park by the title that ventilated his ego?*

'Alambo, for long I have asked for an incubator in the CSCU. For so long have you not heeded the appeal. There is no money, we are always told. Yet cars are being purchased and given to people to use. Please this time, we have incubators, ours for the moving.' As she was finishing her address, Mrs. Green took the letter from Fiona and presented it to Alambo.

'Excuse me Chief Matron, you doctors and nurses use a lot of abbreviations. What or where is CSCU?' The two ladies looked at each other. Fiona was surprised. The Chief of Administration did not know an important unit in the hospital. That, perhaps explained part of the neglect she saw in the University Teaching Hospital. Mrs. Green politely explained what CSCU stood for and reminded the Chief of Administration that it was where the incubator was requested for, several times in the past. He glanced at the letter in his hands and told his two visitors that he would go through it thoroughly and revert to them. Before they left Alambo's office, Mrs. Green, by instinct, got a photocopy of the letter from the Chief's secretary.

Alambo Mungo Park was sharp and smart. However, there aptitudes seemed to be directed to acquisition of money through equally sharp practices. He was one of those who preferred a job from where they, in addition to the official wedge, got some more from the side. His type would prefer a job from which they were paid $100 and there was an opportunity to purloin an extra $50, to the same job on $190, but with no opportunity to steal. After the two ladies left his office, Alambo looked at the letter addressed to Fiona. 'Yours for the moving'. He heard that expression from an American volunteer who was going back to America after a stint of five years in Kiba. Within that period, he had acquired a lot of household effects. His advertisement for their disposal included 'yours for the moving.' Alambo Mungo Park began to work out ways to take advantage of the opportunity. He racked his brain until he came up with a scheme. It was a scam.

When Fiona got to the children's special care unit, she was told that the two babies had given up the ghost in the night. The unit records were accordingly updated. That would be the end for those cases. The parents would grieve. They would not blame the system that has failed to care for its young. They have not become sophisticated enough to know that one of the duties of government is security to life of its citizens and not just for those in governance. They have not become sophisticated enough to recognize that this security should include assurance of protection and care for the young including the premature. But for these parents there would be relief from the burden of travelling to the hospital with all the inconveniences, including the abandonment of their other children in the house. Fiona had expected some protest, even a minor one. She could not help the tears that welled up in her eyes. There was no time for such emotional indulgences. There were other desperately ill children in the ward who required all the attention they could get. There was a tiny yellow baby suffering from neonatal jaundice. She required exchange blood transfusion. The hospital blood bank was empty. The parents of the girl refused to donate blood. For them, 'any child who did not want to stay alive should be allowed to return to the ancestors.' Fiona was confused at what she was experiencing in such a short time. She began to wonder whether she could actually absorb it all. The attitude of everyone worried her. She offered to have her own blood tested. It was compatible with the baby girl's. She donated one pint of blood. She returned to the unit and did the exchange blood transfusion. She was proud to hand the baby over to her smiling mother a week later, when the baby was discharged home in good health. She was in a happy mood at home that day. Okon noticed. He was happy, but asked no questions.

Chapter 14

CASHING THE GIFT

Alambo Mungo Park had typed out the list of items available on condition of 'yours for the moving'. He made three copies and invited three contractors to the hospital to bid. The amount involved exceeded his limit. It was not the first time. There were ways to circumvent that kind of encumbrance. The items were split into three invoices, each within his limit. He approved the purchases. Payment was to be made in dollars. The hospital accountant, with a little nudge in cash, was an easy recruit into the scam. Alambo sent for Fiona without the Chief Matron. He informed her to accept the items on offer. The hospital would pay for the shipment. They had contractors who knew people in clearing and forwarding. Any of them would happily do Alambo a favor in lieu of the next over invoiced contract. Four weeks later, the items, wrapped as if they were new, were delivered in the hospital and taken to the store for inventory. One incubator was sent to the Chief Matron for the CSCU. Mrs Green thanked Fiona profusely. Matron Green went to the Chief of Administration to acknowledge the supply. She had a sneaking suspicion that some money had gone underground in the deal. However, she was not in a position to know and was not disposed to find out.

'Alambo, you have done well to bring us that incubator. Those two babies we came to you on behalf of have made the supreme sacrifice. They died before the incubator arrived. They have sacrificed their lives that others may live. We thank God.'

'It is a pity Chief Matron. Those people in Kumbrujaa do not know what those of us on the ground have to suffer, facing patients and their relations. All they are interested in is churning out jargons upon jargons, which are nothing but red tape. There is a new one, the brain child of the new Minister. They call it 'due process.' They are waiting for the white paper to implement it. If I did not use my initiative, I would have been travelling to and from that place trying to defend this vital equipment.'

Alambo, a sweet talker was wringing his palms as he spoke. He talked meekly as one who was a die-hard defender of the oppressed. He failed to acknowledge that he defended his selfish interest by what he did.

Some months later, rumors doing the rounds had it that Alambo had bought a house in Chichester in Zeland. His son was studying hospital administration there. He had made the announcement with pride at the Senior People's Club where members spent some of their loot and exchanged banters in the process. A nurse who helped her mother in the Club heard the boast and filtered the news into the hospital and wherever else the opportunity presented.

Shady deals were not an exclusive preserve of the ivory tower and her appendages. The roads in Konganoga were roads on the map but not on the ground. Like many projects, the aims, as publicized, were fronts for the opportunity to account for some money. The publicized project was only going to be a collateral event for the people. Thus, the granting of independence had turned out to be a burden for the ordinary citizens, while the new colonialists, 'home-grown' colonialists that was, like wolves in sheep's clothing, plundered the land. Schools were built, not to enable the children get education. It was an avenue to siphon some money into private coffers. The building materials would be of inferior quality. Yet the auditor would file the price of the superior material. Roads appeared to be the fastest source of illicit funds acquisition. While the approved budget was for six inches thickness, the contractor, having paid the officials awarding the contract up front, would take his own 'share'. The remaining would be used to build the road in portions, each with about 2 inches thickness. The road would be started and finished in the dry season. By the rains, the money would have been lost to any form of tracing. The road would be washed out by the rains. Another budget would come. It would subsequently get to the turn of the same road to be 'rehabilitated', perhaps with another government.

Hospitals were not spared this graft. Either a new hospital project would be embarked upon or existing ones were 'upgraded' from a health centre to a community hospital. In this instance, the sign boards would be mounted as soon as the session of the parliament adjourned *sine die*. Nothing inside the buildings would be 'upgraded'. Drugs were something else. They had become better known as o/s (out of stock). Occasionally an official, lower in the corridors of power, would get an opportunity to procure an 'emergency' supply of drugs. Such an opportunity, if missed, would not recur. As one elderly politician crudely put it, power is like getting to the top of an iroko tree.

Once there, take all you can because second chances were non-existent.

As the graft ate deep into the body politic, the perpetrators devised even more bizarre propositions. In one case, a pharmacist ordered expired drugs to scheme off the difference between these and the current ones. In one of his travels for 'budget defense', his mother was admitted into the National Hospital where the Pharmacist worked and was in charge. An urgent prescription was written. It was the expired drug that was dispensed. It caused renal failure in the woman. When the Pharmacist returned, he found out details of the relation's admission and death, from acute renal failure caused by an expired drug. He shrugged off the disaster as "God's doing."

The situation had become an epidemic of bogus proportions. A generation, which had not seen anything genuine, was in the line of succession. As for bigger projects, bigger returns were expected for individual stakeholders and for the party as well.

Dr Johnson had completed two years in the Federal University of Science and Technology, Kiba as a head of department. He was involved in appraisal committees for promotion and confirmation of appointments in his department and faculty. He kept his own promotion in sight. He had to do a mandatory three years to move from one position to another. He learnt the rules. The higher one went, the hotter it became. He was attending medical conferences and writing papers for publication in medical journals. Since the University was recently established, there was not enough time to harness studies from '10 years experience', as he saw published in medical journals. He collaborated with other units to write. Dr Johnson was not used to the system of university politics. He listened to stories of other people's experiences. There was a lot of subjectivity in the assessment of a publication. Assessors used the opportunity to vent their idiosyncrasies and prejudices. People who found it difficult to scale through the assessments resorted to peddling rumors. There is no smoke without fire. There was usually some iota of truth in the stories peddled. One Professor Kaiza was so mean that someone checked his publications. The case was made that, by the current guidelines, that he was not qualified to reach the rank of Professor. Worse was that since his appointment as a professor, he had not published any papers and had not supervised anyone to publish. This led to the joke that among Konganoga professors, after 10 years, they became prophets as they no longer engaged in academic activities like publications and lectures. Many would either be politicians or traditional rulers, with such titles as Majesty or Highness or High Chief.

Dr Johnson noted the nuances of pursuing a career in the ivory tower and took appropriate measures to negotiate them. One of these was to never have enemies in high or low places. His industry and attention to duties endeared him to the Coordinator of the Clinical Program, Dr Ziebu and the Dean of the Faculty, Prof Kemji. The Dean often asked him about his publications tally to date. At the last asking, Dr Johnson needed about three or four papers to meet the guideline requirement for a Reader or Associate Professor. Different universities used one term or the other. The first hurdle was to be adjudged to have met a *prima facie* case for promotion at the departmental and faculty levels. Responsible Deans ensured that candidates they presented to the central university committee scaled through. Professor Kemji was one such Dean. Dr Johnson and Dr Ziebu turned three years in their respective positions and were thus due for appraisal for promotion. The Departmental assessment was a *fait accompli* for each applicant. At the Faculty level, all departments brought the papers of those that met the departmental *prima facie* case.

At the Faculty Appraisal Committee meeting, all heads of department were members and all attended. Dr Ezemtubo, head of Pharmacology was present at the meeting. There was no candidate from his department. He had not bothered to work hard in spite of the push that was necessary to make him a senior lecturer. He had come to the meeting to act as a spoiler. On the list circulated for debate were the two from the Clinical Division, Dr Ziebu for a full Professorship and Dr Johnson for Reader. The first impulse to Dr Ezemtubo was 'this man of just yesterday'. He felt that he must find a fault with it.

At the last episode, Dr Ezemtubo had argued in vain that Dr Johnson, having been employed as a Lecturer 1, could not be considered for promotion until he had done three years. Dr Ezemtubo forgot the argument at the time. The Dean presented the candidates for confirmation of appointment and promotion up to senior lecturer. Once those were concluded, he asked those below the rank of Reader to leave. They could not deliberate on the promotion of people above their ranks. Dr Ezemtubo protested but was left alone arguing, as others of his rank obeyed the instruction of the Dean. He soon found himself among his superiors, including Dr Ziebu. After initial hesitation Dr Ezemtubo reluctantly left the room. All the candidates presented by the Dean were successful to be forwarded to the central university committee. As usual, Prof Kemji presented his candidates there. The central committee approved all his presentations. The candidates for Reader and Professor were to be sent to external assessors. In a few months, the assessments were returned to the University. Dr Ziebu was promoted full Professor. Dr Johnson 'of yesterday' was promoted Reader. He remained head of his department. This was to be the case until two years later two lecturers were promoted to senior lecturers in his department. Prof Kemji asked him to remain head of department for one more year. This would expose him more to the eggheads that were in Senate and some of who were in the university central appraisal and promotions committee. What interested Dr Johnson with the continued headship included the use of the departmental car and driver. Fiona was yet to get used to the driving skills required to pilot cars in Konganoga. She had once observed that one could 'drive in any direction' on the roads. She was amazed that on a dual carriage way, some drives drove in the opposite direction without any qualms or sanctions. Her observation was confirmed by a fellow Scot, Mr. Doul, an engineer in an international oil company. After a few shots of scotch whiskey at a dinner, Mr. Doul quipped 'one thing I like here is that you can drive in any direction. Aye.'

Chapter 15

ON YOUR MARKS, GET SET

Prof Kemji continued to make it clear to Dr Johnson that there were now only three good papers between him and the professorship. To encourage his staff, Professor Kemji had started a book project. The book had gone to the publishers and final corrections were in progress. It was a peer-reviewed book titled Introduction to Clinical Practice. Dr Johnson had contributed two chapters in addition to being one of the editors. If the book was printed and went into circulation by the next appraisal, he would benefit tremendously. Dr Johnson also had about five papers accepted by journals for publication as well as others in preparation. In one year, baring the unforeseeable, he looked forward to another round of appraisals for promotion. Fiona had been behind a lot of the publications that were credited to her husband, Okon. She proof-read his papers and helped with the typing on the word processor.

While Okon Johnson was engrossed in his duties in the

Teaching Hospital and honed into his career enhancement, Fiona was getting to grips with the different environment she and her young daughters were thrust into. For the children with an unlimited capacity to assimilate new facts and acquire new skills, it was a matter of routine. Not so for their mother. The important thing was that Fiona banished any thoughts of returning to Zeland unless it was a collective family decision. She got her driver's license on the basis of her Zeland international driver's license. However, she had to learn to drive the Konganoga way. In Konganoga, driving was not for pleasure although cars were called 'pleasure cars'. Driving was a contest among all road users. If there was a choice between efficient brakes and sharp horns, the Konganoga driver would choose the horns. Driving was on horns. A driver needed to stress to other road users that he was on the road and had priority. He needed to get to his destination faster than the other road users. The major challenger to a driver was the pedestrian. The pedestrian did not have a car because he owned the road. The power of the pedestrian lay in the fact that he was never at fault. He could be dead, right, but that did not seem to bother him. Whoever hit a pedestrian was at least guilty of an offence. Other pedestrians resorted to mete out punishment on the hapless driver. It was as if the driver of a car was responsible for the lot of the pedestrian. There were rituals that evolved with the introduction of pleasure cars and other motorized vehicles regarding fatal accidents. If a female child was the victim, the driver of the offending car was forced to 'marry' the dead victim. Marriage was the fulfillment of marriage rituals without the body. Fiona was told all these. Garrulous Jonas was in his elements at the job of teaching Fiona how to drive *a la* Konganoga Highway code. On steep hills, Fiona was advised to climb with the car in the reverse gear. That was what Jonas did. He did not know that the problem was with his engine. In the event of an accident, 'never stop to assist the victim'. Fiona found it chilling, until the rationale was explained by Jonas. The mob at a scene of an accident lynched any strange face before finding out whether the victim was injured or not. A good Samaritan who stopped to help a 'hit and run' accident victim would be held guilty by the mob. Once, such a good Samaritan was beaten to death, while the accident victim survived. Fiona could certainly be recognized as a strange face from a mile. She was reassured when she was told that she should report to the nearest police station. That was what civilized Konganogans did. The real ones simply 'hit to run', said Jonas. Fiona kept to the golden rule of driving in Zeland. She let the condition of the road determine the speed at which she drove.

Dr Okon Johnson also learnt a few things about Konganoga. He came to his office one morning to find that his lap top, containing manuscripts he was preparing, was missing. He wondered if he had taken it home and forgotten to come with it. That was soon dispelled. Fiona was sure he did not come home with it and it was not in the house. No one admitted seeing who took the lap top. The broken window in the office was fixed before he went home the previous day. The cleaner happened to come late to work the morning the loss was noticed. She could therefore, not be held responsible. However, she was the prime suspect. She was aware that the lap top was often left in the office. She usually reported to work early until that morning that the lap top was missing. When all these facts were laid down to her, she wept, denying knowledge of the theft. A query was issued to her to return the lap top in 24 hours or face the disciplinary committee. She continued to cry until she got home. She explained her predicament to her husband. The husband informed his father. The decision was to go to a native doctor who usually found out who stole things. The native doctor demanded the list of all the people that had been in the office the previous day. There were three men, the cleaner and Dr Johnson. The three men were the driver and the carpenter and his apprentice who repaired to window. They were summoned to the shrine of the native doctor. The carpenter had come along with his 'pastor' who assured him that he would not come to harm. At the shrine, in the presence of everyone, the native doctor tested everyone on the list. The driver was the first. The native doctor went behind him and put two broom sticks in front of his neck, one from each hand. The doctor told the driver to mention his name.

'Jonas.' As he said it, the native doctor pulled aside each hand holding a stick. The sticks separated with the hands. The cleaner was the next. Her husband was present. The native doctor did exactly what he did with Jonas and got the same result. The same happened with the apprentice. Meanwhile the pastor was muttering prayers with his eyes shut. The carpenter was put in the chair. The native doctor went behind him and put the two broom sticks across his neck. He was told to say his name.

'Amakwe.' As he said it, the native doctor tried to pull the sticks apart. They got stuck. As the *doctor* pulled they tightened on the carpenters neck. The *doctor* asked 'Did you steal the lap top?' 'No.' As he said No, the sticks got tighter. This continued until the tongue of Amakwe protruded and was turning blue. It was then that Amakwe admitted to the theft. He was not allowed to go until the lap top was brought to the shrine. The *doctor* explained that he was surprised that Amakwe was still alive. The juju, called *Mpeke*, never let go once it caught a mendacious thief. Amakwe sent his pastor to his house to go into the roof and bring the lap top. Amakwe paid for the exercise and for the goat used for exorcising the lap top. Dr Johnson was dumbfounded at the power of what Fiona called African wonder. The pastor took credit for sparing the life of Amakwe with prayers.

In the second year of her arrival in Konganoga, Fiona missed her period as soon as she stopped taking the 'pill'. It was not by accident. Eight months later, she was delivered of a bouncing baby boy. Okon suggested the names, Alfred Scot, for the boy. Fiona agreed with him. The baptismal certificate read Alfred Scot Johnson. Okon had observed something in the two years he was back in Konganoga. Names were used to profile individuals. From a name, one could assign a tribe to a person. Okon Johnson came from a 'minority' tribe in the university community. Members of that tribe had developed paranoia from stories of discrimination even at the level of submission of application forms. Dr Johnson himself had even begun to entertain the thoughts sold to him by some of his tribesmen. They felt that if he was from another tribe, his promotion would not have followed the three-year regulation. He knew better, but would still not take any chances on behalf of his son. He felt that Alfred Scot Johnson obliterated the trace of any tribe or ancestors from his son. As events unfolded, his judgment was to become vindicated many years later, when Alfred Scot Johnson sought admission into the 'Command Academy.' He was admitted. The administrators could not immediately ascribe any tribe to the name Alfred Scot Johnson.

With her confidence to drive, Fiona was able to take part in many social activities. It was as if all that happened in Konganoga was one social activity after another. There were weddings, burials, naming ceremonies, thanksgiving services and ceremonies. The conferment of chieftaincy titles became rampant. If one was not being conferred with a title, a friend or family member was. There was hardly a dull moment. People were usually gorgeously dressed for these occasions. It turned out that some people had begun to rent clothing for particular ceremonies either individually or in groups. The women reveled in these social events more than their men folk. Kadiri was a middle aged executive of a farm produce company with a large work force. He found out by himself that he was getting randy. Other people felt the same with him. He was good at getting people to laugh. The women liked that. His handicap was short vision. He needed to be quite close to an object or to people to recognize the object or the people. His further confusion was that he met several people in the course of performing his duties which involved travelling to several towns and cities. Having charged himself up with wine and beer, Kadiri usually became loose cannon with women. On one social occasion, he had found an exquisitely dressed young woman who appeared lonely. She had come with paired friends and she was the odd one out. He approached the girl and engaged her in a friendly conversation. One thing led to another. The woman found Kadiri very funny and he made her giggle quite frequently. He set up a date with her. The woman was elated at her boss setting up a tryst with her. She had recognized him but he did not recognize her in her exquisite attire. On the appointed date and at the chosen place, the boss discovered his folly. He had dated the cleaner in his office. This was because the cleaner had searched deep in her box for an exquisite dress. Her boss, Kadiri had not expected her to turn out the way she did at the social event in which the date was set up. They were drinking while waiting for the menu that was ordered. Then, something clicked. Kadiri recognized his date and froze up literally. He pretended that he knew all along the identity of the bird in his cage. He played along until the food was served. He was patient to last the episode. After the meal, he took the girl home.

He neither kissed her nor tabled any amorous lines. It was men who paid for the dresses that were used to entice the women.

Chapter 16

MEETING THE CHALLENGE HEAD ON

With three children and a husband to look after, Fiona was finding life in Konganoga challenging. She wrote so to the mother. Mrs. Fergus and her husband still harbored lingering resentment at Fiona marrying a man of color. They also did not like her leaving Zeland for good. As there was a lingering resentment, there was also a lingering hope that Fiona would return to Zeland with her children and with or without Okon. Fiona described her experience as a challenge. She had obviously taken it up. Mrs. Fergus ruminated after reading that particular letter and wished her daughter happiness. Fiona began to learn the language of Ikara people, the predominant group in the university town. She could not learn Okon's language because the latter preferred that everyone in the family spoke English. He had not seen much utility in his language as far as his children were concerned. The medium of instructions from the primary to the tertiary educational institutions in Konganoga was English. He felt that human civilization had gone too far for his language to develop itself for the sciences, including engineering and medicine. Fiona did not think he was completely right. Okon was surprised one day when Fiona and Jonas conversed in Ikara language. At first, he did not take notice. The next time, it dawned on him that Fiona was now speaking in tongues. After Jonas left on that occasion, Okon asked her to say more things in Ikara language. He was not in a position to know whether she was right or wrong. He had not bothered to learn the language in spite of more frequent interaction with those who spoke it. He lamely congratulated her. His mind was on his career progression. Fiona had also won the admiration of her colleagues in the hospital. Her integration in the university community was complete. She wondered if the same could obtain with Okon's native community. She would have preferred it.

Professor Kemji was a busy academic and was still the Dean of the Faculty of Health Sciences. Professor Ziebu, immediately he got his professorship, applied for a sabbatical leave of one year. In his absence, Dr Johnson combined the duties of program coordinator and head of department. The Dean continued to find favor with Dr Johnson who equally remained industrious. Dr Johnson had come to take Prof Kemji as his role model. Professor Kemji was elected into the governing council of the university to represent congregation. He was on his second and final year in that capacity. When he received a message inviting him to meet with Prof Kemji, Dr Johnson was unaware that a momentous event was in the offing. In his characteristic manner, he went to see the Dean as soon as he got the message.

'Dr Johnson, how are you and your family?'

'We are fine, Dean. Can you believe that my wife, Fiona speaks Ikara?'

'You must be joking because I do not think you speak it.'

'You are right on the second part but not on the first. I am not joking, Dean', Dr Johnson said, smiling.

'Any way, that is by the way. If I may ask, how is your department?'

'There is no problem for now. You recall that there are now two senior lecturers. They are quite helpful.'

'That is good. Congratulations. It is the duty of any head of an academic unit to show academic leadership. On that score, you will agree that you have not done badly. I will not say the same for some of the other heads.'

'You were the inspiration, Dean', Dr Johnson responded.

'Well, Dr Johnson, a lot of changes are about to happen. The Vice-Chancellor will soon get in touch with you. You should begin to assemble your hand over note. What I have said is confidential. Good afternoon.'

It was obvious that the Dean did not invite further comments, as he picked up his coat to go.

'Will do, Dean', Dr Johnson said by instinct, without a clue as to why he was being asked to 'resign'. However, he felt that if he had done something wrong, there would be a process to determine the wrong and apportion appropriate sanctions. These things took time in the system. He did not go back to his office. Fiona was off duty that day. He went home, to take refuge.

'*Ibiala*', Fiona teased Okon in Ikara language. 'You are home early. A drink?'

'Thanks', Okon replied without specifying what he was thankful for.

Fiona did not know either. She went and brought a bottle of chilled beer. That would usually tune Okon up.

'That is what the doctor ordered and that is what I need.' He gave a wry smile. Fiona was not quite sure what was going on. She came and sat closer to him.

'Did you have a meeting today in the department or faculty?

'I guess you are right'.

'Which one then?

'Faculty, but just me and the Dean', Okon tersely replied.

Fiona then relaxed. A meeting between Okon and the Dean cannot be bad for Okon. He usually told Fiona all the official matters that arose in the discharge of his duties in the faculty and department. However, she expected Okon to be more forthcoming. He realized it.

'The Dean called me to his office. We exchanged the usual casual banters. Then he said that the Vice-Chancellor would soon get in touch with me and that I should begin to prepare my handover notes in the department. Then, from nowhere, he said 'Good afternoon.'

Fiona jumped up and went down to sit and hug Okon the way she had done those early courting days in Zeland. She screamed 'Congratulations.'

Okon became confused. Was Fiona mocking him? He had come home for refuge. Or was that the refuge?

'What is going on?' he asked.

'It is obvious, sweet heart. Your papers went out. Remember? Then 'the Vice-Chancellor will soon get in touch with you'. What else about? Sherlock Holmes would have figured it out, Dr Watson, sorry Dr Johnson, my husband.'

It made sense to Okon. However, his instinct was to 'not count the chickens until they are hatched'.

'You could be right, but let us keep it close to our chests a few more days or even weeks, if need be.' He now drank his beer in a mood different from when it was offered. His mind raced back to those courting days. He looked at Fiona the way he used to. His thoughts went the same way as in those days. He was about to let his emotions drive him when suddenly Eno and Kem rushed in with their own story. It was the proceedings from school for that day. That was priority. Meanwhile, Alfred Scot was soundly asleep.

Two days after the Dean, Prof Kemji told Dr Johnson 'Good afternoon', the Senate convened. The Vice-Chancellor announced new Professorial promotions. Dr Johnson, as head of department, was present. His name was called. He was overwhelmed with joy. The Vice-Chancellor asked all the newly promoted professors to stand up to be recognized by the senators. They complied. Each stood up as he or she was called. When he called all the names, the Vice-Chancellor congratulated them. He enjoined them to develop the human resources in their departments. He reminded them to continue to play the role of academic leaders.

'You may sit.'

As they sat, Prof Kemji left his seat and went over to Professor Okon Johnson. Congratulations, Prof Johnson.' He shook his hands and went back to his seat. Nobody had done that before. There was a loud applause. The senators noticed. Prof Okon Johnson became an instant celebrity. When he got home, Fiona was very happy. Her judgment was vindicated.

As was predicted by Prof Kemji, things were to move rather fast for Prof Okon Johnson. Prof Kemji called for a Faculty Board meeting. He used the opportunity to inform the board of the promotions including that of Prof Okon Johnson. He also used the same opportunity to announce that nominations for a new Dean were welcome. This took everyone by surprise. The regulation required that two weeks' notice be given for an election. However, there were only three professors in the faculty. Prof Ziebu was away on sabbatical leave. Prof Kemji was vacating the seat. Therefore, only Prof Johnson was eligible to be voted for.

Yet, all the righteousness was to be fulfilled. An election was called. The only candidate was Prof Johnson. Votes for and against were called. Only one vote was against. It did not make sense. It was cast by his senior lecturer adversary, Dr Ezemtubo.

A few weeks later, there was an election of senate representatives into the governing council of the university. Prof Okon Johnson was encouraged to submit his candidature. Prof Kemji mobilized his friends and stated his interest. His friends told their friends. At the election, Professor Okon Johnson was in the top four and was declared elected. With that election, he joined Professor Kemji in the governing council of the university.

Chapter 17

AT THE PINNACLE

The rise of Prof Okon Johnson from a rejected applicant in Zeland to a member of the governing council of the institution that rejected him was attributed to "an act of God". Although his path had not crossed that of Prof Stans Ewere, the Deputy Vice-Chancellor at the time of his rejection, both the rejected and the rejecter were soon to serve in various committees of the university. Prof Ewere was one of the four representatives of the senate in the governing council. He had been long in the system. He was also conversant with the game. The game had been that of approximating or equating personal interest to public interest. Sometimes, religion was invoked. At other times, it was tribe. The common denominator or bottom line was always self. Vacancies in public service were often left unfilled because a desired but undesirable candidate was waited for. Prof Okon Johnson, soon after he was employed by the university, had come to know that he was rejected at that Zeland interview because of Prof Ewere's personal interest. He however, did not know the plank of Prof Ewere's interest. It could be financial or tribal. It could not be religious as both were supposed to be Christians. More appropriately, they were church goers. Whatever it was for which Prof Ewere's panel to Zeland rejected Dr Okon Johnson's application did not bother Prof Okon Johnson, until now that they came too close for comfort.

When Prof Ewere was Deputy Vice-Chancellor (DVC), he was responsible for development projects in the University but he reported to the Vice-Chancellor. He was the point man for contractors. The department of works in the university was under his purview. This department supervised and inspected completed projects. It was their report that was used by the Vice-Chancellor to approve payments or deny same. The contractors were still active in the university projects. Although new contractors came on board, only a few functioned for a prolonged period. The long lasting contractors infiltrated the system with gratifications in cash or in kind or both. Prof Ewere received both. He had a price for various contract sums. The contractors simply built his price into their quotations. It was assumed that the Deputy Vice-Chancellor made 'returns'. The rumors did not really identify who could have received the 'returns'. In kind, he was sponsored to conferences in addition to his claims for reimbursement of expenses from the University. His cook/steward was an employee of one of the big contractors. The salary of the cook/steward was paid by the contractor. When his term as the DVC came to an end, the contractor did not know how to withdraw the services of the cook/steward. Prof Ewere did not have the decency to send the cook back to the company. After several indirect hints for Prof Ewere to terminate the services he was receiving in spite of losing 'power', a decision was taken by the contractor to recover the cook/steward.

After several unheeded insinuations and many weeks of quiet deliberations on the most appropriate course of action to take to rectify the situation with the cook/steward who was serving Prof Ewere but who was under the contractor's pay, the latter stumbled on what he felt was the only option open to him. There was a native medicine man who concocted all kinds of medicines. On his sign board, he cured every illness known in the orthodox medical dictionary, ranging from cough through cancer to baldness and barrenness. He also poisoned one's enemies through food. On consultation, his client was a Christian and did not want to commit murder. He just wanted his worker returned to his office. He was given a powdery stuff to put in the food of the target as it was cooked. That way the portion of the powder that caused instant death would be cooked out. The first night the cook introduced the stuff, Prof Ewere had a meeting of some of his colleagues. The cook had not been aware of this meeting prior to the cooking. He had introduced the stuff. The next day the guests reported to Prof Ewere that they suffered from diarrhea. He was not surprised because his household was equally affected. The worst case was Dr Nang who recently returned from America. He lived far from the campus. He had run into the incessant traffic snarls at certain times of the day. He was returning to his house on one such time. To find comfort, he was forced to evacuate his bowels on newspapers places on the floor between the front and back seats of his car.

'What the hell, men. Was that a termination attempt, men? I just didn't find it funny.' He complained to Prof Ewere the next day.

'What did you not find funny?' Prof Ewere asked penitently.

'Shit men. I beg your pardon, but that is to tell it exactly like it was. You know what I mean? If it was a restaurant in America, men, I'll sue it to god dam high heaven. Damn it, men. That was cholera, shit.' Dr Nang, looking through the top of his spectacles, his trousers fastened just below the level of his nipples and suspended from shoulder straps, walked away with a swagger.

That was how Prof Ewere suspected food poisoning. Cholera was food-borne disease. He remembered that from his secondary school days. That was probably the most sophisticated science that he knew. He studied Education in the University. Those who knew him then remembered him for unwholesome activities academically and socially. His wife demanded that the cook be dismissed with ignominy. All that Prof Ewere could do was dismiss the cook/steward with immediate effect. He however made sure that he 'settled' the cook very handsomely to ensure that he kept his mouth shut over the fact that the cook's salary had all along been paid by a contractor who did business with Prof Ewere's office as Deputy Vice Chancellor.

Professors Ewere and Johnson were members of the governing council. Prof Johnson was a novice in the system. However, one learnt the ropes by personal experience. He had come back to Konganoga because of his left wing ideas. He had not abandoned those ideas. In his circumstances then, they were hurting Fiona and his two daughters. The circumstances were now different. Whereas back in Zealand he was unemployed and had reason to resent the system, in Konganoga he was employed and was close to the pinnacle of 'power' till retirement. After retirement, he would still be on the payroll of the system, as a pensioner.

The Council of the university had many committees. Some were important by their lucrative nature. The most important of these was the development committee. The other was the tenders committee. Progressive academics in the Council preferred the Appointments and Promotions Committee membership from Council. The development committee decided what projects to embark on, while the tenders committee selected the successful bids. The Chairman of the council was a member of both. The Chairman constituted all the committees and allotted places as he pleased when he pleased. It was only important to distribute the external members who were appointed by the government. Internal members were sent by a kind of lucky dip. Prof Ewere knew the game. As soon as the Chairman arrived for the inaugural sitting, he called on him by virtue of being a past principal officer of the university. The new Council Chairman was obviously interested in the man who was a past principal officer and currently a council member. He could tap on the 'wealth' of experience of the erstwhile principal officer.

'Good of you, Professor Ewere. I am particularly happy you are now in Council and will be a most useful asset. I am about to allot members to committees. Which one do you think you can contribute most to?'

'Thank you, my Chairman. From my experience, there are two main committees: the development committee and the tenders committee', Prof Ewere said.

'Yes, by the way, one person can exceptionally be in both.'

'You mean in addition to the Chairman, sir?' Prof Ewere said.

'That is correct, come to think of it.'

Prof Ewere did not respond to that comment. He felt he should not belabor the point in order not to show enthusiasm for any. Two days later, at the inaugural meeting, the Chairman announced the composition of each committee. Prof Ewere was in both the development committee and the tenders committee. Prof Johnson was in the protocol and logistics committee. He felt honored. The protocol and logistics committee organized important events in the university calendar such as convocation and matriculation. They arranged the travel of the Chancellor who was an elderly senior statesman. Prof Okon Johnson was not aware of the importance of each committee. Prof Ewere was inwardly happy. He had begun to calculate and choose his goals during the tenure of that particular Council. All committees reported to the council. A committee's decisions could still be debated and challenged in the council. In situations that were likely to be resolved by voting, the committee's chairman was expected to lobby members of the council. This was done by inducement in cash or kind. There were only a few who were strategically placed in the university to be able to parade a lobbying potential. If the Chairman had an interest in any issue before the council and he needed to lobby, he would consult a loyal member and advise the council member to lobby other members on his behalf. The Council Chairman put Prof Ewere into the particular committees because of his lobbying potential, first as a past Deputy Vice-Chancellor and now as a councilor. As a seasoned politician who was usually recycled by each government, the Chairman of Council expected Prof Ewere to be a strong ally, if the shove came to a push.

By the end of the first year of the council, Prof Ewere's countenance became noticeably sanguine. Prof Johnson's committee did not have any major program to execute. The Council had come in after convocation. It would be another year for such an event for the next graduating classes. He had been attending council meetings to debate issues that were brought up. He made his intellectual contribution from time to time. All that gave him some incentive for the council was the food (lunch for internal members) and the 'power' of being 'in council' as far as the students and the staff were concerned. The recycled external council members knew they were there as compensation for their loyalty to the party or a powerful politician. These seasoned members applied the principle of self help in the discharge of their functions in the council. Some of the members, including both the external and the internal members, were innocently naïve of the goings on in the council. Soon rumors spread about the activities of the council. So many projects were started. None seemed to be nearing completion. The situation appeared to mimic the scenario in the larger society where abandoned projects littered the landscape. The reason was not far-fetched. Development projects were started with ulterior motives. The arrow head of the motives was personal financial aggrandizement. The tenure of the council was four years or as long as the government did not change. A reshuffle of the governing cabinet was equally expedient to sack a council. There had been no change in the government either *in toto* or *pari passu*. The President of Konganoga was happy with his initially negotiated cabinet. He resisted pressures for a change. His excuse was, 'Why change a winning team?' Yet there were no victories on record, although there was a lot of it in figment. The grumbling on campus filtered into Professor Johnson's ears.

'Johnny boy, we hear you guys are out for the kill, men', Dr Nang teased Professor Johnson in the senior staff lounge. Members of the senior staff club were like a brotherhood. Membership of the club superseded academic rank in the university. Besides, pals who got elevated in rank remained at social par with their pals. Dr Nang with his American background did not really understand the ways of the university system in Konganoga.

'In America', Dr Nang often said to the chagrin of some of his colleagues who had not gone beyond 50 kilometers radius of the university, 'things were different. In America, students and lecturers communicated on first name basis. The word 'sir' was anachronistic in America.'

Dr Nang was not a man to behold if he got angry. In such moods, he spewed out four-letter words with careless abandon. He said that he found the Konganoga beer 'rich in taste, unlike Budweiser, the beer that made Milwaukie famous'. Dr Nang was not interested in 'god dam' promotions.

'We hear you guys are taking the university to the cleaners, Johnny boy. Hey, where's your own project?' Dr Nang asked Professor Johnson.

'Which guys?' Okon Johnson asked his pal.

'Come off it, buddy. Council, men.'

Okon denied knowledge of council members allocating projects to themselves. He would have been more correct if he said he did not have a project. He would have been forthright about himself alone. However, he did not know the self help aspects of council.

Chapter 18

ARETHA IS NOT TARZAN FOR THE JUNGLE

Dr Nang's American wife had not yet been persuaded to join him in Konganoga. The first time she came to visit, she was forced to fetch water from a street tap with a bucket. At first, it was fun to carry the bucket on the head with others. She did not know the others were house girls and house boys. When she found out, she was not amused. She called Dr Nang a son of a bitch. He did not really care. There were worse names to call him. He would not have cared either, however unprintable.

'Aretha, sweetie, you just fetched that dammed water a week and you're grumbling. Men, I had to do it for 20 long years before I come over to America, hugh. Give me a break mamma, please.' Aretha thought she had been harsh on Dr Nang. It was not his fault that water was an essential commodity in Konganoga. Yet, she did not like doing like the 'house people' as she used to group the girls and boys. When she got back to America from that first visit, she began to reconsider the relationship. They had no kids. She decided to take it easy in the meantime.

Dr Nang made do with socializing in the staff club. He had become friends with Professor Johnson soon after they both returned 'home', one from America and the other from Zeland. They needed mutual protection from their colleagues who were conversant with events in the larger society and in the confines of the University. These colleagues did not find the situation of decrepit infrastructure appalling. They often criticized anyone who talked down on the 'father land'. One question that irritated Okon and Dr Nang was 'Why don't you go back to the white man's land since you are no longer black?' Okon Johnson and Thomas Nang weathered the storm together. The only problem was that Dr Nang was a chain smoker of cigarettes. To help his friend and simultaneously extricate himself from passive smoking, Okon Johnson sponsored a motion in the staff club to ban smoking in the lounge. As a doctor, he explained the hazards of smoking. Many lecturers bought his viewpoints. Some others, who found Dr Nang's flippancy with four-letter words irritating, supported the motion to get at him. The motion was passed. Both 'immigrants' still needed each other's company.

'Men, you got me there. That son of a bitch in Philosophy screwed the knife as you stabbed. Hell, *I ain't gonna quit the fag*. Come on.' He told Okon over a bottle of beer. Between sips, he would go out in the open 'to drag a fag.'

The governing council of the University had met to discuss the new projects the Vice-Chancellor requested. The university lacked adequate classroom space. Generally in the campus, both hostels and classrooms often lacked toilets in appropriate locations. Dr Nang had complained that the students and workers were forced to defecate behind some buildings. The students ignored the pit latrines and preferred to abuse places where no 'reasonable' person would ease himself or herself. Many of the lecturers had spoken to condemn the 'barbaric' actions of the perpetrators of the felony that the Vice-Chancellor had outlined. One speaker suggested that the security men should be stationed to capture one or two culprits who would be used to set an example on good behavior and acceptable civilized standards.

As Professor Johnson listened, he was bewildered at the comments of members of governing council. He remembered Dr Thomas Nang's accusation about projects. It was possible that was the plank of the Vice-Chancellor's presentation.

Projects would engender contracts.

Professor Johnson raised his left hand to attract the Chairman's attention to let him speak. As a new member, he took his time to assess the situation. He was new to big administration in the university. He had become Dean and member of council simultaneously. The Chairman was happy to see the new and young Professor get into the discussions.

'Yes, my Professor of TEN, Throat, Ear and Nose.' The Vice Chancellor said.

Okon stood up but was told that he could speak from the sitting position.

'Thank you, Mr. Chairman, sir. May I make a point of correction?'

All eyes, including the Chairman's, turned to Professor Okon Johnson as he continued:

"Sir, we prefer the appellation 'Ear, nose and throat (ENT) or the more jaw-breaking Ortho-rhino-laryngology.

But mine is Ophthalmology. Mine is certainly less jaw-breaking, sir.

In ophthalmology we see, or we make people see. They talk or listen in ENT.'

At that, a few members chuckled.

Prof Johnson having unwittingly attracted attention to himself continued:

'Sir I want to comment on the two issues that have so far been raised. Although the projects requested by the Vice-Chancellor are topical and pertinent, what assurance do we have that when approved by council and started, that they will be completed. Mr. Chairman, sir, if you have time to drive, or better, to get driven around this University, you will see an abundance of abandoned projects. This University, if the trend is not nipped in the bud, may soon after approval and commencement also become abandoned like the projects I have referred to.

The other point, sir, is the issue of toilets or more accurately, the lack of them. There is this rather draconian suggestion that we set security men to lay ambush to catch defecating 'felons', my apologies. These security men probably dump more gallons and kilograms of effluents than the students combined. They will gladly lay ambush and catch some *scape*-goats. If it is a female student, my fear is that it will be the University that will be put to ridicule rather than the student being embarrassed. Sir, if I was a student of this university and I was sufficiently pressed by nature, in the absence of the necessary conveniences, I would probably equally have used any available convenient space to answer any of nature's calls. It is the University that is barbaric not to have decent toilets. It is not those who have been forced into embarking on barbaric actions. Thank you, sir.'

There was a round of applause from many members of

council at the conclusion of Professor Johnson's rendition. Professor Ewere appeared to turn out as a lone pilloried voice and justifiably so. He had come to believe in contracts from whatever source and from whatever justification. He could be daubed Mr. Abandoned Project for the legacy of his four years as DVC. No one else spoke on the subject. The Chairman had no option than to lead the way towards a decision.

'Members of council, my people say that you do not stand at one place to admire a masquerade. It is good to look at an issue from several perspectives and consider various ramifications. The learned Professor of T.E.N, I beg your pardon Eyes, has chewed the bread fruit and has bared his teeth to us. I must admit that I buy into his holistic perception of the University's predicament. He describes a campus littered with abandoned projects. We will drive round and take note. We will set up a campus project monitoring team who will report to council like other committees of council. I think, with apologies to my learned eye surgeon, that it is more salubrious to tackle the cause of a disease rather than the symptoms. These security men are not as cultured as you and I. Imagine the scenario of the man lying in ambush. This undergrad female looks round, sees nothing and goes ahead to strip herself. The security man is more likely to want to secure some carnal pleasure than capture a *scape*goat. There was a roar of laughter

'My fellow council members, let us be realistic. The Director of works is to present to Council through me, a master plan to install toilets at strategic locations in this campus, the type of any one of us can comfortably utilize.'

Thus was the Chairman's ruling.

It was time for lunch. Council adjourned. On the way

to lunch, a few members congratulated Professor Johnson for taking the bull by the horns. One of the admirers whispered that the contract merchants were not very comfortable with the speech, especially as the Chairman endorsed the points that Professor Johnson made.

The contribution by Professor Johnson filtered out of the council chambers into the campus congregation. A version was propagated by those who were fed up with contract merchants like Prof Ewere and others who were camouflaged for the time being. Those in the camp of Professor Ewere took notice of the potential crusader for moral probity. Either way, Professor Okon Johnson had begun to make his mark and attract attention. The university appointments and promotions committee (A & PC) was meeting. There was a petition from the Faculty of Education in which Professor Ewere had been a Dean after a stint as Deputy Vice-Chancellor. The petitioner had been denied promotion to professor on the grounds that he lacked sufficient teaching experience. In the section for 'Teaching experience', an arbitrary score below the minimum for that section for professor had been entered. This was the point observed by a member who advised the committee at the time that the candidate did not fulfill the criteria for elevation to professor. That advice was upheld and the candidate was denied promotion. As was the practice, the candidate subsequently demanded his assessment report and it was given to him, although begrudgingly so. He complained to a few members of the A &PC including Professor Okon Johnson, who advised the candidate to send a petition to council through the Chairman. He advised the petitioner to marshal out his point logically and with humility. It was this petition that was before the committee. The committee Chairman was the Vice-Chancellor. After introducing the matter, the Chairman called for comments and contributions. Professor Johnson had been shown the draft of the petition and its final version that was now on the table. He, in fact, arrogated to himself the role of the advocate for the petitioner. He enjoyed the notion of playing the role of an advocate in the council as obtains in the law courts. He raised his left hand as usual and obtained the 'protection' of the Chairman to take the floor. He cross-examined the Dean of the Faculty, Professor Ewere.

'Mr. Chairman, sir, thanks for allowing me to speak. I need some clarifications. The candidate makes a lot of claims to justify his rejection of the score given to him on Teaching experience. Is there any claim therein that is not true?'

'Dean of the Faculty, please respond.' The Chairman directed.

'The candidate's claims of teaching at another tertiary institution are correct.' Prof Ewere replied.

Professor Johnson straightened himself on his chair and then asked:

'Chairman, sir, does this University accept the years of teaching at such institutions at par with the same years here?'

'Registrar, direct the committee.' The Chairman said.

The Registrar, a lawyer by profession informed the committee that the answer to Professor Johnsons question was in the affirmative.

'In that case, sir, the petition has a lot of merit. In my opinion, the petition should be upheld. Once the appropriate score is entered, a prima facie case for external assessment would have been established.'

Professor Johnson spoke so clearly and so passionately that an interlude of silence quickly followed his assertion.

It was as if the committee members were ruing over his speech. It required the intervention of the Chairman to breach the silence. Even at that, all he was able to say was 'Approved?' The response to this was an encore.

Towards the end of the meeting, they reached the 'any other business (AOB)' item. Prof Kemji sought an explanation over the spate of abandoned or uncompleted projects in the institution. He explained his reason for the concern. He did not approve of a situation where officials shirked their responsibilities with impunity.

The Vice-Chancellor was obviously the target of that concern. Eggheads in the Ivory Tower understood themselves. He took the question but pointed out that the Chairman of the Governing Council had already gone beyond the point of inquest that Prof Kemji alluded to and that the Chairman's directives would be attended to by the next Council meeting. There was no further comment on that item. The VC had successfully parried the concern.

It was as if a wall had developed separating Professor Okon Johnson from Professor Ewere. They invariably found themselves on opposite sides of the fence at discussions in the committees both of them attended. After nearly two years in these committees, they were yet to find a common ground. However, they were not looking for any. There would probably be no common platform for both eggheads.

Chapter 19

ONE INCUBATOR AND THE BUBBLE IN ACTIVITY

With the incubator donated from Zeland, Mrs. Fiona Johnson's work load increased. Word spread in the town about the white matron who was in charge. The availability of the service to the poor was attributed to the fact that she was a white woman. This was true up to a point. That point was that she was instrumental to the acquisition of the incubator. The selfish interest of Alambo Mungo Park, the Chief of Administration was a facilitator. The exploitation of the opportunity by the CA to make money out of the project was not new in Konganoga. Mrs. Johnson was soon to learn this. It affected her psyche. She expected that she would train up some nurses to do what she did with the incubator. Unfortunately, there were many obstacles. The work was tedious. The nurses seemed to want a job. Once they were employed, they loathed the work. Quite a few were employed on the basis of 'federal character', a decrepit principle by which individuals were hired for jobs not on basis of competence or uniform qualification but largely on basis of their areas of origin in the country. Ability was a secondary consideration. Many nurses who were employed came through sponsors, mainly politicians. There was an exception. Obele was the bright student nurse who had worked with Fiona when she started work in the Children's Special Care Unit popularly called CSCU. She had completed her training and had been employed as a staff nurse midwife. Her case was treated purely on merit. Fiona's endorsement and recommendation at the interview did not meet with any opposition. At Fiona's request, the Chief Matron posted Obele to CSCU. The two nurses had a complimentary attitude to work. Fiona invited Obele to her house one evening for a meal. She was pleased to visit. She had known Okon longer than she knew Fiona but on a rather official capacity. Eno and Kem were excited to see a visitor in their house. Scot had started walking and went to stay with the visitor. Not to be outdone, Kem went to her room and brought her books to show Obele. Perhaps, she wanted to show that she was superior to her little brother. Stories were told and questions were fielded to Obele. She hardly had time to chat with her hosts when the food was presented on the table. They all went to eat. Scot still stuck to Obele, who helped him with his food. They finished rather late. Obele left to get home and prepare for the next day's work. The children were put to bed.

At home, Fiona enjoyed looking after her children and her husband. The thought of going to work began to compete with her need to look after her family, especially with the children learning and acquiring skills. While the work in the hospital was frustrating, managing the house chores was pleasant. For the three years she worked, she had not taken a holiday. She was promised that the leave would be deferred officially so that she could take all as an accumulated period. The leave period for each year was 30 working days. By the end of three years therefore, her accumulated leave was 90 working days. She and Okon planned that she should take it during the long school vacation so that the children would not miss school. Okon was too busy in the university to stay away for a long period in a stretch. He therefore, planned to take two weeks and travel to Zeland with all the family. Fiona arranged to get a *locum tenens* appointment in the general hospital where her parents lived. This would enable her mother to help in looking after the children from time to time.

The Fergus family lived in a four bed-room detached house. All the three children had left the house. However, they all still regarded the house as their home. Mr. and Mrs Fergus had wanted to sell the house and move to a smaller holding. This plan was shelved when their eldest daughter had a baby, soon followed by another baby. Each time Agnes visited with her children, Mrs. Fergus seemed to receive a new lease of life. The children enjoyed the petting of 'Granny', as they used to call her. The sale of the house for a smaller place soon got relegated to the back burner. When Fiona informed her parents that she wanted to visit Zeland during her vacation, Mrs. Fergus was delighted. Mr. Fergus did not really mind. After all, he was not the one to cook for them or wash them. Mrs. Fergus cleaned up the whole house in expectation of her daughter and her husband together with her grandchildren. The flight details were sent to her. She looked up the train times to inform Fiona.

Professor Johnson arranged for one of his heads of department to look over the affairs of the Faculty for the two weeks leave he had been permitted by the Vice-Chancellor. The driver was to pack the Dean's car in Professor Johnson's compound until he returned. However, his driver, Jonas, was expected to report to work daily while occasionally looking up in his house from time to time in case the house girl, Umanamaa had a message for Jonas. Professor Johnson fetched the airline tickets for himself and the rest of the family. The fare was high but he and Fiona considered it worth it. From the airport, they took a train to Chisterton where Mr. and Mrs. Fergus lived. From the Chisterton railway station, they took a cab to get to the Fergus's. As the cab driver was bringing down the loads, Mrs. Fergus came out to welcome her visitors. She was thrilled to see her grandchildren from Konganoga. Most of her friends could not pronounce the name because it was a mouthful. That even made her prouder. Her husband was different. He was almost indifferent to the issue of his grandchildren from Africa. He preferred that to Konganoga. However, he did not show any hostility to any of the Johnsons, daughter, son-in-law or grandchildren. He had not been favorably disposed to the marriage between Fiona and Okon. He knew that there was nothing that he could do about it, as Fiona persisted. He had accompanied his wife to visit the couple at the birth of each of the daughters. His rationale was that having 'lost' his daughter, he was not going to lose his wife in the bargain. He was delighted when Fiona informed him and his wife that they were relocating to Konganoga in Africa. That was far enough. When his wife told him that Fiona and her children were coming on a visit to Zeland, he was not aware they were coming to stay in his house. Having arrived, he was told they were going to stay there. There was nothing he could do about it. Mrs. Fergus was good to him. He respected and often depended on her.

Inside the house, Fiona introduced her children to her parents. At the end she said, 'Eno, Kem and Scot, this is granddad and this is grandma.' At that, Scot rushed to his grandddad and clung on to him until they were taken to their two rooms. Mr. Fergus was touched by Scot's affection towards him. Apart from Scot's attitude to Mr. Fergus, his name was also good for Mr. Fergus. At the dinner table that evening, Scot insisted on sitting between granddad and grandma. Kem tried to struggle over it with him. He screamed so loud that granddad Fergus had to intervene. He placed one on his right and the other on his left. It was convenient for Scot on the left side of granddad. Mr. Fergus was right handed. He was therefore able to feed Scot intermittently. That was how the attitude of Mr. Fergus to Fiona's marriage to Okon changed for the better. He was to share the care of the grand children with his wife when Fiona went to work.

Fiona started to work as a *locum tenens* nurse in the children's ward. In the three months they were to stay, she bought a few hospital items for her husband. She also arranged to accumulate discarded hospital equipments from a few hospitals in the region. She would sell these on her return to Konganoga. She had not forgotten how Alambo Park exploited the consignment she had arranged for the Teaching Hospital, Kiba. She had gone round to some of the hospitals with Okon. Mr. Owen and Dr McAndrew were very helpful in this. They were very pleased to see Fiona and Okon again after so many years. To prevent Dr McAndrew from mispronouncing his name, he was quick to inform Clough that he had recently been promoted Professor in his university. Yet, Clough persisted in calling him 'Okn'. The time was soon up for Professor Johnson to return to Konganoga. He was happy to have seen the colleagues who helped him in his career in Zeland. Fiona found a nursery for children, one that was open two days a week. It was designed for mothers in part-time employment. She enrolled her children. Their attendance relieved the grandparents of some of the responsibilities for the time they were at the nursery. This enabled Mrs. Fergus to attend to her usual chores. In any case, Mr.

Fergus was warming up to them. He tried to make up with the rest of the time they were not at the nursery. After two months in Zeland, Fiona began to make arrangements to return to Konganoga. To her surprise, her children were torn between Zeland and Konganoga. They were being spoilt by their grandparents. The refrigerator was stocked full with drinks, fruits, ice cream, yoghurts, etc. There was always light. Kem had asked the grandparents why there was never a blackout in the house since they did not have a generator. Mr. Fergus parried the question. He did not know what generator the little granddaughter referred to. At the same time, the children liked the large space in Konganoga available for them to play. There was life everywhere with chirping birds and insects such as grasshoppers. It was not long and the three months came to an end. The hospital equipments and a three-year old car were put in a container and shipped to Konganoga. Fiona flew back with her children.

Chapter 20

BOARD ROOM GAMES

The government announced changes in the boards of a few government departments. It was looking ahead to the next elections and needed something to show and justify the intention to continue governance. There was a mining company that had become moribund. The earlier members of the board had seen their membership as compensation for support for the president's party. Rather than pay them, they were given appointments from which the members would fend for themselves. After all, it was better to show the people how to fish than to give them fish caught by other people. They would be vulnerable when the fishermen had other things to do and could no longer fish. The Tin Mining Company of Konganoga (TMCK) had been promising when it was set up. The prospects for tin in the foreign market were rated high. Suddenly, the war in the Middle East broke with the effect of sky rocketing of the price of crude oil, which Konganoga also produced.

The board of directors at the time was headed by a former political thug, Comrade Doe. He was a thug who had risen through the ranks to the upper echelon of the party hierarchy. He began slowly to exploit the opportunity of being the Board Chairman. The government had diverted attention to crude oil exploration and sales and did not pay attention to other activities in the country. Comrade Doe first sold off the company's movable assets to himself and a few others who he identified to be equally greedy. Such people could *chop and not quench*. They would not spill the beans. It was betrayal that brought schemers down to their knees. From being Chairman, Comrade Doe built a hotel. This was venue for several party functions. He also acquired three cars. One was for him. The other was for his wife who was yet to learn to drive. The third one was for miscellaneous errands. He did not complain when he was removed as Chairman of TMCK. All that he left of TMCK was its carcass. The entrails were devoured by Comrade Doe.

Professor Johnson had been recognized beyond the confines of the university as an astute physician and surgeon. He often served in technical committees for government development projects involving industries. He had become acquainted with another 'countryman' in Zeland when he was rounding up his graduate studies. Sharma had come for a postgraduate diploma in History. This was completed in one year and Sharma quickly returned to Konganoga. He did not wait for the results to be released before he flew back. He was among the very few privileged Konganogans whose path of progress had been mapped out. Professor Johnson had seen it announced that Sharma was an under-secretary in the Ministry. He recognized the name. He quickly sent him a congratulatory letter, reminding Sharma of their acquaintance some years previously. Sharma remembered and kept the letter perfunctorily without any immediate purpose. He had gone to the Ministry of Establishment when the boards of some *parastatals* were being reconstituted. The officials did not have names submitted for TMCK. After what Comrade Doe did there, no one was keen to go there. Sharma casually dropped the name of Professor Johnson and left, without much thought about it. He was pleasantly surprised when he got another letter from Prof Johnson informing him about the appointment as the Chairman of the Board of TMCK. Although the professor did not know how his name came on the list, Sharma knew. Prof Johnson did not have the profile of the members of the Board. He would get that information in due course. The inauguration of the reconstituted boards was done at the national capital in Kumbrujaa. There, the members of the TMCK Board had their inaugural meeting. The Chairman was able to get the curriculum vitae of the members. Professor Johnson also went to the supervising Ministry to obtain the files of previous transactions of the company.

Following a report on the state of affairs in TMCK, the Chief Executive Officer (CEO) of the company, Dr Adamus, was sent on compulsory leave. He was never to return to the same post. However, he was not dismissed. When the dust seemed to have settled, he was transferred to another Ministry without any sanctions. His subordinate officer with whom he had a turbulent relationship, Mrs. Lakunja, was appointed the Acting CEO. An extraordinary Board meeting was scheduled. There was need to get to grasps with the Company. In a subsequent chat with Sharma, Professor Kemji learnt that the President was keen for results from the Company. The rock bottom share price needed to be raised in an apparent transparent manner. There was an intrigue in financial houses whereby shares were artificially raised by insider interested parties. These parties took huge loans from Banks and bought up shares in a target company to create a fake scarcity. This would stimulate public interest. The insider interested parties would choose convenient times to sell and use their profits to repay their loans and keep some reasonable, often mouth-watering profits. Most often, the original loans were not repaid and the debtors bought up property in foreign lands on cash down payments. The affected banks were said to be distressed and were to receive some cash transfusion to ostensibly "to prevent collapse of the financial system." Nemesis was to catch up with them sooner than later, when the property market also collapsed. This sharp practice soon became rampant internationally. It led to the proclaimed collapse of the international finance market.

Mrs. Lakunja was instructed by the Chairman of the Board, Professor Johnson, to prepare a comprehensive report for the Board for discussions at the extra-ordinary meeting. She had a stake to protect. It was desirable to be confirmed as the substantive CEO. She therefore, spent a lot of effort and time to do a comprehensive report. She knew a bit of the wrong-doings of the former CEO. This was the root cause of the mutual antagonism, which both shared. Mrs. Lakunja felt that the CEO and the former Chairman of the Board went too far with their compensation for their support to the ruling party. The main blame was on the CEO. If he did not agree with the Board's activities, he should have articulated that in writing to the supervising Minister. Although a panel of enquiry was set up to determine the remote and immediate causes of the collapse of TMCK, the report was not *gazetted* in any paper *white* or *brown*. The self-help attitude of the CEO and Chairman of the TMCK Board degenerated to insatiable avarice. The Company was literally looted. No charges were pressed on any of the indicted participants. Mrs. Lakunja listed the problems that existed in the Company as at the time she assumed office as Acting CEO.

Exploiting her experience in the Company over a fairly long period, she went on to suggest counter-measures to redress the situation. The Chairman got an advance copy of the report. The other members of the Board were to get their copies on arrival for the meeting. They had not had time to form cliques for or against the Chairman as was the norm. Before the meeting, the Chairman phoned Mrs. Lakunja and thanked her for the clear and concise report, together with suggestions for correction.

Although the Company had a guest house that could accommodate the members of the Board, the former Chairman stayed in an expensive hotel during meetings of the Board. Occasionally, he extended the same privilege to whoever on the Board, that he wanted to do special favors in the form of support. He was soon to extend his stays to when he had personal and private business interests in town. His next plan was to reserve a suite in the hotel permanently, at the expense of the company. Prof Johnson asked the Acting CEO whether the guest house was in a good habitable state. The latter confirmed that the staff of the house worked during and after Board meetings. In fact, the accommodation was rented to the public in order to keep up the services there. Each room was self-contained. The Chairman's was a suite with a lounge. The meeting circular stated the time of arrival and the venue for accommodation. As the members arrived, they were taken to the guest-house and put in an available room. Each room was fitted with an air-conditioner. There was a reading desk, a king size bed and a wardrobe. Each room had an inter-communicating telephone. A door led to an adjoining toilet and bathroom. There was a general kitchen, a dining room with table and a refrigerator stocked with non-alcoholic drinks.

Each Board member was, on arrival, given a copy of the report in a sealed envelope. It was written by the

Acting CEO. Each was to study it for the morning meeting scheduled for 10 am. The members were informed that coffee would be served a half hour before 10 a.m. By 9.30 a.m. the Board Chairman was in the conference room. He fixed himself a cup of coffee and went to a chair to sit. It was another ten minutes before the first member sauntered in. He expressed surprise to see the Board Chairman, Prof Johnson, already seated, although not in the chair positioned for him. Mr. Dumbe was a retired principal of a secondary school. In his active days, he was a terror to any staff or student. who arrived late to any meeting. He had not expected the Board meeting to start before 11 a.m. although the scheduled time was unequivocally stated. He was exchanging banters with the Chairman when Mrs. Lakunja, the Acting CEO, walked in. On seeing the two men, she was delighted and apologized profusely for her lateness. In the former Board, members were lucky if the entire meeting was not postponed to suit the whims of the Chairman. This new Board seemed to be one with which she could do business. She immediately recognized that she needed to do quite some readjusting and apologized again for being late for the coffee. She gave the excuse that she had to make sure everyone was in order in her home. She promised that she would be more punctual in the future. Both the Chairman and Mr. Dumbe congratulated her for the clarity in which she couched her report. She acknowledged and went to drop some files and documents by her seat. The two gentlemen continued their chat over the coffee. Mr. Dumbe took tea instead of coffee. At 10 a.m., the Chairman excused himself to go to his seat and implored Mr. Dumbe to do the same. Then, five members entered the room, astonished to see that the meeting was being called to order. They were shown their seats. Two seats remained vacant.

'Please anyone who wants coffee can walk across the

table set at the far end and help him/herself. Otherwise, an usher could serve a member where she or he sat. Lady and gentlemen, I welcome you to this extra-ordinary meeting of the TMCK. Being an extra-ordinary meeting, there will be no minutes of a previous meeting. This includes the inaugural meeting that preceded this. Let us go through the Agenda for modification or ratification.'

'Any modification including addition or subtraction?'

He looked up. No hands were up.

'Is the Agenda as presented approved?'

'Approved', the members responded.

The first item on the Agenda was Chairman's opening remarks. He began to address the Board.

'Lady and gentlemen, I welcome you again. I believe that we all had a pleasant night and have had some breakfast. The coffee at 9.30 a.m. was not a mistake. It was to get members to settle down. We shall work with time consciousness. The main reason for this meeting was circulated to all of us yesterday. I believe we took time to peruse it. As we all know, it is important for government to revive the tin mining operations for a dual purpose. There is need to inject resources into the economy and there is also the need to employ the able bodied men and women in the polity. The government has chosen this high caliber of men to accomplish her objective as stated. We shall go through the report one item after another. I hope we can reach some decisions today. Otherwise, we will come again in the morning. Let me suggest that when someone has made an important point, subsequent speakers should not repeat the point. The Acting CEO, Mrs. Lakunja will present her report.'

Chapter 21

POINTS OF ORDER

As the Chairman of the Board of TMCK took his seat, two remaining members of the Board entered the room. One was Mrs. Nabel George, wife of a late member of the party. She inherited the Chairmanship of George Motors a well-known car dealership in town which had often supported the party in power, from her husband. It was not easy with her brothers-in-law. However, invoking the cries of a widow, she was able to see them off her late husband's assets. The company supplied all sorts of vehicles on contract. She was regarded as a female activist. Her activism was in line with the general modus operandi of public institutions in Konganoga. The members were in it for what they could get for themselves. The second late comer, Prince Jakes was a lawyer in his early fifties. He was not a prince and he was not prudish.

'Mrs. George and Mr. Jakes, you are welcome. Please take your seats. The CEO will present her report.' There was silence, as Mrs. George looked round as if to search out anyone in particular.

Mrs. Lakunja stood up and adjusted her cream white blouse over her dark brown long skirt. Next, she adjusted the bangles she wore on her left forearm.

'Mr. Chairman, sir, honorable members of the Board, let me join the Chairman to welcome you to this extraordinary meeting which you instructed me to call. I hope that you had a pleasant night.'

At that point, Mr. Prince Jakes quietly but audibly added: 'It was lonely.' Heads turned to him. Mrs. Lakunja pretended not to have heard and continued.

'Efforts were made to make your accommodation clean and comfortable. Please bear with us if there have been any short comings.' A few people cleared their throats and looked in the direction of Prince Jakes. Mrs. Lakunja continued.

'The report is in two sections. The first section lists the present situation and highlights some of the major problems on ground. The second section includes our suggestion from management on how to make amends for a smooth take off of operations as soon as possible.' She continued until she finished what she intended to say.

'Ladies and gentlemen, we have read the report. We have heard the same report. Let me thank Mrs. Lakunja for this report. However, I ask that we adopt it for discussion.'

Mr. Dumbe raised his right hand. The Chairman gave a nod.

'Mr. Chairman, I move that the Board adopt the document for discussion.'

'Any supporter?' the Chairman asked

'Supported *sine difficultas*,' added Barrister Prince Jakes.

'Point of order, Mr. Chairman,' Mrs. George said with her left hand raised.

'Yes, madam.'

'Then another point of order, Mr. Chairman.'

'You have the floor Mrs. George.' The Chairman did not know where he had provoked Mrs. George's second order.

'Thank you very much, sir. The first point is that we should deliberate in the Konganoga lingua franca, English. The learned gentleman should not think we are in a court chambers where he can communicate in Latin.' There was a roar of laughter. Mrs. George paused to acknowledge the roar and continued. 'The second order, sir, is that the title 'madam' is too patronizing. I am however, happy that you quickly brought yourself to order when you addressed me as Mrs. George. Thank you, sir.' There was more laughter and some applause. Then someone said, 'I suppose she has been *matronising* by addressing the Chairman as 'sir' which is the opposite of madam.' Others, including the Chairman heard it. There was more laughter.

The Chairman let off some wry smile for a change. 'I guess it is therapeutic to tone down tensions. Thank you, Mrs. George for letting me off. I also thank Mr. Dumbe who came to my rescue, although it was after the parole. Let us take the points in the report one after the other.'

The discussion continued until lunchtime. The meeting adjourned for lunch. The members agreed to reconvene after 90 minutes.

The discussions before lunch had been without acrimony. The issues were obvious. From the management, there was need for manpower and its development. Office equipment needed to be provided, repaired or upgraded. Medical facilities for employees were necessary to reduce man hours lost to ill health. Smooth discussions continued after lunch until Mrs. Lakunja reached 'Service vehicles'. She continued, 'a bus or two will be needed for conveying field workers. Some officers also need cars because of the nature of their jobs.'

'The Chairman has no car. For this meeting, he came by bus and was seen on a motorcycle taxi on one of his visits to the premises', the Acting CEO lamented. She pressed on. 'The CEO is still using the official car. This means that I have to depend on my husband to get to work and back to my home.' By the time she got so far, many hands including Mrs. George's were up.

'Mr. Chairman, sir, apologies to Mrs. George, there is no doubt that all the vehicles listed by the Acting CEO are necessary. We the members of the Board should not be left out of any largesse when it comes to vehicles. The special license plate number of government will save us the embarrassment from law enforcement arms of government. What the CEO has not told us is how the resources will be tapped. I would like to hear her view on that.'

Prince Jakes sat down. Mr. Ocha, a member of the Board raised his hand. When he was recognized by the Chairman, all he said was that he supported the last speaker. This was the type of contribution the Chairman had cautioned against.

Mrs. George was the next to speak. She stood up. The Chairman told her to sit since they could all hear her. She thanked the Chairman but insisted on standing up while addressing the Board.

'Mr. Chairman, sir, the humiliation I got from the ignorant policeman who accosted me on my way to attend this meeting will remain indelible in my mind. In fact, the only way I know to delete it is by giving each member of the Board a vehicle with government registration number. I would have asked for one of those second hand vehicles which they call *tokumbo* vehicles. And if I may ask, who is fooling who in this our country? If you go to a permanent secretary's house or a Commissioner's house, you will see all

KONGANOGA

types of new vehicles imported from anywhere they make them. Mr. Chairman, sir, all I am saying is that Konganoga has crude oil. If we ask, and we ask for brand new cars, sir, we are not rude. We will get them because this country can afford them for honorable Board Members. Remember the biblical injunction: 'Ask and you shall receive. Seek and you shall find. Knock and it shall be opened unto you.'

'We have neither asked, nor sought, nor indeed knocked. We should begin from these initial periods in this Board to do these before it becomes too late. Mr. Chairman this is my humble view on this issue of cars.'

There was subdued but audible evidence of support and approval of Mrs. George's short contribution. Prince Jakes indeed gave thumbs-up sign to Mrs. George. And the latter nodded gently in acknowledgment.

The Chairman did not appear to share in the hilarity and emotions. He did not chide or laud the speaker but quietly reminded the Board Members that their primary assignment was to resuscitate a moribund company. That, according to the Chairman must remain the focus. 'It is only when the task of resuscitation has been achieved that we can begin to discuss or dream of brand new cars.' The Chairman said as he ran a quick glance across the room as if to press it home to the members that he was there to do a job even if the other members did not go along with him.

With the Chairman's permission, Mrs. George went on

'Mr. Chairman Sir, a new car for the Chairman does not have to come from a dream. It should be actualized. My Company is ready to supply any or all the vehicles listed by the CEO. By the way, she is here doing the work. You say she is acting. Is she now an actress? Please let me do that one of supply of service vehicles at a generous discount. My people the Igbollas say you cannot be at the river and have soap enter your eyes.'

Many others spoke on the need for vehicles and the Chairman summarized thus:

'Lady and gentlemen the bottom line is the funds. I agree that the vehicles are necessary. But we need to do our jobs to reorganize the ailing and wasteful system and generate the funds first. As soon as funds are available, the Acting CEO will inform us and we will do the needful.'

The meeting continued until dusk and adjourned till the next day to reconvene at the same 10 a.m. The members of council used the first day to appraise themselves. This was important for the Chairman. He had shown that he was a stickler for time. It was too early to reveal his greed or lack of the same. The Acting CEO made a positive impression on him. Mr. Dumbe, the retired Principal could be a dependable ally. It was too early to confirm. He was not sure about Prince Jakes. He was, however, funny. Mrs. Nabel George was someone who still needed to disabuse her mind of her notion of the benefits and privileges of Board membership vis-à-vis the responsibilities, the way Prof Johnson intended to play his role. As an academic and an administrator, Prof Johnson was used to accomplishing tasks in a reasonable time frame. For Prof Johnson, the task on hand was to salvage TMCK not to cannibalize it. The salvage assignment was enormous, especially as he had been told that there were insufficient funds. It was a vicious circle. It was because of need for funds that the necessity to resuscitate TMCK arose. Yet, this task required funds for its accomplishment. It was necessary to develop and sustain the will. Without a grant from the government, the Board would survey the possibility of sourcing funds from commercial banks or private entrepreneurs.

The resumption of the meeting the following day was remarkable in a few ways. Members arrived early enough to enjoy the coffee session collectively. This offered another opportunity for familiarization. Some members wanted an early conclusion to enable them return to their bases. The Board resumed discussions at exactly 10 a.m. The remaining items on the report did not demand a lot of debate. The recommendations of the Acting CEO were accepted. After all, she was to implement the decisions of the Board.

The Chairman made what would aptly be termed closing remarks. He thanked all the members for the fruitful and cordial discussions without rancor. The government had stipulated remunerations for Board meetings. In spite of financial constraints, the Chairman advised the Acting CEO to ensure that sitting allowances and honoraria were paid to all members, including the Acting CEO. She liked that. The Chairman emphasized that without the payments, members may not have the incentive to attend, especially in emergencies. He implored the cooperation of every member towards the accomplishment of the targets the Board set for itself. The next meeting would follow the timetable as laid down in the White paper establishing the Board. Finally, the Chairman wished every member a safe journey back to their respective destinations. Two members could not depart the day the meeting ended because they travelled by air. The rest travelled at the end of the meeting. The remaining two members were taken to the airport the following morning by a driver of the company.

Chapter 22

BECOMING A "LEARNED GENTLEMAN LADY"

Fiona's morale to work in the Teaching Hospital eventually began to wane. The major reasons boiled down to frustrations. It seemed that there was a general lack of insight into the difficulties that confronted virtually everyone. Worse, these were largely contrived and therefore avoidable. She had become infected with the bug of nonchalance in the discharge of one's duties. She had come across the saying that 'if you cannot beat them, join them.' She was handicapped in the conscientious discharge of her duties. She could not join them, even if she tried. She was consoled by some factors. Obele and a handful of the girls she had tutored were hard-working and were not deterred by the pervading attitude of their colleagues. Her children were oblivious of the sad realities that prevailed in Konganoga. Furthermore, Prof Johnson, her husband remained optimistic that things would get better. She seemed to have been infected by this optimism bug. She soldiered on, while pondering over alternatives to her job with her husband. Some days in the hospital were good but most days were not. Poverty and ignorance accounted for a lot of the suffering observed in the hospital.

Meanwhile, Fiona and her husband began to survey the career prospects for Fiona. She could do a B.Sc in nursing but that would require a full time study back in Zeland. This option came up only to be rejected outright. She and Okon simultaneously and independently saw a glass ceiling in Fiona's career in nursing. She had trained enough nurses over the years to do what she could do. Therefore, the times her attention were required were few and far between. She fancied studying Law as a part time student. This appeared to be reasonable and feasible. The children, including Alfred Scot, were fairly independent and could fend for themselves with the help of the housemaid, Umanamaa. Thus, Fiona enrolled as a part-time student in the Faculty of law. The icing on the cake for this program was that with four summer courses, a part-time student could complete the requirements for graduation in the same number of year as a full time student. Law entailed good knowledge of, and versatility with the English language. This was Fiona's mother tongue. Fiona therefore had an edge over other students. Other students often asked her for assistance to explain certain scripts.

One of the constituents of the glass ceiling was the issue of citizenship of Konganoga. This was easy to overcome. The application form for naturalization was endorsed by the University on the recognition of Professor Johnson, her husband. The Teaching Hospital recognized Fiona when the hospital area was filled. The husband was asked to follow this up at the Ministry in Kumbrujaa. This was easy. There was a meeting scheduled to hold at the Universities Commission in Kumbrujaa and Professor

Johnson was a participant. He travelled a day earlier for the purpose of following up Fiona's application. He met the appropriate official on seat in his office in the Ministry of Immigration. The officer was receptive. Prof Johnson introduced himself.

'Oh yes, Professor. I saw your wife's application. It was not the appropriate one since she is married to you, a bona fide citizen of our great Republic. In fact, the application would have sailed through if it had been made in the correct form.'

'Thank you, officer. But, your office issued this to me in person. I had told them that she is my wife.'

'Well, sir, there is also this section that says spouses of citizens should go to section 6. Section 6 is not in this form. It is in the appropriate one. In any case, nothing spoil. I will give you the appropriate form to spare you the time and effort it would cost to go back to that office where this was given to you. On completion of the form, please mail it to me by courier, attention myself. Here is my complimentary card, Professor.'

Professor Johnson knew that nothing would be gained from arguing over the wrong form. Besides, the officer had been magnanimous and friendly to the bargain. He collected the form and the complimentary card which he exchanged with his own.

'I am grateful, Mr. Jifril. I will return to her and get this completed as soon as possible. Is it alright if I call you?'

'Sure, Professor. It will be my pleasure.'

Professor Johnson returned to his hotel room to rest on his back. He mulled the encounter and thought in himself: 'It could be worse.' At least, his meeting with Mr. Jifril was civilized. Money would have been required to exchange hands in other similar circumstances.

The meeting at the Universities Commission went on as scheduled. It was more or less a rehash of the usual.

Why are the universities not doing research? Lack of funds! The allocation for the funds will await passage of the necessary bill by the National Assembly. The universities should source funds internally. Yes, they may need to start to mint the necessary money in campus! Professor Johnson mused

Meanwhile at any one point in time, half of the National Cabinet would be in developed countries to sign memorandum of understanding on how to harness solar energy. They were everywhere else except in those countries that have highly developed solar source of energy. Politics and religion were intertwined inexorably to further reduce the standard of living of the masses. At the end, the Dean returned safely to base. He would claim his *estacode*. The charade would continue *sine die*. Everyone would wonder why the economy was not improving. The Ministry of Establishment had come to accept the futility of statistical data on unemployment. After all, there was no more kwashiorkor and people were no longer scavenging from garbage dumps. Those surely must be indices of progress or stagnation, which is still better than recession. The truth was that no one understood the Kenneth Galbraith jargons in economics. It did not matter. Life just floated on as it pleased the wind to flutter. The ruling party claimed to be the strongest in the black world. Slogans were reeled out while all sorts of woes befell the independent country.

When Prof Johnson got home to his family, there was an air of gloom occasioned by lack of progress with Fiona's naturalization. In the 12 years since they returned to Konganoga, the Professor and his European wife had not owned a new car. Okon Johnson was not particularly welcome in his village. He also had not welcomed himself. He had no house. He could not afford one even on a professor's pay packet. The local government councilor who might not have seen the four walls of a university would monthly smile to the banks. His salary was more than four times the salary of a university professor who was charged with the duty of training out the nation's high level man power and spearheading research and technological development. The salaries of the members of the State and National Assembly when compared with those of the University professors were causes for regret. Initially, the problem had a logical solution. He only needed a roof over his head if he went to the village. It made sense to contain that problem by boycotting home visits.

Thomas Nang the senior American-trained academic staff popped in to see Okon and Fiona one evening when Dr Nang had not seen Prof Johnson in the senior staff club.

'*Men*, it is all over campus that you are generous, man. Are you government? You and Fiona bought stuff to equip the hospital, *men*. Some father Christmas, *huh*? That's real cool. You know what I mean? Give me your five, shit.' That was Dr Nang talking to Prof Johnson. Fiona was attending to the children.

'Who's been giving you some wrong low down, Tommy?' Prof Johnson asked.

'The question is who has not been giving the low down on you and Fiona. Come on, men are you kidding me?'

Professor Johnson took a gulp of the *small stout* alcoholic beverage in his glass and peered over his half moon spectacles at Thomas Nang. He explained to him how they obtained the donation to the hospital. They had taken most of the contents of the second shipment and gave some items they did not need to the hospital.

'Well people are actually saying you should have sold the stuff and perhaps bought a new car. You got some problems, *men*. You got a wife. You need a befitting car, common on.' Dr Nang had a way of saying the right thing but in an inappropriate frame of mind. No one needed to tell Prof Johnson to get himself a car befitting of a man married to a *Zelander*. There was need to change the topic of conversation.

In the past, Prof Johnson used to share a report of his meetings with Dr Nang, often with Prof Johnson attempting to ape Dr Nang and failing to accomplish that task. They would laugh at both the substance as well as the failed mimicry. This time, Okon and Fiona took the encounter with Dr Nang a bit more serious than they did previously. However, there was no regret about getting an incubator or securing discarded but serviceable hospital equipments. While they ruminated, Professor Johnson became convinced that things had not been going as well as he had hoped or expected. His attainment of the rank of Professor did not leave an imprint on the sands of time. He was content with doing his job in a transparent manner. That was the way business was transacted in Zeland. It did not seem to work in Konganoga. Besides, he did not see what point Dr Nang was driving at. Dr Nang had not been bothered about promotion. He lived in a smaller house on campus. He also earned less than Professor Johnson. Was Dr Nang, therefore, pulling Prof Johnson's legs? Yet, whether he was pulling the legs or any other part of the body, there was something not quite right. After supper, the kids came together to bid their parents goodnight. Fiona and Okon filled their portions of the naturalization form. They would send it to the VC and the Chief Medical Director the next day for endorsement.

As he lay back in bed at night, Professor Okon Johnson began to ruminate over his woes as highlighted to him by Dr Nang. He was a professor who had never driven a *tear rubber* (brand new) car. He was a professor who had no house anywhere; neither in the village nor town nor city. He was a chairman of Board of a highly-rated federal government company. The immediate past chairman of the same company the TMCK had made himself a multimillionaire from illicit activities in the company. The latter had built many houses both in Konganoga and in Zealand. He also owned chains of cars all from the resources of the TMCK. The company had almost gone bankrupt thereafter before the former chairman was removed.

The removal of the voluptuous chairman of the Board was not expected to wipe out the long term effects of neglect and of the Tin Mining Company and it did not. The latter's misdeeds were neither investigated nor redressed. The former chairman understood the language of Konganoga's governance, a three word formula which could open doors for the men in power and shut the same doors to men of vision and conscience as well as to men with good governance and progress of the nation in mind. The three word formula in Konganoga was simply known as "Chop I Chop".

Any who ignored the Chop I Chop formula or who like Professor Johnson, preached against it, would drift into ignominy or inexorably sink into penury. And if such a person occupied high office such an office would sooner than latter be on the line. A few individuals like Mrs. George of the Board of TMCK understood this principle too well. A few others like Professor Johnson genuinely believed in a perfect system and would like to stick to the rules. But unfortunately the latter would sooner than later realize to their peril that Konganoga needed God's intervention. Otherwise she would need a drastic French-Revolution-like action for sanity to prevail. She, like many corruption ridden nations before her would probably need painful social hot fires to make their finest social steel. The latter would only be in conformity with John Mitchell's quote that "the finest steel has to go through the hottest fire."

Professor Johnson heaved a sigh. It was not a sigh of relief.

Chapter 23

THE BURDENS OF OFFICE

Fiona had completed her legal education in record time because she was already a University graduate. She studied very hard and later had to reduce her hours of work in the hospital to devote time to her studies. She passed her final exams with honors and had no problems with passing the bar exams.

She had joined a group practice and was getting good patronage from the rich and famous in the community. These saw her as one with a good knowledge of the language and thus one who was best suited to handle complicated cases. Zeland language was her mother tongue. Her impeccable use of it in arguing her cases in court sometimes mesmerized some sitting Konganogan judges so much that all that they could do a good number of times was to involuntarily nod in affirmation as the pretty Zelander-Konganogan who was the wife of a renowned professor of surgery stood tall in all her poise and attorney's regalia and argued her cases in court. Again Attorney Fiona Johnson's integrity was not in any way in doubt and she could not be imagined to be untruthful to her clients. She won most of her cases and was gradually becoming a celebrated Attorney both in Kiba and also in Kumbrujaa the national capital where she was sought after by the rich and powerful.

The success of Fiona's practice also translated into greatly improved finances for the family. Indeed within eight months of her starting her private legal practice, Fiona's contribution to the finances of the family became dominant almost doubling what Okon earned as a professor and a politician who did not take bribes or grossly inflate contracts.

But Fiona's success as a practitioner was not without its toll on the wellbeing of the family. She spent longer hours in the chambers and the long court sessions greatly reduced the number of hours that she spent with the children. The realities of the effect on the family became all too obvious to Fiona when she observed that the children turned more to the company of the house maid Umanamaa even when she, their mother, was home. These events made Fiona greatly unhappy. It became for her a question of choosing between her job as a successful and highly sought-after lawyer and a mother and companion of her children. Fiona loved her family. She always recounted how she and Okon had started, how they struggled, planned, and bore together the vicissitudes of their early years of marriage both in Zeland and in Konganoga. She remembered how she had secretly put in an application for Okon's appointment.

On the other hand Fiona loved her work and the opportunities that her practice offered her both to meet people and at the same time make good money. She therefore decided to strike a middle course, to reduce her hours of work in the chambers and to do some of her cases from home so that her children could have access to her while at the same time she prepared her cases.

On his own part, Okon's profile kept rising in the opinion of the public. It was not difficult for people to hear the deliberations in Board Rooms. They heard mainly about stubborn chief executives who prevented people who should otherwise be going home daily with tons of money from enjoying what should be their own share of the "national cake." Where the national cake was wantonly shared there often were no complaints. But where a chairman played the pious and incorruptible leader and would not "chop", and would also not allow others to "chop" the whole society would hear stories of how bad and stingy the chairman was. That scenario very rapidly became the scenario with Professor Johnson and the Board of the TMCK.

Here was a chairman who sat over a multibillion dollar board which had to all intents and purposes been resuscitated from impending doom and had once again been placed on a very sound footing.

Why would the chairman not allow the other members of the Board to enjoy the fruits of their labor after they had successfully resuscitated a previously ailing federal government company one that had been previously thoroughly run down by its previous Chairman and Board?

The former Chairman of the former Board had made a fortune from the Board before the latter was dissolved and Professor Johnson's Board appointed. This new Chairman Professor Johnson had no good car. He had no house in his village. He lived in university property and later in a rented house in Kiba. He stayed in the company's guest house instead of in the presidential wing of a five star hotel to which he was entitled as Chairman of a Federal Government Board. The Tin Mining Company of Kiba, TMCK, had come alive again and was exporting materials and making lots of money for the Federal Government. And so, *why would this Chairman not allow himself "some fresh air by way of huge financial largesse? In any case even if the chairman "was so daft" as not to indulge himself, why would he prevent others from enriching themselves?*

That was the dilemma of Professor Johnson's office.

Mrs. George the loquacious contractor-member of the Board complained the most among the members of the Board.

"What bad luck brought this devil that they call Professor Johnson to this Board as Chairman? In other Boards the chairmen and members cooperated and became mutual millionaires within the first three months of their inauguration. Nobody would complain. And if any complained, he or she would be settled. But here we are with this devil of an imbecile professor who would sit astride the money guarding it like a hawk." Mrs. George would often complain. It was not long before she coined the name "Agada gbachili uzo" for Professor Johnson. The name implied that Professor Johnson was a dog in the manger. He would neither eat the grass nor allow any herbivores to enjoy the grass.

Dr Johnson's attitude in transparency also impacted on the way he related with the big powers that were in Kumbrujaa. Much as it was his perceived hard work and renowned uprightness that earned him the position of Chairman in the first instance, the powers that were in Kumbrujaa the national capital had apparently only wanted someone who would merely salvage the company from complete ruin and thereafter start sharing the gains as soon as the company recovered and started making profits. It did not appear to have been their idea that they would be left perpetually "empty-handed", not receiving any financial "returns" from their appointee in the company.

It had never happened. All appointees especially the chairmen of federal government-owned companies were expected to make monthly or at least quarterly returns to their godfathers. It had been like that from the time that Zealand handed independence to Konganoga. The new pseudo imperial overlords in Kumbrujaa, much as they wanted TMCK to survive for political reasons, did not wish that any Professor Johnson should set a "bad example" by denying them of their assumed "entitlements".

Chapter 24

THE BATTLES WITHIN

It was getting increasingly difficult for Professor Johnson to contain opposition to his policies of punctuality, transparency and accountability in Board matters in the Tin Mining Company. This was in spite of the fact that such a policy was almost entirely responsible for the progress so far made by the Company's new management to pull out the company from the doldrums which the corruption-ridden former Board had thrust it. Professor Johnson saw himself and his Board as having been appointed into a board for a mission. That mission was to revamp the Board, make it more profitable, more productive and more serving of the needs of the people of Konganoga. To Professor Johnson ingratiation of self was secondary. Achievement of the set goals was primary. But to the other members of the Board and those that appointed them, it was not "nation first". Self for them was the primary motive. The choice of Professor Johnson for the post of Chairman when the Board was economically down was only to satisfy the need for a capable hand that would make the Board more profitable once more for the returns to resume flowing to the masters in Kumbrujaa. It certainly was not the intention of the Kumbrujaa cabal that the goose that laid the golden egg should be killed. The latter needed to be alive for the golden egg to continue to be laid. Members of the cabal were no fools and the appointees to the Board were no fools either. The only apparent fool was the man who saw the appointment as a messiah mission, a mission to save planet Earth from damnation and the notion of such a mission being divinely ordained. It was the latter notion which informed Professor Johnson's oft repeated admonition to the members of Board whenever they complained about his apparent tight-fistedness thus:

"We need to save this Board. We need to make it more profitable for our people. We need to tighten our belts and we need to do this as a sacrifice in the interest of our dear country."

Yes, the Company needed to be saved for the monetary proceeds to continue to flow. But beyond that, the other Board members saw no further need to tighten their belts. Besides they saw no reason why they would continue to tighten their belts when the people in governance and especially in Kumbrujaa and in the seat of regional power in Kiba continued to loosen their own belts.

With time the opposition to the belt-tightening policies of Professor Johnson began to be openly challenged.

During one of the Board meetings the chairman had vetoed the decision of the members who had voted to increase the number of days which they sat so as to increase their monthly allowances.

'This proposed increase in the running cost of this Board even in the face of the economic downturn of the nation is hereby vetoed by me in the interest of the overall good of our country", Dr Johnson had said.

All hell was let loose after the Chairman's veto was announced.

The assault was led by Mrs. George who was still reeling with rage over the refusal of the Board to let her supply cars to the Board Members. The other members of Board were unhappy with the persistent refusal of the Chairman to let them have greater allowances under different guises. Most importantly the godfathers in Kumbrujaa were unhappy with the man who was reported to be the stumbling block to the *returns* which they received from their protégées. Tempers had run to fever pitch during the subsequent day's meeting after the Chairman had vetoed the proposed allowances to the Board members. A meeting of the entire Board members excepting the Chairman had been held in a private residence of one of the godfathers in Kiba to discuss the issue of the "Chairman who wanted the Board members to starve."

All the members of Board including a member who was a bishop of one of the new generation churches in Kiba were present. The reverend gentleman used to be one of the voices of reason whenever there was a division in the house or when issues got thorny. But he was also known to be very insistent on the issue of increased allowances and increase in the number of "sitting days" which increase invariably translated to increased pay for the Board Members. His modesty did not extend to money matters otherwise he and the Board Chairman could be counted as the only voices of reason in the midst of wolves in sheep's clothing. The highly respected Bishop must have been lured into the meeting of "Dissolutionists " with a promise that participants would benefit materially if the Board was dissolved and that they would be either handsomely compensated or they would be re-appointed to a new reconstituted Board under a new Chairman.

The decision after the short meeting of the "Dissolutionists" was unanimous: The Chairman Professor Okon Johnson must be overruled. A second motion that called for pressure on the authorities in Kumbrujaa to dissolve and reconstitute the Board was however narrowly defeated. Some of the members were afraid that if the Board was dissolved that they might not make the new list of appointees especially those of them who had not been making adequate *returns* to their godfathers.

One of the sponsors of the dissolution motion was a colleague of Professor Johnson in the University Hospital. Dr Ezemtubo was the lazy Senior Lecturer in Pharmacology who having been frustrated by his lack of promotion in the University system had resorted to political party activities and had been appointed as a protégé to one of the political godfathers. He had carried his opposition to Professor Johnson a little too far into the Board of the Tin Mining Company. His mission in the Board appeared to be to oppose any and everything that was raised by Professor Johnson.

Dr Ezemtubo had fought very hard to get the dissident members of Board of the Tin Mining Company holding a secret meeting in the residence of his godfather to endorse a motion calling on the Federal Government to dissolve the Board of the Company. He had hoped that he or somebody close to him would be appointed the chairman of the Board in place of Professor Johnson.

When the secret meeting failed to approve the motion to apply pressure for the dissolution of the Board, Dr Ezemtubo and two of his dissolution campaigners had resolved to go it alone. Each of the three dissolution campaigners had a powerful godfather and through them the message was relayed to Kumbrujaa that progress was being made in the University Hospital because Professor Johnson was starving the godfathers of funds and was indeed plotting to cut off all extraneous sources of funding for sustenance of the cabal in Kumbrujaa. They also had alleged that Professor Johnson was indeed secretly working for the political opponents of the powerful godfathers. The "Dissolutionists" as Dr Ezemtubo called their group had also promised their godfathers that success for them in their cause would triple or quadruple the monthly monetary *returns* to the godfathers. With this promise in view and the glaring fact of diminishing returns to the powers in Kumbrujaa since after the commencement of Professor Johnson's era, it was relatively easy to persuade the Kumbrujaa powers to consent to the dissolution of the promising Board of the Tin Mining Company of Konganoga under the Chairmanship of Professor Johnson.

Thus without any forewarning or any prior indication a letter was made to the Board of the Tin Mining Company of Konganoga that they stood dissolved. The tone of the letter of dissolution was however quite mild and adequate recognition was given to the enormous successes of the Board especially in resuscitating the ailing economy of the Company.

A happy twist to the saga for Professor Johnson and a great disappointment to Dr Ezemtubo however was the subsequent appointment of Professor Johnson to the position of substantive Vice Chancellor of the University of Kiba. The position had remained vacant with an Acting Vice Chancellor following the expiration of the tenure of the then incumbent Vice Chancellor.

For Professor Johnson it was a mixture of sadness and joy: sadness that his determination to fully turn around the fortunes of the Tin Mining Company of Konganoga had been dislocated midway and especially when the recovery was gathering momentum. It was however joy for him since a letter addressed to him from the Presidency fully acknowledged his contribution, great courage and hard work. Secondly the position of Vice Chancellor of a Federal Government-owned University was much higher than the position of Chairman of the Tin Mining Company of Konganoga.

For Fiona the appointment of her husband to such high office was also one laced with happiness but with some degree of apprehension. She was happy at the meteoric rise of her husband to the zenith of his profession since the position of Vice Chancellor was the highest that any academician could hope to get to. The ultimate recognition and ascendance to that position did not always come easy or merely through merit or hard work. Political considerations and connections often played a major role. Many who had risen to that position had often had to compromise one thing or another in Konganoga. Often such compromises were either in cash or in kind. Most often it entailed accepting to dance to the tune of the most highly-placed godfathers in the land.

Theoretically the Senate of the University would present a list of three candidates who were often top professors in the institution. From the presented names the Presidency was expected to select one name. The competition for such initial senate selection was often fierce and sometimes rancorous. In other situations as was the case with the appointment of Professor Johnson, the Presidency could make an appointment *de novo* and without recourse to the wishes of the dons of the university. As the "Visitor" or "owner of the university" the President had the powers to appoint any deserving don either from within the University or indeed sometimes from outside the Institution as the Vice Chancellor of the University. Where dons did not like the appointment they could protest, down tools or resign en masse. Either situation often made little difference in Konganoga as universities had been known to be shut down for many months or even for a full year with little worry on the part of the powers that be in Kumbrujaa or the state capitals.

The appointment of Professor Johnson as the Vice Chancellor of the University of Kiba was received with great joy within the rank and file of the University community. The erudite professor of Ophthalmology had widely been known to be one of the few dons who could be said to have remained incorruptible in the midst of the rot and decay that was Konganoga society. Professor Johnson's ability to remain above board among the general madness was often attributed to his being married to a Zelander.

People would always refer to Professor Johnson as: "the incorruptible black *oyibo* doctor who married a pleasant and kind *oyibo* lawyer". *Oyibo* in the native language meant a white person. It was believed that Professor Johnson was a *black white doctor* and since his wife was a lawyer the combination was such that whoever attempted to bribe the doctor or demand bribe from him was looking for trouble. Being a doctor married to a lawyer ordinarily meant that Professor Johnson's household must be swimming in money. They would not need to be bribed. And since Dr Johnson had a lawyer for a wife, whoever sought to take bribe from him was assumed to be angling for jail.

The Vice Chancellor designate soon received a letter inviting him to Kumbrujaa for consultations before his full assumption of duties. It was only normal in such situations of high government appointment. The Vice Chancellor's official car, chauffeur and paraphernalia of office were already placed at the disposal of Professor Johnson even before he was to move into the Vice Chancellor's office and mansion.

KONGANOGA

It was a wonderful and spontaneous transformation, such as Professor Johnson had never imagined was possible. It was akin to a royal treatment.

The name "Professor Johnson the new VC" was on every lip. Despite all kinds of dissuasions people from all works of life had thronged Professor Johnson's office and private house trying either to get noticed by him, to wish him well or "to join (him) in thanking God." After dissuading many of them who called in his private home for some time Professor Johnson agreed with Fiona that since those visitors were well wishers that it would not be right to chase them away or to turn them back. For security reasons chairs were set out in the open garden to sit the many guests. Problems came up when after dropping their cards or expressing their good wishes many of these visitors would now refuse to go home so as to make space for other visitors. They expected to be served not just the traditional kola nuts but also some food and drinks into the bargain. As the numbers got larger the available seats got all taken up and the kola nuts and snacks got exhausted.

It was a most unexpected turn out and even the usually friendly Fiona ran out of patience. The children of the house had to be tucked inside their rooms as every visitor would ask about the children and would want to carry them up and kiss them as a sign of friendliness. Even the dutiful Umanamaa was exasperated after several rounds of serving different sets of guests.

After she had served several sets of visitors and saw more of the crowd surging through the gate Umanamaa dashed to Fiona and complained:

"Madam these visitors them too much. I want make them begin de go. Our food it go finish. Also many of them be bad people. Then go come for night after them see the compound finish for day. I just de see Benja who everybody know him be big thief. The other time Benja steal Madam

Agbomma him goat and they come catch him, come naked him for market place. Benja just de stand there de look like him be good man. When night come, him go come jump wall come steal." (Umanamaa was complaining about one Benjamin who was a known petty thief that was once caught and stripped naked in the market place. Benjamin had sneaked into the party and was seen nosing around).

Umanamaa's fears were not unfounded. It was known that some visitors in similar situations would be friends during the day but turn out to be deadly enemies at night.

Chapter 25

MR VICE CHANCELLOR THE LEAGUE MEMBER

Professor Johnson had arrived at the offices of the Special Adviser Special Duties to Mr. President a full hour before the appointed time of his scheduled meeting with Mr. President. A first class ticket had been dispatched to him in Kiba two weeks in advance of the scheduled date of the meeting with the Konganogan Head of State. A vehicle had been dispatched from State House Kumbrujaa to pick him up from the airport.

It was one of the many bullet proof vehicles that adorned the vast presidential car park. It was assumed that any senior staff of the seat of power or indeed any invited guest to the presidential mansion might be a target for kidnapping for ransom and must be protected. The reason for the paranoia was not difficult to see. The ruling class in Konganoga had turned themselves into a league that was afraid of their shadows. They had embezzled so much of the people's resources and got themselves so detached from the people who they were supposed to be ruling that they were perpetually afraid of reprisals and the anger of the people. They and their invited guests and friends therefore considered it perpetually necessary to go with armed convoys and bullet proof vehicles. They needed to protect themselves from the angry citizenry and the "bad boys" who were growing in numbers commensurate with the increasing joblessness in the oil-rich Republic. The latter having no access to the "brigands in power and the latter's agents who have looted the polity dry" therefore turned to any unprotected ordinary citizens or friends or invitees of the cabal who appeared slightly better placed than they were.

Because of the prevailing injustices and the high profile looting of the polity by expected custodians of the instruments of governance each new day turned out worse for the ordinary citizen than the preceding day. The latter had to sleep with one eye open at night. The marauder might be lurking around the corner. The kidnapper or some agents of the kingpins of insecurity might be just waiting for the setting of the sun. And the citizen had no protection and only trusted to chance and prayed to his God not to be remembered by the evil men. And a government was supposed to be in power for the protection of the citizens. And security to life and property which were supposed to be the first duty of any government to her citizens was glossed over and relegated to the background. And the sirens announcing the movement of the men in power sounded every half hour and chased away the citizens from the pothole-filled roads and highways. Even Konganogans in the womb were not spared the nauseating spate of the arrogance and bad governance as even their pregnant mothers would face the horsewhip of the uniformed security guards of the overlords if they failed to clear the roads fast enough.

Professor Johnson in spite of his previous high positions had never enjoyed the privilege of being waited for at the presidential wing of any airport. He was saluted by a smartly-dressed uniformed officer as he stepped into the lounge from the air plane.

"Professor Johnson Sir?" the officer had asked as he approached the new 'League Member' of the ruling class. It was a big surprise to Professor Johnson how the man managed to know his name and identify him. The officer must have been properly briefed about the Vice Chancellor's looks and his dressing.

"Yes indeed! And how did you get to know me?" Professor Johnson had involuntarily asked.

"We are trained to observe and to recognize people even without seeing them." The officer replied obviously feeling happy and elated that his skills were being appreciated.

The officer immediately took hold of Professor Johnson's brief case and escorted him to the waiting car which sped off to the elitist Konganoga Hutton Hotels.

Professor Johnson was at the waiting room of the east wing of the Presidential Villa by five minutes to 9 o'clock for the 10 o'clock meeting with His Excellency Mr. President.

He did not want to take any chances with the unreliable Kumbrujaa traffic.

A table at the far end of the waiting room had the day's newspapers with coffee and tea at the disposal of any guests.

Professor Johnson had waited for one hour and ten minutes before an usher directed him into an exquisitely furnished office one of so many in the very vast complex.

Sitting behind a glittering semi circular table at the far end of the office was a very refined-looking young man in his middle thirties. He was not Mr. President. There was no name tag on the table. Perhaps it was considered essential that any visitor should not be able to identify the person by whom he was being attended to.

The man behind the table was very courteous. He stood up as soon as Professor Johnson entered the room and stretched out his hand.

"Good day Professor Johnson. My name is Johnson, Mr. Johnson Ayuda. I am the Assistant to His Excellency on "League Member matters".

Professor Johnson was immediately struck by the similarity of the Johnson common name even though one was a first name while the other was a surname. The common name made for easy common bonding and an easy topic for exchange of banters.

Professor Johnson had once heard of the "elite club of Konganogans" who were known to be feeding fat on the oil and other resources of the Konganogan Republic. He had heard of the club whose members twisted the affairs and destiny of the country on their finger tips. He had heard of the "League members" but he had never considered himself a privileged member of such an elite or nefarious club whose membership included the top retired Military Generals and the top politicians in the sprawling country whose top soil was fertile at every turn and whose sub soil was laden with the black gold as well as with all kinds of precious metals. Mr. Johnson Ayuda did not waste any time in explaining to Professor Johnson the reason behind his invitation to the Presidential Villa.

"Professor Johnson your name was brought up to the Presidency as a potential worthy member of the most exclusive and the most highly competitive group of citizens of this country. This is an elite group of Mr. President's men. This is a select group of men and women who rule this country with Mr. President in charge. The group periodically expands its membership by injecting worthy new blood into it. The members hold the most sensitive positions in the polity especially positions that have to do with the economy and potential hot spots like the top academic institutions of higher learning. Membership is by invitation only and admission is purely by Mr. President even though people like me assist with the preliminaries. Money and power are our watchwords. Absolute loyalty to Mr. President is the basic principle. Family, faith and friends come second to this loyalty."

As he spoke, Mr. Ayuda had his gaze fixed on Professor Johnson as if his words were meant to pierce the latter's inner being in quest of assurances that he would be loyal.

He then continued:

"The confirmation of your appointment as the Vice Chancellor of the Federal University of Science and Technology Kiba is predicated on your acceptance or otherwise of membership of this elitist league whose official designation is simply known as 'League Member'. You stand to gain nothing by refusal to be a League Member. On the other hand there is everything to lose by rejection of this offer which straightway confirms you as the Vice Chancellor of this Federal University. Acceptance places your office and the accruing position s and resources at the disposal of Mr. President who may act through his agents. There is no punishment or reprisal for rejection of this very sought-after offer. On the other hand immediate acceptance ensures life-long reward with enough resources for you and your family. The decision is yours to make but it is binding as it is consummated with oath of allegiance which is binding and which can be made on any instrument of faith that is chosen by you."

Again Mr. Ayuda paused as he peered through his gold-rimmed glasses on a bemused Professor Johnson. He then continued:

"Now Professor Johnson, are you prepared on the aforementioned terms to accept the position of the Vice Chancellor of the Federal University of Science and Technology Kiba?"

Mr. Johnson Ayuda even in spite of his youthfulness was succinct and straight to the point. There were no prevarications in his speech. There were no embellishments or equivocations. Acceptance of the offer needed a simple affirmation and would bring on all the glory. Rejection would see him back to Kiba not as an "ex-Vice Chancellor" but as a "non-Vice Chancellor". The latter alternative was simply untenable.

Professor Johnson's mind immediately figured out the mountains of congratulatory letters and the numerous guests of all shades that had thronged his office and his residence since the announcement of his appointment as Vice Chancellor. He blinked once or twice as he tried to divert his eye balls away from the piercing gaze of this young Johnson whose large eyeballs appeared to pierce through the bony cage that shielded Professor Johnson's cerebral hemisphere. Professor Johnson wasted no time in uttering the expected three letter sentence:

"I am prepared!"

What followed was a short ceremony whose brevity was a sharp contrast to the everlasting image that it was to present to the erudite professor of ophthalmology. The latter as if his listener did not hear the first assertion had repeated:

"I am prepared!"

Mr. Johnson Ayuda pressed the call-bell and a smartly-dressed middle aged man emerged from the adjoining room pushing before him an oblong-shaped trolley which

KONGANOGA

contained three simple objects, a Bible, a Koran and a short gun.

"What faith do you profess?" Mr. Ayuda had asked.

Professor Johnson did not answer. He appeared to have been lost in thought about the speed of events. His eyes had caught the trolley and the man pushing it. But he did not appear to have seen the three objects on the trolley. He had come to Kumbrujaa in the hope and belief that he was coming to hold consultations with Mr. President. But here was he being interviewed by a young man whose identity and seniority he could not immediately ascertain.

Mr. Ayuda seeing that Professor Johnson was not fully attentive then repeated:

"What faith do you profess? You swear by the Bible if you be Christian, by the Koran if you be Moslem and by the gun if you be atheist. By your name I presume say you be Christian but you go answer for yourself. What faith do you profess?"

As Professor Johnson appeared to hesitate Mr. Ayuda lifted the short gun and held it in the direction of the dumbfounded Professor Johnson. The sight of the gun being lifted towards his direction appeared to have resuscitated Professor Johnson who now shouted as if in fright:

"Christian! Please Christian!"

Mr. Johnson Ayuda appeared to have played his part. He dropped back the short gun on the trolley and went back to his seat. The oath-taking part now appeared to have been shifted to the middle-aged man who hitherto had remained silent.

As soon as Mr. Ayuda took his seat, the middle aged Oath Administrator now appeared to uncoil. He again immediately lifted the short gun and offered it to Professor Johnson who was already safely holding the bible.

"But I am a Christian and I am already holding the Bible." Professor Johnson protested.

The Oath Administrator then spoke for the first time.

"My name be Muktar Obredu. This one it be my office. You go do whatever me I command. Whether you be Christian or you be Moslem or you no believe nothing at all, you must swear also by gun. It be only this one we be sure say it go kill you when you begin do monkey business. So, hold your bible for your right hand and hold this gun by your left hand. If your right hand no kill you, we go be sure say your left hand go kill you!"

At the repeated use of the word "kill, kill", Professor Johnson started trembling. Trickles of sweat immediately became visible on his forehead as he turned in the direction of Mr. Johnson Ayuda as if seeking the latter's intervention. The high office of a Vice Chancellor did not appear to offer any immunity to Professor Johnson in the presence of a half literate Oath Administrator.

But the oath administration appeared to be outside the control of the President's Assistant.

The latter simply looked Professor Johnson in the face and said:

"Professor, do as the Oath Administrator commands. That one is his office as he said." Professor Johnson for a short while appeared entrapped as he attempted to wipe the sweat on his forehead with the sleeve of the coat which he was wearing.

The air conditioner in the room made no difference to the sweat and the lump in the throat which appeared to be choking the embattled professor.

The two words "Vice Chancellor, Vice Chancellor" appeared to chant melodious tunes in Professor Johnson's eardrums. He desired nothing more at that particular time than to ensure that he retained the position of Vice Chancellor. He therefore stretched out his left hand and accepted the short gun from the Oath Administrator.

As Professor Johnson held the gun in his hand he cast

his mind back to other publicly-administered oaths of allegiance which he had in the past witnessed. What he had always heard people say and what he had expected that he would be asked to say started thus:

"I swear allegiance to the Federal Republic of Konganoga..."

He had never seen or heard anybody swear by a loaded gun. He also had never seen or heard anybody threatened with being killed for defaulting on an oath. But those were at other times and in other saner situations. Professor Johnson's own time and his own situation involved membership of the elitist club as a "League Member". League membership was outside of the ordinary. It was outside of "normal times". It was also outside of "normal situations".

Mr. Muktar Obredu did not appear impressed by Professor Johnson's hesitation. He appeared to have been very sure from the beginning that the professor would accept whatever conditions that were presented to him. He had administered the same oath to a couple of "ordained men of God" and they all succumbed to the lure of office. He was sure that a *simple* professor would certainly not be holier than an "ordained man of God".

The oath taking was simple but stern:

It had already been typed out and pasted on a thick sheet of paper.

"By this symbol and this instrument I stand at the absolute direction of Mr. President or his accredited agents in all matters of money, position and power in my office and out of it for as long as I remain in the office of Vice Chancellor under penalty of action from either or both of this symbol and this instrument."

The oath was at the same time ominous and in clear English.

As Professor Johnson read it out to the hearing of Mr. Muktar Obredu and Mr. Johnson Ayuda his voice trembled. But he completed the oath-taking nevertheless.

At the conclusion of the oath-taking ceremony, Mr. Johnson Ayuda congratulated the bemused Professor Johnson. The latter's inner conscience kept telling him that he had sold his soul to the devil. Perhaps so, but in exchange he had bought the consolidated position of the Vice Chancellor of the University of Science and Technology Kiba. The Professor, who had come to Kumbrujaa ostensibly to meet with His Excellency Mr. President, was not sure whether to laugh or to cry. He feebly replied "Thank you" to Mr. Ayuda even as his mind still tried to wriggle its way out of the oath-taking statements: "under penalty of action from either or both of this symbol and this instrument."

Chapter 26

THE REALITIES UNFOLD

"Welcome to the League" was the opening sentence by Mr. Johnson Ayuda to Professor Okon Johnson. This was after the former had congratulated the latter on the latter's taking of the oath of allegiance.

Mr. Muktar Obredu the Oath Administrator had pulled his trolley back to his room adjacent the office of the President's Assistant Mr. Ayuda. The latter now sat down to explain in greater details to Professor Johnson the full implications of the latter's acceptance of the position of Vice Chancellor.

Mr. Ayuda had a copy of the oath on his table. He again read the full wordings of the oath to Professor Johnson. The latter did not utter a word. He only gazed at Mr. Ayuda as if he was still under a spell.

Mr. Ayuda then continued:

"Professor Johnson, your oath of allegiance entails that every month 40% of all monies accruing to your institution will mandatorily be returned to the coffers of a the *League Members Fund*. This fund is abbreviated as *League Fund*. It is contributed into by all League Members who have benefitted from appointments and other favors from Mr. President or under his directive. It is under the direct control of His Excellency the President of Konganoga."

Professor Johnson opened his eyes wide. The scales appeared to fall off his eyes. For the first time he appeared to understand what he had signed into.

"Do you mean that the university's budgetary allocation will be diverted to other areas outside of the university?"

"Yes, that is how the system works. The league has to remain financially strong in order to continue to win elections and retain its membership in their positions. If the League collapses or is hamstrung by cash all the members will suffer."

"But I don't control the finances directly. There is a University Bursar whose responsibility is the collection and disbursement of funds. I don't have any access to the university's funds even assuming that I would want to get into any form of embezzlement or fund diversion. Also…"

"I have not yet finished, Professor Johnson!" Mr. Ayuda cut in as Professor Johnson was still trying to explain his expected handicap in the directive to hand over a big chunk of the University funds to the League or indeed any organization.

"Professor Johnson you swore a few minutes ago to be loyal to Mr. President or his appointed agents or representatives. Return of 40% of all funds accruing to your institution to the League is one of the many signs of loyalty and it is not optional."

"But…" Professor Johnson tried to cut in.

"There are no *buts*, Professor Johnson, and it is to ensure that *buts* are eliminated from the total loyalty exhibited by every League Member that the butt of a gun is added to the symbol upon which every member swears even if the member is not an atheist." Mr. Ayuda concluded.

As the discussion went on it finally dawned fully on Professor Okon Johnson that he was into a difficult situation from which he might not be able to extricate himself.

Professor Johnson's mind wandered to his family, his profession and the reputation which he had tried all through the years to build. He fancied what Fiona would think of him if ever she got to know that he had to swear by a bible and a gun to exhibit absolute loyalty to the President up to the point of having to embezzle an institution's money that was entrusted to him. He imagined what society would think of him if it ever leaked out that he stood before a fetish priest to swear to steal and to enrich somebody or some organization in order to maintain his job.

Professor Johnson remained silent for a while. He was deep in thought. Mr. Ayuda noticed this and tried to assuage the embattled Professor whose countenance had dimmed from the initial radiance which it had exhibited.

He then said:

"Professor Johnson, the oath of allegiance is not peculiar to you. The modality and instruments used and the words are not designed with anybody in mind. It is routine here but it is binding. Nobody goes about announcing that he has sworn by a Dane gun or a pistol or any other instruments. I have told you that even your Bishops swear. For you to be entrusted with our patronage we have to be sure about your absolute loyalty. You want to be a *big man* and so you must pay the price. Nothing comes from for nothing. Nothing ever does. Mr. President's conditions are even the mildest that you can imagine. In some situations some crude godfathers would send you to fetish and voodoo priests where your blood will be taken and mixed with some concoctions and you would be made to drink the mixture. In other situations you might have been made to sign with your blood. Indeed there are situations where you would have been made to lie naked inside a coffin and from inside the coffin you would be made to read out and assent to the oath of allegiance. And those were indeed relatively inferior positions in the States and not the Federal. When you compare these therefore you will agree that Mr. President is a God-fearing man and a gentleman. And he personally has insisted that this oath of allegiance should be as simple as possible even though His Excellency does not know the details.

The only thing to remember is that you have sworn with a loaded gun just as the Oath Administrator Mr. Muktar Obredu has told you. The consequence of default as regards that one is usually not dictated by me and certainly not by His Excellency, and that makes it worse."

Professor Johnson understood. The consequences of a default after one had sworn with a Bible and a loaded gun must be very ominous indeed. And the consequences would be dictated by a man who was neither God-fearing nor a gentleman. Again Professor Johnson understood.

Mr. Ayuda had made his point. He had noticed that Professor Johnson appeared very unsettled. Mr. Ayuda imagined that the Professor obviously was not one of the diehard ones who would be prepared to dine with the devil and still present a bold and pious face. Mr. Ayuda had seen many of such diehard pretenders in the past. He empathized with Professor Johnson but he knew that his acceptance though reluctantly done was all motivated by ego and greed. He knew that nobody was ever forced to take the oath and nobody was ever compelled to remain in the League. Konganoga had deteriorated since Zealand handed her independence. But it had not deteriorated to the level where people were compelled to accept membership of the League. There was still freedom of choice in that regard and many competitors lay in waiting to grab the position if any invited member declined. But no invited member had ever declined. They would beam in with smiles and beam out again with smiles even after swearing with the bible and a loaded gun.

But Professor Johnson appeared a little different. He beamed in with smiles but was not beaming out with smiles. Mr. Ayuda was aware of the reasons behind the abrupt dissolution of the Tin Mining Company of Konganoga. The major reason for the dissolution was that enough returns were not flowing in. But in the case of the Tin Mining Company no oath had been administered to the helmsman. And so the latter was under no obligation to make returns or to surrender a certain percentage back to source. The Vice Chancellorship was a bigger pie and so it was necessary to be assured of one's loyalty. And since many of the faithful were no longer afraid of the consequences of reneging after swearing on the bible it became necessary to add a loaded gun. And there would be every justification to use the latter if after swearing on it, the oath-taker defaulted. It was a more assured way of securing compliance and all oath takers knew that. There were fewer or indeed no defaults since the loaded gun was added to the Bible and the Koran as instruments for oath-taking.

"Professor Johnson you appear a little downcast. I can understand. I happen to know the background. Nothing has gone wrong. Ours is a civilized administration. I know you are married to a Zelander and the value systems are a little different. But always remember that we are in Konganoga. We have our own value systems and responsibilities. For instance those people in Zeland have only one wife by law. Again often they have only one or two children or sometimes no children by choice. Again, once their children turn eighteen the latter are assumed to be adults and often they can be dispersed like the chickens that have come of age. But you know as well as I do, that our value systems and culture are different here. Even as a Christian you know what I mean. Our wants are more because our culture and value systems are different from what obtains in your in-laws' place. Again don't forget that people contribute to the society in Zeland and the society in turn takes care of them in their old age. But here most people loath the idea of paying their taxes and contributing to society while they work often because you and I will invariably embezzle what they have paid or contributed. And so the overall polity is poorer and we have to make private arrangement for the rainy day when we are still in office. You know what I mean. So brighten up. You have just been admitted into the membership of the most progressive League in Konganoga if not in this region of the world. The sky is your limit and you must strike while the iron is hot.

"Your wife's people will always say: 'Make hay while the sun shines'. You know what I mean?"

Mr. Ayuda spoke with such apparent candidness that even Professor Johnson with all his sincerity and honor started to rationalize on whether he should indeed be happy or whether he should be sad.

There was no doubt in Professor Johnson's mind that he had bitten a little more than he could chew. But having waded so far into the sea of sin he felt that it would be defeatist not to try to catch the fish. And the big fish in this particular instance was the enormous material resources of the Republic of Konganoga. Professor Johnson silently promised himself that there was no going back. He resolved to go to the devil if need be in order to make it big. Hitherto he had always felt contented having risen to the top position of professor. But as the love of having grows with having, his appointment to the Board of the Tin Mining Company of Konganoga and later to the even higher position of Vice Chancellor opened up the political arena for him. He had this time come close to visiting the President and if he could under cover of the oath of allegiance facilitate the diversion of university funds into the big League, he might at last be able to dine personally with Mr. President. The gloominess instantly disappeared from Professor Johnson's face. He consoled himself the more by repeating to himself the revelation which Mr. Ayuda had made to him much as there was no evidence supporting the assertion:

Even men of God also took the oath of allegiance with the bible and the loaded gun!

Professor Johnson was driven back to his five star hotel suite by another chauffeur attached to the presidency. Before he left Mr. Ayuda's office he was informed that there would be a presidential banquet that night and that selected League Members would be invited. He was thereafter handed a beautifully-designed and embroidered invitation card which had the lion and elephant symbols of the Coat of Arms of the Republic of Konganoga conspicuously displayed on its front.

On the card was boldly written
"This card admits. Please bring it with you."

At the center page of the invitation card was written:

"His Excellency Commander in Chief of the Republic of Konganoga has the pleasure to invite Professor Okon Johnson to a banquet in honor of the visiting Head of State of the Republic of Tughana…"

Professor Johnson nodded his head in appreciation. He was now being invited to dine with visiting Heads of State. He read the invitation again and pinched the back of his hand to reassure himself that it was truly him and not merely a dream. It was him indeed!

Professor Okon Johnson had indeed "arrived!"

An oath requiring the surrender of even up to 90% of the monthly allocation of Professor Johnson's institution would be worth the opportunity to dine with visiting Heads of State. An oath over a bible and a hundred loaded guns would be no impediment.

Professor Johnson nodded again in affirmation. He reached for his cell phone to call Fiona his wife to inform her of the invitation. He wished that the distance between Kiba and Kumbrujaa was only a couple of miles apart. He would have taken Fiona along. It would have been worth all the troubles. But Fiona could not answer the call. The battery of her cell phone had run down and there was no public power supply to charge the battery. The stand-by generator which was almost becoming the hallmark of every household in Konganoga could also not be used. It had run out of diesel the previous night and all the gas stations were closed as a result of strike action by the gas tanker drivers over harassment from soldiers and policemen. The latter had the previous day beaten up one of the tanker drivers to death allegedly for refusing to *settle* them with money at a check-point on the highway. After several fruitless attempts at reaching his wife, Professor Johnson gave up trying and simply sank back into his hotel room bed conjecturing how sweet it would be to sit at close quarters with the President and the other dignitaries at the presidential banquet and dinner.

Professor Johnson had alighted from the car that took him to the Palace Hotel venue of the presidential banquet. As he walked towards the entrance to the hotel lobby there was a near-stampede as security men attached to the President and his visitors used their batons to chase away people that had gathered in small groups at the entrance of the lobby. It was announced that Mr. President would arrive shortly and so the policemen had on their own, swung into action. A mild drama had occurred when Professor Johnson showed his invitation card at the gate and was informed by one of the security men that his invitation card was a fake one. Most of the attendees to the banquet were escorted to the gate by one or more security guards, some in uniform others in plain clothes but visibly armed. Professor Johnson has alighted from the car and had walked to the gate unescorted. He obviously had not graduated to the level of the privileged League Member who would be accorded personal security outfit at state expense. The security man obviously must have noticed that this particular attendee had arrived unescorted. His invitation card therefore needed more scrutiny. Even if it was a genuine invitation card the fact that the owner had no personal security outfit meant that such attendee must still be a junior League Member who was more vulnerable to extortion. Professor Johnson's invitation card was therefore declared fake. The sum of $200 was required to "un-fake" or validate the card otherwise the card owner would be turned back from the gate. He would thus miss the opportunity of dining with the "movers and shakers of society". The suspected fake card carrier would not be charged to court with impersonation because there was the likelihood that the card would be discovered to be genuine. All that was needed was some dollars to grease the palms of a poor *gate keeper* in uniform.

"Where you get this fake card from?" The security man had asked Professor Johnson. It was most embarrassing for professor who had to go to the details of how he was given the invitation card by the Special Assistant to the President.

"But this card it no get police stamp and signature for back. Who give you this fake card?"

Professor Johnson was dumbfounded. Here was an official invitation card given to him by a high official of government right in a wing of the presidential villa being declared fake by a security official.

Could Mr. Ayuda have deliberately set me up? Could there have been a conspiracy that was set up to entrap me and label me a gate crasher? Could there have been a mistake somewhere by which Mr. Ayuda gave me an invitation card that was meant for somebody else and would have needed extra validation before it could be used?

All kinds of questions crossed Professor Johnson's mind as he stood there glued to the spot. He looked like a fake and was almost completely at the mercy of a group of security men at the gate.

He thought of phoning Mr. Ayuda but he did not have the latter's phone number.

As Professor Johnson fumbled through his pocket for his phone to call one of his friends that were resident in Kumbrujaa the security man probably fearing that his prey might wriggle himself out of the entrapment quickly searched through a paper box that was lying on the table in front of him and brought out a piece of paper on which was written "Pass" and on which was attached a blank name tag.

"Chief this one it be pass. It go cost you $200!" The security man told Professor Johnson.

"But I was officially invited to his banquet. What I have given you is my official invitation card and I was told I would collect an official name tag at the gate." Professor Johnson insisted, emboldened by the fact that the security man appeared to be backing down.

At the mention of name tag, the security man quickly asked "Who give you the card and wetin be your name?"

'The Special Assistant to His Excellency Mr. Ayuda gave me the card and my name is Professor Okon Johnson."

The officer took down the name on a sheet of paper and walked off to his superior officer who was reclining on a chair and table a few meters away. The latter searched his list, conferred briefly with the junior officer and the latter walked back to Professor Johnson.

OK professor. You may go in. But you fit still find something for your boys. We dey loyal Sir. Even fifty dollar go do."

Professor Johnson was already fuming with anger. But he knew that it was risky to completely ignore those uniformed security men or to go too far in exposing their unwholesome practices att the gate; certainly not in Konganoga. One would never know where and when one might again encounter them. It might be on the lonely highway or even in one's place of abode after a false report might have been lodged against the individual by a distraught neighbor.

Thus it was, that Professor Okon Johnson was

reluctantly allowed to get into a banquet to which he was duly invited.

The first thing that struck Professor Johnson when he entered the banquet hall was that almost every other person had a name tag on him. But since he had been allowed to go in, Professor Johnson did not feel that it was necessary for him to get back into an argument with the rather rude security men at the gate. At least he knew the name and office of the person who invited him. He could always ask any person who would want to question his presence to verify from Mr. Ayuda the Special Assistant to Mr. President. It was a very exquisitely arranged hall. Most of the high and mighty who were at the hall had come with their spouses. There were ambassadors and several heads of diplomatic missions, senior government officials and lots of press men and women.

Shortly after 8.15 PM the President of the Federal Republic of Konganoga was ushered into the Hall along with his guest the Head of State of Koghana. Everybody in the hall stood up as the National Anthems of both countries were played.

It was a very grand occasion and Professor Johnson not having come with his wife and not being familiar with many people in the hall simply kept himself busy with the buffet and the good wine. It was during one of the rounds of servings that he met a rather over-dressed gentleman who had a name tag on which was written "Okon Johnson" which was Professor Johnson's name. Out of curiosity Professor Johnson moved up to the man and introduced himself.

"Hi, I see you are Okon Johnson. That also happens to be my full name. How are you, and are you resident here in Kumbrujaa?"

The man hesitated and Professor Johnson continued:
"I teach medicine at the University of Kiba and I am here on a visit."

Professor Johnson noticed that the man was ill at ease. He simply said to Professor Johnson.
"I dey fine, thank you Sir."
The failure of the new supposed "Okon Johnson" to get into a discussion coupled with the furtive behavior that he exhibited did not immediately ring a bell to Professor Johnson. Some 30 minutes later Professor Johnson walked up to the table where the man had carried his food to and could not find the man any longer. It was then that it occurred to the Professor that the man might have been a fake and must have absconded after he introduced himself to him. The man might not have been properly invited to the banquet. His actual name might not have been Okon Johnson. It was widely known that people's names and identities were often stolen and sold even by security agents who were expected to be the watch dogs and custodians of such identities.

Mr. President had taken a walk around the banquet hall to interact with the visitors. He had gone almost from table to table briefly chatting with people and having some of the well known faces introduced to him. Professor Johnson had wished that there was a way that His Excellency could stop at his table. He was not familiar with anybody within the hall but he was determined to introduce himself if Mr. President would stop by the table which he shared with five other people. Such a meeting, Prof Johnson believed, would greatly increase his chances of getting into the inner caucus of the League membership some day. He had got into the group and had been invited to a presidential banquet. He was beginning to enjoy the company of the big and mighty.

It was his intention to exploit every available opportunity to get to the apex of the group. He believed that his education and his profession would be great advantages as there were not likely to be many professors of medicine in the entire gathering.

As the President walked towards a table close to where Professor Johnson was sitting, the latter briskly sprang to his feet accidentally upsetting the well laid-out plates and cutlery. The brisk movement attracted the attention of both the President and the four security details who accompanied the latter around the hall. The security details immediately readied themselves for 'action'. But it was a false alarm. The movement however had turned the attention of the President in the direction of Professor Johnson.

From his table Professor Johnson immediately said "Good day Mr. President, my name is Johnson, Professor Okon Johnson from the University of Kiba. I thank you for the opportunity for me to be here."

Even though it was an uninvited self introduction, it was one that was brief and refined, one that was quite different from the verbosity and poor English of many of the semi educated or crude political appointees who were only being rewarded for roles played in election-winning or election-rigging. The introduction might not have been necessary or expected, but it worked.

Mr. President immediately diverted his course in the direction of Professor Johnson.

"Hi Professor, you are welcome to Kumbrujaa. I hope your journey to this place was smooth. And how is the University Community?" The President said while stretching out his hand for a handshake with Professor Johnson. Obviously there were not many other professors in that gathering which was mostly populated with professional politicians and diplomats.

The president even when he had never known or met with Professor Johnson was quite polite and exhibited the warmth of one who had known the professor for quite some time.

Beaming with smiles Professor Johnson grasped the president's outstretched hand with his two palms and meekly replied:

"We are doing well in the University Sir." Professor Johnson replied.

The press photographers clicked away at their cameras every step of the way.

The President was soon off to the next guest.

The joy on Professor Johnson's face was palpable. He needed no further evidence to convince himself that he had truly joined the celebrated ruling class. The scene at the oath-taking event in Mr. Ayuda's office flashed through his mind but he quickly dismissed this as one of the growth pains that he needed to endure to become of political leadership age.

Chapter 27

FULFILLING THE LEAGUE MEMBER'S PROMISE

Professor Johnson had faithfully narrated to his wife Fiona his experiences at Kumbrujaa.

Fiona was initially excited at the red carpet treatment accorded to her husband. The issue of oath-taking involving a bible and a loaded gun as well as the threats that accompanied use of the loaded gun were however issues which greatly troubled her. She had subtly told her husband that it might have been better for him to simply remain a professor and maintain his integrity than to accept the position of Vice Chancellor and mortgage his conscience.

She had even quoted some passages from the Bible to convince Professor Johnson that they might have been better off without the position of Vice Chancellor with all the burdens and strings that were attached to the position.

She said:

"What will it profit us to gather all the accolades and perhaps all the wealth and mortgage our consciences and perhaps the future of our children?"

Professor Johnson had no answer to that question.

The office of the Vice Chancellor was again abuzz with activity after a substantive Vice Chancellor had taken over from the acting Vice Chancellor who stood in for a while after the retirement of the former holder of the post.

The political party chieftains of the ruling party were regular visitors.

Fortunately for Professor Johnson his appointment had emanated, not from the State Government but straight from Kumbrujaa the National Capital.

Right from the day that he assumed duties the 40% revenue returns which Professor Johnson had been told must be made monthly from revenue accruing to the University was like a Sword of Damocles hanging over the Vice Chancellor. He often wished that he could have the opportunity to ask the retired Vice Chancellor whether the latter was burdened with such a load during his own tenure. Bu since he did not wish that anybody else would know about the discussions, Professor Johnson had kept the burden to himself.

It was relatively easy for Professor Johnson to adapt to the administrative office of the Vice Chancellor from his experience as the Chairman of the Tin Mining Company of Kiba. The caliber of personnel which he had to deal with was however grossly different. In the Tin Mining Company most of the Members of Board who he had to deal with were political appointees whose main qualification for appointment to the Board was the fact of their membership of the ruling party. Many of the Board members were not very educated and their main focus was the money which they would make from the Company and the extra which they needed to extract from the system so as to make maximum returns to their political godfathers. In the case of the University senate and University Council, the dramatis personae were a different caliber of people. They were highly educated people who were not only knowledgeable but who were also highly analytical and critical of actions and events around them. The latter were not groups that the Vice Chancellor could easily hoodwink or cajole into actions that were against their will or against acceptable civilized norms.

Before Professor Johnson departed from Kumbrujaa Mr. Ayuda had held another round of discussions with him. During those latter rounds of talks Mr. Ayuda had told the Vice Chancellor that the latter would be given one month of grace from the commencement of his administration as Vice Chancellor after which the stipulated 40% of money accruing to the University would need to be remitted monthly to the League.

Professor Johnson had sought to know from Mr. Ayuda how he would have to get the bursar and the auditors to also comply with the directive to have 40% of the University's revenue diverted monthly to the League's account. In answer to that question Mr. Ayuda was very emphatic.

Looking Professor Johnson in the face Mr. Ayuda had said:

"Professor, the resolution of this issue of 40% monthly deduction and remittance to the League is mandatory. It is supposed to be part of your job. The bursar and the internal auditor are all subordinate to you in the University. You have been appointed to be in charge. And you must be in charge. That is precisely why you, as a very educated and articulate professional, were appointed to that high office in preference to the many contenders to that position. You must use the influence, power and respect which you wield within the academic community to get the relevant staff members to cooperate with you. You have the power and authority of the presidency behind you. Whoever you hire is hired and whoever you fire is fired. This is as good as ultimate power and you must use it!"

Professor Johnson felt enormously empowered and rejuvenated.

He had immediately started to figure how sweet it would be to wield the power that had been conferred on him. From the time of the order on him to divert 40% of the University budgetary allocation back to the President's league, his whole attention was diverted from good governance and advancement of the University's cause to strategies which would make it possible for him to make the necessary returns to the President's League.

He became less attentive both at his job and in his home. He daily replayed in his mind's eye the different scenes which he encountered in Kumbrujaa. He remembered the Oath Administrator Mr. Muktar Obredu. He remembered the latter's wry and sarcastic smile. He remembered the trolley that contained the tray, a Bible, the Koran and the loaded gun. He remembered the last few words of the oath itself. He missed a few heartbeats at the thought of the possibility of use of the loaded gun. He knew that people had disappeared mysteriously or had been gruesomely assassinated in the system with no trace of the killers. He thought of his wife Fiona and his lovely children. He then got up and walked towards the window of his office. He looked out through the window and remembered that he was now in charge of all that he saw. He nodded his head with satisfaction and quietly declared:

"It has been a hard climb and I am prepared to retain the prize."

To retain the prize Professor Johnson knew that he must keep the promise. And the promise was to satisfy the cabal that went by the name of "The President's League". The members of the League were called "League Members." And the League Members were expected to have ultimate power over the finances of any institution over which they were appointed. That was the only way they could divert as much a 40% to 50% of the revenue accruing to the establishments back to the League. Whatever atrocities that they committed in the process of achieving that goal were overlooked. Any obstacles including staff members that stood on the way for realization of these objectives were ruthlessly done away with. And the chief helmsmen were certain of the support of the presidency in whatever measures that they took to ensure the realization of these objectives.

To satisfy the cabal Professor Johnson knew that he had to embark on measures which would drastically maul the polity. There was no doubt in the professor's mind that the system would be greatly traumatized by his keeping the promise. But the stakes were too high and the reprisals for reneging were severe. Professor Johnson again thought of the loaded gun. And he remembered that he was made to hold the loaded gun in his hand while he took the oath of allegiance. Professor Johnson heaved a sigh and went back to the well-padded seat which was the seat of power in the University. Even as he took his seat the wordings of the oath again reverberated in Professor Johnson's ears:

"By this symbol and this instrument I stand at the

absolute direction of Mr. President or his accredited agents in all matters of money, position and power in my office and out of it for as long as I remain in the office of Vice Chancellor under penalty of action from either or both of this symbol and this instrument."

Professor Johnson again heaved a sigh. It was not a sigh of relief. It was one of burden; a burden which he realized was iatrogenic. It was a burden which he knew only greed and avarice had made him thrust upon himself.

A promise had been made. And it had been made under oath. And the instrument of oath was double barreled. If the Bible did not kill him on default because of the infinite mercy of the Almighty, then certainly the loaded gun would do the job. It was more of a double-edged sword.

Professor Johnson remembered the medicine man in his Akunwanta native home. The name of the medicine man was Okpani. Okpani worshipped a shrine which was called Udogwugwu.

Udogwugwu was said to be a particularly vicious shrine which would kill anyone who swore falsely by it or who broke a promise after swearing by it. For many generations people had come from far and near to swear by Udogwugwu or to seal agreements by it.

Okpani's ancestors had been the known priests of Udogwugwu and Okpani had inherited the tradition of chief priest of Udogwugwu.

Udogwugwu was known never to spare or take pity on any who defaulted or swore falsely by it and the death of its victim was known to be within days of the default or false swearing. For generations people wondered how Udogwugwu was able to identify the culprits. It was much later that one of the errand boys of Udogwugwu who was apprenticed to Okpani for many years turned to

Christianity and revealed that Okpani and his Udogwugwu community had a very powerful secret service group which carefully but secretly investigated all cases that were brought to Udogwugwu for adjudication. After the secret investigations murderous agents of Okpani and his Udogwugwu community would move fatally against any of the culprits or persons who had been proved to have been guilty. Thus was the popular statement among the Akunwanta Community:

"Udogwugwu egbuhu, Okpani egbuo" which translated meant "If Udogwugwu fails to kill a transgressor, its chief priest Okpani would help."

Professor Johnson again remembered the loaded gun with which he swore. He remembered the Okpani and Udogwugwu story in his Akunwanta Community. In this particular instance he knew that if he reneged in his promise and the all merciful God whose Bible he had sworn by spared him that certainly the Okpani which was represented by the loaded gun would certainly do him in.

Professor Johnson immediately reached for his intercom. Within minutes the bursar was in his office. The first stage of discussions which would engulf the university in an unprecedented wave of embezzlement and graft had come underway!

The issue of setting out some chunk of money every month for the godfathers in governance did not sound strange to Mr. Amajide the bursar.

He had listened attentively to the Vice Chancellor as the latter sounded him out on the need to set out a lump sum every month "for the benefit of the friends of the university in Kumbrujaa."

The Vice Chancellor had started thus:

"Mr. Amajide, I thank you again for your congratulatory message to me on assumption of office as Vice Chancellor. I feel happy that I can count on your support and understanding in ensuring that jointly we work to ensure a smooth sail for this administration.

I will particularly seek your cooperation in ensuring that we set out something every month for the friends of the University in Kumbrujaa. These are the lubricating oils for our wheel of progress and we need to ensure that the engine is well oiled."

Professor Johnson paused for a while to watch the effect of his feeler. He did not need to say more. Mr. Amajide understood. He nodded his head in affirmation but said nothing.

Professor Johnson then continued more boldly but more cautiously.

"I am happy you understand Mr. Amajide. But what percentage of the budget do you think we need to set aside for them every month?"

Mr. Amajide remained silent for a while and then said.

"It depends upon you Sir. I am an obedient servant."

"No, Mr. Amajide, you have been longer in this business than I am. You have worked with several administrations. What is it that had been your practice in the past?" Professor Johnson asked.

Again Mr. Amajide remained silent. He was a seasoned administrator who knew a lot but was often reluctant to say much.

As Professor Johnson stared him in the face and made it obvious that he expected an answer, Mr. Amajide then again reluctantly volunteered:

"It depends on you Sir. Every administration has its style. It depends upon your understanding with the auditors and more importantly on what you have agreed with Kumbrujaa. They own the government. Theoretically we are bursars, auditors, accountants and all. But these things are effective in the developed world where accountability is the watchword. But you know as well as I do Sir that we are in the jungle. Pardon my use of the word jungle Sir. But that is what it is.

We are in the jungle and the law of the jungle obtains. Might is right. Of course as an obedient servant I take orders."

The matter was getting a little more complicated for Professor Johnson. Mr. Amajide did not appear willing to give any clue as to the percentage that he knew had in the past been set aside for the Kumbrujaa overlords.

But Professor Johnson had been told a percentage and he knew that he was committed to a percentage. But he had wanted to know first from the Bursar who also happened to act for the Chief Accountant, how much had been the practice for similar situations.

Professor Johnson then remembered Mr. Ayuda's statement:

"Whoever you hire is hired and whoever you fire is fired."

He then said:

"OK then Mr. Amajide, we shall consider setting out 40% of the monthly budget towards servicing the *friends of the University* in Kumbrujaa.

It was at the mention of 40% that Mr. Amajide who had

hitherto remained almost taciturn about figures opened up and shouted in amazement:

"40%? Then what would the University run on. 40% off the monthly budget of the University would be a killer for any meaningful development. Professor Solomon the retired acting Vice Chancellor used to set out 25% for those sharks in Kumbrujaa and the University was almost choking economically. He had unilaterally reduced the *returns* to 20% so that services would not grind to a complete halt. It was alleged that the reduction in what was accruing as kickback to the vampires in Kumbrujaa was one of the reasons for the former Acting Vice Chancellor's non-confirmation and his premature and sudden retirement. 40%? I fear Sir that you may not be able to pull through with even 30%. Both Professors Kemji and Ziebu were luckier. The sharks in Kumbrujaa hadn't gotten so greedy during their tenures. They were still making do with 10%. And even with 10% deduction the university was suffering. But Sir, like I said, I am an obedient servant."

Professor Johnson was stunned at the inadvertent disclosures by Mr. Amajide. Rumor mills had it initially that one of the Former Vice Chancellors Professor Williams had been under great pressures from the political powers in Kumbrujaa but not many people actually knew what those pressures were. The official reason for that particular Vice Chancellor's retirement was quoted as "personal reasons". Professor Johnson was just beginning to know what those "personal reasons" were.

He again largely remembered part of the wordings of the oath which he had taken in Mr. Ayuda's office:

"By this symbol and this instrument I stand at the absolute direction of Mr. President or his accredited agents in all matters of money, position and power in my office and out of it for as long as I remain in the office of Vice

Chancellor under penalty of action from either or both of this symbol and this instrument."

Professor Johnson had a streak of sweat running down his forehead. He brought out his handkerchief and wiped his face. He felt like a man under bondage. He again heaved a sigh of exasperation.

Chapter 28

THE DOWNWARD DRIFT

The first few months following the first month of grace were uneventful in Professor Johnson's administration. The system was still able to sustain itself due to the resilience that the immediate past administration had built. But by the 4th month of the administration the crushing effects for the 40% *returns* to Kumbrujaa coupled with the nearly 10% internal pilfering of funds in the system had started to manifest adversely on the quality of teaching, research and other services within the university community.

For the first time the University started considering retrenchment of some staff of "non-performing Departments." Criteria for determination of the non-performing Departments were not very clear cut. A lot depended on the whims and caprices of the man who had been given almost ultimate power to hire and fire. Fees began to be introduced for services that were hitherto offered free. The financial burdens on the students began to manifest, imperceptibly at first but more noticeably with time. Resentment by the students and staff alike began to spring up. Dislike of the once adored name of Professor Okon Johnson gave way rapidly to hatred and tension and unease pervaded the once tranquil university environment.

As a possible response to the growing tensions, Professor Johnson remembered the powers which he had as Vice Chancellor, especially one who had the strong support of Kumbrujaa. But the power to hire and fire did not place food on the tables of the students and staff of the university. It did not collect the garbage. It did not pay electricity bills or the gas bills. And so as money for the running of the University ran short, services stagnated. Payment of some salaries got delayed and the lecturers started to grumble.

Back in his home front Professor Johnson became increasingly detached from his family. He left home early and returned late. He started missing the routine Sunday services which he used to take his family to and which his children often enjoyed so much.

At first he explained the situation away by telling Fiona that the pressure of work was weighing too much on him. But it soon became increasingly clear that what was actually weighing much on the Professor was the burden of the dinner that he had had with the devil. So much time was spent in the office computing how to cover up and make up for inadequacies after the 40% deductions for the President's League. The situation got so bad that Fiona had to make out some time to talk candidly to her husband on one of the days that he came back to the house a little after midnight.

As usual Professor Okon Johnson had blamed "too much outstanding work" for his continued lack of attention on his family. But the truth was that Professor Johnson's time was spent manipulating figures and projects so as to be able along with the Bursar/ Accountant to set out the 40% money for his godfathers in Kumbrujaa.

After fruitlessly trying to reason with her husband Fiona had in desperation told Okon:

'Honey, you may begin to think of choosing between your work as a Vice Chancellor and your roles as a husband and a father. You may have to choose and you may need to do it soon."

Johnson who had allowed his new position to overcome his usual humility and sense of direction had apparently taken offence at the innocuous statement by his wife.

He had replied angrily:

'Fiona if your statement is supposed to be a threat or blackmail, rest assured that I will not succumb to either of them."

Professor Johnson probably forgot that he was talking to his wife and one from Fiona's background where the wife was not expected to be a disposable tool as obtained in some uncivilized cultures. The unwarranted arrogance of office as Vice Chancellor appeared inexorably to be taking the better half of Professor Johnson. The hero worshipping in the system appeared to be intoxicating him. The winner-take-all mentality and the oligarchic culture inherent in the system had literally infused into a once meek and humble loving husband such misdirected sense of self importance that all reason for a while appeared to be relegated to the background.

Fiona recoiled at Johnson's statement and sneering countenance. She was not the quarrelsome or nagging type of wife. She was a very well-groomed lady who had carried the initial burdens of living and practicing in a foreign land with all equanimity and joy.

She had seen her husband from the time he was a near-helpless medical resident in Zeland to a position where he had to struggle to overcome the hurdles instituted by real and imagined competitors in his native land. He had seen him inch his way through thick and thin to the top of his profession as a Professor and Dean of a medical school. He had watched as the husband was offered the top position in the academic community as Vice Chancellor, a position which she easily observed was rapidly destroying his family life and detaching him from reality and humaneness. She had watched helplessly as her once loving Okon appeared daily to be getting snatched away from her and tossed up to the wind of societal hollowness and irresponsibility. She was initially enjoying the spotlight as the spouse of a rising star. But it was beginning to hurt her. It had of late persistently hurt her to the extent that for a brief while the idea of divorce flashed in her mind if only for her to once again take hold of her life away from unnecessary playing to the gallery. She had quickly dismissed that apparently wicked and unreasonable thought. She had prayed over the idea and had, as a Catholic, thought of going for Confession 'to cleanse the unholy thought.'

But Professor Okon's outburst against her had once again aroused Fiona's concerns. She again began to think of the 'unholy' prospect of divorce or separation. This time she did not easily dismiss the idea even when she struggled not to succumb to it.

As Fiona struggled to maintain her sanity in the midst of a deteriorating family situation Professor Johnson sank deeper into the abyss of moral decay. The quest to discover new ways of diverting university funds into the League Fund in Kumbrujaa had assumed center stage in virtually everything the new Vice Chancellor did in office.

Fictitious contract awards were made. Fake projects were advertised for and contracts awarded. The money for the non-existent projects was diverted en-block to the League account. Professor Johnson had ordered the disbanding of the projects Committee and the Projects Monitoring Committee of the University. The Appointment and Promotions Committee was reorganized and filled with professors who would dance to the tune of the Vice Chancellor. The few principled people who still remained in the system were blatantly side tracked and ignored. Money was demanded from people who sought appointments in the University and at the directive of the Vice Chancellor such money, often huge amounts, were officially known as application fees and were paid directly into a fund affiliated to the League account. Professor Johnson never touched the money and so could not be accused of stealing it. But he overtly diverted such monies into an account which was not in the service of the University for the benefit of his godfathers. The maintenance Department of the University was almost crippled as no funds were provided for repairs and servicing.

The internal network of roads of the University was filled with potholes. The internal power supply plants of the university which supplemented the epileptic public power supply had almost become nonexistent as most of them broke down and were never repaired. The few that were still serviceable did not have diesel on which to run. The money for emergency diesel supply had been diverted to service the league Fund for the Kumbrujaa masters.

The University of Kiba was dying and everybody knew it. The students had staged series of demonstrations and were threatened with permanent shutting down of the institution if they did not learn to manage. The outspoken professors were muzzled and either put on suspension or had some fictitious charges placed against them. The once budding pearl of a nation was rapidly fading away. And Professor Johnson the once highly respected ophthalmologist –turned administrator had assumed a new image, the image of some curse which had descended upon an institution and a people.

Back in the house a once happy family the family of Professor Okon and Attorney-at-law Fiona Johnson was in great distress. The emotional distress which her disintegrating family had placed on Fiona had started affecting her work. She skipped court hearings and subsequently her practice began to diminish. She later decided to dispense with her cases and planned a holiday to Zealand ostensibly to put the children in school there since the educational system in Konganoga just like everything else was going into shambles. Whoever that could afford it had sent their children abroad. Fiona had no problems securing a school for her children.

Okon even in the midst of the maddening spell of acquisition to enrich the League did not fail to see the gathering clouds that were about to engulf his family. He had protested against Fiona's moves to secure a school for the children but Fiona had insisted on having them continue their education in Zeland. Professor Okon already had enough problems with the University to want to make more troubles at home. He let Fiona have her way. His protests were as feeble as they could be and he could not muster the forceful voice of a father in moments of great decision as had erupted in his own family.

"I would have preferred our kids to remain here with us. Even though the schools have deteriorated we can afford to hire private home tutors for them" Professor Johnson had said. His entreaties fell on deaf ears as Fiona had indeed completed all travel arrangements for her children and her.

In the traditional Konganogan society the final word about such major decisions concerning the education of the children would often emanate from the father who always was the head of the family. But Professor Johnson in his complete immersion into the fulfillment of the oath that he swore to had literally mortgaged away his fatherly rights. He did not even have the time to look into such issues. On the evening of their proposed journey Fiona had kept awake till past midnight when her husband would as usual saunter into the sitting room after being dropped from his official car by a half-dozing chauffeur.

"As I had earlier told you, Okon, the children and I are travelling tomorrow on our annual vacation." Fiona had unceremoniously told her husband.

The sleepiness and weariness suddenly disappeared from the busy and overburdened Vice Chancellor. The children were already all asleep in their rooms. There was no evidence of elaborate packing in the house. The chairs, drapes, shoes, laundered clothes in the hangers, living room, kitchen and even the bedrooms were looking intact. Only two medium sized bags that were fully stuffed suggested some preparation for a journey.

"Did you say tomorrow?" a bemused Okon asked.

"Yes, tomorrow, and we shall be away for a while!" Fiona coldly replied.

"But Fiona we ought to have planned this properly. You don't really mean you are travelling tomorrow when the children will be restarting school in ten days time from their two weeks break. Will Umanamaa be able to cope with them in your absence?"

An apparently confused Okon asked. He was apparently

inattentive to Fiona's explanation that she was travelling with the children.

Fiona looking away from her husband and making to walk off to the room quietly replied:

"Umanamaa will not need to look after the children. I can afford to look after them. I told you that we are travelling tomorrow."

It was only then that the impact of the "We" struck Professor Johnson as he exclaimed:

"You mean you are travelling with the children?"

"Yes I am. The children need no visas to Zeland!"

Unguarded gas escaped from some professorial rectum and the man who had sworn to put himself and his institution's resources at the disposal of the President suddenly came back to his senses albeit momentarily.

"But you can't do this to me Fiona. We never planned this together!"

But it was too late. Fiona walked briskly off to their common bedroom where Fiona for many days each week slept alone as her Vice Chancellor husband gallivanted between Kumbrujaa and Kiba.

"No, Fiona, this is very unfair! You can't do this to me!"

It was too late and Professor Johnson even in his momentary period of sanity could read this.

He dashed to the drawer where the family's travel documents were usually kept. Only his own passport, his Konganogan passport, was left there. Both Fiona and the children were all dual citizens of both Zeland and Konganoga. None of their passports was still there inside the drawer.

In a brief moment of rashness, Professor Johnson grabbed both bags that lay on the floor at one corner of the room. He had thought of impounding the passports that might have been kept there. But sanity prevailed as he quickly realized that force and violence in a case like this would only escalate a bad situation. Fiona neither fretted nor made any dash to counter her husband's move when the latter momentarily grabbed her loaded bag. She simply donned her sleeping garments and slipped under the comforter and proceeded to have a good sleep.

Chapter 29

**AN EYE ON THE PROMISE;
A FAMILY IN RUINS**

Mr. Ayuda the Assistant to the President in Kumbrujaa had kept a close eye on the returns from the Federal University of Science and Technology Kiba. There were other Assistants and Special Assistants in different Ministries under the Presidency. Mr. Ayuda happened to be the Assistant in charge of *returns* from Institutions of Higher Learning. After the one month of grace it was expected that the agreed percentage between the Head of the institution in Kiba and the Assistant to the President must have started to flow in. It was estimated that once the inflow started that it would not diminish. Rather it was expected to grow just as the fortunes of the mineral-rich Konganogan Republic grew in revenue. As the nation grew in revenue, the greed of the ravaging masters in governance also grew. Consequently even as the revenue accruing to the state grew the average Konganogan got poorer. The highways got worse. Infrastructural facilities decayed faster and were never refurbished. Morality and humility in public office grew in reverse gear and the fortunes and prospects for the young Konganogan dimmed by the day.

The expectations by the President's League from The Federal University Kiba also grew.

On the other hand the man who was saddled with the responsibility of ensuring that the diverted funds got into the coffers of the League was facing mounting opposition both domestically and at his place of work. The goose that laid the golden egg the Federal University in Kiba was boiling internally. The teachers and students were in revolt. Much as most of the account tinkering was done between the Vice Chancellor and the Bursar Mr. Amajide, it was not possible for the entire transactions to be kept secret from the other senior staff of the accounts and Bursary Departments. Very soon tongues started wagging.

"This new man is even worse than the retired man that we were complaining against." The workers in the Accounts and Bursary Departments would say while comparing Professor Johnson with the immediate past Vice Chancellor.

In order to save costs the meal subsidy that was in existence for the students since the establishment of the University had been withdrawn. The scholarship scheme which was available for the overall best student in each department every year was scrapped.

The University had become an old caricature of itself since the dawn of the Professor Johnson administration.

By the eleventh month of Professor Johnson's administration things had deteriorated so much that Professor Johnson, from reports reaching the latter, was afraid that there would be an open rebellion in the university. Most of the professors were on the side of the students and many of them attended rallies organized by the students to protest the deteriorating situation. By the twelfth month of his reign, Professor Johnson had summoned the Bursar and asked him what his opinion was about the deteriorating situation.

Mr. Amajide was a principal player in the packaging of the graft. He lived among the students and other staff. He must have witnessed the groans from a once bouncing academic community. He knew that the funds being made available to the university would have been sufficient for the running of the institution if well managed. He was part of the mismanagement but as usual, in answer to Professor Johnson's inquiry from him about what should be done to avoid a catastrophe Mr. Amajide had replied: "I am an obedient servant."

Professor Johnson had heard this affirmation several times before. This time he needed solutions. And when none were seen to be coming Professor Johnson felt that it would be to his great discredit if he allowed the system to collapse completely. He had therefore decided to take unilateral action even in defiance and violation of the oath which he had taken in Mr. Ayuda's office. He had resolved to cut back on the percentage of the University's revenue which he ploughed back to the *President's League*. He had consequently summoned Mr. Amajide and peremptorily instructed as follows:

"Mr. Amajide, it will be tragic if we allowed the system to collapse on us because of this 40% deduction. Please cut back on this figure to 30% and if necessary with time to 25% so that the institution can stay afloat. We have a career here to protect. If the system collapses Kumbrujaa will float other institutions. We may be hard put to find our footing in that event. A cutback will amount to a violation of a promise but what can we do under the circumstances in which we find ourselves. I will head to Kumbrujaa to reason with them on this matter.

Mr. Amajide even when he was in the full know of what was going on and the fact that the institution would not survive with the heavy deductions in place had simply as usual replied:
"I am a loyal and obedient servant. I will do as you say Sir."

Professor Johnson's trip to the office of Mr. Ayuda the Special Assistant to the President was not this time as grand as it was when he first went for the swearing-in in the latter's office. There was no official car to wait for him at the airport. There were no exquisite hotel bookings except for the one which the University did for him. However, even in spite of the dire economic situation of the University the public relations section of the University had gone ahead to book first class for the Vice Chancellor and book executive suites for the latter too. That was in a situation where the workers in the University were being owed two months arrears of salaries.

Professor Johnson was no longer given red carpet treatment at the time he arrived Mr. Ayuda's office. He was kept unusually long at the reception even when he was the first to arrive to the office of the Assistant to the President. By the time he was called in to see Mr. Ayuda the Oath Administrator Mr. Muktar Obredu was already seated in the office with the same trolley displaying the same instruments which Professor Johnson had sworn on by his side.

It looked as if Mr. Ayuda had fore-knowledge of

Professor Johnson's mission and had assembled all the personnel and instruments necessary to counter him.

As soon as Professor Johnson entered the room Mr. Ayuda, wearing a mien which was a complete opposite of his initial self, announced:

"Professor Johnson, you swore by the bible and the gun. You have violated the vow. You have reneged on your promise. Mr. Muktar Obredu is here to inform you of what happens in such situations."

Mr. Ayuda paused for a while and looked at Professor Johnson from head to feet and then up again from feet to head as if to size him up for swallowing.

He then continued:

"The League is the noblest organization in this country and only men who keep their promises are allowed to belong there. People who cannot keep their promises made on oath are not deserving of the honor of membership. They are not even deserving of being with us. I am off to a meeting with Mr. President. But I will allow you and Mr. Muktar the honor of use of my office. The last time that we met here, remember that I advised you as an educated man and as a man whose family still had need for, to keep your promises especially those made under oath which included the Bible and a loaded gun. We are all architects of our own fortunes or misfortunes.

I wish you best of luck. Have a good day."

As soon as Mr. Ayuda left his office Mr. Muktar Obredu pulled closer to Professor Johnson and said:

"Professor, my own be to carry out instruction. I only pass message and do message. Them say you renege for the oath. That one it be violation and you know the thing that go follow. The gun here it no de shoot people. The Bible and the Koran, them no de kill people. Them be only symbols for this place. The things wey de kill people, them dey for inside that room. Make you follow me go see them."

Professor Johnson hesitated as the Oath Administrator Mr. Muktar Obredu got up and walked up towards the adjacent room. It was the same room from where he had rolled out the trolley during Professor Johnson's first visit.

Professor Johnson did not miss any bit of Mr. Muktar Obredu's statement: "The things wey de kill people, them dey for inside that room; follow me go see them!"

It was the same professed deadly room that Professor Johnson saw himself being invited into. The professor saw himself being invited into a room which had unequivocally been declared as one which killed people!

Even without giving a thought to it, Professor Johnson the highly respected Professor of Surgery and Vice Chancellor of the highly respected Federal University in Kiba sprang to his feet. The little *pot belly* that he was beginning to develop from too many parties and relative physical inactivity since he was appointed Vice Chancellor constituted no hindrance to the flight. Professor Johnson sprang to his feet. He walked gingerly as if in compliance with Mr. Muktar Obredu's order to follow the latter. Half way towards the door of "the things wey de kill people" Professor Johnson suddenly made a U-turn and took to his heels. Instead of continuing towards the door of the apparently intended room, he made a detour towards the door that led into the Secretary's office to the outside. He dashed out of the room, past the Secretary's office and into the street.

"If they want to kill me let it be in the full glare of the public." The erudite professor muttered to himself his fingers trembling and his feet wobbly and barely strong enough to support him. He again immediately remembered the often repeated story of Okpani and Udogwugwu in his native Akunwanta village. He succinctly remembered the slogan: "Udogwugwu egbuhu, Okpani egbuo" (If Udogwugwu fails to kill a transgressor, its chief priest Okpani will help).

Professor Johnson had no intention of being the object of Mr. Muktar Obredu's *help*.

Professor Johnson did not want to take a chance by going back to his hotel room. He was not sure of the plans that had been hatched out against him. Even though neither Mr. Muktar Obredu nor any other agents came in hot pursuit of the reneging and fleeing Vice Chancellor, the latter was not sure if they would not come after him in his hotel room. *The things wey de kill people* might have the singular capacity for relocation. They could momentarily relocate, or be relocated, to a hotel room in town.

The fact that Mr. Ayuda left the room soon after accusing me of violating the oath and reneging on my promise could be an alibi in the event of my demise, Professor Johnson thought. The Professor felt for his wallet and having found it he stopped the next taxi and requested to be taken to the airport, abandoning his belongings in the hotel room. The flight for Kiba had just taken off but that was no problem. The fleeing professor could make do with an unscheduled flight on any other available flight to any other city. Luckily there was space to the country's commercial capital Leko. In less than two hours Professor Johnson was in a taxi headed to one of the airport hotels in Leko.

As he laid his head on the pillow in a hotel room in Leko, Professor Johnson felt every inch like a fugitive. He felt like a man who had cheated or stolen and was hiding in an undisclosed location far away from justice and from home. He felt that Muktar Obredu and his men might be looking for him in his hotel room in Kumbrujaa. They might have called his office in Kiba to no avail. He wished he could straight from Leko dash out of the country to join his estranged wife in Zeland. He began to regret having accepted the position of Vice Chancellor in the first instance. His peace of mind, family cohesion and joy disappeared soon after his appointment as Vice Chancellor.

Professor Johnson had not called Fiona for nearly a month prior to the latest visit to Kumbrujaa. Most of his conversations with his largely estranged wife had been lately sketchy. All he could gather from Fiona was that the children had been enrolled into schools. He had initially felt some sense of relief at the children's enrollment into schools in Zeland. But he equally knew that the implication was that they were gone for good. Education had almost collapsed in Konganoga except for a few private schools in the large cities. Even at that many of the teachers in most of those schools were also products of the flawed system of exam malpractices. It was not always easy to know who was genuinely well trained and who had bought the grades. But certainly it was not due to lack of intelligence on the part of the teachers or the students. The blame lay largely on the doorsteps of flawed governance.

Professor Johnson would have wished that he fled the system completely from his hotel room in Leko. But he knew that even such a move was fraught with problems. As he chewed his chicken in one quiet corner of the hotel's restaurant, he found the saliva in his mouth scanty and the otherwise tasty food unpalatable. Professor Johnson was an unhappy man but he knew that he must make the best of a bad situation …if only the oath Administrator Muktar Obredu would not make good his apparent promise for a pound of flesh!

Chapter 30

**DASH FOR REPARATIONS;
DINNER WITH THE DEVIL**

Professor Johnson did not narrate his experience in the office of the Special Assistant in Kumbrujaa to anyone. He did not wish to appear as a fugitive or a frightened dog that fled a hunt with its tail between its legs. He quietly slipped back into his office in Kiba and sat back on the *throne* of his fast crumbling empire. His greatest confidant, the one person that he would have narrated the story to and expected genuine sympathy and understanding from, was four thousand miles away in her country of birth Zeland.

The order that the Vice Chancellor had given to Mr. Amajide to cut back in the deductions for sustenance of the 40% League fund was still in force and had already started to yield some positive results in form of savings. These savings were already being ploughed back and were helping to restore certain amenities like increased power supply to the beleaguered University.

Professor Johnson knew that his flight from the office of the Presidential Assistant Mr. Ayuda would not go unpunished. He knew that both Mr. Ayuda and the vicious-looking Oath Administrator Mr. Muktar Obredu would be exceedingly cross with him. But he knew that he needed to be alive first to witness and possibly counter their wrath. He knew that a dead man would not be able to tell any tales. His safe arrival back to Kiba was a vindication of his wisdom in fleeing from Mr. Ayuda's office to escape a visit to the room of which Mr. Muktar Obredu had spoken thus:

"The things wey de kill people, them dey for inside that room."

Even though he had escaped from "the things wey de kill people" in Kumbrujaa, Professor Johnson knew that his escape might only be temporary. He knew that he had dined with the devil without having a long spoon. He knew that having crossed the path of the devil and having provoked the latter's wrath that he would not run far for as long as he was in the system. For the third time within one month Professor Johnson, a devout Catholic again remembered the saying in his native Akunwanta village:

"Udogwugwu egbuhu, Okpani egbuo" (If the cult Udogwugwu does not kill a transgressor, his chief priest Okpani would lend a helping hand).

Professor Johnson again expressed his firm resolve not to allow himself to be the victim of this version of Okpani which apparently was manifesting itself in the form of a man called Muktar Obredu.

Professor Johnson felt that he had come under siege and that an immediate escape was his only recourse.

With the power of the Presidential Assistant behind Mr. Muktar Obredu and the power of the Presidency behind Mr. Ayuda himself what can I do all by myself? Who will protect me and who will believe my story.

Professor Johnson asked himself.

As expected it did not take too long before a response to Professor Johnson's flight arrived from Kumbrujaa.

On the twelfth day of his return from Kumbrujaa, the Vice Chancellor while making some calls in his office was informed that an *important visitor* had arrived to see him from Kumbrujaa. The business card of the important visitor bore the name Mr. Muktar Mumudu. The majestic and unmistakable Coat of Arms of the Republic of Konganoga was beautifully embossed in green and white on Mr. Muktar Mumudu's beautiful business card. The lion and elephant symbols of the once promising Republic of Konganoga were prominently displayed on the high quality business card and the words "The Presidency" were clearly detailed below the Coat of Arms. The beautifully designed card was as neat as it was awe-inspiring.

The front desk officials as well as the personal secretary to the Vice Chancellor saw the business card and were subdued. All other protocols were immediately waived for the august visitor.

Professor Johnson was on the phone in his office chatting and giggling like a teenager. At the other end of the line was Ms Stella, one of the staff of the Admissions Department. Professor Johnson, in spite of his many problems, had developed a soft spot for Ms Stella since the departure of his wife back to Zeland.

When Titi the senior receptionist brought in the business card and dropped it on the table in front of Professor Johnson, the latter was too deeply engrossed in chitchat with his new heart throb Ms Stella. He therefore did not take immediate notice of the delivered business card.

Without looking at the business card brought in by Titi, Professor Johnson had taken hold of it and had kept rolling it between his fingers. He was laughing hilariously over the phone in the chat with Stella as he inattentively rumpled Mr. Muktar Mumudu's beautiful business card.

Titi stood in great apprehension as she saw the business card of the august visitor being rumpled inadvertently. She wished that her boss' attention could immediately be diverted away from the phone to the important business card which she had just brought in. Having seen the words "The Presidency" embossed on the card and feeling that it must be an important visitor that was waiting, Titi did not want to leave Professor Johnson's office immediately after delivering the visitor's card as she was wont to do. She had not even bothered to ask the visitor to fill out a proper visitor's form prior to her collecting the business card. The visitor's form would have stated why the visitor wanted to see the Vice Chancellor and whether there was any prior appointment with the VC as the Vice Chancellor was often called. Such protocols were however often for lesser mortals and were in most cases waived for the so-called *men of timber and caliber.*

Titi had waited behind so as to draw the Vice Chancellor's attention to the card which she had just brought in. She was also subtly interested in hearing what her boss, who had indeed only recently dated her, was saying to a possible new heart throb that was making him giggle so much and smile from ear to ear even in the midst of the mounting economic and other problems of the university.

Visitors from "The Presidency" always had a pride

of place and priority treatment wherever they visited in Konganoga. It was known that staff of Ministries that were allied to "The Presidency" often bribed their ways to be issued business cards that bore the inscription "The Presidency" on them. A few staff of other government Departments sometimes printed business cards bearing "The Presidency" on their own for greater attention and enhanced rite of passage wherever they visited in Konganoga.

As Titi would not leave the Vice Chancellors presence before the latter attended to the card which she had just brought in, Professor Johnson got a little furious and waved her away. But Titi before she left pointed the Vice Chancellor to the card which she had brought in.

Titi herself was a tall and very pretty lady who at a time commanded the attention of the Vice Chancellor before Stella came into the picture. Titi indeed was working as a sorting clerk in accounts Department before Professor Johnson directed that she be relocated as a Senior Clerk and Receptionist in the Office of the Vice Chancellor. She had noticed the entry of Stella into the Vice Chancellor's life. She knew that her former admirer was speaking to Stella that afternoon. She was certainly jealous and the entry of the important visitor from Kumbrujaa was a good excuse for her to interrupt the discussions with her rival.

Titi's insistence directed Professor Johnson's attention to the business card which he was inattentively rolling and almost mutilating between his fingers.

Professor Johnson's attention was by reflex directed to the business card following Titi's finger motion.

A single glance at the business card on his hand almost literally froze Professor Johnson. The card bore the Coat of Arms of the Federal Republic of Konganoga. It further bore in bold print the words: "The Presidency"

Worse still the card bore a name which Professor Johnson had come to dread over the many days since he first took the Oath of Allegiance to the President and the League in Mr. Ayuda's office. The card bore the name Mr. Muktar Obredu. So Professor Johnson had misread. But indeed the card bore the name Mr. Muktar Mumudu. As soon as he saw The Presidency, the Coat of Arms and the name Mr. Muktar, the next thing that entered Professor Johnson's visual center was not the word "Mumudu" but rather the word "Obredu".

An immediate transformation occurred in Professor Johnson's countenance. The phone slipped from his hands and fell off the table dangling ungainly by the cord as if inadvertently nodding mockingly in ridicule of a married man who appeared to have decided to regress into second childishness in terms of his family life.

The words that immediately erupted from Professor Johnson's lips only went to confirm the fright in the man who only a moment earlier was laughing and giggling like a twenty year old who was falling in love for the first time.

"Muktar Obredu in my office! My God, I am finished! Titi, please come back! Shut the door and bolt it."

Titi obliged her boss by locking the door. For a short while she wondered what her boss was up to. Could he have suddenly fallen out with Stella? No, the panic must have stemmed from the business card which the boss had just glanced at. Titi watched with equal apprehension the trembling lips of his boss who only a moment earlier was laughing and giggling. She was full of apprehension about what had come over her boss and what he was indeed up to.

Professor Johnson looked like a scared pupil who was

caught cheating in an examination hall. He trembled like a kidnap victim in the clutches of the ever-menacing armed robbers and kidnappers who operated almost unchecked in the increasingly unsafe streets of Kiba. He bent forward towards Titi and in a whispering tone inquired from his equally scared receptionist thus:

"Please tell me Titi, is this visitor still in the waiting room? Did he come alone or in company of other people? Is he carrying any boxes? How many and how big are his luggage? Is he armed? Did he ask any questions? Did you tell him that I am in the office?"

The barrage of questions coming in an uncoordinated sequence and not pausing for an answer only went to display the level of fear which had suddenly overcome the once powerful lord of an empire that was reeling under the crushing load of mismanagement, financial insanity and unbridled human insatiety.

Frightened by the obvious and inexplicable panic of her boss Titi started trembling.

Her fright exacerbated the fright on the face of the boss as Professor Johnson continued:

"Titi please lock the door properly. Do me a favor. Stay behind here in the room until I leave. I will explain to you at a later time. My life is in danger. Kumbrujaa's *room of death* has come around town."

Mention of "the room of death" which was a direct reference to "the things wey de kill people" as used earlier in Kumbrujaa by Mr. Muktar Obredu, made no meaning to the greatly terrified Titi but it was akin to life or death for Professor Johnson. The latter felt that having missed him in Kumbrujaa his assailants had pursued him down to Kiba through a direct visit to his office. And the pursuit was supposedly led by no other person than Muktar the Oath Administrator himself.

As Professor Johnson hurriedly gathered his eye glasses, his cell phone and his house keys from the table into the pockets of his coat, a terribly frightened Titi opened her mouth wide and was about to scream when the once solemn and reserved Professor and Vice Chancellor again pleaded:

"Please Titi I am not running away but I don't want to see this man. Stay for a few minutes while I excuse myself from the back door. Then go out and tell the visitor that Vice Chancellor is not on seat. If he insists on coming to check the office you can let him in thereafter."

As Titi still held her right palm over her mouth, and wondered who this visitor could be who had frightened the hell out of his boss, Professor Johnson donned his coat and hurriedly slipped out of his office through the back door.

Professor Johnson did not want to be seen around Kiba while the suspected Oath Administrator Muktar Obredu was in town. He did not wait to be driven down to his house by his official driver. Such a move would easily give away his whereabouts to a second party which the Vice Chancellor considered dangerous in the presence in town of a man who in his opinion had come to Kiba with the sole purpose of exacting his pound of flesh for his failure to deliver on his sworn promise. Just before he got out of the Administration Building's main block, Professor Johnson for disguise quickly removed his coat and necktie and pulled out his shirt from the trousers. He flew the shirt over the trousers in a rather careless way for further disguise. He then walked more briskly than he used to walk as a Vice Chancellor. He also removed his glasses making him look very simple and inconsequential except for his pot belly which he tried to hold in by holding his breath periodically. He then stopped by a nearby small kiosk and bought a few fruits and requested for a large-sized polythene bag into which he tucked in his wearing apparels, coat, neck tie and eye-glasses.

For further disguise Professor Johnson also started eating the guava fruits which he bought from the kiosk. This he did even without washing the guava. It was in his estimation better to be attacked by worms from the unwashed fruits than to get detected by his assailant from Kumbrujaa.

Instead of taking the campus taxi, Professor Johnson walked briskly across the street and stopped and entered a town taxi straight to a hotel in the outskirts of the city.

In a moment of great mental and physical stress such as he was going through Professor Johnson was again reduced to a reluctant fugitive by choice, for the second time in less than three months. He did not want to go to his house where he could be easily traced. He did not want to get to his village which was another likely place for a search by his assailants. He thought of calling and heading straight to the home of the lady that he was speaking with when the message about the arrival of the visitor from Kumbrujaa was delivered to him. He had dialed Stella's number and was about to request her to come home to let him in. But he quickly aborted the call realizing that people already knew about the romance that was going on between him and Stella and were likely to direct the search party from Kumbrujaa to the home of his known mistress. As an alternative Professor Johnson settled for another Stella, this time, Stella Hotel a small two star hotel that bore a similar name to the woman who was at that time very close to Professor Johnson's heart in spite of his marital status.

KONGANOGA

As Professor Johnson checked into Stella Hotel under a false name, he had a brief moment of introspection.

If anything ill should occur to me in this hideout how would I be identified and what would people eventually think of me, a highly revered professor of medicine and Head of the one biggest Federal Government establishment in the entire region?

Who would I say I was running away from? Who would be there to identify me?

In spite of his reservations Professor Johnson had checked into Stella Hotel with an assumed name, Mr. Innocent Okoko a businessman from Leko. As *Mr. Innocent Okoko* settled down to the rather poorly-kept room in Stella Hotel, for the first time in many weeks he remembered his wife Fiona who had in protest against her husband's new careless way of life relocated along with the children to her home country Zeland.

Professor Johnson remembered how proud and contented he was as a Professor of ophthalmology living happily with his wife and three children. He recognized that he did not have or control much money but that he was happy and much fulfilled. Now, he figured, he had power, position and money as a Vice Chancellor. But he had lost his independence, his cheerful looks his innocence and most importantly his family. He had had to check into a fairly run down hotel room in disguise lest some executor of a murderous oath-taking from Kumbrujaa would catch up with him and execute the wordings of the oath of allegiance and control which he had sworn to.

Professor Johnson sat up on the single bed in his *emergency* hotel room and again recounted his ordeal.

He knew that he had not committed any offence known

to law and yet he was on the run. He knew that he could run but could not hide.

He knew that the measures he was taking, slipping out of his office to avoid meeting a man who knew his name, his address, his contacts and virtually everything else about him was futile and puerile. He knew that the man with the power of the Presidency behind him could afford to lay siege on his office until he surfaced. He knew that he had been hemmed in. He acknowledged to himself that the options open to him in the face of his commitment to the League and his abysmal failure in the administration of the University as Vice Chancellor would forever haunt him. Professor Johnson felt like a fleeing robber that had been chased into a cul-de-sac.

For the first time since the loss of his father over twenty years earlier, in the face of the unfolding scenario of loss of his family and the looming loss of the position for which he had mortgaged his conscience, the once ebullient and highly respected Professor of ophthalmology fell back in bed and wept.

Chapter 31

MAKING THE BEST OF A BAD SITUATION

Fiona had enrolled her three children back into school in Zeland. The school curriculum in Konganoga was fashioned after the Zeland system since Konganoga was a colonial creation of Zeland.

The children did not find difficulty fitting into classes since they had no difficulty understanding the language which was indeed their *mother tongue*. Fiona did a lot of teaching lessons for the children at home from the little time that she could squeeze.

Her Konganogan law degree was recognized in Zeland but she needed to do some refresher courses before she could be allowed to take the Zeland bar exams to be allowed full license to practice.

It was not easy for her trying to find her footing again in a system from which she had been absent for so long a time. It would have been easier for her to get back into the nursing profession for which she had a Zeland practicing license. Bu having practiced law in Konganoga and having enjoyed what she saw she decided to quit nursing in favor of law.

It certainly was not easy but Fiona had decided to weather the storm especially as her mother Mrs. Fergus was still strong enough to take charge of the children while she struggled with studies.

For long periods after Fiona departed Konganoga for Zeland Professor Johnson was seething with anger that his children were literally taken away from him to Zeland by their mother without full consultations with him. Much as he did not fully approve of the journey he knew he could not afford to object too strongly without incurring the wrath of the law and condemnation from his neighbors many of who had already taken sides with Fiona while the Vice Chancellor position took the greater hold on Professor Johnson.

What pissed Fiona off the most was the fact that Okon did not care to take them up to the airport. On the morning of the family's departure to the airport Professor Johnson had deliberately left the house very early in the morning leaving his wife and three children to get down to the airport by a self-arranged public transport. Indeed the children were still in bed when Professor Johnson left the house. He did not as much as care to say farewell.

Okon himself was under the impression that taking Fiona and the children to the airport would give the wrong impression that he endorsed or condoned Fiona's un-Konganogan decision to take the children away from their biological father or without the former's expressed permission.

He did not appear to have also considered Fiona's sensibilities.

Fiona had considered formal divorce from Okon after her two letters to Okon were not replied to. She did not feel that the differences between them were irreconcilable. She had felt that some moment of living apart from each other would perhaps rekindle the desire of one for the other. She remembered the aphorism in her native Zeland which stated that absence makes the heart grow fonder. She did not however fully reckon with the many fair weather friends and gold diggers who milled around her husband's place of work. She apparently overestimated the ability of the Okon Johnson that she knew to resist such temptations from the ubiquitous daughters of Eve many of who roamed the main campus of the Federal University of Science and Technology Kiba.

On second thought about the divorce issue however, Fiona had decided to let the situation linger for a while so that she would bring up the children up a little more.

When Okon recovered from the great distress of taking shelter in a shabby hotel room in disguise, there persisted only one person in his mind who he could call and confide in at that moment of need. He had dialed Stella and requested her to come down immediately to Stella Hotel. He had requested her to keep her movement top secret until he ascertained that the suspected Oath Administrator had left his office.

It was getting late in the evening and Professor Johnson knew that he did not tidy things up in his office. All sorts of ideas had entered his mind. These ranged from absconding from the hotel room and taking a flight out of the country to escape the assured pursuit by the men from Kumbrujaa. But then he considered the permanent damage that such a move would do to his reputation and his career. He knew that *come what may* that his progression to the position of

Professor and Vice Chancellor was only because he was in Konganoga. He remembered that if he remained in Zeland that the competition would have been much more acute ad that he would never have been able to make even the position of a senior lecturer at the same time frame. Again Professor Johnson recognized that even with his marrying from Zeland and even in spite of the subtle discriminations that he had endured in the Federal University Kiba that it would be very difficult for him to be fully accepted in Zeland. He easily recognized that his best bet was to remain in his native country Konganoga unless it became impossible to function there.

Even when he did not completely shed the possibility of an eventual escape back to Zeland to try rejoining Fiona, Professor Johnson had decided to fall back to Stella's company and confidence.

"Stella, it's me. I am a guest in Stella Hotel in Harbor Road. Could you straight way take a cab and come down. Please make your movement strictly secret." Professor Johnson told Stella in a phone call to her.

"But Prof, what is it that went wrong. There is this fast circulating rumor this afternoon that you ran away from your office a short while ago because some detectives were after you from Kumbrujaa. I have been very worried. People are gathered in small groups in the University discussing this. A few of my friends have already called me to ask whether I heard." Stella told Professor Johnson with an obvious trembling voice.

As Stella settled down to a chair in the not-so-cozy hotel room of the married older man who had been dating her for some three months, she saw a frightened and near-broken man who looked every inch a shadow of his old ebullient self.

Professor Johnson was still in his purposely-disheveled state which he had assumed for greater disguise while leaving the University environment. Stella who had always seen the Vice Chancellor in his well-kitted-up state could not quite recognize the University boss at first when she entered the single hotel room.

Professor Johnson did not go into any details. The worried look on the face of the Vice Chancellor had suggested a man who had a lot of stories to tell. But this was not to be so with the obviously very intelligent and calculated Professor of ophthalmology who had weathered many storms in the past. None of Professor Johnson's experiences however compared with the prevailing situation in which an Oath Administrator had apparently come for his pound of flesh from him who had sworn with a Bible, a loaded gun and adjacent to the room which harbored *'the things wey de kill people.'* There was every reason for any delinquent of such an oath to fear for the worst.

"I would like you to take a trip back to the University and check out my office. Without declaring your mission find out whether the man from Kumbrujaa has left. The man's name is Muktar, Mr. Muktar Obredu. But you will feign ignorance of that name. Get into a conversation with the receptionists especially the one called Titi. Gather as much information as you can and get back to me by phone."

Professor Johnson then dipped his hand into his pocket and gave a hundred dollar bill to Stella.

"This will cover your transport and other costs." Professor Johnson said.

His days of struggle in and out of job in Zeland had fashioned Professor Johnson into a fund-conserving man. Even Stella during her dates with the Vice Chancellor had easily observed the fact that this Professor and Vice Chancellor was rather too conservative with his dollars. She had stuck with the much older and married man not necessarily out of love but more with the hope that the association would earn her the much needed uplift in her job. She was aware of how her rival Titi had prospered with rapid promotions and improvement in her job placement because of her association with the Vice Chancellor who appeared to be getting more randy by the day since after the exit of his wife Fiona.

Professor Johnson had become increasingly paranoid and suspicious of people since after his stint in the Department of ophthalmology and his rift with Dr Ezemtubo the pharmacologist.

He had also learnt from stories he had often heard since he became chief executive not to make his location readily and generally accessible to people. He had heard several stories of hired killers and stalkers. And much as he did not intend to become reclusive he did not appear to trust even Stella well enough to keep her mouth completely shut about his location which he had reluctantly revealed to her.

He started conjuring in his brain a scenario in which Stella would get back to the University compound and tell one or two friends that she had just been with the Vice Chancellor and the story would filter into the ears of people in his office and subsequently into the ears of Mr. Muktar Obredu (or the man who was mistaken for Mr. Muktar Obredu). He imagined a scenario in which the dreaded Oath Administrator would, within a few hours of his checking into Stella Hotel, also check into the same hotel and stalk him until he left or even complete the mission for which apparently he had come looking for him.

After Stella had left the hotel room Professor Johnson decided to take a closer look at the business card which Titi had handed over to him in his office to announce the presence of the suspected Mr. Muktar Obredu. Unfortunately the Professor in his haste to escape from the office had dropped Mr. Muktar Mumudu's card on his table after rolling it around his fingers before he read the dreaded name "Muktar".

A closer look at the card would have confirmed to Professor Johnson that the emissary from Kumbrujaa who he was running away from was indeed Muktar Mumudu and not Muktar Obredu. Such a discovery would perhaps have lessened the embattled Vice Chancellor's apprehension.

Professor Johnson had not stayed more than three hours in his hotel room when he decided to leave. His reason was that he did not want to leave a trail just in case Stella opened her mouth too wide.

With no luggage except the polythene bag stuffed with his jacket and his neck tie and a few fruits the guest Mr. Innocent Okoko again walked down to the front desk, paid his bill with cash and checked out of the hotel room. He did not wish to use his credit card for obvious reasons.

Not sure of other cash needs that he might have along the way, Professor Johnson walked across a nearby ATM and cashed some money. He would not want to pay certain bills with his credit or debit card until he was sure that he was not being stalked.

As he stood waiting for a taxi, Professor Johnson overheard two ladies discussing and repeatedly mentioning the name of University of Kiba. That abbreviation was what the Federal University of Science and Technology Kiba was known as by the local population.

Professor Johnson's interest having been sufficiently aroused, he tarried a while and eavesdropped.

One of the ladies told the other that stories were all over the university that the Vice Chancellor of the famous University was on the run after security operatives swopped on his office.

Professor Johnson wished he could hear more. He was even tempted to get into the conversation and ask the ladies for more details. He was however worried that he could easily be identified. He therefore decided to make do with the much information that he had heard and move on.

He walked across to the next hotel around the corner and decided to check in to recollect himself and to reflect. The latter hotel was much smaller than Stella hotel but was certainly newer and neater. This time Professor Johnson decided to check in with his actual name. He figured that it was dangerous to keep using false names just in case there was an accident or something that would necessitate correct identification. "After all, I am not a wanted man and I have no reason but for foolish fear, for which I should have absconded from my office." Professor Johnson said.

Having checked into the room as Benjamin Okon Johnson, Professor Johnson settled down in his room and decided to reflect. Benjamin was his middle name which Professor Johnson rarely used. He found it expedient to use it at this time as his first name.

Professor Johnson tuned on the TV in his room to have the greatest surprise he ever had. On the TV screen was his photograph. The news was that the Vice Chancellor of the Federal University of Science and Technology Kiba suddenly absconded from his office following a visit from some officers from Kumbrujaa. It was a mere news summary. Professor Johnson wished to heaven that he could get the full news. His heart beat faster and more forcefully.

After taking a cold shower and a hot cup of coffee professor Johnson contacted his lawyer and narrated the episode to him. He however only narrated how he left his office stealthily and what he had just heard in the news. He carefully left out the aspect that dealt with his encounter with the Oath Administrator in Kumbrujaa. The latter was a well guarded secret which only the ears of Fiona had heard.

"I have committed no offences and I am very sure about this" Professor Johnson told his lawyer. I only left my office because I did not wish to deal with the persistent demands of these chaps from Kumbrujaa" Professor Johnson further advised his lawyer.

The lawyer had advised Professor Johnson to get back to his office immediately so that it would not be misconstrued that he was a fugitive.

Emboldened by the advice of his lawyer, Professor Johnson who had within a space of a mere twenty four hours lost quite some weight, dressed up neatly and was at the premises of the university by 8.30 AM the following day.

It looked like an eternity. The university was swarming with activity. News men appeared to have laid an overnight siege on the entire campus scooping for news, interviewing students and staff and reporting back almost on hourly basis to their offices.

Professor Johnson had driven to the administration building incognito in a rented vehicle ostensibly to evade the prying lens of newsman. But the escape was not quite successful. As soon as he alighted from the rented car

Professor Johnson saw newsmen chasing him and almost sticking microphones to his lips.

Professor Johnson who ordinarily was publicity shy kept mute until one newsman asked him:
"Sir, it is alleged that you promised to make returns of 50% of the monthly budget of the university to your backers in Kumbrujaa, what do you say to that?"
Professor Johnson was stunned. He initially said "No Comments" but realizing how damaging the allegation might be, he added:
"Where did you get those figures from?"
Another newsman had followed up the question with another question thus:
"Sir there is this other allegation that you ran away from your office because you made the deductions from the University and failed to remit same to your backers in Kumbrujaa; is that the true situation Sir?"

Even in spite of Professor Johnson's earlier decision to leave the details of his Kumbrujaa trips secret, the vivid details which the journalist had introduced meant that the stories had leaked and that he needed to correct any exaggerations or excesses in the story. Besides, he felt that it would be counterproductive to keep mute or pretend that all was well even when the other party was busy dishing out exaggerated aspects of the story. Professor Johnson knew that he told the story of his Kumbrujaa experience only to his wife. Mr. Amajide knew only the sketchy aspects of the Kumbrujaa agreement. The only source from which the story could have leaked to the press therefore must have been through the office of the Assistant to the President and most likely through the most dreaded of them all, Mr. Muktar Obredu himself.

Professor Johnson would not like to have any contest with Mr. Muktar Obredu. Indeed the name Muktar sent shivers through his spine and that was why he misread the name Muktar Mumudu for Muktar Obredu. A rift or dialogue with Mr. Johnson Ayuda the Assistant to the President would have been preferred by Professor Johnson. A rift or dialogue with near illiterate oath administrators the likes of Mr. Muktar Obredu, in Professor Johnson's opinion, was not only reprehensible but was also certainly to be avoided.

The journalist had repeated the question which Professor Johnson had parried:

"Sir, is the allegation of a 50% kickback to Kumbrujaa true or false?"

There was no hiding place for Professor Johnson who not only did not want the question to linger on but also wanted to put an end to all future speculations about any such deals.

Professor Johnson paused for a short while and then in a low and calculated voice replied:

"Not so sir! Certainly not 50%!"

The vague answer of course prompted more questions.

"What then is true Sir? Which version should the public believe?"

A dialogue had inexorably developed, one which Professor Johnson would have liked to avoid as the latter replied:

"Unfortunately the public is free and should be free to believe what they wish to believe. But there is certainly no truth in the 50% story."

Professor Johnson was about to beat his chest that he had deftly parried the vexing question of kickback. But then another prominent journalist from the *Konganoga Guardian* one of the most prominent national dailies shouted another question:

"Mr. Vice Chancellor, will you contest a documented evidence of a 40% or 50% kickback deal?"

There was silence among the group of journalists and a few staff of the university who had assembled at the spot.

There was no parrying the question which was not only outstanding and direct but was also asked at a very auspicious moment when all else was very quiet.

The crucial part of the question asked was "Will you contest the 40% or 50% kickback deal?" It was relatively easy for Professor Johnson to parry the question of a 40% or 50% kickback by denying the 50% aspect while remaining silent on the 40% aspect.

But the question from the erudite journalist from the Konganoga Guardian had tied the two figures by asking whether the Vice Chancellor would contest documented evidence of a 40% or 50% kickback deal.

The mere mention of documented evidence demonstrated to Professor Johnson that there must have been evidence which was available to the journalist or his associates or sources.

The question reverberated in Professor Johnson's ears: "Will you contest a documented evidence of a 40% or 50% kickback deal?"

Professor Johnson from his many years of dealing with students and various kinds of gatherings of intellectuals had come to know that the best way to generate interest in a question was by parrying the question or trying to dodge it. He also knew that interest could be generated by *dancing* around a question or by refusing to answer it. He had come to realize that it was always easier to downplay a vexing question by answering it even if incorrectly than to try to avoid it or by dismissing it outright. The latter solution would inevitably re-invite the question often in another form.

And so Professor Johnson in an apparent offhanded manner tried to give as direct a reply to the question as he could. And so he said:

"Ladies and Gentlemen of the Press, 40% kickback from the coffers of any institution will certainly cripple that institution."

The professor had hoped that his reply was simple and straightforward enough and that it would settle the issue. He was wrong. Rather than settle the issue the direct response fuelled more questions. All hope that the factual but indiscreet reply would settle the issue was dashed for Professor Johnson when the follow up question came from the same journalist:

"So, professor, is 40% kickback occurring at the Federal University of Science and Technology Kiba?"

Professor Johnson was at first stunned stiff by the latter direct question. He remained silent for a while before he responded.

A more indiscreet but killer response then came from Professor Johnson. His many years in public administration had taught him quite some new lessons. He was beginning to learn the art of public speech diplomacy and talking from both sides of his mouth.

He then replied:

"Gentlemen your guess will be as good as mine!" With that response Professor Johnson disappeared into his office.

Chapter 32

THE LIMITS OF DIPLOMACY

Dr Johnson was back to his office from a temporary self-imposed vagabond status. He had heaved a sigh of relief as he sat back on his throne behind his large table and the large pack of files that had accumulated during his short period of absence. It all looked like a dream. But certainly to think that he had to escape from his office through the back door at the mere mention of a name of a suspected oath administrator appeared so unreal to him. It looked like a dream. But if it was a dream it must be a very costly dream.

If the flight did nothing else it had brought to the fore a topic which Professor Johnson had least intended to discuss. The issue of 40% kickback which he had sworn to was one that he thought was shrouded in utmost secrecy since it was done in the privacy of the office of the Assistant to His Excellency the President.

But an agent of the Assistant had come calling and the

fright that he generated had generated a chain of events which started with the flight of the Vice Chancellor and culminated in the massive presence of the members of the Press in the University Campus.

As professor Johnson reclined back on his seat he began to ask himself the question:
"Why did I have to behave so cowardly? Why did I not face up to Mr. Muktar Obredu since this time he had come to my office? Why did I allow Titi into the picture? Why didn't I just slip out through the back door if I must flee?"

It was while he sat there deep in thought that professor Johnson's attention was caught by a note written on a memo sheet. The sheet had been placed on Professor Johnson's table by the office secretary on a rack marked "For Immediate Attention". The memo had as header the bold inscription: "The Presidency." The unmistakable Coat of Arms of the Federal Republic of Konganoga was at the top center position of the memo sheet.

The power which a combination of the Coat of Arms and the sign "The Presidency" wielded, had become something of an enigma to many senior government officials especially in the States outside of Kumbrujaa the capital of Konganoga. The Coat of Arms and its twin brother "The Presidency" constituted the emblem of ultimate power of the State and it often foretold great things either for good or for ill. The twin signs would ordinarily be the harbingers of some form of evil, threats or command. If they conveyed something useful, commendable or graceful then in more cases than not a big price must have been paid either in form of gratification or promise of same.

Indeed Professor Johnson himself a year earlier in one of the talks that he gave in a symposium had stated thus:

"Most times before a document bearing the Coat of Arms would come for good some money would be expected to have exchanged hands. If it should come freely as a harbinger for good, in most instances, it would be a big surprise."

The professor was severely criticized by the government-owned radio and television for making that statement. He had at that time been made to withdraw that statement under penalty of his losing his senior position as a staff of a government-owned tertiary institution. He had made the withdrawal even when he strongly believed in what he had written.

The contents of the official memo awaiting Professor Johnson's attention were unambiguous. The Vice Chancellor was asked to report to the Assistant to the president in Room 404 of the Federal Administration complex Kumbrujaa not later than 72 hours from the date of the letter. On arrival Professor Johnson was to report to one Mr. Muktar Obredu!

The letter was signed by one Mr. Muktar Mumudu.

The complimentary card which was brought in for Professor Johnson while he was talking to Stella, the same complimentary card which Professor Johnson was rumpling on his fingers and whose misread name tag had chased the professor away from his office was neatly arranged by the office clerk at one corner of the Vice chancellor's office table. It was from that complimentary card and the name on the memo sheet that Professor Johnson realized for the first time that the name for which he ran away from his office two days earlier, was indeed Mr. Muktar Mumudu and not Mr. Muktar Obredu the dreaded Oath Administrator. Mr. Muktar Mumudu must have been a lesser devil than the man Mr. Muktar Obredu who sent him. But Professor Johnson had got so paranoid about the name Muktar that mere sight or hearing of that name was enough to conjure up the surname Obredu.

It was after comparing the names on the complimentary card and the memo sheet that Professor Johnson realized that he was a few days earlier running away from an emissary of Mr. Muktar Obredu. Now he was being more or less ordered to report in person to the much dreaded Mr. Muktar Obredu himself. Professor Johnson again immediately remembered the statement from Mr. Muktar Obredu during the Professor's last visit to Kumbrujaa: "The things wey de kill people, them dey for inside that room."

Even when he had taken a decision to remain strong, a second wave of fear and apprehension seized Professor Johnson. He was born and raised as a Catholic and had practiced the Christian religion all his life. He was never fanatical about religion and had indeed occasionally seen religion and the deeply religious as an institution and a people who were somehow weird or who were or might be on the brink of some psychological problems.

Since the departure of Fiona back to Zeland Professor Johnson had indeed slipped further away from religion and had often remembered his prayers only when he was in some form of troubles.

Now the renewed problem of Muktar Obredu had reared its ugly head again.

Professor Johnson shut his eyes for a while. He ruminated for a while over his entire tenure in the various positions in the university commencing from the moment of his first appointment as a lecturer after his rejection at the interview in Zeland to the time of his meteoric rise that culminated in his appointment as the Vice Chancellor of the University. He acknowledged that he had not set out to soil his hands

He realized that it was merely the system that was pushing him to extremes in diverting as much as 40% of the revenue of the institution that he had sworn to serve into the pockets of some economic vultures in governance. He knew that there was not likely to be any reprieve and that the situation could only get worse as long as the powers that were in control in Kumbrujaa were on seat. He also acknowledged that those powers that were in power would only continue in power at least for some time since the chances were that they would only continue to be in power as they would invariably recycle themselves in the absence of any credible elections.

Finally Professor Johnson ruminated over the state of his family. He remembered his wife Fiona. He remembered his three lovely kids. He knew that the departure of Fiona and the life of virtual separation which he was living were not unconnected with his new position as Vice Chancellor. He tried to exonerate his developing randy relationships and the crass immorality of diversion of University funds by blaming these on the exigencies of office. But again he acknowledged that the situation might not last forever and that he would sooner or later have to relinquish the position of Vice Chancellor whenever it suited his Kumbrujaa overlords who appointed him to relieve him of that position.

Professor Johnson was a very intelligent man. He could easily read the hand writing on the wall. He was afraid of Mr. Muktar Obredu. He would not wish to be subjected to the shenanigans of a barely-educated native medicine man who was hoisted within the premises of a high government official to terrorize, intimidate and extort concessions from other government officials and appointees and beat them into shape as it might please the political overlords. He knew that Mr. Muktar Obredu might wish to find fun with trying out all sorts of tricks and magic on him simply because he had wanted to remain as Vice Chancellor. He knew that he had already fallen short of the tenets of the oath which he swore over the Bible and a loaded Dane gun. He reasoned that the visit of an emissary from Mr. Muktar Obredu to him soon after he halted the return of full 40% of the University revenue was not a mere coincidence. He reasoned that the timing of the visit was a sure reminder to him Professor Johnson that he had fallen short of the agreed terms of his appointment. The visit of the emissary of Mr. Muktar Obredu was directly in connection with the shortfall in the agreed 40% monthly revenue.

And now he, a very senior government official a professor of medicine and a Vice Chancellor of a University, a chief executive of a tertiary institution and the highest Central Government official in the State was being directed to proceed to Kumbrujaa and to report to a native medicine man who was christened as an Oath Administrator who was not up to the rank of his office attendants.

The embattled Vice Chancellor then reasoned thus:

This is certainly the ultimate humiliation. I know that the idea is to break my will. They will take great pleasure in disgracing me out of office if they cannot get me to steal on their behalf. They will thereafter plead as the innocent ones in case of an inquiry.

The ultimate is the relinquishing of office and they may want me to do so in disgrace. I may have to do so but on my own terms. I will disappoint them by complying with their wish but at my own time, the place of my wish and on my own terms."

Since the onset of rot and decay in the university the circle of friends of the Vice Chancellor had continued to diminish. It was a highly intellectual society and a lot of the senior members of staff of the institution knew of the returns being made monthly from the coffers of the University to the powers that were operative in Kumbrujaa. They did not know the details but they knew that huge amounts of money were paid out into the accounts of some fictitious characters who would be said to have completed certain contract jobs. It was even rumored especially among the junior workers that Professor Johnson used to share the money with the overlords in Kumbrujaa. It was believed that Professor Johnson did not complain about the deteriorating situation because he was benefitting from the sleaze. But deep within him Professor Johnson knew too well that apart from the patronage which he received in being appointed Vice Chancellor without any strong godfather behind him that he had indeed never benefitted directly or indirectly from the remittances that were made monthly to Kumbrujaa.

Perhaps the only benefit that Professor Johnson knew that he could truly be said to be receiving was that he was allowed complete free hand in the management of the University. As long as he continued to remit the required 40% of the institution's revenue as kick back, it would not have mattered to the powers that were in Kumbrujaa if Professor Johnson and his acolytes stole another 40% or 50% into their bank accounts. But Professor Johnson even if he were predisposed to steal, knew that the 40% *returns* to Kumbrujaa was already severely hurting the University. Any more deductions would certainly lead to certain collapse. And Professor Johnson would not want the institution to collapse on his hands, not after his friends and benefactors like Professor Kemji had successfully shepherded the institution to maturity before him.

Convinced about his innocence and eager to demonstrate that he was "clean" as far as embezzlement of funds or self enrichment was concerned, Professor Johnson had summoned a meeting of some top professors and Deans in the University to brief them on his efforts "to stem the tide of decline in the University."

Professor Johnson had also sought to use the opportunity of a meeting with the Deans to let them have a little insight into his administrative handicaps "Just in case the expected happens and (he) would not be coming back as Vice Chancellor."

Of the twenty six Deans and other professors that Professor Johnson invited to the meeting only fourteen turned up. So much had the Vice Chancellor's image sunk that many top academic staff openly defied his orders or openly shunned him as "a rubber stamp and stooge of the political powers in Kumbrujaa."

No good reasons were given by the absentees to the meeting. To those that came Professor Johnson had tried to be as candid as official protocol, libel and ordinary decency would allow. The embattled Vice Chancellor more or less was walking between the devil and the deep sea. He was not sure about the intentions of the authorities in Kumbrujaa. On the other hand despite the smiles and the compliments and camaraderie that were freely exchanged Professor Johnson and the other Professors had little love lost between them. Some of the other professors felt that they were senior to Professor Johnson in the system. Some others felt that Dr Johnson used the opportunity of the ready availability of cases for publication in his specialty to pad his curriculum vitae so much that he got promoted professor rather too early. The Professor of Fine Arts who for instance took very long before he could be promoted professor based on his alleged inability to publish papers based on his drawings was particularly hostile at first but had to be pacified with jokes and pleadings for understanding from Professor Johnson.

The Vice Chancellor looked sullen and harassed even when he tried to put up a cheerful mien. He attempted to crack some jokes and lighten the prevailing air of moodiness that had for some time enveloped the university environment. Since the monthly 40% deduction from the university resources under Professor Johnson started the fortunes of the academic community had plummeted. The quality of the infrastructure had nosedived. There were rampant complaints from staff and students alike.

Appeals to the Vice Chancellor and demands for explanations fell on deaf ears. Information had filtered from staff of the bursary and accounts departments about how University funds monthly found their way into the coffers of agencies that were set up by operatives in Kumbrujaa.

Indeed staff of the bursary who daily witnessed the drain while their salaries were being owed had developed the habit of greeting each other every morning they arrived at work with the slogan: "Monkey de work!" On hearing the three-word greeting the other party would immediately respond thus: "Baboon de chop." And so, as far as the staff of the university community under the Vice Chancellorship of Professor Okon Johnson was concerned, it was simply "Monkey de work, baboon de chop!" It was certainly not a very healthy slogan and the debilitating effects manifested in virtually everything in the university from declining academic performance to dilapidating infrastructure.

Expectedly the productivity was only to plummet in an institution where the staff had got so disillusioned with the frustrated greeting of "monkey de work, baboon de chop." And it did, so rapidly that revenue collection dwindled to less than 30% of its pre-Johnson era with disastrous consequences.

Professor Johnson's address to the gathering of deans and professors started without any preambles. The Vice Chancellor knew only too well that his rating among the staff and students was at its lowest ebb. He had seen the administration collapsing on his hands. He had initially tried to redeem the situation by cutting back on the percentage of monthly deductions going to the authorities in Kumbrujaa. He knew by doing the latter that he was going against the agreement which he swore to with the Bible and the loaded gun and under the watchful eyes of the dreaded Oath Administrator Mr. Muktar Obredu. He had embarked on a salvage mission knowing full well the consequences of such blatant defiance of a loaded gun. He knew full well the consequences of reneging on a promise made to ravaging politicians and their stooges and acolytes, men and women who had no qualms whatsoever in mauling the polity.

It was not in Professor Johnson's character to be a thief of public funds, a stooge of the powers that be, a licker of boots or a pawn at the disposal of some overbearing and patronizing godfather. When he was appointed Vice Chancellor up from the position of Chairman of the Tin Mining Company of Konganoga he had taken it to be an acknowledgment of the good work that he did at the former post. He was exhilarated and had characteristically decided to give his all to the pursuit of excellence. But then the invitation to Kumbrujaa came up. And the Bible, the Koran and the loaded gun on a trolley were laid bare before him. And the room within which lay "the thing wey de kill man" was there by the corner. And the erudite professor of ophthalmology whose appointment as Vice Chancellor had been so greatly orchestrated and publicized was standing in a room alone before the agent of death and the Oath Administrator. And the man who with his ophthalmoscope had looked into the depths of so many eyes, now with his own two naked eyes looked at the agent of death and was asked to choose. Ostensibly he had the freedom to choose or refuse to abide by a decision to relinquish 40% of the monthly revenue accruing to his institution to the powers that appointed him.

Ostensibly Professor Johnson had made the decision to say "No!" But Professor Johnson was only human. To say "No!" was permissible. But was it feasible, especially under the circumstances?

To say "No!", as Professor Johnson knew only too well, might be tantamount to saying "Yes!" to *justified enemy action* from the loaded gun. The action might not come directly. But it had in the past been known to come indirectly. An announcement over the state-controlled radio station that a certain professor and Vice Chancellor was attacked and murdered by armed robbers in his house or in the streets of Kumbrujaa or Kiba would only be one of the many similar stories that had become only too common in the news that emanated from Kumbrujaa. The megacity had inexorably degenerated to one huge Sicily where, in the past the only sure way of staying alive was to conform, remain silent or to go underground.

Yes, Professor Johnson had the option of saying "No!" even as he literally looked into the barrels of a loaded gun. But again the erudite professor was only human. He had worked into the offices of the Assistant to the President as a professor and Vice Chancellor of a Federal University.

He did not wish to walk out as only a professor, a non-professor, or indeed on a stretcher en-route a morgue.

Some of the powers that were in Kumbrujaa at the time had no qualms. They often acted as outlaws. They had the powers of coercion and persuasion. They could look the civilized world in the face and tell barefaced lies. They did not come to power with the mandate of the people. They therefore owed little or nothing to the people.

Professor Johnson, therefore even in spite of himself and his convictions had opted to conform. He had therefore sworn allegiance, not to the flag or the nation Konganoga. No, he had sworn allegiance to the powers that were. And he had done so using a benign agent of life and a malignant agent of death.

And so, that day in the Chambers of the University Council, the Vice Chancellor had addressed the gathering of Deans and Professors, those who either out of some tenuous respect or out of pure curiosity had heeded his call.

Standing, not on the podium but on the floor at the same level with his colleagues in the once revered ivory tower, Professor Johnson had addressed the gathering thus:

"My fellow teachers and administrators,

I have summoned you Ladies and Gentlemen to brief you, not on the situation in the University as far as learning and infrastructure are concerned since you already know about these, but on efforts that we are making to set things right. I also wish to bare my mind to you, and rub minds with you about whatever misgivings and grievances that any of us may have against the other." Professor Johnson had started.

The initial silence gave way to a few grumblings and one or two hisses. But Professor Johnson had continued:

"I speak to you not just as Vice Chancellor but more so as one of you who has a strong stake in the education of our people. I take full responsibility for the failings of this institution since I happen to be the chief servant of this institution and would have taken glory if we had succeeded."

As Professor Johnson paused to take a look at the countenances of his listeners he could not make much out of their faces. But he needed no seer to let him know that his audience was only sneering at his crocodile tears. Most of his listeners knew the true story behind the falling standards and deterioration of infrastructure in their cherished institution. They had relations or friends or at least informants who fed them with almost the day to day happenings in the accounts department.

A few more religious ones among the listeners only took sympathy at the Vice Chancellor. They saw him as a man who had inadvertently dined with the devil with a short spoon.

Some felt that rather than condemnation that the vice Chancellor needed redemption. They wished that they possessed the means to cast out the devil in him and the multiple demons with whom he obviously was associating. But then they knew that the demons were in far away Kumbrujaa and that they too were employees of the demons directly or indirectly. They therefore were handicapped even if they had wanted to deliver their Vice Chancellor. They themselves could get their fingers burnt in the process. They therefore sat there and listened as the primary victim tried unsuccessfully to bare his mind.

Professor Johnson did not have much explanation to do. He had very little to offer his audience except an acknowledgment that he held himself culpable for the failings in the system. Besides that he had little else to say. It would have been more heartening for him to assure his audience that the situation would improve soon. But the situation would certainly not improve soon, not when a good percentage of the dwindling resources of the University had to be shifted back by stealth to some voluptuous leaders and politicians in Kumbrujaa. It would have been more reassuring for the vice Chancellor to say thus:

From now on, I wish to assure you that all the resources meant for the university would be channeled towards services of the university.

That sort of statement would have elicited good applause. But the Vice Chancellor did not say that. He could not have said that; certainly not when the Sword of Damocles was hanging over his neck in form of the oath which he had sworn to.

By the time the Vice Chancellor completed his short address it was obvious that he had little or nothing new to offer to the expectant professors and deans. He did not promise them a radical change in the fortunes of their beloved institution, the livewire of their economic existence.

Some of the Vice Chancellor's listeners had expected that since he had accepted responsibility for the failures in the university that he would offer to resign. They expected that he would have told them that if things did not improve by a certain time frame that he would resign. But people of Professor Johnson's tribe hardly ever tendered their resignation. Even when their world was collapsing over their heads all through their fault, they never resigned. They would rather sit tight and feign ignorance of the problem. They could alternatively attempt to blame their failings on their subordinates, the system or any other person but themselves.

Chapter 33

THE LAST STRAW

Professor Johnson had left his hotel room in the Kumbrujaa hotel where he had lodged preparatory to his invitation to meet with Mr. Muktar Obredu. His letter of invitation had indicated that he would meet Mr. Obredu preparatory to his meeting with officials of the Ministry of Education which oversaw the running of all Federal Universities.

Professor Johnson knew that the proposed meeting with officials of the Minister of Education was only a diversionary tactic. He knew that the major reason he was being invited to Kumbrujaa was his failure to continue to fulfill the 40% monthly deduction as kickback to the "gods of Kumbrujaa" as the top officials of the government in power were often called.

A proposed meeting with the officials of the Federal Ministry of Education was only an embellishment.

Unlike during his very first visit when he was feted and treated like a prince, Professor Johnson was this time on his own from the airport to the hotel and to the office of the Assistant to the President where Mr. Muktar Obredu had his office.

Banters were exchanged between the visiting Vice Chancellor and the officers in the front room of the Presidential Assistant's office. The front desk officers were in the habit of receiving lots of gratification from visitors to the boss. More often than not, gratifications and other gifts offered to the front room officers facilitated access to the Assistant to the President. Persistent failure to appreciate the people in the front office might result in the response thus: "The Assistant is not on seat."

But ironically even after the statement declaring the Assistant not to be on seat, if money suddenly exchanged hands between the visitor and the front room officers, the Assistant would suddenly be on seat!

In his first few years after his return from Zeland Dr Johnson would never give gratification to anybody to have people perform jobs for which they were employed.

He would usually tell people: "That's your job!"

Over the course of time however the Konganogan professor who was married to a Zelander had come to realize that in Konganoga that the statement "That's your job" would almost always result in the job not being done. Complaints to the boss would hardly ever rectify the situation as the boss himself might be expecting some gratification too. If he did not get his gratification directly from the customer, he would seek to get it by way of *returns* through the subordinate staff. Thus the senior police officer at a police check point would sit in duty car and look away as his subordinate officer fleeced motorists. He would expect to have his subordinate officer make account at the end of the day. A motorist complaining to the senior officer about the activities of his subordinate officer would be a waste of time or might even complicate matters for the complainant.

Collection of gratification by officers in, and outside their duty posts was not a new phenomenon in Konganoga. Even Professor Johnson could remember stories which his uncle who was a police officer during the latter colonial days used to tell him. The officer had narrated stories about how as young officers, he and his colleagues often cut holes in the pockets of their baggy police trousers. Through those holes some of the money that they collected from motorists would drop into some secret inner pockets which they had sewn inside their trousers. At the end of each shift the young officers were required to empty their pockets on a table in the presence of their superior officers. The latter through the shift, had stood at a distance and watched their subordinate officers fleece motorists and deposit the proceeds directly into their pockets. While the money from the emptied pockets would be shared between the junior officer and the superior officers, the money that had dropped into the inner secret pocket through the hole cut in the pocket, would belong solely to the subordinate officer.

Even with the latter practice, there was still some measure of sanity during those colonial days. Konganoga had retrogressed greatly since then, as the new sets of officers would negotiate bribes which they had christened as "rojers". The statement "Rojer me!" was no strange statement at police check points or government offices. It was not just the police. Hardly any profession or office was above board in Konganoga. No position was considered too sacred, too dignifying or incorruptible by any means. Gratification was expected. Not accepting it was considered unusual. A rejection might only connote that the amount offered was considered too small, too inadequate, or required augmentation before it would be accepted. From the gate man to the messenger, up to the senior officer of government, it had become one huge cauldron of corruption that might require the virtual *wastage* of an entire generation to cleanse the rot and rid the society of the souls that had sinned.

Only one military regime in Konganoga had in the past attempted to challenge the monster head on. They succeeded while they lasted on seat. But their tenure was cut short. Konganoga regressed and even got worse than before the coming on board of the duo of the "no nonsense Generals." It soon once again took a turn; a turn for the worse. It has since become a way of life, and the turn that it has taken has contributed positively to making Konganogans "the happiest people in the world"; a largely metaphorical statement.

And so, life would go on and public utilities would work *well*. And the roads would get done, the taps would run, power would be available uninterrupted and the schools would turn out products that would place Konganoga on the world map of nations heading for space! All these, with the turn that events had taken would of course be in the negative direction.

Sometimes officers on road check points or what many motorists chose to call "toll gates", would even give change to motorists for high denomination bills which they collected as bribes or illegal toll. Often that would be done in the full glare of other motorists and passers-by!

And so, Professor Johnson did not hesitate in *paying his dues* to the officers in the front office of the Assistant to the President. He was thus allowed to get into the waiting room. It was a far cry from what obtained at his inaugural visit when he was given express service at the instance of the Assistant to the President. In this particular instance he was being invited for some sort of reprimand for failing to fulfill a promise he had made on oath. He had unilaterally reduced the *returns* from the agreed 40% to a mere 25% of the revenue accruing to his institution.

As Professor Johnson exchanged banters with the clerks and other officers in the front office he momentarily forgot the fear and apprehension about what might befall him in the office of the oath administrator Mr. Muktar Obredu. As soon as he sat alone on a chair in the inner waiting room, Professor Johnson's worst fears again came up in full force. Muktar Obredu's loaded gun stared him in the face. For the first time since he left Kiba for Kumbrujaa on that trip he started entertaining fears that he might not return alive. Hitherto he had only entertained fears that he might leave Kiba as a Vice Chancellor and come back as a mere professor just like any other. He had more or less braced up for such a scenario. It would not be the first time the latter situation would happen in Konganoga's volatile political environment. High officials of government had on many occasions learnt of their dismissal only over the radio or television. And by the time they would get back to their duty posts their replacement officers would be on seat. A few people had been dismissed from their posts while on duty tours and while on active service. No reasons needed to be given. That was Kumbrujaa a beautiful and greatly blessed country that appeared to be condemned to live in perpetuity in the political past.

Professor Johnson had not been summoned to come to Kumbrujaa to see a senior officer of government. He had been commanded to report to Mr. Muktar Obredu a barely literate oath Administrator in the office of the Assistant to the President.

A call bell soon rang and a smartly-dressed young man emerged from a side room adjacent to the entrance to the room where Professor Johnson had once met with Mr. Johnson Ayuda the Assistant to the President. Professor Johnson had never taken notice of the presence of that door. He had thought that Mr. Muktar Obredu's office was a sub office within the office of the Assistant to the President. He had believed that the room that housed "the things wey de kill people" according to Mr. Muktar Obredu, had its entrance only through Mr. Ayuda's office.

Professor Johnson was to immediately understand that the Oath Administrator was a "big man" in his own right replete with his own ushers and other attendant staff.

The smartly-dressed young man on entering the inner waiting room had loudly asked as he looked straight in the direction of the anxious-looking Vice Chancellor:

"Mr. Okon Johnson?"

Professor Johnson was a little taken aback. As a surgeon and a fellow of the royal College of Surgeons in Zealand he was used to being addressed as Mr. Okon Johnson. But since he came back to Konganoga he had always been addressed as Dr Johnson and later as Professor Johnson since after he became a professor of ophthalmologic surgery. For many years he had never heard himself addressed as Mr. Okon Johnson. At the mention of the latter name therefore Professor Johnson looked around him to ensure that there was no other person who bore a similar first and surnames as he did. Already the Assistant to the President bore the name of Johnson. It was possible that there might be another double coincidence. But there was none.

Professor Johnson hesitated. Could the young man be making a mistake?

Or could he already have been stripped of his professorship and consequently the Vice Chancellorship? Anything was possible in Konganoga.

Again Professor Johnson hesitated even as the smartly-dressed young man again announced: "Mr. Okon Johnson, please!"

There were five people waiting in the room. Each of the five looked at the other. None appeared to go by the name of Mr. Okon Johnson. But there was a Professor Okon Johnson. The latter hesitatingly got up and almost timidly asked the young man: "Is that the same as Professor Okon Johnson; I am Professor Okon Johnson?"

At that juncture a massively-built young man who sat close to Professor Johnson reclining back on his seat also said; "Me, I be Chief Okon Akpan if na only Okon you de call!" (I am Chief Okon Akpan if you are actually calling for only Okon).

The young man spoke in such a rough and carefree manner that it was obvious that he must have been one of the political thugs who probably had come for some more *duties*.

The bulky young man who introduced himself as Okon Akpan had a relatively small head which was completely shaved of all hair. He scratched his head repeatedly as one who had chronic ring worm of the scalp which had defied all treatment.

It was at this stage that Professor Johnson took a closer look at the other three people who were waiting for Mr. Muktar Obredu. It then occurred to Professor Johnson that all the other four people who were waiting with him were burly young men in their late twenties and that they all looked rough and impatient. Professor Johnson then remembered the story of how some heavily-built political thugs were often hired during political campaigns to apprehend political opponents and readily break their necks and dump them at the road sides. Such attacks were often attributed to "armed men" or "men of the underworld". Professor Johnson was afraid.

The smartly-dressed young usher was still waiting. One Chief Okon Johnson and one Professor Johnson Okon had established their presence.

The smartly-dressed young usher soon went back into the room as none of the two Okon's appeared to fit perfectly into his name description.

As the young man left, Professor Johnson realized that he was the person who was being called as no other person who was waiting fitted into both the title, first name and surname of professor Okon Johnson. But he was apprehensive. He was too afraid to follow. The room which lay adjacent Mr. Johnson Ayuda's office was certainly the same room of which Mr. Muktar Obredu had said: "The things wey de kill people them dey inside that room!"

Professor Johnson immediately thought within him of a possible corollary pidgin English which might easily fit into the scenario:

"The people wey de kill people dem dey inside this room."

The above translated would mean that the hired assassins were right there in the waiting room.

Professor Johnson was so afraid that he started trembling visibly. He thought of leaving immediately. As the embattled professor was considering his next line of action, the door again opened and the same young man came out and motioning to Professor Johnson he said tersely

"Oga make you enter!"

With wobbly legs Professor Johnson impulsively followed the young usher into a massive office almost as massive as the office of the Assistant to the President where Professor Johnson had taken his initial oath of allegiance.

Behind a large semi circular table in the office sat no other man than the dreaded Mr. Muktar Obredu. The latter did not as much as look up at the entry of Professor Johnson.

At the far end of the room was the unmistakable trolley on which still lay two of the instruments on which Professor Johnson had taken the oath of allegiance: a Bible and a gun. The Koran had been removed. That, to Professor Johnson was evidence that judgment was about to be delivered against him based on the two instruments upon which he had sworn. And the massive bouncers who lurked around might constitute *the people wey de kill people*!

Professor Johnson's real fear came on when he saw sitting behind the trolley two other very bulky young men each of who wore a face cap. Professor Johnson could easily observe that the eyes of the two men who sat by the side of the large table were deep red. He could easily perceive the deep and unmistakable heavy smell of marijuana.

Mr. Obredu neither welcomed Professor Johnson nor even offered him a seat. He merely sat there behind the large semi circular table and appeared to be piecing together some loose beads which were scattered on his otherwise bare table. As he pieced the beads together he only occasionally looked up at Professor Johnson who between deep fear and apprehension had managed to utter the words: "Hello Mr. Obredu."

Mr. Obredu did not respond. He only took up his face and appeared to size Professor Johnson up scrutinizing him from his shoes up to his scalp. He looked at Professor Johnson as a hawk which perching on a tree sized up a cockerel before pouncing on it.

The young man that ushered Professor Johnson into the room soon left the rom. Mr. Muktar Obredu then looked in the direction of the two bulky men and motioned on them.

The two men sprang to their feet and immediately started rolling the trolley in the direction of the trembling Professor Johnson.

Could they be coming to administer another oath? Or, could they be coming to enforce the letters of the previous oath? And what was it that was wrapped in deep brown cloth that was lying by the side of the gun. Could it be another weapon or could it be another more sinister instrument of terror and intimidation?

In either situation Professor Johnson did not wish to take a chance.

The man who invited him to Kumbrujaa would not want to speak to him. Did he feel that he had a recording device or was he so pissed off by the reneging on the oath that he would not wish to engage his victim on another round of discussions?

Either situation in Professor Johnson's view was enemy action. Either situation was ominous.

The approach toward him of the two bulky young men immediately brought back to Professor Johnson the memory of his Boy Scout slogan: "Be prepared!"

And Professor Johnson was prepared. At least his two legs though trembling and almost wobbly were prepared. And his medical school physiology had thought him that in moments such as he was the adrenaline pump in him would prepare him for one or all of the three f's: fright, fight or flight. Professor Johnson wasted no time in opting for the last of the three f's. He had done it before in his office at the danger of a mere mention of the name of Mr. Muktar Obredu. Now Mr. Muktar Obredu was present in flesh and blood. And this time he was not alone. He had with him two muscular young men who were rolling the trolley of death towards him!

Professor Johnson immediately remembered the saying in his native Akunwanta village in Ikot-ikoro town:

"Only a tree would stand still at the sight of the chain-saw and the discussions about the direction in which the tree would fall." A more reasonable object or being would flee if it could.

And so, the erudite professor of ophthalmology and Vice Chancellor of a well renowned University for the second time in less than a month immediately turned towards the direction of the door and took to his heels! He bolted out of the room shouting at the top of his voice: "Help! Help!"

Neither Mr. Muktar Obredu, his trolley-wheeling assistants, the clean-shaven skin head visitors outside nor even the well-dressed usher tried to stop Professor Johnson as he bolted out of the office past them. Even the people in the front office did not appear to express much surprise at the flight of the suit-wearing professor who had only a short while earlier shared some money out to them. It was possible it was not the first time that they witnessed people fleeing from Mr. Muktar Obredu. Only the handful of visitors in the outer waiting room appeared surprised at what they saw. All was soon again quiet within the office of the Assistant to the President on Higher Education.

The next four hours saw Professor Johnson back in his office in Kiba. He was very busy and had given instructions that he did not want to see any visitors no matter from wherever.

Professor Johnson was busy. He was however not busy with signing the many papers that had piled up on his table awaiting his signature. He was busy gathering a few personal effects after he had written a brief resignation letter addressed to the Chairman of the University Council. He had done the letter by himself and had had it printed out by himself in his office. He did not want to set up some panic that might lead to Kumbrujaa sending in some security men to either stop him or harass him in some ways. He had chosen to resign quietly and not set in a stampede in the process.

Professor Johnson had fled twice from the office of the Assistant to the President who apparently was charged with ensuring compliance with certain norms among the institutions under him. He had reneged on an agreement which appeared to be one of the main reasons he was appointed Vice Chancellor of a university which needed someone who was prudent and hard-working enough to make it financially viable and thus to sustain 40% monthly deductions without caving in. Unfortunately the institution was caving in under the weight of the big financial burdens.

The embattled Vice Chancellor therefore guessed that what would follow would be summary dismissal perhaps over the radio or on television. He had therefore decided to disappoint his 'tormentors' by resigning suddenly on his own volition. Retirement or dismissal of unwanted officers over the radio was not an unusual event in Konganoga.

Professor Johnson had requested immediate relief and had called the Deputy Vice Chancellor to take over in the interim in an acting capacity pending the appointment of a substantive Head for the University.

He had assembled a few trusted senior staff and confided in them that he was on his own volition proceeding on immediate terminal leave according to him "on health and personal grounds."

There were enough grounds to involve "health grounds" since the issues involved were indeed almost driving a once amiable and level-headed professor crazy with every passing day.

In the midst of situations which daily threatened his sanity and made him an unwilling accomplice in mauling the polity, Professor Johnson found himself with little choice than to resign immediately.

Chapter 34

THE BIGGER FLIGHT

Professor Johnson had given "health and personal grounds" for his sudden resignation from the top notch position of Vice Chancellor of the famous Federal University in Kiba. But almost everybody in the University knew that health issues were not the issues that drove him from the position. Following the celebrated visit of the emissary from Kumbrujaa and the Vice Chancellor's publicized flight from his office through the back door, it was obvious to most close observers that the famous Vice Chancellor of the high-brow university was having troubles with his employers. Closer observers of the goings-on in the university were also quick to remember that from information that constantly leaked from the university bursary and the accounts departments, that all was not well with relations between the Vice Chancellor and his backers in Kumbrujaa on the one hand and between the Vice Chancellor and the university funds on the other.

Again, apart from his many problems in the university, Professor Johnson had family problems. Everybody that was in the know in the University was aware that his wife had left him back to Zeland with his three children. People had thought that he would long have joined back his family or found a way to persuade the wife to come back with the children. But none of these had happened. Rather what had happened was that Professor Johnson had for a while found fun from within the enclave where his word was law. If he had stayed a little longer he probably would have created scandals within the institution as one or two ladies that he had dated and dumped for others were in the process of ganging up against him. Even within his office his receptionist Titi who he had transferred to his office before dumping her was not happy with the complete take over by her former competitor Stella. Even Stella knew that there was another one down the line who was on the verge of displacing her.

Under the circumstances Professor Johnson felt that it would be suicidal for him to remain back in the university as a professor of ophthalmology without first taking a long leave. Under normal circumstances this would have been a very good opportunity for him and his family to travel jointly to Zeland or to some distant destination of their choice far away from the maddening crowd of the university community or what was left of it. But those were not normal times. First, the circumstances under which Professor Johnson vacated his seat were not normal. Secondly the circumstances under which Fiona had departed back to Zeland with the children were not normal either.

Above all, the consequences for violation of Mr. Muktar Obredu's oath still hung on the neck of Professor Johnson like an albatross. The latter always felt that the loaded gun on which he swore might be used as a justification for following him around through the agency of Mr. Muktar Obredu just like the Okpani component of *the Udogwugwu and Okpani saga* in Professor Johnson's village. Certainly Professor Johnson did not want to be the object of a story that would be told in the future to exemplify the power of a fetish oath-taking ceremony. A morally dwindling and decadent society was bound to be awash with such retrogressive stories that had no scientific basis and served no useful purposes except in teaching the individual the need to abide by any oath or agreement reached mutually and freely between individuals or groups. Such stories flourished as far as they went to satisfy the unproductive imaginations of some fetish-minded individuals. That was the fate that was rapidly beginning to befall Konganoga.

Professor Johnson had invited the staff of the Vice Chancellor's office into his office and spoken briefly to them. Everything was being done in such a hushed manner that most of the staff did not actually understand what was going on. When the Vice Chancellor ended his short speech with profuse thanks to his Secretaries, and personal aides, many of them thought that he was simply proceeding on one of his many travels or that he was at the most, travelling overseas, on a long tour. It was only when he appealed to them "to extend the same level of loyalty to whoever might be (his) successor" that the very observant ones among them began to have an inkling that some major changes were about to occur. As the Vice Chancellor stepped out of the office his official driver Mr. Jonas who Professor Johnson had pulled over to his office from the Department of Ophthalmology ran up to pull the official car closer to the front of the office. But Professor Johnson had declined a ride in the official car. He had rather told Jonas to get him public transport. Jonas was taken aback but after some hesitation had complied.

As the Vice Chancellor boarded the taxi cab members of his office staff all trooped out of their offices partly out of curiosity and partly in an effort to get more information about the actual motives behind the movements of their obviously departing boss. They waved him good bye in response to his hand of good bye that continued to wave until the taxi was no longer visible in the distance.

As the taxi dropped off Professor Johnson and the latter walked up to the front door and pressed the door bell Umanamaa would not open the door. She was not used to entertaining visitors at that time of the day. The security situation in Kiba had deteriorated so much that people never even peeped out to see who was calling or knocking unless they were expecting someone. It was only when the gateman came in and shouted out to Umanamaa that the latter felt confident enough to open the front door. Umanamaa was not left out in the expression of surprise at the sudden turn of events with her master.

Professor Johnson thanked his stars again that he had refused to move into the Vice Chancellor's lodge but instead had opted to remain where he lived privately outside the university compound It would have been more psychologically upsetting to have started parking out of the Vice Chancellor's mansion within the university. It would have caused some more sensations. Professor Johnson's adversaries would have procured Press Photographers to record the scene of the exit of "the big man". If nobody else did, Dr Ezemtubo would ensure that he recorded the scene "for future reference" as Dr Ezemtubo was wont to say.

The first night out of the office of Vice Chancellor was one of sober reflection for Professor Johnson. He had resigned from his position of Vice Chancellor but he did not resign his position as professor of ophthalmology in the university medical school. His big fear however was that he was not very sure how vicious Mr. Muktar Obredu could be; whether he would still wish to pursue him for the balance of the unremitted 40% revenue deductions which he swore to remit, or whether he would decide to leave him alone and face the new occupant of the Vice Chancellor's chair. Professor Johnson was aware that people of Muktar Obredu's *clan* were known to be ruthless especially in matters concerning money. They could also be very vindictive.

Professor Johnson therefore figured out that it would be best if he made a clean break from the system. But the jobs were not there for the asking especially at such high positions. Professor Johnson had therefore taken a decision to make peace with his family and if possible seek sabbatical leave and return to Zeland even if only momentarily.

Professor Johnson had not visited Zeland for almost nine years. His relationship with his wife since two years had been as good as a protracted separation. Professor Johnson had for two years been riding the waves and basking in the sunlight of his new, glamorous and elitist position as Vice Chancellor. He had been walking and dining with kings and had almost lost the common touch. He had even fallen for the lust that often came easy with high positions. He had abused his position with his subordinate female staff on a number of occasions. But coming from a culture and a society where such abuse was rarely investigated and even when discovered, rarely punished, he had gone scot free except for the occasional pang of conscience that could not be completely suppressed.

Fiona had completed the refresher course in Law and having done the necessary prerequisite courses in Zeland law had taken and passed the Zeland Bar exams. She had joined one of the leading legal firms in Zeland's capital city Bondon. She was still operating from the home of her parents Mr. and Mrs. Fergus. There her children were receiving the maximum attention from their happy grandmother.

Professor Johnson even in the midst of uncertainty about whether and how he would be received by his estranged wife had made hurried arrangements to travel to Zeland in search of his family. He had taken the middle course of submitting a letter for leave of absence from his primary duties as a consultant to the Department of Ophthalmology. He had initially thought of an outright resignation but was advised to take the whole thing in stages just in case things went wrong in his calculations and planning.

He knew that even though he did his post graduate training in Zeland he knew that getting absorbed into the job market there was a tall order. Professor Johnson easily remembered how he had to wait for a long time without a job even with his fellowship qualification. He again remembered the multiple "locum" jobs that he had to do and the many moments of uncertainty that he had to endure. He remembered the psychological and emotional torment that he had to go through being rejected at an interview by interviewers from his own country not because he was not qualified, not because of any particular disability on his part but simply because he came from "the wrong tribe". He remembered how a foreign national who was not as qualified as he was, was given a job for which he was fully qualified and for which he had applied. He again remembered the double jeopardy which he faced for being from where he was. He finally remembered the enthusiasm with which some of his medical colleagues in the University received him. He remembered how some of them like Professor Kemji and others, fought to ensure that he got his due in terms of appointment and promotions. He even remembered the recommendation and suggestions from a benevolent foreign national Professor Vanchees. He deeply regretted how he must have disappointed some of them when he toed the path of bad reasoning by embracing Mr. Muktar Obredu and the latter's oath, starving the university of the good leadership which his friends and associates had expected from a man like him who rose to the top of the ladder through support of well meaning friends and associates in the Faculty of medicine of the University in Kiba.

After deep and painful ruminations about his obvious failure and the abrupt and almost disgraceful end to an otherwise very promising family and career, Professor Johnson sorrowfully bent down his head and wept.

But it was some tears that were being shed after enormous damage had been done; some crocodile tears that were shed after the milk had been spilled and the victim had been swallowed; some belated remorse that had followed a premeditated and unwarranted participation in mauling of the polity. And the sad aspect of the whole saga as was appreciated fully even by Professor Johnson himself, was that the mauling was emanating from someone who had benefitted from the system; someone who was well positioned to help salvage the system; someone who could have done without participation in furthering of the rot and decay.

Professor Johnson had wept to no effect. But at least he wept. He showed remorse. The likes of Mr. Muktar Obredu would never weep even if they had the opportunity to repent. And it was the likes of Mr. Obredu that were in power, or were near the corridors of power.

Chapter 35

THE STARTLING REVELATION

Professor Johnson had proceeded to Zeland in spite of the prevailing uncertainty and the possibility of failure of reconciliation with Fiona. He had checked into a hotel near the home of the Fergus family. He had hoped that even if he was not allowed into the family home of Mr. and Mrs. Fergus that he would at least be able to catch a glimpse of his children as they went to, or returned from school.

Unknown to Professor Johnson stories of his escapades while in office in Kiba had filtered steadily into the ears of his estranged wife in Zeland from Konganoga. His adversaries in Kiba notably Dr Ezemtubo had succeeded through their friends in Zeland to secure the mailing address of Fiona and they had on a weekly basis feed the latter with the latest information about Professor Johnson's escapades both with his female friends and with the funds of the University.

Naturally Fiona was more worried about the stories of her estranged husband's relationships with people who were supposed to be his subordinate staff. These latter were issues on which Fiona by her background and upbringing would not compromise on.

Unknown to Professor Johnson, Fiona had several months before after assuring herself of irreconcilable differenced between her and Okon, and after consultations with her parents and friends, filed for divorce from Dr Okon Johnson. She had filed for the divorce in the divorce court which was located close to the same church in which she and Dr Okon were married several years before then.

The divorce papers had indeed been mailed to Dr Okon both to his last known address in Zeland, in a national newspaper and to his last known address in Konganoga. Of course the mail to Konganoga as in many other things that followed the rot and decay in the polity might have found its way into some thrash can in frustration after being opened in search of foreign currency or other valuables. The dead line for response having expired all that remained for the court was to rule the case in favor of the petitioner. A date had not been fixed before the arrival of Professor Johnson.

It did not take long for Professor Johnson to connect with his former friends. Dr Clough McAndrew and many others of Dr Okon's former benefactors had retired from active medical practice. Most of them had heard of Dr Okon's meteoric rise in status in the Konganogan educational system and the medical school. They had equally heard of his arrogance of power and his orchestrated fall, the failure of his marriage and his orchestrated links with the vampires in the Konganogan polity. Professor Johnson's adversaries in the system appeared to have been more vocal overseas than his few remaining friends. Chief among those adversaries was Dr Ezemtubo. These, while Professor Johnson was busy administering the Tin Mining Company and the University in Kiba were busy making oversea tours and fanning the embers of the damage to the image of the man who had started off with much promise and had ended up dining with celebrated devils. Damage to a reputation which might have been in doubt could only be made more rapidly when the image of rot was authenticated by a spouse to the orchestrated *devil*. Fiona's arrival with the three children of the orchestrated *devil* and her stories of abandonment, neglect and infidelity provided the missing link to the full credibility for the circulating stories.

By the time that Dr Johnson arrived therefore the damage to his image was complete and almost irreversible.

Most of the former family friends of the Johnsons were naturally sympathetic toward Fiona. Dr Johnson when therefore he arrived presented the image of an undeniable and unrepentant devil, a wife deserter and a child abuser judging from stories of how he did not care about the welfare of the children just before they departed for Zeland and after they had arrived back to Zeland with their mother.

Indeed hardly any of the people that he thought were his family friends wanted to see him.

The divorce suit instituted against him by Fiona was granted four days after Dr Johnson's arrival.

Dr Johnson did not get to know about the case until the eighth day of his arrival when he visited Dr James Golden a former colleague in the hospital where he had met Fiona as a nurse. The former colleague had introduced Dr Johnson to his wife thus:

"Honey, here you meet Dr *Ok'n* Johnson the former

husband of Miss Fiona Fergus. He is from *Konagona*, I presume, for the unfortunate incident of last week."

Apparent sympathy as vocally expressed, but undisguised despise and disdain as manifested by countenance, could easily be recognized from Mrs. Golden as the latter grudgingly stretched her hand out to Dr Johnson and said:

"Hello doctor, happy to see you. I hope the court decision was not too hard on you. I know you will be able to overcome these. Fiona too is a poor unfortunate fellow. I feel greatly for those lovely kids. Poor souls! They will grow up without a father to guide them through life."

After he was first introduced as "the former husband of Fiona Fergus", Dr Johnson had thought that his friend was making a mistake. Even the sympathy statement from Mrs. Golden did not ring the full bell to a thoroughly bemused Dr Johnson as the latter stood interchanging glances between the Goldens. Another friend of the hosts soon entered and the host Dr Golden again introduced his Konganogan guest as 'Dr Johnson the former husband of Ms Fiona Fergus'. It was only then that the former husband of Miss Fiona Fergus mustered courage and asked:

"Dr Golden did you say former husband? Are you assuming some sort of papal role to unilaterally annul my marriage to my wife Fiona?"

Dr Golden had thought that Dr Johnson was already aware of the divorce. The story of the divorce of an absentee husband was already known by almost everybody in the neighborhood except the erstwhile husband himself.

Dr Golden had therefore jokingly said:

"No, Dr Johnson it was neither the Pope nor I, who culpably annulled the marriage. If there was any culprit it was purely Her Majesty's government through her courts."

Even with Dr Golden's elucidating statement Dr Johnson did not appear to understand. He simply also jovially had said:

"Her Majesty's government will do well not to tamper with my marriage. Fiona and I will resolve all issues between us before any courts set in."

Dr Golden was a little confused by his friend's response and had asked:

"Do you intend to contest the divorce?"

It was at the subsequent exclamation of "Which divorce?" by Dr Johnson that Dr Golden's wife who knew that the divorce was not contested made a sign to her husband to terminate the discussion.

Dr Johnson was beginning to get the message.

He remained sullen for the rest of the remaining thirty minutes which he spent with the Goldens.

Dr Johnson on his way out of the residence of Dr and Mrs. Golden had sought indirectly to prod the couple to talk more of the divorce which was under discussion. He had by way of a forced joke muttered to the hearing of the Goldens:

"I came into your house a married man, and I am leaving a divorcee, Dr Golden."

It was a ploy to extract more information about the purported divorce and it worked, as Dr Golden said:

"Your divorce took so long to be granted. At a time we started wondering whether you cast a spell on the courts and prevented them from taking an early decision in favor of Fiona from five thousand miles away. Everybody started calling you a sort of magician hiding somewhere in the wilds of some far off country and pressing the buttons in Her Majesty's courts here in Zeland.

I am sure Fiona must finally have felt some big sense of

relief, having been kept in suspense about the granting of her request for so long."

As Dr Golden made the latter statement he paused momentarily and cast a glance at his visitor before he continued:

"But tell me my friend Dr Johnson, how does it feel being a divorcee, a father of three lovely children and now staying so close to your former wife and seeing your children come out and go in with you being completely denied access to them?"

Dr Johnson almost collapsed. He had gotten the message. He strode off from the Goldens without any further talk.

Back in his hotel room Dr Johnson lay back on his bed for hours on end praying for sleep to come to no avail. Early the following morning he worked the phones on end trying to contact as many old friends as possible and trying to get as much information as possible. But it looked like everybody had already heard his story. Everybody appeared to have heard of the scoundrel who took a lovable wife from a land that had been so kind to him down to his native enclave and almost starved her and her children to death. Everybody had heard of the sex and power maniac who had thrown all decency to the wind and abandoned his innocent wife in favor of fleeting political appointment and women of easy virtue, acquiescing to fetish oath-taking administered with human blood and the wings of bats and wild pigeons and hung around the neck of a learned professor of ophthalmology who sat in his office on a chair padded with the bones of dead men and dead dogs in an effort to dispel other aspirants to the high office of Vice Chancellor of a renowned University! Everybody had heard of one Professor Ok'n Johnson who had what was the best education that Zeland could offer but who had descended back to the voodoo practices of the medieval ages simply because of quest for, and retention of power. Even the courts in Zeland had been told of "the evil man" called Professor Okon Johnson who would therefore not be trusted with either a daughter of Zealand as a wife or the three grandchildren of Mr. and Mrs. Fergus who were respected citizens of Zeland. The courts had been told the whole story which were collaborated by a pharmacologist who taught in the same university where "the evil man" was committing the atrocities and who had willingly testified during the hearings which "the evil man" had been invited through many avenues to, but which he had willfully shunned.

The courts had therefore decided 100% in favor of the plaintiff, former Mrs. Fiona Johnson. The courts not only had granted the divorce in its entirety but for the safety of the plaintiff and her children had granted a restraining order on "the evil man" from being seen closer than five hundred yards from either the now Miss Fiona Fergus and the latter's parents and three children.

Professor Johnson had obtained the details of the ruling on the divorce from a friend who had obtained same from the court registry since those were public records.

Immediately after reading the court verdict Professor Johnson stood up momentarily. He then again sat back on his hotel room bed for a minute or two. He pinched himself and pulled his ears. He then walked up to the mirror in the bathroom and looked himself in the mirror and blinked a couple of times on the mirror, all to convince himself that it was all in reality and not just a bad dream. He then immediately went down on his knees and for the first time in almost one year prayed to God for strength and presence of mind and the courage to be able to withstand what he felt was an onslaught on him from all sides. Yes, Professor

Johnson prayed. And as he prayed his mind drifted back to the Bible and the gun on the trolley in Muktar Obredu's office. He also remembered the two bouncers inside the room and the four or so that were outside. And even as he grieved he thanked God that he survived that ordeal.

Having mustered some strength and the courage to stand upright Dr Johnson reached for the nearest glass on the tray in his room and gulped a cupful of cold water. For the first time in over ten years he wished that he also stocked gin or at least some alcoholic beverages in his room. And for the first time in his life he thought of drugs or indeed anything that would dissociate his mind from the realities of the moment.

The next thing that cropped up in Professor Johnson's mind was to ascertain that he had not run afoul of the restraining order. He immediately picked up the phone and called the front desk of the hotel.

Speaking in a frantic voice Professor Johnson had asked:

"Hello, Sir, Please how far is this hotel from number 12 Richards Street?"

The response was frightful to Professor Johnson;

"Oh! Pretty close."

"Tell me Sir; is it up to two miles from here?"

"No! No! It's just a short walking distance."

Professor Johnson did not wait to say thank you to the informant. He made straight for his luggage and quickly stuffed his clothes and other belongings hurriedly into his suitcases. He hurried back again to the phone.

"Please Sir, this is Mr. Johnson; Mr. Okon Johnson from Room 16. Please prepare my papers for immediate check out. I will be down there in ten minutes!"

Professor Johnson had become very used to hasty

fleeing from potentially dangerous or presumed dangerous situations and locations. It therefore did not ruffle him in any way fleeing again from his hotel room. He would not want to be charged with violating the court order not to be seen within a range of 500 yards from the Fergus family and from his children!

As He boarded the next available taxi, Professor Johnson kept muttering to himself:

'Thank God I got out early enough. The worst thing would have been to be caught violating a court order by being seen within five hundred yards of my wife and children at number 12 Richards Street!'

Professor Johnson was not sure of where he was heading to. Deep in thoughts he did not hear the cab driver when the latter kept asking him for his destination.

After repeated prodding of "Your destination Sir" as the cab driver drove out of the hotel security check point, the cab driver had cleared by the side of the street since he was not sure of which direction his passenger wanted to head to.

After clearing on the road side the cab driver had again enquired "Where Sir?" In his absentmindedness Professor Johnson had simply said 12 Richards Street!" The driver was very surprised that someone should take a cab to a place so close. Nevertheless since it was a fixed rate for each drop within the city, it was good business for him. Within three minutes the driver took a turn into the vicinity that appeared a little familiar. He then announced to his passenger who all along was busy perusing a small pocket diary:

"We are home Sir!"

Professor Johnson instinctively asked, "Is this the hotel?"

"No Sir, this is number 12 Richards Street which you requested."

"My God! Please take me out of here. Take me out of here quickly." Professor Johnson yelled with his head bent down towards the floor of the back seat of the cab as if to hide his face from the damning vision of some bystanders.

Half raising his head from its hiding position with his eyeballs turned towards the cab driver the embattled professor said in a half pleading and half commanding voice:

"I requested for the next nearest hotel! The next nearest hotel not number 12 Richards Street. Please, please drive off from here."

The bemused and thoroughly embarrassed cab driver had no option than to drive off immediately occasionally looking back at the house through the rear mirror to ascertain that some evil men were not coming in hot pursuit. When after some five hundred yards away he did not visualize any pursuing evil men, he immediately concluded that there must be some evil man occupying the back seat of his cab.

When he was some half a mile down the road from the apparently bewitched 12 Richard's street the cab driver in a sterner and obviously less courteous voice now asked:

"Now Sir, tell me for certain where you want to be taken to.'

The response was this time unambiguous but still not precise:

"Any hotel at least two miles away from here; any hotel at all, but I want it at least two or more miles from here."

It immediately became obvious to the cab driver that his passenger was on the run from something or from somewhere, as he mused.

Obviously this passenger must be running away from some people or from the law. He must be a fugitive if not a terrorist from the horn of Africa or from some terrible country. This must be one of the people causing trouble for us here in Zeland. See how red his eyes were, and how disheveled and ruffled he was. He must be on drugs. See how every hair on his head appears to be standing on end. He must be a terrorist or something close to that. He must be on the run from something in number 12 Richards Street. He might have committed some murder or some robbery there and so did not want to be seen around there! Vigilance and patriotism dictate that this must be reported to law enforcement. You never know whether he had robbed or even murdered the people in number 12 Richard's street that makes him mention the number inadvertently and at the same time want to escape from that house number.

Immediately after dropping off his passenger at Celestial Star Hotel, the cab driver had made a call to the police to alert them of the "suspicious passenger" who he had just dropped off at the Celestial Star Hotel.

Professor Johnson for his own identity concealment had checked into Celestial Star hotel under a false name.

"My name is "William O'Connor" Professor Johnson had told the check-in clerk.

"I want a detached room at the end of a corridor.' Professor Johnson requested.

Of course a detached room at the end of a corridor was a privilege and cost a lot more. Professor Johnson paid advance and indicated an approximate stay of about a week. He wanted enough time to study the situation and possibly reach across to Fiona and make appeals.

Professor Johnson had relaxed for a while on the sofa in his hotel room before going to bed. About an hour after checking in he was still tossing about restlessly on his hotel room bed. He did not sleep well the previous night after the visit to Dr and Mrs. Golden. His mind had meandered between his houses in Kiba and his former office as Vice Chancellor. He remembered the room which housed 'the things wey de kill people' in Kumbrujaa. He ruminated over his several escapes from apparently near-death situations, once in his office in Kiba and twice in Kumbrujaa. Finally he remembered the latest escape from number 12 Richard's Street, the vicinity which he knew so well but which had changed so much during the decade and a half that that he was away to Konganoga. He then went deep in thought about his children and his once loving wife. He calculated the different measures which he intended to take to win back his wife. But he was greatly worried about the restraining order which he learnt of the night before and which he almost violated inadvertently a short while earlier.

Professor Johnson was still deep in thought when a loud knock was heard at this hotel room door.

Anger welled up in Professor Johnson's mind.

Why should these room service people or house-keepers come to disturb a guest so soon after check in? Professor Johnson mused.

Professor Johnson ignored the knocking at first but later decided to respond when the knocking persisted.

"Who?" Professor Johnson asked.
"The police, please open!" The command came.
"The police?"
"Yes, the police, please open!"
Professor Johnson's heart sank.
He took a deep breath and said:
"Please just a minute, let me dress up."

Two burly looking policemen in uniform and fully-kitted were soon in the room.

They were very polite but very firm.

"Good evening Sir! May we see your ID, please?"

Professor Johnson did not utter a word. He simply reached for his jacket in the wardrobe and brought out his international passport. As he opened the wardrobe each of the two officers had their hands on their service pistols apparently to counter any wrong move. *One never knew. A terrorist taken unawares might still be reaching for a loaded weapon from a wardrobe!*

Professor Johnson took notice.

He remained calm even when his heart was palpitating.

One of the officers collected the international passport and took a quick glance at it. He then flipped through the pages and brought out a piece of paper from his pocket and appeared to compare the two names on the paper and on the passport.

"Are you Mr. William O'Connor and did you by any chance visit number 12 Richards Street earlier today?"

Professor Johnson started trembling. His lips quivered with fright and apprehension but he tried to calm himself down.

"My name is Johnson, Dr Okon Johnson. William

O'Connor is an alias that I occasionally use to conceal my identity" Professor Johnson responded calmly.

"Sir, are you Mr. William O'Connor and did you visit Number 12 Richards Street today?"

"No, I am not Mr. William O'Connor. I am Dr Okon Johnson and a taxi cab mistakenly took me to number 12 Richard's Street earlier today."

"Why would a taxi cab mistakenly take you to Number 12 Richard's Street? Did you mention that number to him, and do you have any issue with that number?"

As the exchange continued, Professor Johnson hesitated, wondering what to say so as not to go wrong, the other police officer went to a corner of the room and started talking to someone else on phone.
"Yes, we have got our man!"
The real name is O'Connor Johnson. Yes! Yes! We have him. It is O'Connor Johnson."

As the second officer kept saying "O'Connor Johnson", Professor Okon Johnson felt it necessary to make the correction lest the mistake be listed as another misinformation or forgery charge against him.

"It's Okon Johnson Sir, not O'Connor Johnson"
The second officer did not acknowledge the correction. He kept calling O'Connor Johnson. They already "had (their) man". And their man had proved that he could tell lies by checking into a hotel with false identity.
He obviously must be a criminal. Who knows what else he wanted to do in number 12 Richard's Street?

"Sir, you need to come with us to the office briefly for further questioning. We understand that you checked in only a short while ago and we regret the inconveniences. But further clarification is very essential in view of the prevailing security situation in the country."

The officer said. He was very polite but firm.

Professor Johnson understood but tried to do some explanation.

"Thank you officer, but I checked into this hotel not quite two hours ago. I have not even taken a shower. I have shown you my identification and it is very explicit. The mix up or ambiguity between my actual name and the name with which I checked into the hotel was for personal reasons and certainly not for any criminal intent. I simply did not want my many acquaintances and colleagues to locate me here and disturb the quiet time which I think I am entitled to. My name is, and remains Okon Johnson, Dr Okon Johnson from Konganoga on a private visit to Zeland. The brief stop which the cab driver conveying me made at number 12 Richards Street was entirely an error on the driver's part as I never intended that he should take me anywhere else except to this hotel. I did not even step out from the car as the cab driver can testify if he can still be traced."

Professor Johnson paused for a while to weigh the impact of his explanations. He then continued:

"I understand the need for security alertness Sir, but can't we have the situation fully cleared here and now? I am only here on a short visit as I am a professor of medicine in my home country and not a dubious character by any means." Professor Johnson said.

The officer listened attentively and then said:

"Yes Sir. I understand and I apologize for the

inconveniences. But we need you to come with us to the office for further clarification in view of the dual identity."

Professor Johnson knew that impersonation or presentation of false identity was a fairly serious offence. He subtly wished that it were in Konganoga. He might have negotiated his way out with some large purse which would have ensured *settlement*. But that would have been possible only four thousand miles away, certainly not in Zeland.

As the officers and Professor Johnson got close to the front office of the hotel, the officer paused and pointed Professor Johnson to the notice pasted conspicuously at the checking in counter warning against false identities.

The notice pasted right in front of the checking in clerk was unambiguous and in simple English:

"Customers are warned that checking into the hotel under false names, or with forged identities are criminal offences and violators will be handed over to the police for necessary prosecution."

Professor Johnson read the notice which indeed he had earlier ignored at the time that he checked in. His heart sank as he imagined how bad it would be if he started having troubles again in Zeland when he was indeed running away from Konganoga precisely because of troubles.

Even as the officer pointed out the offence to Professor Johnson, he was very polite. Professor Johnson took note.

The officers who were dispatched to Celestial Star Hotel as well as the ones dispatched to number 12 Richard Street had all returned to the police Station. The officers dispatched to the hotel had returned with the man who was earlier in the day reported by an anonymous vigilant citizen, the cab drive. The police had also discovered that the suspicious man had checked into a hotel under a false name in violation of the laws of her Majesty's government. The checking in clerk at the hotel who did not confirm the identity of the guest but insisting on seeing a proper identification document like a driver's license or a passport was not brought into the picture. That issue would probably be dealt internally by the authorities in the hotel.

The owners of the house on number 12 Richard's street had also confirmed that a man by the name of Okon Johnson was prohibited by a court order from being seen within 500 yards of the abode or presence of six of the inhabitants of the aforesaid number 12 Richard's Street.

The charges against Professor Johnson were twofold:
That you Okon Johnson, foreign national had on the 19th day of July… falsely checked into a public hospitality by the name Celestial Star Hotel in Huntington Zeland using a false identity in violation of section 419 subsection 26 of the criminal code. ..
That you Okon Johnson on the same 19th day of July …violated a court order banning you from being seen within 500 yards of the residence, or presence of Miss Fiona Fergus and/ or any or all of her three children and her two parents.
Professor Johnson had pleaded not guilty despite persuasion to plead guilty for a lesser sentence.
He had secured a lawyer and had been granted bail. Hearing was fixed for six weeks time during which time Professor Johnson had planned to have returned to Konganoga.

Hotel costs for six weeks stay was as burdensome as flight ticket to and from Konganoga. Professor Johnson had opted to travel only to find that he would not be allowed out of the country with two counts of criminal charges hanging around his neck. The prosecution counsel in opposing bail for the professor had argued that being a Konganogan that Professor Johnson could not be trusted with not jumping bail if he was allowed to leave the country.

A heavy bail bond was thus entered into before the once powerful Vice Chancellor could be granted bail.

As the days in the hotel room dragged to weeks and the resources available to Professor Johnson ran thin the embattled professor was forced to request for accelerated hearing.

The verdict was easy to reach: guilty as charged and on both counts. Professor Johnson was to go to prison for six months on the first count and was to go to prison for 18 months on the second count. Both prison terms were to run concurrently.

Luckily for Professor Johnson each of the sentences had option of a fine.

The Konganogans resident in Zeland had rallied around Professor Johnson at his moment of greatest need and had contributed money to pay off the two fines since the professor had run completely short of cash.

The fines having been paid, Professor Johnson once more became a free man. But he had become an ex-convict.

Dr Okon Johnson, Professor of Ophthalmology, former Chairman Board of the Tin Mining Company of Konganoga, and former Vice Chancellor of the University of Science and Technology Kiba came in to Zeland legally clean and untainted. But he was leaving a besmeared man and an ex-convict.

He came in a married man with three lovely children in his own estimation. He was leaving a divorcee, a broken man and officially a man of doubtful integrity.

Chapter 36

BACK TO BASE TO MAUL THE POLITY

After he learnt of the divorce, and before the Celestial Star Hotel incident, Professor Johnson had hoped that he would be able to meet with Fiona and perhaps be able to plead with her to reconsider her position on the divorce issue. He had hoped that he would be able to persuade her for the sake of the children to give him a second chance. He had planned that he would perhaps do that which was unheard of in his part of Konganoga, go down on his knees and plead for forgiveness before her and promise never to offend her again, never to look twice at anything and anybody in skirts except her, never to be away from home latter than 6 in the evening, always to profess his love of her every day of his life and to truly adore her as his one and only loving wife for the rest of his natural life. All these he had planned to communicate to Fiona if only she would agree to give him a second chance and have the divorce repealed. It would have been unheard of, a man going down on his knees before his wife in Ikot-ikoro, Professor Johnson's hometown in Konganoga. It was usually the other way round. A wife would go down on her knees and plead with the husband for forgiveness when she transgressed. But the man in the lopsided society would often bluff his way through and expect his wife to understand that it was a man's world and that the man as head of his family would do no wrong even when he did.

Professor Johnson understood the customs of his people to his fingertips. He grew up in Konganoga and he was very familiar with the customs and traditions of Ikot-ikoro. He did not need Okpani who doubled as the chief servant of Udogwugwu shrine and the chief custodian of the customs and traditions of Ikot-ikoro to interpret that aspect of the customs to him.

Tucked inside the Celestial Star Hotel on the night that he considered going on his knees to plead with Fiona, Professor Johnson knew that he was four thousand miles away from Ikot-ikoro, from Udogwugwu and from Okpani the chief servant of the latter for him to have been seen as violating the customs and traditions of his community if he prostrated before Fiona begging for forgiveness. It might have been humiliating and an abomination in Ikot-ikoro for Professor Johnson as a man to be seen begging for forgiveness from his wife. But it was not seen as humiliating for Professor Johnson to have been found guilty of being seen in the vicinity of his ex-wife and his own children. Such were the vagaries in human existence. Such were the lessons that ought to have been learnt even by people who saw themselves as mighty and strong in one culture but who if they were to venture to other cultures would have seen themselves as Lilliput or at best as mere mortals like the rest of men.

When Professor Johnson stepped out of the plane back in Kumbrujaa airport in Konganoga he heaved a sigh of relief. From the day that the two count charge was read out to him and a possible jail term of two years for the two counts read out along with the charges, the erudite professor of ophthalmology did not stop imagining himself wearing the light blue and pink colors of Her Majesty's prisoners. He shuddered as he thought of that possibility. He there and then promised himself that he would never again allow himself into such a humiliating situation. He resolved that since he could no longer fit into the Zeland society or even possibly have access to his wife and children that he would delve into Konganoga politics head on and sink or swim with it. He had been reduced to a nonentity, an ex-convict in Zealand. But he was now back to what he felt was his natural base for good.

Back in Konganoga Professor Johnson was once more king. A new Vice Chancellor had been appointed in his place for the University in Kiba. Another victim must have sworn to the oath of allegiance with a bible and a loaded gun. Another promise of 40% monthly deduction from the coffers of the University in Kiba must have been made. Mr. Muktar Obredu's attention must have been diverted to another puppet, another vampire who would help some men and women who lacked conscience, vision or indeed reason, to sit in judgment over their poor countrymen and their resources and daily without qualms or remorse, severely maul the polity.

Professor Johnson knew that he had reached the peak of his academic career as the ex-Vice Chancellor of a University. He had crashed from that position and would certainly not have any new grounds to break in the administrative ladder of any higher institution in the country. He knew that he was already an ex-convict in Zeland. But officially his records were still clean in Konganoga. Even when it was known by all and sundry that he had collaborated with the wreckers of the economy in Kumbrujaa nobody had ever for once accused him of stealing. Mr. Muktar Obredu might accuse him of failing to adhere to the letters of an oath but those would not appear in Professor Johnson's records anywhere. And as regards the failure of his regime as Vice Chancellor, Professor Johnson was well aware that Konganogans were a people who could pass as having poor memory for remembering evils wrought on them by their leaders. They would rather praise a leader for sparing the nation 10% of what belonged to the nation than blame or punish such a leader for denying the nation 90% of what rightly belonged to her. They would indeed choose to forget that a leader out rightly stole 90% of the resources of the nation. That was Konganoga and Mr. Muktar Obredu knew that only too well. And they took maximum advantage of it. Knowledgeable foreign nations and nationals who understood the mediocrity or imposed mediocrity in the governance of Konganoga also took full advantage of this situation and helped the men of power in Konganoga to fleece the polity.

Professor Johnson had tasted power. It was sweet; indeed sweeter than honey. And it was only administrative power that he had tasted. How much sweeter it indeed would be to taste political power!

Professor Johnson had lost his administrative power as Vice Chancellor. He had lost his family as it were. Simply going back to the clinics to take up the ophthalmoscope to look into the retina of people's eyes was out of the question for him.

The elections were coming close and the political landscape was populated mainly by die-hards many of who had little or no good education. Some that were said to be educated among the lot of possible and serving contestants actually bought their certificates or had cheated to secure their certificates.

Most were men and women who had stumbled on money by fair means or foul, either by frank stealing, by embezzlement, through drugs or often through inflated or unexecuted contracts. A few were however honest and otherwise noble men and women who had been made to mortgage their consciences to godfathers who would sponsor them. These latter did not have the money or the reach. Having been sponsored and thus *selected*, since selections rather than elections were often the order of the day, such sponsored men and women found themselves almost completely at the legislative beck and call of those who sponsored them. A few would succeed in breaking away from the clutches of the ubiquitous sponsoring godfathers after a few months or years on the saddle. Those few would even at great threat to their personal and political safety attempt to drum up support for political reforms and some form of moral re-armament. These latter often remained the underdog consciences of the nation, the only solace for genuine patriots who might be few in number but on who all men of conscience truly pegged their hopes for a greater, more humane and just society in Konganoga.

Professor Johnson was decided on joining politics. It did not matter to him how he would get there but he was prepared to get there. He had immediately resigned his appointment with the University and after setting up a small private practice at which he attended only three days in a week, he had joined the political party in power in the center. The ward leadership of the party was overjoyed at having among them a man of Professor Johnson's caliber and clout. They immediately rallied around him and mounted pressure on him to run for office.

The party leadership at the center soon learnt that the former Vice Chancellor of the University in Kiba has joined their party and sent for him to come to Kumbrujaa. It was a big catch for the party and Professor Johnson was treated to various evening cocktail parties in the nation's capital. Professor Johnson once again found himself in the limelight. This time it was in his self recognition and there was no Mr. Muktar Obredu to swear an oath to.

The campaigns were soon in full swing for the Senate seat which Professor Johnson had decided to run for. The party primaries were expected to pose only little challenge for Professor Johnson. Of the two other candidates who showed interest, one was a wealthy grocery stores magnate and the other was one Chief Ozomee a wealthy contractor who had made his billions of dollars through unexecuted government contracts. None of Professor Johnson's opponents in the primaries was well educated. But each of the two men had tons of money to spare. The campaigns were fierce as most of the delegates were ordinary village folks who had paid their ways through ordinary party members to become delegates. Having spent money to rally the village folk to support them as delegates, many of these delegates felt that they needed to recoup the money from the highest bidder among the contending candidates.

The delegates were to vote to elect the party's flag bearer against the candidate of the opposing party.

Professor Johnson had only a handful of strong loyalists who he could camp in his residence and who carried out the day to day ground work and contacts for him. He had set up a campaign office right in his residence in Kiba as he did not have enough money to rent a prominent office in the center of the city as his other two opponents had done. One of his opponents the contractor had furnished his very large newly-completed apartment complex at the city center and had decorated the whole vicinity with party flags. He had also pulled out lots of cars painted in party colors. He had mounted loud speakers on cars and the name "Ozomee" which was the candidate's surname was on every lip. Scarcely anybody except the few well-educated people in the party remembered the name "Johnson" even when they had received his entry into the party with fanfare before the dollar-rain from the Ozomee camp.

Two days prior to the primary elections Chief Ozomee had dispatched vehicles to almost all the nooks and corners of the state to freight the party delegates to a camp which he had set up to house them. He had also purchased almost all the available hotel rooms in Kiba where he housed the party leaders in the state as well as the leaders of opinion among the party delegates. On the eve of the elections he had made available the sum of $100,000 in cash to each of the delegates to ensure that he had their votes!

Kiba the state capital was agog with Ozomee's colors on the eve of the election. Only two cars bore Professor Johnson's colors, his personal car which he had only recently repainted and an old car which one of his friends and classmates had donated to him. On each of the two cars Professor Johnson had pasted his photographs and had his newly-acquired chieftaincy title "Ojimmuta" boldly written below his name. The title "Ojimmuta" meant "Knowledge is power."

On the eve of the elections Chief Onunkwo the third candidate in the primaries had withdrawn from the race and had declared his support over the radio and television for Chief Ozomee. It was said that Chief Ozomee had repaid Chief Onunkwo's expenses and also paid him an undisclosed large sum of money. It was said that he had also approached Professor Johnson but that the latter had felt confident that the delegates would collect Chief Ozomee's money, eat his food, enjoy his hotel camping but cast their votes at the end for *Ojimmuta* since they all said that they valued education and knowledge. It was also believed that most of them knew that the source of Chief Ozomee's wealth was the money which would have paved the roads and built the schools and supplied water to the citizens but which found its way into Chief Ozomee's bank accounts. It was therefore believed, at least by Professor Johnson and people in his camp that the delegates would collect Chief Ozomee's money and reject him at the polls.

Indeed one of Professor Johnson's election slogans to counter Chief Ozomee's money flaunting was: "It is your money! Collect it but vote Ojimmuta!"

The results of the elections were as good as known even before the elections were over.

Of the 385 delegate-votes Chief Ozomee scored 384 votes while Professor Johnson scored only one vote. Since each candidate also voted in the elections it therefore meant that the only vote which Professor Johnson scored was his own vote. It therefore meant that Professor Johnson's aides and staff some of who were also delegates must have collected money and voted for Chief Ozomee! One of Professor Johnson's uncles was also a delegate and was indeed in charge of publicity for his nephew's campaign. It was said that lots of 'last minute delegates' had lined up about midnight in Chief Ozomee's campaign head quarters to receive their own $100,000 and take the administered "oath of compliance." Nobody disclosed the nature of the oath. When Professor Johnson later heard of the oath-taking exercises he was curious to know whether it involved the bible and a loaded gun. The memories of Mr. Muktar Obredu easily came to his mind.

Professor Johnson had committed all the money that he received as gratuity into the campaigns for the primaries. Banking on the hope that the party would shoulder all subsequent expenses after he must have won the primaries, he had thrown in all that he had into the purchase of the nomination forms and the campaigns. He had indeed mortgaged his only house two weeks before the elections when reports came back to him that his opponent was outspending him 32 to 1.

With loss of his family and loss of all that he had materially the only thing that kept Professor Johnson going was the consolation that he had his pension. Short of that reassurance the thought of suicide had crept up in Professor Johnson's mind on the morning after the election results were announced.

Having emerged as the candidate of the top political party in the country and the State, winning the Senate seat presented no problems to Chief Ozomee. A few weeks into the main election for the Senate seat every road junction, every tree that stood by the road side, every commercial bus and indeed almost every taxi that plied the roads in Kiba and the other major streets of the state and even in the rural areas bore the banners of Chief Ozomee. The three words "Ozomee for Senate" became such a common slogan that even very young school children recited it as they walked to school. The opponents of Chief Ozomee started dropping off one by one and by the eve of the main election only two remained. Ozomee easily trounced each of these and each did the unusual thing among politicians in Konganoga. Each congratulated Chief Ozomee both in the electronic and the print media. In other situations in Konganoga they would have rejected the results of the elections and proceeded to the election tribunals and the courts where in many cases the candidate with the heavier purse would expect to win. In the election tribunals in the case of Chief Ozomee it would have been futile for his opponents since in all probability they would be greatly outspent and out-maneuvered.

After losing the party primaries Professor Johnson ensured that he was present at all the rallies organized by Chief Ozomee. It was obvious that he as an individual did not have much political following despite the hilarity that initially greeted his coming on board. When the professor issued a statement requesting his "teeming supporters to queue behind Chief Ozomee", every discerning observer found the statement as a huge joke. Everybody knew that there was nothing teeming about Professor Johnson's supporters. Indeed there were virtually no supporters any more as demonstrate by the zero vote that he scored outside of his personal vote.

Chief Ozomee was very magnanimous in victory. He was very aware of his shortcomings in terms of education and legislative experience. He recalled that even when he and his campaign aides were heaping insults on Professor Johnson that the latter never for once retaliated with abuses or foul language. He was aware of Professor Johnson's previous high office. He therefore immediately after the results of the elections were announced extended an invitation to Professor Johnson to his house and offered him either the position of his legislative adviser or any position of the latter's choice in his constituency office.

Professor Johnson even though he realized that whatever position that he would take under Chief Ozomee was not going to be an executive one, nevertheless realized that acceptance of the post of a chief legislative adviser to a Senator of the Federal Republic of Konganoga would straight away take him up to Kumbrujaa. And Professor Johnson knew that whatever that was worth having in the governance of Konganoga emanated from Kumbrujaa. Konganoga was a nation of federating states. But the reality on the ground was that successive military administrations in the country had so whittled down the powers of the states that the latter had become merely like puppets ever waiting on the center to provide the guidance and the funds without which most of them could not function.

Professor Johnson further knew that as a senior special adviser to a Senator that he would get into the circle of the so called 'men in corridors of power" He knew that he might not have any executive powers. But he knew that he would be able to participate in the crumbs as one in the corridors of power. And he knew that participating in picking up the crumbs was better than having no crumbs at all. He believe that with a position as Chief Adviser that he would be able to make contacts and in the process prepare himself for any future available political position.

Chapter 37

COALITION OF POLITY'S WRECKERS

Professor Johnson's office in Kumbrujaa was usually a beehive of activity. He was the most learned of all the chief advisers. It did not take long for people to know that a chief adviser to one of the *distinguished senators* was indeed a professor of medicine and a former Vice Chancellor of one of the nation's foremost universities.

Even the presidency noticed Professor Johnson's presence. The addresses delivered by Chief Ozomee and the bills which he sponsored as well as the motions which he moved were always distinct and impeccably done even when people knew that Chief Ozomee was not a properly educated man. His beautiful presentations very soon attracted attention to the poorly educated but agile and intelligent Chief Ozomee. With time Chief Ozomee who was known to possess a questionable college degree began to earn the nickname of "the Doyen of the Senate" because of the finesse with which his speeches and bills were prepared and delivered. It did not take too long for it to be recognized who the architect of all the finesse was. It was soon recognized that the brain behind Chief Ozomee's success was indeed the highly-educated professor of ophthalmology who manned Chief Ozomee's senate and advisory team. These made Professor Johnson a very popular commodity both behind the scene and even in the presidency.

Professor Johnson's excellence did not escape the attention of the presidency.

It was no wonder therefore that eight months into his serving as the chief adviser to Chief Ozomee, Professor Okon Johnson was invited by the presidency and offered the post of Senior Adviser to the President on Educational Affairs. The office which was very highly regarded was usually known as SAPEA. SAPEA's were always known to be right hand men of the President since education theoretically enjoyed a pride of place in each year's budget of the Federal Government. The budgets of both the Federal and State Governments in Konganoga almost always had education enjoying the lion's share in fiscal allocation. Whether this translated to the realities on the ground was another question.

The appointment to the post of Senior Adviser to the President on Educational Affairs was a big turning point in the life of a man who had once been rejected in an interview for a post which he was fully qualified for in his country. The rejection then was simply because the man spoke the *wrong* language and came from a part of the country which simply did not sound right.

It was to the great credit of the officials of the presidency that they easily discovered Professor Johnson and offered him the position of SAPEA irrespective of his circumstances and his immediate past which security checks had readily made available. Security checks available to the presidency had revealed that the man Professor Okon Johnson had subjected himself to Mr. Muktar Obredu's 40% returns oath but had defaulted down the line. The mere fact that he acquiesced at a stage was safe enough reason for getting him on board to the new SAPEA position.

It was hoped that he would also in his new position cooperate for some time, and also utilize his great knowledge positively before possibly once again reneging. If he did, certainly he would not be the first and certainly he would not be the last. If he brought a few positive changes to education especially higher education, made some good financial returns before perhaps *repenting* that would be good enough. He would be quietly eased out of the system without any explanations to the people whose resources were being spent. And he must not open his mouth too wide if he had a change of heart and reneged on returns and subsequently got fired without explanations. He would still be subjected to the oath of allegiance with the Bible and the loaded gun. He would soon be made to know that although Mr. Muktar Obredu's office was under him, that he would still be subjected to the oath with a Bible and a loaded gun. And if he dared open his mouth too wide after getting fired for reneging, the loaded gun would be employed to do its job. And the operators of the trigger would never be found. "Unknown soldiers", "unknown policemen" or "unknown armed robbers" would always be available to absorb the blame.

Default after an oath taking could also bear the blame. "Udogwugwu egbuhu, Okpani egbuo".

If Udogwugwu failed to kill an oath defaulter, Okpani, the high priest of Udogwugwu would help. And the muscular men who waited outside Muktar Obredu's office would only be too happy to help; just for a small fee.

Professor Okon Johnson by his new position had an office that was even bigger in size and higher up in hierarchy than that of Mr. Johnson Ayuda the Assistant to the President on matters of higher education. Professor Johnson was in charge of the office and all that went with monitoring of the progress in, and advising His Excellency the president on higher education in the Federal Republic of Konganoga. Even Mr. Johnson Ayuda's office was directly within Professor Okon Johnson's area of control. Mr. Muktar Obredu the Oath Administrator therefore came under Professor Johnson's *jurisdiction* as a relatively junior staff.

Despite the fact that he was now the boss of both Mr. Ayuda and Mr. Muktar Obredu, Professor Johnson still felt jitters whenever he encountered Mr. Muktar Obredu. The thought of "the things wey de kill people" was constantly in Professor Johnson's mind. The latter had the uncanny feeling that somehow the curse of the Bible and the loaded gun upon which he had sworn and reneged were still on him for reneging on the 40% deduction from the resources of the Federal University of Science and Technology Kiba.

He had decided that he would still make out time to visit the office of the Assistant to the President and that he would want to know the contents and functioning of the dreaded room which harbored "the things wey de kill people."

Professor Johnson did not have the chance to take a tour of Mr. Muktar Obredu's office before he was instructed to go to the office of the Assistant to the President on Higher Education for his swearing in. When he received the directive professor Johnson knew that he was in for a second round of ordeal with Mr. Muktar Obredu. Luckily this time around Mr. Obredu was his subordinate in the government. The fear about what he would encounter was no longer there for Professor Johnson. At least he had been there before. On this second visit Professor Johnson did not have to sign any papers to see anybody. He did not have to wait in any queue. He was indeed ushered into the room with all dignity and respect. This time he had the boldness to ask Mr. Muktar Obredu:

"Why do you have to have a gun along with the Bible?"

The response was stunning:

"Our people no longer fear the bible. But they will have no choice but to fear the gun."

Mr. Obredu looked around him to ensure that there was no other person in the room and stealthily said:

"But if you no like the gun Sir, we fit swear you for only bible, for sake of you be oga, boss. Only make you remember say, for this office we no de do mercy or nepotism or any favor for even big man at all, at all. These boys when them come smoke them stuff finish, they fit take gun or other means follow even big men when them big man swear for one thing and them go outside de do another thing, because them be big man. Me, Muktar Obredu I no de follow those boys to go kill. My own be only to show them the man wey default and to authorize for them to be paid them money. After that, the hit boys them go know what to do."

Mr. Obredu's offer of exemption on swearing with the gun was supposed to be a special concession to his boss. But the supposed beneficiary had sworn with the gun and the Bible before. Even though he defaulted and was still alive he was under the subtle belief that it was the default in the previous oath-taking that cost him his job and had been responsible for his many woes so far. This time around, with a much more influential job Professor Johnson did not wish to take any more chances.

"Whose interest am I protecting?" Professor Johnson asked himself.

The polity has already been badly mauled. The system is thoroughly broken. I am not responsible for the breakdown of the system. I had tried in the past to be part of the solution but it cost me my job." Professor Johnson muttered to himself.

Looking straight into the face of Mr. Muktar Obredu Professor Johnson asked: " Do you give this choice to everybody?"

"No!" Mr. Obredu replied.

"Then I would prefer to take the oath the normal way." Professor Johnson replied.

It did not now matter to Professor Johnson. He would abide by the full dictates of the oath.

Even if it means diverting the entire coffers of the education sector under me, I will do that to ensure that I keep this job. Mr. Johnson Ayuda and Mr. Muktar Obredu had spelt out 40% and I reneged and lost my job. Now I know better. Even if the presidency and the powers from above today desire 90% of the revenue from the education sector, I will cooperate.

Professor Johnson mused.

Professor Johnson then remembered the decision that he took after he discovered that his delegates in the senate election had defected to his opponent because the latter was dishing out large amounts of money to the delegates. He remembered that even people who were his personal staff and even his close relatives had abandoned him to go and collect money from his opponent.

Professor Johnson had at that time resolved that if ever

he had a second chance to embezzle the entire money available to his office that he was going to do so since apparently that was what the system understood. That was what obtained in the system. The people appeared to understand that officials of government should steal money and perhaps give back a little part of it to the system. It did not appear to matter how much the system was mauled, the people would hail the big thieves and happily receive back crumbs and be grateful for little gifts from their stolen wealth.

Professor Johnson had realized that it was lack of money which made him lose the election against Chief Ozomee. He was nevertheless grateful to Chief Ozomee for the opportunity to serve in his team in the senate. He fully recognized that it was his tenure in Senator Ozomee's office that earned him recognition by the presidency.

Professor Johnson had decided from his first day of appointment that he would make as much money as possible from the presidency. To further this decision he had proceeded from the first day at work to lay the foundation for as much money as possible to be paid to him by anyone who would have cause to use his office. He was also determined to use his offices to divert as much funds as possible into the accounts of his benefactors and the political party that brought him and his associates to power.

He had lost his wife and his children to the job. He had lost an election because he did not have the money to throw around and buy up the delegates. He had resigned his high office in the university simply because he did not have the callousness to continue to divert 40% of the university revenue to his bosses in the capital city. All that was left for him was the SAPEA position that was kindly given to him.

To start with, Professor Johnson proposed a staff reshuffle and enlargement program which ensured that only staff who would cooperate with his illegal demands and sleaze were accommodated in his Department.

He had announced that there would be a fresh auditing of all staff in his department. The staff auditing would be done concurrently with scrutiny of the academic certificates of the relevant staff. He said that he wanted to root out al staff who had joined the department with forged certificates.

Of course Professor Johnson knew that well over 75% of the staff of the ministry were employed either with forged certificates, with no certificates or were simply placed on wrong job positions because they had paid some huge amounts of money to some recruiting staff.

A few years earlier such a verification exercise emanating from Professor Johnson would have been genuine. But that was before the former erudite professor of ophthalmology decided to join the gang of looters. That was before Professor Okon Johnson lost his family, resigned his university job, and delved headlong into the gang of people who, with careless abandon and with all temerity, were mercilessly mauling the polity in Konganoga.

Within a short period of three months Professor Johnson had set up such a monstrous embezzlement machine which was diverting close to 50% of the entire money budgeted for education at the federal level into two private accounts that were surreptitiously set up overseas by his bosses. Those accounts were said to be supplying educational materials to higher institutions in the country. Not a single pin was ever supplied.

The lot of the Universities and higher institutions got so bad under Professor Johnson's supervision that the Association of University Teachers decided to lead a delegation comprising former friends and associates of Professor Johnson to go and consult with their former colleague and friend in the presidency in Kumbrujaa.

For greater effect the team was led by Professor Kemji who was known to have been Professor Johnson's mentor and friend. The team after several attempts was able to be granted audience to see the Senior Adviser to the President for Educational Affairs in the country's seat of power. It was as difficult as seeking audience with the gods.

Professor Kemji was very surprised at the many security screenings that he now had to pass through before he could be allowed to see his old protégé and friend.

Professor Johnson even in spite of his transformation into the elite club of "Men and Women in Power" (MEWIP) an amorphous organization of the top political elite in Kumbrujaa, had not forgotten his days as a young and inexperienced lecturer in Professor Kemji's Department.

As soon as he saw the visitors' form with Professor Kemji's business card attached he ordered that the team should be let into his office. He had walked up to the door and embraced Professor Kemji who had become an emeritus professor in the University at Kiba. The discussions were very cordial.

But even with the presence of his old friend in the team that came to negotiate a better deal for the universities, Professor Johnson found his hands were largely tied as far as to what he could do to increase the percentage of the allocation to universities that were actually released to them. Having violated Muktar Obredu's oath as Vice Chancellor and after getting into trouble for it, Professor Johnson did not wish to take any chances with his new hard won position. Only 50% of budgeted and appropriated revenue that was supposed to be released to educational institutions was actually being released to them. The rest was usually brazenly stolen and deposited into private accounts of fronts in foreign and local banks. And this time around Professor Johnson always ensured that he had his cut upfront. That was apart from the millions of dollars that he smiled to the banks with every month as donations and gifts from favor seekers in the presidency.

The team that went to see Professor Johnson had at least tasted the flamboyance and opulence in Kumbrujaa. Many of them had never had the opportunity of coming closer than a mile of the seat of power. There were the ever vigilant eyes of thousands of security personnel ever ready to chase away visiting citizens and other visitors who might be anxious to have a mere close look at Konganoga's presidential mansion in Kumbrujaa. Even the mere precincts of the so-called "Rock of the People", as the presidential mansion in Kumbrujaa was called, were completely out of bounds for the people. Even mere look from a distance was denied the people. Only the charlatans, wealthy contractors and the vultures in flowing robes who paraded as leaders of the people were welcome to the "Rock of the People". All else were suspect and must be warded off.

The visit to the offices of their former colleague offered the university dons the opportunity of setting foot on the nation's seat of power. It was like a new world to them, an Eldorado which was way out of what the rest of the country was experiencing: well paved roads, covered drains, uninterrupted power supply, functional traffic lights, order and apparent discipline and low noise level. But that was only as far as selected areas of Kumbrujaa, Konganoga's capital, could go. For all else, it was "a goodly apple rotten at the heart", an enticing yellow banana-like make-believe alluring the unwary into a life of unimaginable rot and decay. It was the continent's hot bed of corruption and graft; a new version of a *sin city* that produced nothing but basked with majesty in the sunlight, flaunting the gains of undisguised plunder of the natural resources that truly belonged to some more richly-endowed but weaker neighboring nationalities.

The visiting dons were feted during their visit. It was all smiles on their faces as they departed.

Indeed each of the visitors went home with pricy souvenirs.

But again that was all that the dons could achieve. Broad smiles and promises had greeted them but nothing changed. The leeches that were sucking dry the lifeblood of Konganoga had not been dislodged. They could not be dislodged. Critics and all forms of dissent were either suppressed or were intimidated with charges of treason. Others were made to have a day with "unknown soldiers", "unknown policemen" or "unknown armed robbers".

Recruits into the privileged class easily assimilated the culture of detachment from the people as they warmed their ways into Konganoga's version of George Orwell's *Animal Farm* where initially it was "Four legs good, two legs bad", but later after assimilation into the group of *Men and women in Power*, it would immediately become "Four legs good two legs better."

Thereafter all animals would be declared equal but some would, for the rest of their natural lives, remain more equal.

Dr Okon Johnson had become a major player in the politics of Konganoga. He had failed as a Vice Chancellor of a University. He had also failed an election. But he had become selected in a different way to participate in the governance of his country. Having been given an unprecedented third chance he could easily have turned his energy and talents into advantage for the good of Konganoga. But having been mauled by the polity and having failed as a family man he had found it expedient to join in the rot and decay that were plaguing his society.

Professor Kemji and the other members of the delegation that visited Professor Johnson in his office in Kumbrujaa could not but notice that the Okon Johnson that they used to know was no longer the same man that they met in the big office of Special Assistant to the President on Educational Affairs. Even when Professor Johnson tried his best not to appear to be talking down on his former colleagues, the opulence and the arrogance of power in Kumbrujaa radiated all over the place. Governance had become so elitist and detached from the people that the privileged class of politicians and politician-appointed cronies would have done well to create a nation of their own completely detached from the rest of the society. But No! The people who were part of the polity but who daily engaged in the abhor-able policy of mauling the polity in Konganoga still needed the riches of the country even when from their utterances and actions they did not appear any longer to need the country. The wealth which they exploited and the lesser men and women who served them and ministered to their every-day needs still emanated from the country. But they despised the country and held everything about her with palpable disdain. They were like leeches which parasitized on the country contributing nothing in return, benefitting maximally from Konganoga but continuing to be economic and moral burdens on the nation that was very richly endowed but which, because of her unfortunate political circumstances, had little or nothing to show for her enormous natural endowments.

Yes, Professor Johnson had joined the big league. The name of the game was "Money, Money, More Money, Political Power, and More Money." And for Professor Johnson and his associates in power and corridors of power it had become a competition about who would accumulate more of the money; who would milk the country drier and who would maul the polity the most.

Academic excellence that would have been utilized to the advantage of the country was wasted in plotting how to outmaneuver or outsmart the other leech and how to subjugate the society the more, lest some others got up to the level where they would ask questions. It was a very vicious cycle.

As the infrastructure decayed in schools and everywhere else in Konganoga and the morale of the populace sagged, a generation of youths evolved who knew no better days. All they encountered while they grew up was bribery, corruption moral decadence and embezzlement. To these breeds of youths these vices were the norm. These breeds of youths had encountered no better. And these were the future leaders of Konganoga. The sough-after light at the end of the tunnel was thus either non-existent or had greatly dimmed. But only few in Konganoga appeared to appreciate the dangers. And even those like Professor Johnson who appreciated the dangers and tried to change the system were greatly discouraged by the ignominy and the hardships that were visited upon them by the very society which they sought to protect. And so, many of them had recoiled and had indeed joined the bandwagon of looters. For many like the professor it was "not in their DNA" as the saying went.

Professor Johnson had gotten very wealthy. The 5% which he got from every 50% that was deducted from the budgetary allocation to education had greatly swollen his bank accounts.

His overseas bank account had swollen greatly. His political influence had also greatly increased. He was assigned a jet from the presidential fleet for his travels around the country. This was more of a reward for his loyalty in religiously executing the duties of deducting 50% from the allocations for education. It was also an appreciation for his great *honesty* in remitting all that he collected only short of the 5% that was privately allowed back to him from his collections. He had been a faithful servant of the system howbeit a poor and unfaithful servant of Konganoga.

But deep down within him, Professor Johnson was not happy. He felt fulfilled as an economic success. But the once erudite professor of ophthalmology deep inside him did not feel all fulfilled. He was not a happy man. Despite his enormous wealth he still felt a sense of hollowness each time he remembered Fiona, his once loving wife whom he had betrayed. The faces of his lovely daughters and his young son Scot flashed through his memory with great regret every now and then even as he tried to brush these aside and try fruitlessly to find peace and contentment by daily looking through his mounting dollars in his local and foreign bank accounts. He would yawn with inner despair each time the thought of his once lovely family crossed his mind. But he would try to find unfulfilled solace in the world of make-belief that prevailed all over the city of sin whose mounting graft and injustices perpetually cast an invisible dark shadow of cloud in the minds of all who truly loved Konganoga and wished her well.

However, despite his dining with the devils, Professor Johnson still had a conscience. And that conscience was beginning to prick him at every turn as he began to persistently ask himself:

"For how long will this period of darkness envelope my country?
For how long will my bank account continue to swell at the expense of the young in my country?
For how long will my compatriots and I, hold our society to ransom?
For how long will we, the rich and famous, continue to hold our people down?
For how long...?"

"Wait a minute!" Professor Johnson said.

"There appears to be some commotion around the corner.
There appears to be a stampede.
Some people are running in one direction.
Many others are running in the opposite direction.
There appears to be loss of a unanimous sense of direction.
We can hear some voices shouting as they run.
They say a new strong man had just come on the saddle.

Will the new strong man spare a thought for Konganoga?
Will he insist on 50%, 40%, 10% or 0% for himself and his team?
Does anyone know the name of the new strong man?
Will he be a better man than his predecessors?

Will he spare a thought for Konganoga and her people?

Will he have the goodness and the will to halt this mauling of the polity?

We can hear the voice of the new strong man.

But does Konganoga actually need strong men?

Will she be better off with strong men rather than strong institutions?

We can hear the voice of the new strong man but we cannot yet see him in person.

Perhaps with the first rays of tomorrow's sun we may be able to see his concealed face.

Perhaps the new strong man may be gracious enough to fulfill a longstanding dream.

Perhaps he may look with pity at the tears of Konganoga's distressed pupils.

Perhaps he may for God's sake practice what many had in the past merely preached.

Perhaps he will not insist on swearing people on the Bible, the Koran or the loaded gun.

Perhaps he may proceed to wipe the tears of a long-suffering people.

Perhaps! But only perhaps ...!"

THE END

Bibliography of some proper names in the book:

1. Jonas...Departmental driver for ophthalmology
2. Dr Ezemtubo.... The lazy and cantankerous Senior lecturer in pharmacology
3. Umanamaa...Dr Johnson's housemaid
4. Dr Ziebu...Coordinator of Surgical Sciences; promoted to Reader
5. Dr Usene...Faculty member who supported Dr Johnson's appointment
6. Professor Vanchees...Indian Ophthalmologist; did the accreditation team that approved the University Hospital for ophthalmology
7. Dr Jumbo...Minimal access surgeon who rejected appointment in the Fed. University Kiba
8. Dr Clough McAndrew...Dr Okon Johnson's Pen pal who helped the latter tremendously
9. Fiona.....Dr Okon Johnson's wife
10. Ingrid...Dr McAndrew's girlfriend and later wife
11. Naomi ....Departmental Secretary for Ophthalmology
12. Kem...Daughter to Dr & Mrs Johnson
13. Mrs. Ama Green...Chief Matron at the University Hospital
14. Mr. Pretty Abatt...Deputy Chief Matron at the University Hospital
15. Professor Abatt...Mrs. Pretty Abatt's husband

16. Obelle......Student nurse and Fiona's friend at the University Hospital
17. Mrs. Allis Barton The Manager who Fiona directed letter of request for discarded hospital equipment
18. Alamba Mungo Park...Chief of Administration , University Hospital
19. Professor Kaiza...Professor in University Hospital promoted Professor with very few publications
20. Mr. Doul...Scottish Engineer with an oil Company from same place as Fiona
21. Amakwe... The apprentice who stole Dr Johnson's lap top
22. Mpeke ...The shrine which detected Mpeke's theft
23. Alfred Scot Johnson..The Johnson's son
24. Agnes...Fiona's elder sister and eldest daughter of Mr. and Mrs. Fergus
25. Sherma...undersecretary in Ministry of Establishment
26. Dr Adams...CEO of Tin Mining Company of Konganoga TMCK
27. Mrs. Lakunja...Acting CEO of TMCK
28. Mr. Dumbe...Retired Principal of Secondary School
29. Mrs. Nabel George...Wife of late party Member and Board Member
30. Prince Jakes...Lawyer; Board Member of TMCK
31. Mr. Ocha...Board Member of TMCK
32. Mr. Jifril Immigration Officer in Kumbrujaa
33. Mr. Johnson Ayuda... Assistant to the President
34. Mr. Muktar Obredu...Oath administrator in Mr. Johnson Ayuda's office in Kumbrujaa
35. Okpani....the native medicine man in Akunwanta Village Chief priest of Udogwugwu
36. Mr. Johnson Ayuda....Assistant to the President on League member matters
37. Mr. Muktar Obredu... Oath Administrator

38. Mr. Benjamin Okon Johnson: Professor Johnson's fake name in the hotel in Kiba
39. Udogwugwu…The shrine which Okpani was chief priest to
40. Mr. Amajide…The Bursar in University of Kiba
41. Titi… the messenger in Professor Johnson's office
42. Innocent Okoko…false name in Stella Hotel Kiba for Professor Okon Johnson.
43. Muktar Mumudu… the messenger from the presidency in Kumbrujaa
44. Mr. and Mrs. Fergus….Fiona's parents/ Professor Okon's parents in law
45. Dr and Mrs. Golden…..Professor Johnson's friend in Zealand who first informed the Professor about the divorce
46. Celestial Star Hotel… the hotel into which Professor Johnson checked in Mr. William O'Connor… False check in name of Professor Johnson at celestial Star hotel at Huntington, Zealand.
47. Ikot-ikoro….Professor Johnson's hometown in Konganoga
48. Ozomee …the contractor-politician who beat Professor Johnson in the elections for Senate party primaries
49. "Ojimmuta"…Knowledge is power; Professor Johnson's traditional title
50. Chief Onunkwo … House of Reps Party primaries candidate who withdrew in favor of Chief Ozomee
51. Sule Ojo… the son of a member of the ruling house in Jalango Province of Konganoga. Met with Dr Okon Johnson as a political science PhD student in Zeland
52. Kirkurd General Hospital …the hospital where Dr Johnson worked in Zealand
53. Mr. Wadinga …Secretary at Konganoga consulate in Zealand
54. Ikot-ikoro, Professor Johnson's hometown in Konganoga.

55. Udogwugwu...The shrine which Okpani was chief priest to
56. Mr. Amajide...The Bursar in University of Kiba
57. Muktar Mumudu... the messenger from the presidency in Kumbrujaa
58. Titi... the messenger in Professor Johnson's V.C's office
59. Innocent Okoko...false name in Stella Hotel Kiba for Professor Okon Johnson.
60. Benjamin Okon Johnson: Professor Johnson's fake name in the hotel in Kiba.
61. Dr McAndrew...Dr Okon Johnson's pen pal who helped him obtain hospital residency in Zeland
62. Prof Ozanda First Vice Chancellor Of Federal University of Science and Technology Kiba
63. Professor Timothy Kemji...Dean of Medicine and medical Sciences later Vice Chancellor of the Federal University in Kiba
64. Vylin... Wife of Professor Kemji
65. Dr Usene...Head of Dept. of Ear Nose and throat
66. Kadiri...The randy CEO of the Agric Equipment Company who mistakenly dated his cleaner
67. Ikara...The predominant linguistic group in the Federal University in Kiba
68. Mr Sharma...The old friend who put up Professor Johnson's name up for Chairmanship of the Tin Mining Company in Kiba TMCK
69. Dr Adams...CEO of The Tin Mining Company
70. Mrs. Lakunja...Acting CEO of TMCK
71. Bondon...Zeland's capital city
72. Dr Nanji...Professor Johnson's American-trained lecturer friend.
73. Mrs. Allis Barton...The Manager in the Zeland Hospital who Fiona directed letter of request for discarded hospital equipment